I0603556

TELL ME HOW IT ENDS

LAUREN JONES

Copyright © 2021 by Lauren Jones

All rights reserved.

No part of this book may be reproduced in any form without written permission from the author.

This story is a work of fiction. Any reference to people, places or historical events are used fictitiously. Names, places, events and characters are products of the author's imaginations. Any similarities to real people, places or events is entirely coincidental.

For my sister, Nicole.
You're the real magic.

CHAPTER ONE

I'm having one of those moments where you zone out then back in later and have no memory of the time that's passed. It's a sensation reserved for boring necessities, like driving home from work. One minute I'm leaving the car park, the next I'm in my driveway. It's muscle memory. I don't remember the drive, but it was an obvious success. Tonight, I remember getting ready. It took six tries to get the winged eyeliner right, and I ripped a belt loop off my jeans while pulling them up. Now I'm at a tapas restaurant, looking across at a man whose name I cannot for the life of me remember.

I met him at a taxi rank last weekend and must have seen something I liked because he's in my phone as Hot-T. Which my Moscato-addled brain deemed a fun nickname because he signs all his messages off with 'T'. Now we're a week's worth of flirty text messages in, and I'm trying to remember if his Uber driver called out Tim or Tom amid the symphony of

Prius hubcaps scraping the curb outside 7-Eleven on Saturday night.

One thing is certain though, Tim-Tom is far more dynamic over text. He had witty anecdotes and displayed some light, yet topical humour. Now, he's inspecting himself in the mirrored wall behind me like a parrot. Moving his head from side to side to find the right angle and catching himself by surprise when he sees it.

He has made an effort with his hair, its side swept and tacked to his head. He smells of artificial caramel, and he's ironed his white linen shirt. It's unbuttoned because I have to know that his chest is hairless. I already know this from the handful of shirtless pics he sent through with no context two days ago.

'You said you're working with a marine conservation group. How's that going?' I say as I take a sip of the gin he ordered for me when he arrived twenty minutes late. He was trying to be suave. However, the magic was lost because I told him how much I hate gin when he suggested this date take place at a gin distillery.

He opens his mouth as my phone buzzes on the table. It's that unknown number again. The one I've ignored four times today. I put my phone back in the tiny black clutch I bought for this occasion, realizing too late I could have used the call to bail on Tom. Or Tim. I still don't know.

'Sorry.' I look up to see him using the mirror to fix his hair.

'So, my parents said if I didn't start looking for a job instead of joining activist groups, they'll kick me out.' He wrinkles his flawless, twenty-six-year-old forehead. 'Don't get me wrong, I love the turtles, but rent is expensive, and my parents' house has high ceilings and a chef's kitchen. Not to mention, I'd have to pay my own car rego. That's like six hundred bucks. Who's got that kind of money to spend on registration? They don't even give you a sticker anymore. It's all digital.'

I raise a brow at his Apple watch, Gucci belt, and choice of restaurant. 'I'm sure the turtles will understand.'

He leans back in the chair, stretching his arms over his head and in a wide arc back down to his side. 'It's not like the turtles will know I left the conservation group. I mean, they're turtles.'

There are too many red flags here to digest.

'Yeah, they're too busy trying to get those plastic ring things off their necks to worry about rental prices in the greater Brisbane area.'

'You're funny, Halliday.' He adjusts his shirt, dangerously close to flashing me a nipple. 'I like that on you.'

I lift my shoulders. 'Glad you're impressed.'

'You should be. It takes a special woman to impress me.'

How life affirming that this gin swilling, part-time friend to sea life that lives with his parents has given me his stamp of approval. I stifle a laugh, but it doesn't matter because I've lost his attention to the mirror wall again. It's clear he isn't worth a fake emergency call or going to pee and not coming back.

'Cool, well I'm going to go.'

He sits up in his chair. 'Wait, what?'

'I can't see this working.'

His face pinches and his head tilts to the side like a dog registering sounds the human ear can't hear. 'Thanks for the gin, Tom.'

'My name's Tim.'

'Okay.' I collect my bag off the mosaic-tiled table and give him a nod. 'See ya.'

He says something, but I'm already weaving through tables with the fervour of a child who's spotted a fairground in the distance.

On the drive home, I blast seventies classics and try to ignore the unknown number that calls two more times. By the time I cross the river, Tim has messaged to say I'm a bitch. It showcases his heightened level of maturity.

Tim-Tom is my fourth date in two weeks and none of them have gone well. I hit it off with the first guy, but he was keeping his options open. He didn't call me back, so I assume I'm no longer an option. The second guy lied about his age. Not just rounding up or down to the nearest whole number. He tweaked that number so hard he had to research what music people my age are listening to. At twenty-eight, I'd even prefer an older guy. What I'm not looking for is a fifty-three-year-old who corners me in a dimly lit Thai restaurant and opens with 'okay, just hear me out.' I deleted the dating app for a few days after that mess. The third guy was the winner. Intelligent, great sense of humour, and had a jaw that could cut glass. The downside, he wanted kids as soon as possible, and I'm not looking to be impregnated in the next year to keep his five-year plan on track.

Which, in hindsight, doesn't seem that bad since I'm now waiting in the McDonald's drive-thru, ordering extra biscuit bits in my McFlurry, and ensuring the fifteen-year-old employee doesn't skimp on the caramel topping because I've already popped the button on my jeans to prepare for this.

'You're home early.' Violet whispers from her darkened perch outside the townhouse that neighbours mine. 'Tom wasn't all that?'

I drop onto the step beside her and hand over the dregs of the McFlurry.

'Tom was too busy staring at his reflection to notice I was there, which is a shame cause I wanted to try the food at that place.'

'Was it the tapas place at Southbank?'

'Yeah. The one with too many mirrors.'

Violet laughs. 'I know the place. Brad and I went there before Archie was born. You aren't missing much.'

I stretch my legs out, flexing my toes in my new, strappy black heels. They cost too much, and I'm disappointed I wasted them on stupid Tom the cockatiel.

Vi hands back my dessert and I flick my chin at the baby monitor on her lap. 'How is the freeloader?'

'He didn't sleep at all last night, and I don't have high hopes for tonight.'

In the soft glow of the complex's driveway lighting, I can see the dark circles under her eyes. Her first and, judging by how well it's going, only child, Archie is almost one. He's an adorable little thing. Chubby cheeks and strawberry blonde hair. But the lungs on that kid could shatter all the windows in a skyscraper.

'Is it too late to give him back?' I ask.

Violet hangs her head and a few oily strands of blonde hair fall out of the messy bun piled on top of it. 'Yeah, I think it might be and I've gotten kind of attached. Motherly love and all that.'

I chew gently on the plastic spoon. 'Rock and a hard place, hey.'

Violet and I met five years ago when I went against the advice of my mother and invested in high density living on the north side of Brisbane. Violet and her then-boyfriend, now-husband, Brad bought the place next door around the same time. We were introduced over a parcel delivery mix up and we've shared a lot of big life moments since then.

Mostly her big moments. The engagement, wedding, and birth of Archie. I don't have much going on aside from a pipe bursting in my laundry and my childhood friend, Wes, moving in to contribute to my mortgage. He's six foot three, does not understand the importance of cooking chicken all the way through, and enjoys playing Call of Duty at two in the morning.

'That sucks about Tom.' Violet yawns so wide I'm sure her jaw unhinges. 'You've still got Evan on Saturday, so there's hope.'

I shake my head, half expecting her to pull out a scorecard and tiny pencil like they have at mini-golf. Or worse, a big whiteboard with lots of newspaper clippings and red string.

'Don't put your eggs in Evan's basket. I'm cancelling and then deleting that stupid app. It's a time suck.'

'No, please don't delete the app.' Violet holds her hands like she's praying. 'It's fun, and they can't all be shit. Statistically speaking.'

'Don't start with your law of averages theory.' I pull myself up off the step. 'I'm too old and tired for how much work this is.'

Violet has become invested in my romantic endeavours of late because she says Archie wants a friend. Archie does not. Archie wants to put everything he can find in his mouth and then throw it across the room. I made that argument and Violet caved, confessing she wants someone to share in the joy of having a child. She attends two separate mother's groups to fill this void and Brad's sister announced she's expecting. It's enough people to share the joy without getting my uterus involved.

To be honest, I'm still scarred from Archie's arrival into the world. That night, fragmented by strawberry daiquiris, still haunts me. It was close to midnight when Brad called to say Vi was in labour. We were already on our way to the hospital because Wes fell off a retaining wall at his birthday party and broke his arm in two places. I split my night between the emergency waiting room and the maternity ward. I'm not sure who screamed more, Violet pushing a human out or Wes getting a tetanus shot because he landed on a rusty nail when he fell.

The unknown number calls again and I ignore it as my front door opens. Wes's mop of dark blonde hair appears around the decorative hedge that separates my front steps from Violet's.

'Thought I heard you.' He's got a beer in one hand and the TV remote in the other. 'Didn't go well with Tom then?'

'His name was Tim.'

Wes's face wrinkles. 'You sure?'

'It's what he said when I called him Tom.'

Wes chuckles and steps outside, swigging his beer. He gives Violet a nod in greeting as I help her up off the step.

'I'm going to wash my hair before Archie starts screaming again.' She takes a deep breath and rolls her shoulders like she's prepping for battle. I doubt the water will even be warm before Archie demands her attention.

'Tell us if you need anything.' Wes calls out, knowing he'd be no help if our friends did in fact need anything. Violet's aware of this but thanks him anyway.

My beautiful heels make a hollow clunk on the driveway as I round the hedge to stand in front of Wes. He offers his half-drunk beer and I take a swig before shuffling into the house.

'Did you eat?' He asks. 'I got pizza and picked the pineapple off the Hawaiian for you.'

'That's so nice.' I hand him back the beer, dump my bag on the bench, and throw my McFlurry cup in the bin. He asks for more details about my date out of politeness, but there's no need to waste his time. Instead, we drop onto the couch, cooling pizza in hand, and I let out a sigh befitting an eighty-year-old.

Soon my belly is full and my eyes close. The TV noise gets further away, and my limbs are heavy, but I need a shower because the longer I sit here with perfect winged eyeliner, the worse I feel about tonight.

Wes is watching the late-night news bulletin when I return from my shower, and he mutes it as my foot clears the bottom step.

'Is it too late for coffee?' I ask, heading for the mug cupboard. 'Maybe tea is a better idea.'

'Hallie.' Wes breathes and I glance up to see him standing

in the middle of our cosy lounge room. His shoulders slump and his heavy brows draw together, like he's been kicked in the guts.

'What?'

'Halliday.' His voice shakes as he rounds the couch and gives me an unobstructed view of the television. I'm not that tired anymore, but it still takes far too long to register what I'm looking at.

My dad's face is plastered all over the crystal clear, sixty-five-inch screen. His once dark hair is grey at the sides, and his pale green eyes crinkle thanks to the grin he's sporting. The ground shifts for a second and I brace myself on the corner of the bench. The image on the TV changes to him wearing a knitted beanie and holding up a salmon. He's smiling at me, but my eyes fall to the thick white banner beneath with text that reads:

Blood of Gold *author, Ellery Yates, dead at forty-eight.*

It's like opposing magnets are clunking around in my head, and I'm vaguely aware of Wes gripping my shoulders. The news is now showing b-reel of Dad's most recent interview on a morning show before changing to more photos of him at book signings and the cover art of his novels.

'Turn the sound on.' I mumble.

Wes's voice is a whisper, and he attempts to hug me. 'Hal?'

I push away and shout, 'Turn the sound on!'

My pulse thunders in my ears and my ribs contract. I can't catch my breath. Wes is speaking, but it's garbled, like we're underwater. He guides me to the couch and picks up the remote as the news anchor with a smooth black bob appears on the screen. She drops her voice an octave to sound sincere, but it's robotic.

'The author of the bestselling fantasy series was rushed to hospital near his home outside Fairbanks, Alaska, in the early hours of Friday morning. Authorities have yet to confirm the cause of death; however, it is not being treated as suspicious.'

As quickly as the story appears, it's replaced by aerial shots of a factory fire in Melbourne.

'I'll call your mum.' Wes says as he grabs his phone off the coffee table with trembling fingers.

CHAPTER TWO

The sun is up when Wes pushes my door open and gingerly steps into the room. I'm cocooned in my quilt, face covered and eyes stinging from lack of sleep. The Dove soap scent gets stronger as Wes approaches and leans down to give my lower leg a squeeze. I peer over the blanket to see he's dressed in a black polo shirt with his carpentry company logo on the pocket. I feel emptier knowing he has to go to work soon.

'Your mum is on her way over,' he says as he hooks his index finger over the top of the blanket and pulls it down to expose my mouth. 'She didn't find out about your dad until this morning, and she's been trying to call you.'

I roll over and collect my phone off the bedside table. I have six missed calls from her and three more from that unknown number. It's on silent, but I heard it vibrating. I just couldn't bring myself to answer. If I did, I'd have to face reality and I like that it's not real yet.

'I have a decent job on today, but I can send one of the other guys.' Wes's leg bounces as he waits for my response. I want him to stay, but he has so much on at the moment he can't even afford Sundays off.

'I'll be fine. Mum will stay with me.'

His lips press together. 'You sure?'

I nod and this placates him enough to stand. He still hovers around my bed for longer than necessary, and when I tell him he'll be late for work, he forces out a reluctant good-bye. I listen to his boots thump down the stairs and out the door. The emptiness of the house is immediate and heavy.

It isn't long before I move to the tiled floor of the shower and watch the water rise as I cover the plughole with my foot. I haven't cried yet, and I don't think that's normal. When I tear up, something in my brain short circuits and assures me he's still over there, in Alaska, living his life. I've never considered what losing a parent would feel like. A sharp pain maybe? Like breaking a bone. In reality, it's a darkness. Something weighty, unstable, and lonely. I move my foot and watch the water disappear with an angry gurgle.

Wes and I sat on the couch in silence for hours, but I couldn't look at him. He didn't know what to say, he just kept apologising and asking if I needed water. Neither of us knew what to do, but I should have been crying. The expectation of it scratched at my bones along with the overwhelming guilt of not being able to make it happen.

I haven't seen my dad in person in six years, but we still talk often. Well, as often as the time difference between Brisbane and Fairbanks allows. We've had a contact drought over the last few months thanks to his writing and touring schedule.

Late last year was the tenth anniversary of his first book, and his publisher released a special edition and routed a tour to mark the occasion. Dad sent me photos from all over the US and Europe as he hopped around eclectic bookstores. He tried to call a few times, but we kept missing each other. The one time I did answer was a thirty-second conversation in which he wished me a happy birthday while I was on my way to dinner.

If finding the time to call was hard, visiting was harder. The last time I went to Alaska, I stayed for a month. Dad was on a strict deadline for the release of his fourth book, so I stacked up pillows on the bay window seat in his lounge room and read through each of his chapters as he wrote them. It reminded me of sitting in his office as a kid and doing the same thing with his earlier work. Thinking about that now causes a sting in my chest.

After my shower and putting on fresh pyjamas, I'm twisting my hair up when a clattering noise sounds from the kitchen.

'Mum?' I wander down the stairs to find her spooning instant coffee into a Texas Longhorns mug along with some sugar.

'Hal.' Her eyes are puffy and her voice gravelly as she pulls me into a hug. She smells like Elie Saab perfume and a coconut hair mask. At forty-six, she's still the stunning young woman in all the old photos at my grandparents' place. The only difference is her long blonde hair is now a blunt bob and there are wrinkles around her eyes. She's a masterpiece, and our similarities are limited. She gave me her hazel eyes and general bone structure, but I'm half a head taller and thicker around the hips, which could be thanks to high-level pasta intake. My abundance of dark hair is courtesy of Dad, though.

'Sorry I missed your calls,' I say.

'Wesley said you found out last night.' Mum pushes the coffee toward me. 'I'm so sorry my phone was off. I would have come straight over.'

'It's okay. It was late.' I take a sip and try not to let it show that Mum can't make coffee to save herself. 'Are you okay?'

She nods, but her eyes fall to the floor. 'I think so. They said it was a brain aneurysm on the news this morning.'

A brain aneurysm? The articles I read last night only said his death was sudden. There's a shift in the room and I'm struggling to breathe. Not knowing the cause made it possible to reject the idea that he's gone. It feels real now, and I want to go back to not knowing.

I clear my throat and set the coffee down on the bench. 'Is there anything we need to do?'

'I don't know. It depends on who the executor of his estate is.' Mum wraps her arms around herself. 'I'm assuming it's Marie.'

Even though it's been seventeen years since she and Dad parted ways, Mum doesn't trust herself not to say something judgmental about Dad's long-term girlfriend. Mum and Marie have only met once. It was immediately after the split, so the wounds were fresh. I don't know if it was Marie who convinced Dad to move back to Alaska, but it was easy to blame it all on her. Mum and I never quite kicked that habit.

'I've called Nora, and she's available to cover the store today.' Mum rubs my upper arm. 'I'm staying with you.'

Mum has owned a homewares store for over ten years now.

Two years into the venture, she moved from a poky old shop front at a busy intersection to a major shopping centre. I'd helped her out a little during university, but as soon as I graduated with a double degree in English and Business, her shop was booming, and I became her full-time help.

'Go sit down and I'll make you something to eat.' She paints on a smile and stares at me until I'm settled on the couch.

I watch her potter around my compact kitchen, looking for something that resembles breakfast ingredients. She says nothing, but as she works, I see her wipe a few silent tears off her cheeks.

A welcome numbness takes hold as I slide down into the cushions, and I push at the reality that's pressing in. The disconnected part of me thinks there's a chance he'll answer if I try to call. The rational part of me knows he won't.

I drag my phone from the top pocket of my pyjama shirt and tap the screen. There's a missed call from Wes, but I disregard it and open Facebook. Most of my feed is stories about Dad and I can't bring myself to tap on any of them. The headlines vary, but the content is the same. The internet's biggest concern is what will happen to his book series. Tens of thousands of comments appear on each article, and fans everywhere are being propelled through this turbulent time by false information and speculation.

Dad has been working on book six for the last year, and even though I've been prodding him for information, he's remained tight lipped. Aside from a short first chapter, which needed a lot of work, I've seen no other material. It makes sense because he's been busy with his tour schedule. Not to mention the promo stuff he's been on the hook for now the TV adaptation is a massive success. He placated my fantasy novel addiction by sending over books by his fellow author friends. I've since become attached to a debut by an author he'd been mentoring. It's called *Red Reign* and I've read it cover to cover at least four times. Dad's influence drips off the pages.

I put the phone down and rub my eyes. Those articles will keep coming, but I'm thankful that Dad used a pen name and I've been able to fly under the radar regarding his fame. Fame that is exponential since the show came out and his publisher reprinted the whole series. Dad's renewed popularity has brought old acquaintances out of the woodwork, too. People I went to school with who want to see the kind-hearted battle axe of a sidekick from book three resurrected. I ignore those messages, mostly because there is no coming back from being shredded to ribbons by a wyvern. Usually, I get a kick out of my anonymity and enjoy listening to people talk about which storylines they love and hate. I've only engaged once, when a guy at a pub trivia night said Brialla The Oracle deserved exile. Brialla deserved a castle for the shit she had to deal with at the hands of the Karrakan King, and I made strong and engaging points to that effect...I haven't been back to trivia since.

Mum stays with me all day. We watch renovation show reruns and she tries to feed me every forty-five minutes. It's not her fault. She doesn't know what to do. Neither do I. She opts for cooking. I opt for silence.

At six, Wes arrives home, and he and Mum have a handover in the kitchen. She gives him a run-down of my sedentary day and asks him to monitor me while she goes to get groceries for dinner. She's fed me all the food she could find, and there isn't much anyone can do with a squashed peach and a jar of passata.

'Are you doing okay?' Wes asks as he slides down onto the couch beside me. 'You didn't call me back today.'

'I've been trying not to look at my phone.'

'Yeah, I wouldn't recommend it.' He nods. 'At least Ma was here to keep you company.'

The blink I offer in response is slow and heavy.

'That good, hey?' He laughs as he shifts to retrieve the phone from his back pocket. His head falls back when he looks at the screen. 'Ah shit, I'll be back.'

His tone has changed so I know it's his business partner, Teddy, calling with another problem he's stumbled across. It must be a big one since Wes is still pacing the backyard and making wild hand gestures when Mum returns with an over-flowing enviro bag.

She hums Cat Stevens songs while buzzing around the kitchen, and it encourages me to get up and set the table. Mum smiles as she produces three placemats I didn't know I owned.

'Dinner's not far off,' she says. 'Can you get Wesley off the phone?'

I finish setting the table before shuffling out onto the grass patch that was advertised as a backyard on the property listing. Whatever Wes's phone conversation is about has him riled up and I can tell he's been tugging at his hair. He rubs his eye while arguing about the lead time on a job and frowns when he looks up at me.

I cross the lawn, wrap my arms around his midsection, and

squeeze as tight as I can. He drapes his arm over my shoulders, and I listen to his voice rumble through his chest. Teddy's voice is faint on the other end of the phone, but I hear him say they'll deal with the rest of it tomorrow.

As expected, our dinner conversation is stilted. Mum and I don't want to talk about Dad, and Wes isn't keen on using his work as a filler. That leaves us with lamb chops and how inconvenient it was that Mum drove back to the supermarket because the butcher ran out.

'It's a lamb chop, not a woolly mammoth,' she says. 'They only ever seem to have a kilo on hand so it's first in best dressed.'

'I hear mammoth is popular again.' I poke at my potatoes. 'It's a surprising resurgence considering the current environmental challenges.'

She smirks. It's the first time today I've mustered sarcasm.

'They know they have the best chops, and they already charge a premium. Their supply doesn't meet the demand, and it's intentional. They've got us all over a barrel, and they know it.'

'Maybe there's a secret underground chop ring keeping a tight hold on the supply chain.'

She lets out a laugh but covers her mouth straight away as if to force it back in. Laughter feels inappropriate, so we resort to eating in silence, which becomes suffocating almost immediately.

Mum attempts to break it by telling me about the order of Art Deco-patterned tea towels she ordered for the store. She can't decide whether to put them with linens or kitchen goods. I sink back into my chair and Wes carries the conversation when the subject changes to Hampton style side tables. He doesn't know what he's talking about, but Mum enjoys the back and forth.

'Shouldn't someone have contacted us about Dad?' I interrupt something about dust ruffles and Mum's deep-set hazel eyes settle on me.

'You mean Marie?'

'Yeah.'

She shakes her head, perfect bob swishing. 'I'm not sure she has my number.'

'Maybe we should call her?'

Mum smooths the front of her dress and averts her eyes to her empty plate. 'I'm not comfortable with that.'

There are a few seconds of tense silence before Mum gathers our plates and carries them to the kitchen.

'I'll take care of the clean-up.' Wes jumps to his feet and takes over packing the dishwasher, nudging her out of the room.

By eight o'clock, Mum gathers that I'd like to be alone. It's not so much a hint as me telling her I'm tired and I want to go to bed. She holds me on the driveway for too long and promises to call me in the morning to check in.

As the taillights of her car disappear, my brain feels like it's swelling in my skull and all I want to do is crawl into bed, pull the covers over my head and hope tomorrow is different.

I lean my back against the front wall of the house, sucking in the night air and enjoying the sweet smell of rain that lingers. It isn't long before Wes comes outside.

He leans on the wall beside me, eyes glassy, and his mouth shifts into a sympathetic frown. 'I'm sorry, Hal.'

I mimic his expression. 'Are the condolences for my dad or because Mum tried to make me feel better by discussing vintage credenzas all afternoon?'

'I don't know what a credenza is but yes, the second one,' Wes deadpans as he pulls me to his side.

'I don't think she can bring herself to talk about him.'

'Do you want to talk about him?'

'Yeah, I do.' My voice cracks. 'He was always a call or a flight away. I could visit him whenever I wanted, and I didn't. Now, he isn't over there anymore. He isn't anywhere anymore.'

'He was the one that left, and you did the best you could. It hasn't been that long since you visited.'

'It was six years ago.' I put my head in my hands. 'That was the last time.'

Blinding pressure builds in my head, and it's not right to dump it all on Wes now. I excuse myself, and he doesn't protest as I go back inside and up to my bedroom.

An hour later, I'm sitting cross-legged on my bed with the guilt of not seeing Dad still weighing me down. I'll find my place on the spectrum of grief at some point, but for now I'm untethered. It's like scrambling for purchase on something I can't see.

In reality, nothing has changed. He doesn't live a few streets away or come over every Sunday night for dinner. I wouldn't wake up tomorrow morning and see him, so tonight is no different to last night or the night before. But my ribs feel wrenched open and my heart torn out, one piece at a time. I've lost the option of seeing him. The choice has been snatched away.

Midnight ticks over and I stare at my phone screen,

pressing the button on the side every time it goes black. Tomorrow has arrived, so I close my eyes and note that it feels different. Everything feels emptier than before.

Phone in hand, I pull myself off the bed and sneak out into the hallway. Wes went to bed a while ago, but I can see his door is ajar. I tread over the charcoal carpet, and the boards underneath groan slightly in the stillness.

'You okay?' He's groggy but in the moon's glow I can see his eyes are open. I shake my head. He lifts the corner of his quilt and I crawl in next to him, settling with my back against his chest. My nose tingles, and he says nothing as I pull out my phone and open the last text message from Dad. It's a photo of the northern lights he took two weeks ago, followed by a message that says *Dreamland*. There's a sting behind my eyes and though he'll never receive it, I type a reply.

HALLIE

I'll miss you

That's when I cry. I break down, my body heaving as tears soak Wes's faded pillowcase. I've never felt so relieved and so devastated at the same time.

CHAPTER THREE

After a night of crying and little sleep, I'm dazed. It's like a hangover with none of the drinking, dancing, or 2 a.m. kebab with extra garlic sauce. Wes and I didn't talk at all last night, and when the tears stopped, I pretended to be asleep so he'd relax. It didn't take long for him to roll over and start snoring. I went back to my room then.

He'd left when I surfaced this morning, and I feel bad. He has a massive day today. Teddy secured them an obscene amount of work at a new housing estate and despite Wes's laid-back nature, it's obvious he's beginning to fray at the edges.

I text Wes a thank you for the coffee he left on the bench for me as I climb into the car. Mum said I don't have to come to work, but I can't sit around the house all day. I don't want to be on my phone, scanning thousands of tweets and reading overblown news articles. Dad's publisher, Harcourt Press, released a statement this morning, and it opened up a fresh can of worms about how they're going to wrap up his book series. The sixth and final book was due for release this year, and without Dad there's no book. It makes my heart heavy to think of it being left unfinished. A feeling that appears to be universal.

I'm at the store for all of an hour before Mum asks me to go home. After those flood gates cracked open last night, I haven't been able to stop tearing up. Mum doesn't seem to understand that if I'm alone for more than a minute, I think.

That never seems to end well for me.

But Mum catches me wiping my runny nose on the sleeve of my lavender blouse a few too many times, so we agree that I should keep busy somewhere else.

When I get home, I assemble a snack with the sparse contents of our fridge. Mum bought a few essentials last night, but there's little to work with. Wes and I hate grocery shopping so the person responsible for our weekly shop is the loser of a fifteen-round game of rock, paper, scissors, which Wes is terrible at. Our fridge often contains only bacon, beer, and the occasional block of cheese. Today is different: we have bread and I find a suspiciously single egg in the fridge door.

I burn the toast, and the omelette is overcooked and tasteless thanks to the dwindling Gouda supply. Still, it provides a small boost and soon I'm rearranging the bookshelf in the lounge room. The rearranging doesn't last long because the fourth book I pull out is *Red Reign*. Before I know it, I'm lying on the tiles, seven chapters deep, and my back is screaming. I twist into a better position and keep on reading.

Around five o'clock, there's movement next door, so I sneak out to the yard and hear Archie gurgling. I stick my head over the fence to see him balanced on Violet's barely protruding belly as she lies on the outdoor lounge.

'Hey there.' I wave my arm. She looks downcast at the sight of me and scoops Archie onto her hip as she stands.

'Wes told me what happened. I'm so sorry. Are you okay?'

I intended on telling Violet about Dad, but I was hoping to avoid it for at least a few more days. Shuffling forward on the raised garden edging, I grip the fence to hold myself up. 'I'm coping.'

She holds her hand up as a visor to block the afternoon sun. 'I wanted to come straight over when Wes told us, but I thought you might need some time.'

'Yeah, I'm trying to get my head around it all.' I look away when my eyes mist.

'He lived in America, hey?'

I nod. 'Yeah, he moved back there when I was fourteen.'

About three months into knowing my neighbours, I thought about telling them who my dad was because both Violet and Brad are fans of the books. Big fans, *huge* fans. It seemed like a fun nugget of information to drop at one of our backyard barbecues, but the more I talked to Violet, the more interested she became in me. She asked about my hobbies, dreams, career, love life. I told her I'm an average surfer, a fast reader, have failed three separate cooking classes, and always correctly guess which house the couple picks on House Hunters. She said she loved my sense of humour and knew that we'd get on like a house on fire. We hung out a lot after that, and I decided she didn't need to know who Dad was because he wasn't the only interesting thing about me.

Wes, on the other hand, found it difficult to keep a lid on

my secret, especially when we started attending the viewing parties Vi and Brad held for the TV adaptation. Even I'll admit it was hard to keep my mouth shut watching scenes unfold that I remember being written.

I was first to read the completed manuscripts, and Dad sent me the first finished copy of each book. I even have some framed artwork from the series and the official artist rendition of the character that's named after me. Violet would get a kick out of the Nike shoebox in my wardrobe filled with hand-written notes about the characters, Dad's original sketch for the map, and the first draft of book one. I can't bring myself to show that stuff to anyone though, that's just between me and the famed Ellery Yates.

'You're welcome to come over if you don't want to be alone. You can watch me change nappies and struggle to make the sound work on the TV now that Brad got that new speaker system thing.'

'That sounds fun.'

She watches me for a moment as errant strands of blonde hair blow across her face in the breeze.

'Are you going to the funeral?'

I shake my head. 'I haven't heard if there is one.'

'Where did he live?'

My back straightens, and I shift my feet. It's a simple ques-tion but answering it might draw some dots closer together. Violet has a radar for lies, though.

'Just north of Fairbanks in Alaska.'

She looks down, brow furrowing as she fiddles with Archie's toes. His chubby cheeks puff out and he squints into the sunlight. When Violet looks back up at me, she presses her mouth into a line.

'What did your dad do for work?'

She's got a wild hunch, and she knows it, but her stare makes me want to sink behind the fence. She must see how much of a stretch this is.

'This and that. He was a university lecturer for a bit.'

She's not buying it. Her eyes are too narrow and the wrinkle in her forehead is turning into the Mariana Trench.

'For a bit, hey? What did he do after that?'

'Stuff in Alaska. Salmon fishing and what not.'

'Like on a commercial fishing boat?'

We've reached the part where she presses for detailed information to catch me out. I know nothing about fishing in Alaska and will barely last a minute under scrutiny.

'I've heard it's a demanding job.' She's making an unnatural amount of eye contact. 'What position did he have? Deckhand? Foreman? Steward?'

Fuck. I forgot about her obsession with Deadliest Catch. This threadbare lie is falling apart.

'I think it was more logistics than anything. You know, moving fish around and all that.'

She makes a humming sound. 'Interesting. Seems kind of weird that he'd get into that industry when he lives so far from the Alaskan coast.'

She's got me, we both know it. That radar of hers is pinging off the charts but I might be able to salvage this.

'Yes. He did say that was tough, but the sea called to him and he answered.'

'Was he based out of Dutch Harbour?'

'Yeah.'

'Wow, that's got to be over two thousand Ks from Fairbanks.'

I've changed my mind. I can't salvage this. 'Alright, you got me. He was a writer.'

'You suck at lying.' She moves Archie to her other hip in preparation for the final round of questioning. 'Has he written anything I would have heard of?'

Yes. Dad's entire works are the only books on her shelf.

'Probably not. He only wrote a few fantasy books.'

Her eyes narrow further and I know she's got me. 'I can't believe you kept this a secret.'

'There is no secret.'

'Then tell me his name.'

I lower myself back down, disappearing behind the fence.

Violet's voice grows louder as she approaches, 'Tell me his name.'

'No.' I shake my head even though she can't see it.

'Hal, tell me your dad's name.'

'It's not important.'

'Get your head back up here and tell me your dad's name.'

I step back up onto the garden edging and peek over. Violet looks threatening even though she's all of five foot five with a vomit stain on the front of her shirt.

'Stop yelling at me.' I hiss. 'I'm grieving.'

'What's his name?'

I grumble. 'Elliot Townsend,'

'And what's his pen name?'

I steady myself using the top of the wooden fence. Violet

waits, her foot tapping on the grass and her hips rocking Archie from side to side.

'Halliday, tell me his name.'

'Fine.' I let out an exaggerated breath. 'It's Ellery Yates.'

Violet's inner turmoil paints her face like a flush of watercolour. She's in shock at the confirmation, elated that she worked it out, and heartbroken because it's still my dad's death we're talking about.

'Jesus Christ.' She exhales as she looks at Archie, who is poking at the side of her face. 'Why didn't you tell me before?'

'I don't tell anyone. All they do is ask me questions about his books and hope I drop spoilers.'

She takes that in and nods slowly. I know what's gnawing at her now.

'I don't know how it ends.'

Her pale blue eyes dart from her son to me, and a smirk tugs at the corner of her mouth.

'Not even a little?'

'I read the first chapter about six months ago. It picks up right where book five left off and gives nothing away.'

She frowns but doesn't push the issue. I wanted Violet to take my mind off things, but she's done the opposite.

I appreciate it when Archie screws up his face and makes that sputtering sound that precedes a mini meltdown. We say our goodbyes and I go back to bed, ready to swim in the loneliness of waiting for Wes to get home. As a distraction, I keep reading *Red Reign*. I'm up to the first battle scene and even though I love that scene, Dad still occupies all of my brain space. I close my eyes and concentrate on the humming of the air conditioner.

Mum once told me Dad wasn't worth the effort it took to think of him. She only said it once and tried so hard to take those words back she was near silent for days. I was only fifteen at the time and even though they'd been apart for four years and Dad had been back in Alaska for one, it was obvious Mum still thought about him all the time too.

Looking back on it, the breakdown of their marriage was straightforward. There was a tense year of separation where we were all trying to find our footing. When nothing improved, they went through with the divorce. To his credit, Dad tried to make life here work, but he missed his home too much and moved back to Alaska three years later. It wasn't an easy decision for him, and though Mum and I shared the heartbreak, we handled it in different ways. I stayed at Wes's place for a week and scolded him every time he asked if I wanted to talk about Dad. Mum cried for hours on end, like the preceding four years hit her all at once and she couldn't process it. I was young and didn't understand why she wasn't spitting venom. I needed to be angry for the both of us, and I liked the feeling of my blood boiling. It was easier than missing him.

I'm on my back watching the fan spin on its lowest setting when my phone rattles across the bedside table.

Dad is calling me.

My heart jumps into my throat and my hands shake. Is this a joke?

'Hello,' I say, catching it just before it goes to voicemail.

'Halliday?' a delicate female voice asks.

I sit up, pulling my legs underneath me. 'Who is this?'

She exhales into the phone. 'Hallie, it's Marie.'

The line is silent for a long moment, and I don't know

what to say. I haven't spoken to Marie since the last time I saw Dad, and at the time I was still getting used to them being a couple. They'd been together for a while, but since I'd only ever known her as his neighbour, it was a little weird to see her cooking breakfast in his kitchen.

'Are you there?' Marie asks, worry edging into her voice.

'Yes.'

'I thought the connection might have dropped out. I'm calling about—'

'To tell me about Dad?' I cut her off, and it sounds harsher than I intended.

'Yes,' she answers but the word cracks with emotion. 'I tried calling. I wanted to tell you before the media got hold of it.'

The news bulletin flickers through my head. I should have answered those calls from an unknown number because hearing it from Marie, as opposed to a Botoxed stranger with a lapel mic, would have been the lesser of two evils.

Marie clears her throat. 'I know it's last minute, but we're having a memorial on Thursday, and I wanted to invite you and your mom. It's a private gathering, but we'll be spreading his ashes up on the hill behind the property.'

There's hope in her voice and I don't feel good about dashing it, but I can't get to Alaska in three days' time.

'I'd like to, but I don't have the money for that and it's such short notice.' I try to keep my tone even, but the guilt is a cat-o'-nine-tails lashing my entire body.

'I understand.'

I press my teeth into my lower lip. 'Thank you for including me though.'

She's silent, and if it wasn't for the slight crackle on the line, I would have thought she was gone.

She takes a deep breath. 'It doesn't feel right to talk about this now, but you are his next of kin. There are things that need to be taken care of like his house and his will, so you'll need to come over soon. I can pay for your ticket if that helps.'

'Please don't do that.'

'It's no trouble at all.' She sounds more upbeat, but there is lingering sadness in her voice. 'I've passed your number onto Dana Robinson, Elle's attorney. She's the executor of his estate, and she needs to get in contact with you.'

I roll onto my side and curl into a ball as if it will absolve me of any responsibility.

'I'll work something out and come over.' My voice is small.

'Thank you,' she says. 'It'll be nice to see you again.'

We swap stilted goodbyes before the call disconnects and a fresh wave of guilt rolls in.

CHAPTER FOUR

On Mum's advice, I spend the next couple of days at home. I feel bad about the time off because both of her casual staff members just resigned. Another good reason not to jet off to Alaska: it'll leave her and Nora to hold the fort alone. Not ideal for Mum's blood pressure, that's for sure.

With that in mind, I intended on keeping Marie's phone call to myself for a bit, but Wes said I'd have to go to Alaska at some point. I distract myself from the inevitability of this conversation with my mum by finishing *Red Reign* and going hunting online for clues about the sequel, *Blue Horizon*. It doesn't have a release date, but according to the author's Instagram, he's working on the first draft. I fight the urge to privately message him and ask where he's at so I can establish a timeline of misery thanks to his cliffhanger ending. He must get stacks of messages about it, and Dad promised I'd meet him in person one day. I'll save my questions for that magic moment.

Now, I'm at a loss for what to do. The bathrooms are clean, and I made my bed this morning for the first time in years. An hour of aimlessly wandering the neighbourhood convinces me to just go to Mum's place. She'll be at work for a few more hours, but we can talk when she gets home.

Upon arrival, my intention is to sit on the couch, close my eyes, and see if the change of location helps me sleep. It doesn't, and I end up staring at my reflection in the dormant TV screen while picking at the dark strands of hair that have slipped free of my bun.

I don't know how long I do that for, but eventually I pull myself off the couch and wander down the hallway, stopping at one of the spare rooms. It was Dad's office when I was a kid; now it's a storage room for shop stock overflow. I step forward and curl my toes into the high pile cream carpet as my lungs fill with stagnant air. Dad's extensive library is long gone, now replaced with boxes of linen and bubble wrapped end tables. The walls aren't the same colour anymore. Deep forest green now hidden under multiple coats of off-white. The notches on the door frame that measured my height are still there though, and I run my fingers over them before lying down on the only available section of carpet.

When I close my eyes, I can see the bookcases overflowing with various editions of Dad's favourite books. With a little more concentration, I can hear the tapping of his fingers on the keyboard and I hate that I haven't thought of those moments in so long.

When my parents first separated, I wanted to be mad at Dad to make Mum feel better. I know it killed her when I went over to see him or answered his calls. Maybe she missed her connection with him and resented mine. I never pushed the subject. But she seemed angry at his success, like he wasn't owed it because he left. I sometimes wondered if he was a success *because* he left. Like any kid, I looked for someone to blame, but even that wasn't straightforward. They might have gotten together because of me, but they made the choice to hang on for as long as they did.

Dad was twenty when he came here on a trip with some friends from college, he met an eighteen-year-old girl, spent three weeks with her, and now I exist. Dad stayed, and marrying Mum made that easier. After the separation, Dad got a small apartment nearby and focused on his book and his job teaching creative writing at the university. I spent weekends with him, and he'd make fried chicken every Saturday night while I watched movies on the big couch in his unit.

For the few years he stayed past the divorce, it was obvious he wasn't happy and his relationship with Mum had deteriorated significantly. Two months after my fourteenth birthday, he sold all his stuff, resigned from his job, and shipped what he could back to his parents in Alaska.

Lying here, I can see myself, clear as day, sitting on the old shag pile rug in this room with my Harry Potter collection while he typed away on what would become a bestseller. My mind wanders to the times Dad told me bedtime stories about princesses who slew dragons and saved ancient cities. We both grew up, but deep in my bones, I know we never grew apart.

I'm still on the floor when Mum arrives home. She calls my name, and the sound of her keys hitting the marble-topped table in the entryway echo up the hall.

'Where are you?' she sings out on approach. 'I didn't know you were coming over. I made plans tonight.'

She appears in the doorway, beads of sweat on her forehead from the gut-punch of a summer we're in. Her hair is a little flat, but it still frames her frowning face.

'What are you doing in here?'

'I got a call from Marie two days ago,' I say by way of explaining why I'm sitting on the floor of the stifling spare room.

'Are you okay?' She inspects me, like she's searching for visible wounds. 'What did she say?'

My brow wrinkles. 'She needs me to go over to help with his house. I've got to talk to his lawyer, too, about the will.'

Mum clears her throat. 'I figured that would be the case. Do you have to go all the way over there, though? You know how you are with flying.'

'I know, but I think I should go.'

'Well, it's your decision.' She rolls her shoulders back and fixes her face into a placid smile. 'I can cancel my plans. Maybe we could get pizza and watch MasterChef.'

I pull myself up to a sitting position. 'What plans have you got?'

'It doesn't matter. I can postpone.' She waves it off.

'Mum.' I eye her, lips thin and brow raised. 'What plans?'

'Nothing. Just dinner...with a man.'

I grin at the blush creeping up my mother's neck. 'Where did you find this man?'

'He came into the shop a few weeks ago.' She straightens her back. 'He asked me to dinner, and I said yes.'

'Does he have a name?'

'Eric.'

I hold my arms out and Mum pulls me up off the floor. 'And is Eric financially independent, well-adjusted, and able to hold a job?'

'Oh, stop it.' Mum turns and steps out into the hall, but I'm on her heels.

'Does he know you have a dependent?'

'You're not my dependent anymore. You have a mortgage, for God's sake.'

'I was talking about Wes,' I joke and see the side of her face pull up in a grin.

'He's your dependent, not mine.' She laughs. 'I do love having him around though. Can you bring him over for dinner?'

I nod. 'Yeah, I'll do my best, but speaking of dinner I have to go. It's taco night.'

Mum gives me a hug and a tray of frozen beef casserole before walking me out.

'When are you thinking of going to Alaska?' She leans against the car and folds her arms across her chest.

'I'll look at flights when I get home.' I tighten my grip on the casserole. 'Will you come with me?'

She swallows. 'No, I don't think that's a good idea.'

'Why? Marie said you were welcome.'

There is a flicker of irritation in her eyes. 'I don't need permission.'

'I know that, all I'm saying is that the offer is there.'

She sucks in a breath. 'And I'm declining the offer.'

'Okay,' I mumble as I press the button on my keys and the car unlocks with a beep. I don't want her to spend the rest of the night wracked with guilt, so I wish her luck on her date and hug her before saying goodbye.

By the time I get home, the day has caught up with me, and I'm looking forward to a warm shower and bed. Wes greets me with two taco options. The chicken is too salty, and the mince is too dry, but he's proud of his efforts and I refuse to crush his spirit.

'Are you sure you can't talk your mum into going with you?' Wes asks as he scrubs the skillet with a sponge that desperately needs replacing. 'Or does she not want to see Marie?'

'I know she doesn't but I'm not sure that's the real reason.' I shrug. 'I don't think she knows how to handle him being gone.'

'That's fair.' He puts the skillet on the dish rack and dries his hands with the dish towel. 'No one knows how to deal with something like this.'

'I know, but part of me thinks he deserves something from her, even if it's just coming with me to say goodbye.'

Wes lifts his broad shoulders in a shrug. 'Are you sure you aren't forcing it on her because you feel guilty about not seeing him for six years?'

His tone is gentle, but the content is a sledgehammer to the guts. I hate his natural ability to get to the heart of a problem and this one hurts ten times more because there's nothing I can do to fix it. I can't call Dad and tell him I'm sorry. When I get to Alaska, he won't be there to hold me, to say he's missed me and give me chapters of his books to read and critique like he used to.

'I wish I'd made more of an effort,' I whisper. 'And I wish he had too.'

Wes puts his arm around my shoulders and pulls me to his chest. His cotton t-shirt is soft against my cheek, and I listen to the steady beat of his heart. We stay like this for a while, swaying from side to side as my cluttered mind ticks over.

'I'll come with you.' Wes's deep voice vibrates against my cheek. 'Teddy can handle things for a week or two.'

I pull back and look up at him. 'Are you sure? I know how busy you are and it's an enormous expense.'

'It's fine. And I have money. I don't waste it on shoes and expensive shampoo like you do.'

'I have dry ends. We talked about it. Remember?'

'The two in one stuff does the job.' He laughs and I cringe as I pull my phone out of my pocket. Wes leans against the bench, shoulder to shoulder with me as I look up flights.

The only affordable flight is this coming Sunday. Wes hands over his credit card and says he'll cover my ticket, but he isn't paying any rent for a while.

The few days before our trip are a flurry of activity. I take care of all the arrangements because Wes has enough going on with work. Teddy said he can manage until Wes gets back, but I can tell Wes isn't comfortable leaving. Mum is ecstatic that I won't be going alone. She's always loved Wes, but this gesture has elevated that love to complete adoration. He might replace me in her will.

'Passports?' Wes asks on the night before we fly out.

'Yes. I've got mine and yours in my travel wallet.' I hold up a pastel pink billfold, and he nods.

He's sprawled on my bed, watching YouTube videos of horrific sporting injuries. He should finish his packing. I've Googled the temperature, and it's going to be a brisk minus twenty-two degrees Celsius while we're there. I've explained this, but I still don't think he's taken it onboard. We'll be finding a department store to get him a decent jacket the second we land.

'Right. I've got my wallet, phone, and charger.' I pat my brown leather messenger bag. 'Did you remember your toothbrush?'

Wes nods as I double check all the documents I've saved on my phone. It's a long list, including the details of our hotel in Fairbanks and the one in Seattle. It also has the addresses of all the people I'm supposed to meet with while I'm there. Dana Robinson called on Thursday and Marie put me in touch with Dad's agent, Cecelia Harris, and a guy named Jordan who works for Dad's publisher. I wasn't sure what to make of all this but agreed to the meetings, and considering the publisher and Dad's agent are both based in Seattle, it's not out of the way.

'Are you going to be alright with all these flights?'

'No, so you better get comfortable holding my sweaty claw the whole time.'

I paste on a smile even though a hot ball of anxiety has already formed in my stomach. It will spend the evening maturing until it's ready to be released as irrational thoughts about plane crashes for the entire flight.

'Don't I always?' Wes pulls himself up as I zip up my suitcase and position it at the end of my bed.

'Thank you for coming with me. I know you've got heaps on your plate and this is the last thing you want to be doing.'

'It's not the last thing I want to be doing. Getting teeth pulled is the last thing I want to be doing.'

'Or listening to your dad talk about the housing market and how you need to get in on the ground floor if you want real estate to be a key part of your retirement plan.'

Wes laughs. 'Yeah, that is worse.'

'I seriously don't know what I'd do without you.' I swallow to get rid of the tightness in my throat as my eyes mist. 'Not just with the flying thing, but all the Dad stuff too.'

He pulls me into a hug and kisses the crown of my head. 'Come on, you know I'd never let you do this on your own. We've been looking out for each other since we were kids, it's not going to stop now.'

'Thank you,' I mumble.

'How about we take your mind off things for a bit,' he offers as I pull back to look at him.

'How?'

'I have literally not packed one thing for this trip.'

I groan as I drop my head forward onto his chest.

The next morning Mum picks us up on her way to work. She's in high spirits but artfully dodges Wes's line of questioning about her date with Eric.

'Are we sure he isn't hiding a wife?' Wes taps his chin.

'He isn't hiding a wife, thank you, Wesley,' she scolds. 'We went back to his house and there is no way a woman lives there. Not one piece of his furniture matches.'

'That's a deal breaker, then.' I smirk.

She narrows her eyes and cranks the radio to end the conversation. Cat Stevens is playing, and Wes starts singing along. Soon, Mum and I join in. It reminds me of her and Dad dancing to it when I was a kid. She must have been hit with a similar memory because she changes the station.

When we arrive at the terminal Mum tears up, and I'm not sure whether it's for me or Wes. She pulls him into a hug and says something that I don't quite catch. He smiles at her, and she ruffles his hair but refrains from pinching his cheek.

'Message me as soon as you land,' Mum says as she issues me with a less enthusiastic hug. 'I printed out your flight and accommodation details, so I can keep track of where you are.'

'Mum, we're twenty-eight and I've done this a few times before,' I scoff even though my hands have started sweating in preparation for take-off.

'It's Wesley I'm worried about.' She glances over at him. 'You know he can't sit still for more than twenty minutes.'

'I'll be fine, Ma,' he calls out as he hoists our suitcases up to the curb. 'But can you let my parents know I've gone to Alaska? I forgot to tell Dad when I was over there yesterday.'

Mum's eyes widen and I stifle a laugh. 'Mum, he's kidding. Trish had to dig his passport out because he didn't know where it was.'

Wes's enormous grin confirms this, but it doesn't stop the concern plaguing her features as she climbs back into the car.

CHAPTER FIVE

As expected, the flight from Brisbane to Los Angeles is an endless struggle of trying to sleep and trying not to panic. I've never been a confident flyer, but since it's been a while, I'd forgotten how debilitating it is. Wes tells me over and over that thousands of flights take off every day, and the chances of being in a plane crash are so slim it isn't worth the worry. It makes no difference; I still shake at the hint of turbulence and forget how to breathe. I hate not being able to escape the feeling. It's torture. Thirteen hours of it. Wes, to his credit, tries to distract me with little bottles of wine and listing the order in which he'll be watching the onboard movies.

My stress levels get a little closer to normal when we land in LA, but two hours in an immigration line and then scurrying to the neighbouring terminal to board the flight to Seattle has them rising again. I'm tense on the second flight as well, but it's so much shorter. I listen to the captain give his brief introduction, and my heart flutters when he says we'll be landing in Seattle ten minutes early. The joy is short-lived; he predicts some rough air around the halfway point.

'I don't think this pilot knows what rough air means,' Wes points out as the flight attendants rush through the drinks service so they can get to their seats.

My jaw is aching from being clenched for so long and for the entire four-hour layover at SeaTac I'm a ball of anxiety. When they call boarding for the flight to Fairbanks, I freeze, and Wes eventually has to drag me off the chair while the attendant at the podium gives us a pointed look and announces that the aircraft is in the last stages of boarding. He's even a little snatchy when I hand over my boarding pass.

Crippling terror aside, the flight out of Seattle at night is incredible. It requires a lot of deep breathing and squeezing Wes's forearm, but I dare to look out the window as we bank over the Space Needle and study the veins of the city before they fall away. The pilot on this flight promises a smooth journey, but I'm dubious after having been burned earlier.

Once I've settled as much as possible and Wes has closed his eyes, I pull out my phone and connect to the onboard Wi-Fi. I shoot Mum an update on our whereabouts before opening Facebook to see my feed still flooded with articles about Dad. With each passing day, the internet is in more of a frenzy about what's happening with the last book. Harcourt has been quiet since that first statement and isn't engaging with any commenters on social media. I wish I had some insight because I'm panicking along with the rest of the population.

I read a handful of articles before the frustration gets too much and I stuff my phone in the seat pocket. It's like the internet forgot he was an actual person. Most of them say how disappointing it is that Dad died before he finished the story. There are petitions to use different authors to finish it and a list of authors that would ruin it if given a chance. The comments are so hate-filled it's uncomfortable to read and I can't imagine how awful it would be, as an author, to see your name on a list for something you have no involvement in.

It's one in the morning on touchdown in Fairbanks, and Wes and I watch in awe as we taxi past the snow-covered planes parked at the gates. It takes a while for my nerves to settle, but before long, we're corralled off the plane and waiting at baggage claim while admiring the taxidermy animals around the place. Wes collects our luggage while I approach a sweet, albeit exhausted-looking woman at the information desk who calls the hotel to dispatch their shuttle service.

Outside the terminal it's freezing and, as predicted, Wes's hoodie is not suitable. He shivers beside me, hands in pockets and letting out lazy puffs of steam into the air. Sucking the cold into my lungs helps with the crippling exhaustion. It's a burn I haven't felt in a while, and I love watching the snow fall while catching flakes on my gloved palm. I see why Dad loved it here. Even the airport is a winter wonderland.

We're almost frozen solid when a smiling, middle-aged man in a bright green jacket arrives to collect us. It doesn't take long to get to the Regent Inn, and soon we're being checked in by a woman with a smile far too bright for someone working at this hour.

Wes stifles several yawns as I check out the stag heads fixed to the walls, shabby patterned carpet, and the massive antler chandelier that hangs overhead. There is a slight musty smell, but it's not offensive; it adds to the feel of the place.

The receptionist slides a key with a hefty yellow tag over to me and returns my card a moment later. Once checked-in, Wes and I follow her complex instructions to get to the room on the first floor.

Like the lobby, the room is dated but clean and comfortable. Wes collapses on one of the queen beds and is snoring in a matter of seconds, but I keep my eyes open long enough to amble over to the window. The panes are freezing, and I'm enamoured by the icicles that cling to the tree outside. It's a world away from where I was yesterday, and the evidence of that is all around. I'm too tired to appreciate it though, and as soon as my head hits the pillow, I could be anywhere.

I wake the next morning feeling groggy and at a loss for where I am. The brilliant blanketed trees outside are a welcome reminder, and I pull my legs up to my chest as I watch a clump of snow tumble from a branch.

Wes makes us some terrible instant coffee while I shower, and I thank him again for coming all this way to keep me company. This trip won't be fun for him, and we both know it. For the moment, though, he seems content to lie on his bed and watch reruns of The Office. He's already learned the jingle for Arby's fish sandwiches and can't stop singing it to himself when it plays during every ad break.

I'm fighting through the cooling coffee when a call comes through from a number I don't recognise. Last time this happened, it was Marie trying to tell me about Dad, so I answer without a second thought.

'Hello?'

A man clears his throat. 'Hi, would this be Halliday Townsend?'

'Yeah, who's this?'

He clears his throat again, and it's phlegmier than the first time. 'This is Anthony Holt, I…um worked with your dad.'

I put the coffee mug down on the desk-cum-luggage bench and sit back on the bed, as Wes turns down the volume on the TV.

'Oh, are you from Harcourt? I thought I was dealing with Jordan.'

He takes a breath, and it sounds shaky. 'Yes, Jordan Fisher. I figured he would have contacted you, but…'

Anthony seems to be alone with his thoughts for a moment, and I have to snap him back to our conversation.

'Jordan and I have emailed about meeting when I'm in Seattle, but we haven't spoken about anything else.'

'Oh really?' Anthony asks. 'So he hasn't said anything about your dad's work and his last book?'

'Not yet. Why?' My tone is uncertain, even though I have a niggling curiosity about what's going to happen.

'Well, his last book is set for publication this year, and there are some things to go over before then. Like, who is going to write it?'

'Right.' I tuck my legs up underneath me and press the phone closer to my ear. 'And what does that have to do with me?'

He sucks in a breath. 'A lot. Are you free to meet at all?'

Harcourt is based in Seattle, so I'm confused by the request. 'I'm in Fairbanks, but I'll be in Seattle in a few days' time.'

'Oh, I know,' he stammers. 'I came up for the memorial and was hoping to meet you as soon as possible.'

Even though he's piqued my curiosity, it doesn't make sense he would hang around to meet me when I'll be at Harcourt by the end of the week.

'It won't take long,' he offers. Wes raises an eyebrow at me.

'Where do you want to meet?'

His tone changes to one of sheer delight. 'I'm staying at the Eastbridge on Tenth. They have a restaurant if you'd like to meet there?'

Our hotel is on tenth, so I'm assuming Eastbridge is the not-too-opulent high-rise we passed in the shuttle on the way here.

'Sure. I'm at the Regent down the street. Give me an hour and I'll be there.'

'See you then,' Anthony agrees before the call disconnects.

'What's going on?' Wes swings his legs over the side of the bed and pulls himself up.

'That was a guy from Dad's publishing company. He wants to meet me in an hour.'

'Do you want me to come with you?' Wes asks.

I tell him I'll be fine, but my head is swimming. Two weeks ago, I was helping Mum up-cycle a Singer sewing table, and now I'm meeting with a major publishing house over the fate of one of the world's most successful book series. I don't feel like the right person for the job, and that means I'm probably not. It doesn't stop the bubbles of nervous excitement that pop in my belly, though.

The restaurant at the Eastbridge is much fancier than the outside of the building would suggest. The thick ruby carpet is pristine, and tall arch windows look out over the snow-covered street. Each table has cloth napkins with little silver rings around them, and the servers are all wearing skinny black ties. I have time to take all this in while I wait for Anthony, who is running late even though he's staying here.

'So sorry, Halliday.' An out of breath voice travels across the empty restaurant. I turn to see a person, who I assume is Anthony, zigzagging between the floral upholstered chairs with another man at his heels.

'It's all good, I haven't been here long.' I stand up and hold out my hand. 'Call me Hallie.'

Anthony shakes my hand. Up close, he's short and not much older than me. His light brown hair is thinning, and he's sweaty for someone this close to the Arctic Circle. After a beat of inspecting me, likely checking for some family resemblance to ensure I'm Ellery Yates's daughter, he steps to the side and gestures for the man following him to step forward.

'This is Fletcher Larson,' Anthony announces. 'He was a close friend of your dad's.'

I reach out and shake Fletcher's hand, trying to ignore how dry my mouth has gotten. I recognise Fletcher from his infrequent Instagram updates, but more notably from the dust jacket of *Red Reign*. In person, he's splendid to look at. Defined features, tall and lean with hair so shiny my expensive shampoo couldn't match it.

'Nice to meet you,' Fletcher says as he takes the seat that

Anthony ushers him into. I sit beside him and my stomach twists with the rising pressure. I'm out of my depth: I thought I was meeting with Harcourt, not an author. Especially not *this* author. I fight the urge to gush about how much I love his book and ask the list of questions I have about *Blue Horizon*. I'm glad I didn't message him now.

'Thanks for meeting with us,' Anthony says as he flags over the server hovering near the small station by the kitchen door. She passes out menus before scurrying off and returning to fill the water glasses from a hefty silver jug.

'Not a problem at all. Though I'm not sure how much help I'll be.'

I look across at Fletcher, still fighting the urge to ask about *Blue Horizon*, but Anthony wastes no time.

'Let's get started. The publication date is set for book six, but they've hit a snag with Ellery's death, and now someone has to finish the manuscript.'

Why did he say, 'they' and not 'we'? It doesn't make much sense, but I'm too distracted by the fact that this sweaty little man has called the sudden death of my dad a *snag*. Fletcher is staring daggers at Anthony and the solidarity is appreciated.

Anthony carries on, unperturbed. 'I've done some research and spoken with Harcourt. All of Ellery's notes are the property of his beneficiary. That's you. So, I wanted to meet and discuss the possibility of Fletcher writing the sixth book.'

This has more red flags than my date with Tim-Tom.

'Don't you work for Harcourt?' I say. Anthony shifts in his seat and gives Fletcher a sheepish look.

'I've dealt with Harcourt in the past,' he stammers. 'I represent Fletcher…and they published his debut novel.'

'Right, but you don't actually work for them?'

He shakes his head and I throw a glance at Fletcher, whose deep brown eyes are on Anthony.

'No, I don't work for them directly.'

I keep calm and try to take this information on board. 'You're telling me you somehow got my phone number, misled me into thinking you worked for Dad's publisher, and then met up with me before them to convince me to hand over his notes?'

Anthony straightens his back. 'It's important that we make this process as seamless as possible for you. Fletcher is a talented author and we know he'll be able to finish your dad's series the way it should be written.'

My skin prickles with frustration and I stand up from the table. 'You have got to be kidding me.'

Anthony opens his mouth but snaps it shut when my eyes widen at him. Who has the nerve to do something like this? It's insensitive and unprofessional. Spikes of rage prickle down my arms, causing my fists to clench.

'You've ambushed me a week after my dad's death, which you just called a snag, to get me to let someone I've never met take over Dad's work?' I lower my voice. 'What is wrong with you?'

I collect my coat off the back of the chair and storm off, narrowly missing the waitress on my way out of the restaurant. My eyes are stinging, and I feel that urgent tingle in the back of my nose.

I won't cry in a public place.

'Hallie, wait,' Fletcher calls out, but I keep walking until I'm through the lobby and out of the building. The city outside is blindingly white and frozen air pricks my face as he catches up to me. He calls my name over and over until I come to a stop on the sidewalk beside the hotel driveway. A cluster of tourists waiting outside the hotel are looking at us.

'Hallie, we didn't mean to upset you, and I can see we've gone about this the wrong way. I'm so sorry.' Fletcher's teeth chatter as he stands in front of me without a coat. 'I was close with your dad. He helped me a lot when I was writing my novel.'

Dad had promised that I would meet Fletcher the next time I came over—I guess he was right, but I didn't expect it to be like this. It makes me wonder if he and Dad were really friends or if Dad was just someone of influence who could advance Fletcher's career.

'If you were close with Dad, then you of all people must know how hard this has been,' I say. 'What on earth would make you think this is an appropriate way to get what you want?'

He sets his jaw. 'I know, but this...his work...it means a lot to so many people. You don't have any experience and you're not an author. I knew him and his work, and I won't let it fall into the wrong hands.'

I don't need a coat because my blood is liquid fire. He doesn't know anything about me.

'Wrong hands?' I scoff. 'I know more about my dad's books than anyone on the planet. So don't come to me thinking you know what's best for his series. You have no fucking idea.'

My eyes are brimming with tears and the pink flush in Fletcher's cheeks fades. 'If it means that much to you then you know how important it is that this series is finished properly, and I'm the one to do it.'

'I do understand how important it is, but until five minutes ago I didn't even know I was responsible for what happens with it. You've dumped a ten-tonne weight on my shoulders and now I'm being railroaded into choosing you. Why? Because you're here? I haven't even seen Dad's girlfriend yet and you've cornered me, expecting I'll make this huge decision.' I raise my voice, ignoring the tourists. 'I just lost my dad.'

His expression softens and he opens his mouth to speak. I cut him off.

'You know what sucks about this?' I say. '*Red Reign* is one of my favourite books, and when you walked through that door I couldn't believe that I was finally meeting the man who wrote it.'

Fletcher's brow furrows. 'I'm sorry I disappointed you.'

I look at him for a painfully long moment.

'Me too,' I say as I move past him and continue down the street toward my hotel.

CHAPTER SIX

'So, let me get this straight.' Wes scratches his cheek. 'These guys you've never seen before, ambushed you to get you to sign your dad's book over to them?'

'Dad and Fletcher were friends.'

'Not an excuse though, is it?'

I shake my head. 'Absolutely not. And he said that I'm not the right person to make this decision.'

Talking about it reignites the kindling in my belly. The audacity of that guy. It blows my mind. I understand fans become protective of their favourite authors' work, and Fletcher Larson is closer to Dad and his work than most, but what gives him the right to accost me like that?

I lean my back against the hotel room window. The chill from outside seeps through the glass and the sensation eases some tension in my body.

'I think you should ask Marie.' Wes joins me at the

window. 'If this guy was friends with your dad, then wouldn't she know him?'

'You're right.'

He grins. 'Say again?'

'No.'

'I swear you just said I'm right.'

'And that's the only time I'll say it.'

'But you said it.'

'Shut up and get your coat. I'm taking you sightseeing.'

It takes some convincing, but I get Wes layered up and out onto the snowy streets of Fairbanks. He's still enamoured with the snow and takes every opportunity to drag his ungloved hand over the fences and mailboxes before shivering and tucking his frozen fingers back into his pockets.

The first place I direct him to is the Golden Heart Plaza, where he snaps some photos of the First Family statue, which is obscured by the afternoon's powdery deluge. Wes has the same wide-eyed expression I had the first time I saw this much snow. He comments on how insane it is as we walk along the Chena River until we reach the Moose Antler Arch and take another zillion photos. We're walking the same path Dad took me on the first time I visited Fairbanks, right down to the burger at Brewster's.

On the way back we swing by an outfitter to get Wes a decent jacket and some gloves because we're walking the fine line between bitterly cold and hypothermia.

'Wait, can we go in here?' I ask as Wes looks up from inspecting the non-slip fingertips of his new gloves.

'The bookshop?' He lifts a brow. 'You have heaps of books at home though.'

'I just want to look.'

He doesn't believe me for a second but still follows as I push open the glass door with a cheery little open sign swinging from it.

'Good afternoon,' an elderly woman with pink cheeks and a wide smile greets us from behind the counter. She's knitting what looks like patches for a quilt, and with our greeting, her gaze returns to her work with renewed focus. The eclectic little shop has rows and rows of bookcases. Not one of them is made of the same wood. Wes takes a seat on a small chair in the front window and pulls out his phone. Something has happened at work, and now I feel bad for keeping him away from decent Wi-Fi. His brow furrows, and he stares down at the screen while I read the handwritten signs on each row of shelves, noting that literary fiction is spelled wrong.

When I find the sci-fi and fantasy shelves, I scan the markers until I spot the Y section. All of Dad's books are there in various editions. I inspect the paperbacks with the US covers before moving along to the anniversary edition of the first book. I pull out a paperback and flip it over to see his smiling face on the back. My chest constricts when I look at his picture. He looks so young. His hair is still dark, no salt and pepper peeking through. For a minute I wonder where the photo was taken because the bookshelves in the background look similar to the ones in his old office at Mum's house.

I remember standing in that office when he got his first rejection letter. There was a light in his eyes when he saw the publisher's logo on the corner of the envelope, and he couldn't contain his face-splitting grin. He pulled me to his side and kissed my cheek. He was shaking with excitement and it was infectious, albeit short-lived.

'This is it.' He beamed as he ripped it open. I waited, and as he skimmed the single-page letter, his face fell.

'What does it say?' I'd asked, squeezing his arm.

'They loved it. Especially Princess Halladora and her magic.' He smiled as he referenced the character he'd named after me. 'Unfortunately, they're about to publish a book that's similar so we have to keep looking.'

He folded up the letter and dropped it in the bin under his desk before walking straight to his bedroom and closing the door. When I was sure he wasn't coming back out, I pulled out the letter and read it. It was harsh. They'd suggested a full rewrite—it wasn't sellable, apparently. I put the letter back in the bin only to discover it sitting on his desk a few days later in a wooden photo frame. I never understood why he wanted to look at it all the time, and when I asked, he told me that the rejection letter was one step on a long road, and it was important to remember that he was moving forward.

I pick up the US paperback edition of book five. It's been almost six months since I read it, and as I don't have that particular book, I grab the anniversary edition of book one.

'Found everything?' the woman asks as I round the end of the shelves and place the books on the counter.

'Hang on, one more thing.' I smile and hold up my index finger before hurrying back to the fantasy section. The scanner beeps as I pluck the hardback of *Red Reign* from the shelf. I'm not impressed with the author, but the book is still great. Plus, this edition has foiling on the cover and sprayed edges. I can't not get it.

'Thought you said you weren't getting anything,' Wes comments as he looks at the brown paper bag that's going to disintegrate in the falling snow on our way back.

Hours later, after dinner and three episodes of a chaotic cooking show, Wes is asleep, but my eyes are wide open. I stare at the snow that weighs heavy on the tree branch outside the window. I've been resisting the urge to look at my phone for the last hour, but the temptation has grown too strong to ignore.

I pick it up and Google Fletcher Larson for the hundredth time in my life.

The first hit is his author website. It's sleek with lots of thick lines, muted grey colours, and proportioned boxes of text. On the home screen is a portrait-style photo of him looking at something out of frame. The top button of his charcoal shirt is undone, and he's wearing a black jacket with no tie. His eyes are whiskey coloured, and his hair swept back like it was today. It's a decent photo, he's handsome, and it does him justice. I keep scrolling and read the praise for *Red Reign* before moving on to the biography page. I know all of this.

Born in Chicago, now lives in Seattle and studied creative writing at college. He cites my dad as his biggest influence and got the inspiration for his novel while on a family trip to the UK a few years ago. At the bottom of the page, I click through to his social accounts and skim his Instagram and Twitter. His last post was an announcement about adding Dallas to his book tour schedule. That was three days before Dad died and there's been nothing since.

I've never been one to judge what people post on social media, but something about him having a public platform and not acknowledging Dad's death rubs me the wrong way.

I'm looking for excuses not to like him. Or validation that my anger toward him is justified.

CHAPTER SEVEN

When I wake up, it's still dark and the weather outside has increased to what I would call a blizzard. The snow falls in blustering sheets, but now and then, I spy someone trudging down the buried sidewalk. It's a stunning place to be, even in the dark, with only a few yellow streetlights showing off the blanket of powdery white that coats the city.

Wes is already up, sitting at the desk with his laptop, and from the severe bunching of the muscles in his back, something is going on.

'What's happened?' I ask as Wes leans back, his spine flexing over the low back of the chair.

'Nadia didn't follow up the council approval for a job we're supposed to be starting on Tuesday, and now the client is pissed.'

'Shit,' I sympathise. 'Is Teddy sorting it out?'

'He's on site out at the estate all afternoon, so I have to call the council and see how quickly we can get the approval.' He groans. 'Hopefully it won't take too long.'

'It's okay. Marie will be here in a couple of hours, but I'm happy to go out to the house by myself if you're working.'

He shakes his head. 'I said I'd be here to support you, so I'm coming out to the house.'

I crawl out of my bed and stand behind him, wrapping my arms around his shoulders. 'Thank you.'

He pats my arm as I release his neck, but all the tension that's been holding him hostage is back. In the space of three minutes, he's received five emails and a missed call from Teddy.

I sit back down on the bed with Dad's first book in my hand. The anniversary edition has to be my favourite. The cover is matte black with a shimmering crown dripping in gold-foiled blood. I run my fingers over the foil before opening to the dedication. I've read it a million times, but I know this time it will hurt.

> *For my Halliday.*
> *You are magic.*

My nose tingles and I close my eyes. The last six years are a weight on my chest. All that time wasted and there is nothing I can do to get it back.

My phone vibrates on the melamine bedside table, and I scoop it up to see Anthony's name on the screen. He owes me an apology and I'm in the mood to collect.

I press the green button. 'Hello.'

'Hallie, great to see you yesterday, and I'm so glad you had time to meet Fletch. He's a great writer. He's going to be perfect for the project.' Anthony's words come out in a whoosh, like he's running up a flight of stairs.

I shouldn't have answered. An apology means nothing if I have to work for it.

'What gave you the impression yesterday was in any way successful?'

Anthony forces a laugh. It does not lighten the mood. 'We may have come on a little strong, but this is a once in a lifetime opportunity for Fletcher. He and I are such fans of the series, it feels like it belongs to us as much as anyone.'

'It doesn't though. It isn't even mine, and I was sitting on the floor next to Dad when the first one was written.' I pick up Fletcher's book and stare at the ruby-toned cover. It feels good in my hand, but when I flip it over to see Fletcher's smiling face on the back, I'm irritated again.

'I'm heading back to Seattle tomorrow, but I'd be happy to have a contract drawn up before you meet with Jordan.' He sounds distracted. Like our conversation is a loose end, he needs to tie up before he can get on with his day. 'Jordan agrees Fletcher is the one for this project and having something drawn up for the meeting will fast track things.'

My back teeth grind. Why do I feel like I'm being left out of the loop? I've never met Jordan. We had one polite email conversation about meeting while I'm in Seattle and that's it. Has Fletcher cut me out and gone straight to Harcourt? Do I even get a say in what happens or is it all lip service? A headache starts building and I roll my shoulders and take a breath as Wes turns to look at me.

'Anthony, don't do that.' My voice has an edge. Razor

sharp. 'I will meet with Jordan on my own to talk about this before any decision is made.'

'It has to be finished and Fletcher is the right choice, trust me.'

'I don't trust you because I don't know you. Or Fletcher.'

Anthony is silent for a long moment, and it's a victory. They aren't going to railroad me. I don't care how talented Fletcher is, or how well he knew Dad. If I get as much say in this book as Anthony thinks I do, then I want to work with the author. I can't work with Fletcher.

'I understand, but the sooner we start, the easier this process will be. Harcourt is already on board. Fletcher has a great relationship with them.' He exhales loudly, and I feel my blood boil. *He* doesn't have the right to be pissed off.

'Anthony, I'm not giving Dad's notes to Fletcher. The way you ambushed me and led me to believe you were from Harcourt wasn't just unprofessional, it was a lie. I get that Fletcher wants this, but you're both out of your minds if you think this is the way to get it. Don't call me again.'

Anthony doesn't respond before I hang up the phone.

'Nice work.' Wes gives me a thumbs up.

I slump back down and drag a pillow over my face to muffle the scream I've been holding in since yesterday.

By sunrise, which is ten-thirty, I'm ready and waiting for a text from Marie to say she's downstairs. We've never had much to do with each other aside from Dad telling me she says hello at the tail end of a phone conversation. I'm not sure how this is going to play out, but it's a pressure cooker of a situation.

My previous visits to Fairbanks were short, and she was always busy running her family's lodge on the property next door to Dad's. Maybe she kept her distance because she wanted Dad and I to have all the time we could together. If that was the case, I appreciate it, but it means I know next to nothing about her. I'm older now and moderately more mature, but nerves still spike in my belly at the thought of seeing Marie without Dad as our buffer.

We're layered up and Wes is typing an email when we reach the hotel's front doors to find Marie waiting by the car. She's wrapped in a thick green jacket and woollen beanie. Her eyes go wide at the sight of me.

'Hallie.' She pulls me to her, but it's far from a comforting embrace, it's stiff, like she isn't sure the situation calls for it. She's the same as I remember, though her long, fiery red braid is now cropped to a bob that clears her chin and there are a few more wrinkles around her eyes.

'It's good to see you.' I pull back, and she releases me like I'm a lump of hot coal. I don't take it personally, I know she's trying to navigate the situation, same as me.

'This is my friend, Wes.' I step aside and my six-foot-three shadow holds out his hand.

'Great to meet you, Marie.' He smiles. 'Hope you don't mind if I tag along.'

'Not at all.' She shakes his hand and jerks her head toward the late model Chevy Tahoe parked behind her. 'How about we get in before we all freeze?'

'I'm already halfway there,' Wes jokes as he tugs down the sleeves on his jacket.

With a nod, I loop around the car and climb into the passenger's side. Wes slides into the back seat and reaches over to squeeze my shoulder.

Dad's house isn't far, but the drive feels endless thanks to our stilted conversation. Marie asks about the flight over and how we're coping with the temperature. I can't muster anything other than short, factual answers and occasional comments about how pretty the landscape is. Wes does a good job of carrying the conversation and asks Marie a series of random questions about Alaska. She answers them, but I can see her anguish by how tight she grips the steering wheel. She can't bring herself to look at me, and I'm certain she doesn't need or want me here.

I remain silent as we follow the highway. It cuts through a forest of snow-caked trees, and I grip my knees harder with each bump in the permafrost-affected road. It's an old habit, just like squinting into the blinding white to glimpse Alaskan wildlife. I was never good at spotting a moose, but Dad had a keen eye. We used to make bets on who would spot one first. Suffice to say, I owed Dad a tidy sum but never paid my debts.

Marie slows the car, and we turn onto a narrow trail that's marked by a metal stake with a yellow cap on top. The trees are thicker along this road, and as we crawl through the fresh snowfall, I squint to see what's ahead. Another stake is visible peeking out of the snow, but this one has a small metal barrel attached with *Wentford* painted on it in fading black paint. It doesn't feel like it's been six years.

'Here we are.' Marie exhales as she turns into the

driveway and accelerates a little harder to get up the incline. I lean forward to get a better look at the three buildings. Just as I remembered, they're a scene inside a snow globe. The perimeter of the property is thick forest, and to the left is a small log house with wide windows and a Christmas wreath still fixed to the front door—Marie's family home. A couple of hundred metres away and separated by a smattering of trees is Dad's house in the same log cabin style. It's three stories with a small porch and a double garage underneath. From the front it looks plain, but on the other side, there's a large deck and floor-to-ceiling windows that have a beautiful view of the empty yard behind and the woods beyond. Alongside Marie's house is a sweeping, snow-covered driveway that leads up to the two-story rectangular building at the back of the property. It's the lodge that's been in Marie's family for years. For much of the year, she opens it to guests as a holiday rental that provides off-the-grid living while being close to Fairbanks. At least that's what the website said when I went snooping.

We climb out of the Chevy, and my boots make a delightful crunch on the snow as Wes and I follow Marie up to the house. The wind has picked up since we left Fairbanks, so my face is burning, and Wes's teeth chatter as we wait for Marie to open the front door.

'Clover,' she sings out when she steps inside, and the sound of paws thumping on timber greets us at the threshold. I close the door behind us just as a cloud of white fur bounds into the entryway and launches itself at Marie. She drops to her knees and wraps her arms around the dog like she's hugging a small child.

'Clover, this is Hallie and Wes.' Marie grins, and I crouch down, so I'm level with them.

'Nice to meet you, Clover.' I scratch the Samoyed's neck, and her bliss-filled black eyes watch me as her tongue falls out the side of her mouth. I can't recall the last time I saw any living creature this happy. Though Wes gets pretty excited when the ten-dollar nugget bucket promotion is on at KFC.

Marie stands and makes a whistling noise; it sends Clover scuttling over to a puffy tartan bed by the unlit fireplace.

'Would you like some coffee? Or tea, maybe?' She pulls off her coat and hangs it on the wooden hook beside an archway that leads to the kitchen.

'Coffee would be great,' Wes says as he helps me with my coat and hangs it on the other wall hook.

Marie's kitchen is a perfect square with cabinets running along the far wall and around the corner to the fridge nestled between the sink and wall. In the centre is a small, circular table and several heavy pine chairs adorned with patchwork seat cushions. Behind the table is a set of timber doors that open out onto a snow-covered deck. I look up to the lodge on the hill and notice how unfathomably quiet the world is out here. Aside from the gentle rustle of the wind and the clicking of Marie lighting the stovetop, there's nothing.

'You can sit down.' Marie points at the dining table, and Wes and I do as we're told. While she continues to prepare the coffee, I look over at the small side table by the back door. It's overflowing with framed photographs. There are pictures of the lodge being built, an elderly woman with Marie's red hair, and so many of my dad. He's smiling while shovelling snow and looking over his glasses as he sits in front of his computer.

There's a photo of Dad's parents and Marie's parents drinking on the deck, and another one of them all decorating a Christmas tree. Marie's parents passed away in quick succession right before Dad moved back to Alaska. Not long after that, my grandfather had a heart attack in the kitchen of what is now Dad's house, and my grandmother struggled for a long time afterward. She died of heart failure seven years ago, and Dad took it hard. I was thankful for Marie then. I try to shake the memory as another photo piques my interest, a larger one at the back of the cluster, it's Dad when he was young, teenage young with a beautiful redheaded girl in his arms. Dad and Marie were close long before Mum or I came along.

Marie places my coffee down, and I collect it quickly, enjoying the warmth of the ceramic mug in my hands. She hasn't looked at me and I'm worried if I mention Dad, she'll unravel.

'How is the lodge going?' I ask after I take my first sip. 'Last time I was here you had it booked solid for months.'

She dips her head and threads her finger through the handle of her mug. 'It's closed at the moment for some renovations. The bathrooms and kitchen need updating. There's a waitlist for when it reopens though.'

'It must be hard to get that sort of work done in these weather conditions.' Wes lifts his mug to his lips.

She shrugs. 'Yes, and no. We're used to it, so we find a way.'

Silence blankets the room, and it's as thick as the snow on the ground. I turn my attention back to the photographs and wonder if my likeness to Dad is the reason she can't look at me for any length of time. If Wes notices any of this, he doesn't point it out. Instead, he continues with a line of questioning about lodge renovations.

I need to be gentle with Marie, but I've never been one to navigate complex emotional situations well. Wes reads this uncertainty in the stiffness of my body language because he reaches under the table and squeezes my knee.

Marie silently stares at a knot in the wooden table. I can't keep the words in my mouth any longer.

'Was he sick or anything?'

There is another beat of silence, and Wes takes my hand. I grip it tight and close my eyes for a second.

'No, it was fast. He was here, then he wasn't,' Marie says. 'It wouldn't have been painful.'

'I'm sorry.' My words sound rehearsed and insincere as I work overtime to keep the crack of emotion out of my voice.

Marie pushes her chair back, the scraping sound of timber on timber echoing through the kitchen. 'Would you excuse me for a moment?'

She hurries from the room, and a few seconds later I hear a door close. Wes looks at me with heavy brows and squeezes my hand.

'You okay?' he asks.

Tears sting my eyes and I shake my head. 'I'll be back.'

Clover is startled by the thumping of my boots down the hall. When I reach the bathroom, I close the toilet lid and drop down onto it with my head in my hands. I'm not ready for this. Any of it.

I stand up and pace the room. It's three strides from one side to the other, and it's getting smaller every time I take a breath. The lavender candle on the toilet tank is too strong, and the sound of my boots on the tiles is too heavy. Clover scuttles past outside, no doubt confused by all the sudden movement and closed doors.

There's a gentle knock on the door, and I ease it open to see Wes.

'Come on.' He opens his arms wide and pulls me into him. 'This is gonna hurt for a bit. We know that.'

His words lessen the tightness in my chest, but it doesn't stop tears streaming down my cheeks.

CHAPTER EIGHT

Wes and I stand in the compact living room listening to Marie sobbing in the bedroom. Clover stands guard at the door, whimpering for her owner.

More framed photos crowd the mantle of the stonework fireplace, and the coffee table in the centre of the room is handcrafted. It's Dad's handy work because the legs are uneven. He wasn't great at DIY, and it reminds me of the wonky step stool he made me and the dodgy concreting under the clothesline with my six-year-old handprint in it.

Marie surfaces a few minutes later, puffy-eyed, and places a set of keys in the palm of my hand.

'I'm not feeling up to going over there today,' she whispers. 'Come back when you're ready, and I'll drive you to the hotel.'

I take the keys, and the jangling sound has Clover running for us. She isn't bounding like before, but her tail is wagging as she rubs her body against my legs, leaving tufts of white fur on my black jeans.

'You can take her with you if you'd like. She loves it over there,' Marie says as she turns and walks back to her room.

'Come on, Clover.' Wes leans down and pats the dog's head. 'You can lead the way.'

I pull on my jacket, gloves, and scarf while Clover sits at the door. Her tail wags when Wes twists the handle, and she's out the door and down the stairs like a shot. Watching her collide with the snowbank beside the path brings a smile to my face, and I keep an eye on her as we trudge up toward Dad's house.

When we cross the threshold, Wes sucks in a breath. 'Shit.'

Dad's house is nothing like I remember. The large open living room with its enormous vaulted ceilings used to look like something from a House and Garden magazine. The long lounge suite is still there, but it's buried under piles of notepads, loose-leaf paper, and leather-bound books. Behind the lounge is a thick mahogany desk, which is as cluttered as the couch. At one end of the desk is an old desktop computer with a mass of twisted black cords spewing from the back.

'What happened here?' I mutter.

'I didn't think he was a hoarder.' Wes bumps a stack of books with his foot, and it falls to the floor with a thud. Clover takes off, weaving through the cardboard boxes and book towers with her fluffy tail bouncing above the stacks like a periscope. I follow her path, but it becomes too narrow, so I break off toward the stairs leading up to the loft. They're buried under more boxes, but I navigate my way up and inspect the open space. The walls are lined with empty book-shelves, and a near new sofa bed sits under the large window at the back. The books from the shelves are piled high on the carpet.

'He wasn't a hoarder. He must have been clearing it out,' I say to Wes as I track back down the stairs. 'He used to do that when he had writer's block.'

Wes offers his hand to help me down the last few steps while Clover zips past us, treating the lounge room like a maze. She doesn't notice when Wes and I disappear into the hallway and stop at the first door on the left side. It's my bedroom and when I push the door, I expect resistance. It swings open with minimum effort.

'Your room?' Wes says as we cross the threshold.

I nod but say nothing.

It hasn't changed in the last six years. The roughly hewn four-poster bed in the centre of the room topped with the red and black checked bedspread I picked out when Dad took me on an eye-opening trip to Walmart. Strings of fairy lights are still wrapped around the bed canopy. Dad put them up the first time I visited because they looked like the ones in my room at home. I was fifteen at the time and refused to admit I wanted them. It warmed my difficult teenage heart, none-theless. Under the large window is a chest of drawers made from the same timber as the bed. There's nothing on top of it now, but I remember it being covered in my cheap makeup and hair ties.

'It's nice.' Wes drags his foot over the fluffy red rug that takes up most of the floor. The smell of fresh fabric cleaner hangs heavy in the air. It's Marie's doing, but there's no evidence of her in this house. No flowers in old wine bottles or patchwork quilts. There aren't any photos, unless they're buried somewhere.

I continue down the hall, now accompanied by Clover, and peek into the bathroom. It's been gutted and redone in the last six years. The exposed pipes now gone, and it boasts a crisp white, freestanding tub with shiny silver taps and a large glass shower beside it. I linger in the doorway a little too long, shooting side glances at the closed door of Dad's bedroom. Clover is tired of waiting and sits down on the floor, splaying her legs out and groaning.

'Give me a minute.' I exhale and she looks up at me. 'This is hard.'

Her tail wags, and it makes a sweeping sound across the timber. We stare at each other for a moment before she gets to her feet and wags her tail with more enthusiasm.

'I don't know what's in there, so stop pushing me.' Clover's tongue falls out of her mouth as I address her. 'Alright, fine.'

Wes chuckles as I reach for the handle, and Clover's tail wags so hard I'm worried she'll hurt herself. She pushes her nose through the crack, forcing it wider and bounding onto the bed to settle amongst the pillows. I open my mouth to call her down, but there's something in her dark eyes that makes my chest ache. She lets out a whimper as she lays her head on Dad's pillow.

'Are you okay?' Wes asks. 'Because I don't think I'm ready for this.'

I squeeze his hand and pull him into the room. He pats Clover on the head as I lay back on the tufted charcoal quilt and stare at the rough wood and cross beams above. It's so quiet and clean in here, nothing like the chaos of the living room. Wes lays down beside me, and Clover, feeling left out, twists around so her cold nose presses against my hand.

'Can you do me a favour?' My throat feels tight. Wes turns his head to look at me. 'Can you tell me that I should feel bad for not visiting Dad more?'

'Is that what you want to hear?'

I nod as a few tears break free.

Wes clears his throat but keeps his tone soft. 'Your excuses for not coming were always weak. You blamed it on your Mum once too. Telling yourself that spending time with your Dad would make her think you were choosing him, like they were both demanding your attention. They weren't and you know it.'

I let out a sob, and Wes panics, rolling onto his side and pulling me into him. 'You said that's what you wanted.'

'It is.' I continue to cry even though it feels good to hear someone confirm, out loud, that I could have done better.

'Don't beat yourself up though, Hal,' Wes says. 'You can't change it now.'

We sit in silence for a few minutes before going back out to the living room. Facing the mess for a second time makes it look worse. Even Wes seems to be hit with another wave of shock. He tiptoes through a couple of teetering magazine stacks to sit down on the only vacant section of the couch, which is far too narrow for his frame.

Clover goes off, periscoping again as I make my way to the desk and collapse into his office chair. Dad must have been suffering through some severe writer's block to get the house in this state. I wonder if Marie knows.

'He was a good dad,' I say. 'He used to sit with me and

drink water from my plastic tea set. He took me to school on my first day and stayed until the teacher asked him to leave. Then he sat in the car outside for most of the morning in case I lost it and came running out.'

Wes smiles. 'Yeah. I remember that. He gave me beer sometimes too. What a legend.'

I run my fingers over the desk again, a faint streak in the dust appearing. It's comforting to be in his space, but I don't feel close enough to him—like we're separated by a thick pane of glass.

The cold has crept in, and my fingers are stiff as I open the desk draw. The chill makes way for a pinprick of excitement when I see the well-worn and cherished red leather notebook with its little gold 'H' stamped on the bottom corner of the cover.

I crack it open to a random page and see Dad's familiar handwriting. My heart swells before I finish the first sentence.

I'm trying not to overthink this, but you're on a date. With a boy. That's what he is, a boy. You're only thirteen and some BOY has taken you to see a movie. I sat in the parking lot while you stood outside waiting for some boy whose name I refuse to commit to memory. Alright, it's Justin and I've already memorized his face from the school picture on the fridge at your mom's house. I don't like his hair. I have to say that. It's too long and trying to gel it is probably why he left you standing there for ten minutes when he should have been on time for his date. What kind of man, sorry BOY, would leave my daughter standing there, in the evening drizzle, wearing the new sundress she spent all of her money on? Justin doesn't deserve you Halliday, no matter how excited his dad said he was. That's right, I spoke to his dad after you both went inside. He said Justin was late because of piano practice, but I know it's his hair. That unruly mess of curls is nothing but a plaything for Queensland's humidity.

I'm having second thoughts about moving back to Fairbanks now and that curly-haired piano-playing Justin has caused it. He's set his sights on my little girl and for all we know he wants me out of the way. He may have been orchestrating this from the start. Every little thing that led to this moment was set in motion by a thirteen-year-old with poor time management.

You should think yourself lucky I didn't buy a ticket for the movie and sneak in after the previews. Instead, I got a Big Mac and hurried back to my vantage point outside the doors of the movie theatre. When you come out in an hour, I know you'll accuse me of hanging around. I'll lie and tell you I went home, but you'll see right through me because I can't lie to you. I'll apologize and tell you we can get ice cream so long as you promise not to see Justin again. You'll say yes to the ice cream and insist on mint choc chip (the worst flavor), you'll negotiate the terms of our agreement and I will lose. I don't mind losing to you, and I don't regret staying.

'What have you found?' Wes cranes his neck over the desk to check out the book.

'It's Dad's journal.' My voice sounds wistful even to my own ears. 'He told me he was writing me a book of letters and he'd give it to me on my thirtieth birthday.'

'Want me to hold on to it for the next two years?' Wes lifts a brow. I close the journal and hold it against my chest.

'No, I want it now.'

Wes picks up a small box from the floor and empties its

contents before placing it on the desk in front of me. 'Anything else you want to take back with you?'

I look around the room. It's in such a state I don't even know where to begin. Or if it's my responsibility to organise any of it. Is that something that falls to Marie?

I get up from the chair and pull the fleece hoodie off the back of it, folding it and placing it in the box. It smells like the soap Dad's been using for the last fourteen years, and the smell reminds me of him and this house.

'Is that it?' Wes asks as I scan the room again.

I know what I want, but don't know where I'd find them or if it's appropriate to take something so important.

'There's something else,' I say.

Wes shrugs. 'Alright. What is it?'

'The notes for book six,' I whisper. 'Is it wrong to want to take them with me? Like, too soon maybe?'

Wes shakes his head. 'I don't think so. Won't you need them when you meet the publisher? Saves you getting Marie to send them to you later on.'

He's right, but I don't know where to start the search for them. There are yellow legal pads and notebooks strewn all over the place. Those were his weapons of choice when he outlined the first five books.

'We'll start with the computer then I guess we'll sort through all this.' I gesture at the living room.

Wes gives a resigned nod and rubs his hands together. 'Let's get stuck in then.'

CHAPTER NINE

'There has to be an outline.' I put my head in my hands. 'Are we missing something?'

Wes stacks the last boxes along the front wall of the living room and pats it triumphantly. So far, we've found nothing relating to book six aside from the rough draft of chapter one that Dad sent me ages ago. Outwardly, I'm confused. Internally, I'm screaming but trying to convince myself that it's fine and we just haven't looked hard enough.

'Is there another computer somewhere? A laptop at Marie's place?' Wes comes over and perches himself on the side of the desk.

We've been at this for hours and with every box and digital file we sift through, I become more panicked. Dad had an outline for every book, right down to the finest detail. Post-it notes all over walls and stacks of index cards categorised by character point of view.

He didn't trust his brain to retain ideas, so he drew them

out onto anything he could find. You name it, there are notes on it. In our search we came across cardboard bar coasters, old bank statements, and even a hand towel with a topographical map scribbled on it. We found nothing new, though. Only more character backstories.

We have nothing.

I'm supposed to meet with Jordan, and I have nothing.

'Can you put it together from the other books?' Wes asks.

'I don't know. Dad would have had the arcs planned out. I just don't understand why he didn't write any of it down. It's so unlike him.'

We continue to search, but when Wes starts yawning, it's time to head back over to Marie's. It's been a hard day and the force of it hits me when I sit down opposite Marie in her living room. My body aches from shifting boxes, my eyes sting from crying, and there's a gnawing sensation in my stomach because I have no idea what the hell is going to happen in book six.

'Will you be back?' Marie asks as she stares at the fireplace.

'Yes, but I'm not sure when,' I say. 'The boxes are stacked for now, but I'll come back and help go through them.'

Marie nods and I ask if she's seen any notes that could be for book six or, as Wes suggested, a secondary computer. She says everything is at Dad's place and not hers. She's adamant, so I don't push the issue.

'I thought you'd call, that's all.' Mum's hurt is clear down the phone line. 'Are you alright?'

'I'm fine, Mum.'

'You don't sound fine. You sound like you've been crying.'

'I was at Dad's house.' I'm despondent as I tug on the hem of my pyjama shirt. Mum takes a deep breath, and I hear the crunch of the pricing gun. She's at work.

'Did you hire a car? I'm not sure I like you driving in the snow, Halliday.'

'Marie picked us up and dropped us back a little while ago.'

Mum makes a noncommittal humming noise, and the pricing gun stamps more tags.

'Is Wes still alive?' she asks. 'I've made some lasagnes and chicken risotto, so you don't have to worry about cooking dinner for a week when you get back.'

Wes's ears prick up as his attention snaps to me. 'Did she say chicken risotto?'

I nod, and he pumps his fist.

'Thanks Mum.'

We chat about the store for a few minutes before Mum has to go. She doesn't mention Dad or Marie but says she misses me twice. She says she misses Wes four times.

After my call with Mum, Wes returns to his laptop to schedule projects and I thumb through the wafer-thin pages of Dad's journal.

You, Halliday Elisabeth Townsend, are more terrifying than any agent or publisher I could send this manuscript to. Even at twelve, you have artfully dissected the fifth draft of my masterpiece like no other. I'd be hurt if I wasn't so impressed. I don't have time to ponder this though because you handed me your notes on my first chapter and asked to see the changes tomorrow. Whose kid are you? A valid question if you didn't look like me so damn much. I'll make the changes and resubmit the chapter. The way you smirked at me when I told you that was priceless.

You have to go back to your Mom's place now, but I don't want you to go. I love having you here, reading my story and telling me that the prince sounds like an idiot and that no one would want to marry him. I think you're right.

I'm so glad I chose this entry because, despite the tears streaming down my cheeks, I'm grinning from ear to ear. I reread the entry three times before closing the book and hugging it to my chest.

The next morning, I leave Wes at the hotel for my appointment with Dana Robinson.

The law firm is small but modern with patterned wall-paper and the kind of brightly coloured chairs you'd see in the office of a tech startup. It's out of place compared to the rustic nature of every other building I've entered in Fairbanks.

'Hi, I'm Hallie Townsend. I'm here to see Dana,' I say to the middle-aged woman sitting behind the glossy white recep-tion desk. She says Dana won't be long and asks me to take a seat. I'm cracking open a magazine when a stunning young woman in a tight, bottle green dress appears at the mouth of the hallway.

'Hallie.' She strides toward me with her hand outstretched. 'Great to meet you.'

Her handshake is firmer than I expect, and it makes me self-conscious about the pathetic grip I offer. 'Hi, Dana.'

I follow her down the short hallway to her office at the end. She offers her condolences and lightens the mood by mentioning how flustered the receptionist was the last time Dad stopped by. She's a huge fan and even had him sign the plastic container she brought her lunch in.

Dana's office is spacious with minimal furnishings. That colourful geometric wallpaper covers one wall, and a large window offers a spectacular view of the blanketed city. I imagine it doesn't look anywhere near as beautiful in the summer months as we're in an industrial park.

'Have a seat. There isn't much to go over. I need a few signatures and some personal details so I can execute your father's will.' Dana takes a seat on the high-backed leather chair and gestures at the chair opposite her. I shrug off my jacket, feeling underdressed in my jeans and a long-sleeved grey t-shirt. I'm still trying to get comfortable on the angled plastic chair when she pulls out a Manila folder and skims the first few pages.

'It's basic. There's no mortgage on the house, and the rest of his estate is cash aside from his investment in Harcourt Press.'

I nod. 'He mentioned something a while ago about Harcourt. What was his involvement with it?'

'None. He was an investor. No role in the day to day, only earnings from the company's profit.' Her eyes are fixed on the contents of the folder. 'You're the only beneficiary, so it's up to you what you'd like to do with his assets. If you're not interested in the publishing house, you can sell your dad's stake back to the owners, and if you aren't interested in keeping the house, I can get you in contact with an agent to manage the sale.'

I sag back into the chair, and the fabric of my jeans makes a squeaking noise.

'No, that's fine,' I mumble as my brain catches up. I hadn't thought about selling the house. Is that something I should do?

'No problem at all.' Dana lays out several documents. 'Just a few signatures here and here.'

Her cherry lacquered nail taps the dotted lines on each page, and I scan them. They're like the ones Wes had to sign when his grandmother died, and he got her old Volvo and a set of salad spoons. The Volvo hadn't run in a decade, and the salad spoons were electroplated. He wasn't the favourite grandchild.

'Do I need to do anything else?'

'You'll need to get in contact with an attorney in Australia to work out any outstanding taxes you'll be required to pay. The entire process is straightforward. Do you have someone that can help with it, though?'

I sign on the last dotted line. 'I'm sure I can find someone.'

A smile curls her lips, and her pale green eyes settle on me. 'Email me if you have questions.'

I hand the pen back, and she gathers the paperwork and returns it to the folder with Dad's real name attached to the side on a printed label. In the surreal whirlwind of this meeting, I forgot to ask a rather obvious question.

'How much did I just inherit?'

'About sixty-six million.' She's flippant as she shuffles paper.

My heart skips several beats, and when I ask Dana to repeat the number, she obliges.

'That's too much money,' I whisper. 'How is he worth that much?'

'Advances, royalties, merchandise, and selling the rights for the television series.'

My weak heart continues its erratic thumping.

'What about Marie Wentford?'

'What about her?'

I can hear my thunderous pulse in my ears. 'Doesn't she get anything?'

Dana lifts her slender shoulders as she stands from her desk. 'Elliot's will wasn't updated, and he passed suddenly. He and Marie weren't legally married either, and they have separate residential addresses. She can contest the will if she chooses to, but that would mean excessive legal fees for you both.'

It feels like I've swallowed a boulder.

'She should get something.'

'Well, that's your decision.'

I search Dana's ageless face, hoping she'll tell me what to do and give me precise instructions on how to execute it. Instead, she holds her hand out and shakes mine with that vice grip again.

I'm in a daze as I exit the building, and my head still hasn't cleared upon arrival back at the hotel.

'How did it go?' Wes greets me with a smile. I stand in the middle of the room with my fingers gripped around the papers I signed, now marred with a sizeable red stamp that says *Client Copy*.

'Sixty-six million, Wes.'

'What?'

'Sixty-six million.'

He exhales a rush of air. 'He left you sixty-six million?'

'Yes.'

'Fuuccckkk. That's a lot of money.'

Wes drops back down on his bed with his mouth hanging open. He's at a loss for words, but after a moment, says the most Wes thing possible. 'Does this mean we can get a new washing machine? The other one keeps trying to escape the laundry when I wash towels.'

'Sure.' I brush off the request. 'Dad also had a stake in Harcourt too. That has to mean something for the last book, right?'

Wes shrugs. 'You'll have to ask them.'

My limbs tingle as I drop the paperwork on the bed and start pacing. This is all so weird. A week ago, I was on the periphery of Dad's world and now I'm in quicksand.

CHAPTER TEN

By the time we leave Fairbanks, everything has gotten on top of me. I'm overwhelmed by the money, I'm waiting for Marie to ask about it, and I've got no idea what to say to Harcourt about the book six outline. Or lack thereof.

My world is turning on its axis and I'm struggling to hold on.

This feeling doesn't ease because when I enter the airport terminal, I see an unwanted, familiar face.

Fletcher Larson is standing in the Alaska Airlines check-in queue. I take a step back toward Wes, who's returning a call over by the door, but it's too late, Fletcher's spotted me.

'Ten o'clock to Seattle?' he says as I join the line two places behind him.

I nod and pull out my phone, hoping it will discourage conversation over the heads of other passengers. As we shuffle along in the queue, he looks back at me, but I turn away and he doesn't try to interact again. The sight of him forces my brain to play back our interaction on the sidewalk. The anger has faded, but the disappointment is still weighing on me. Why did he have to do that? I had ideas about our first meeting. The questions I'd ask and the conversation we'd have. He ruined all of it.

Wes joins me in the line as Fletcher reaches the desk.

'That's him,' I whisper and flick my chin in Fletcher's direction.

Wes inspects him for a couple of seconds. 'I expected some old guy.'

'I told you he was young.'

'Yeah, but when you say fantasy author, I picture a bushy grey beard and a bit of extra weight around the middle.' He's still studying Fletcher. 'That dude's like, I dunno, handsome?'

I don't respond—no matter how handsome he might be, I can't bring myself to say something nice about him.

Once checked in for the flight, I try to avoid Fletcher. It's a small airport, so of course he's everywhere I go. We're right behind him in the TSA line and after I drop Wes off at the gate with our bags, Fletcher walks into the store where I'm purchasing a bottle of water.

'Are you following me?' He raises a brow as he saunters up behind me in the check-out line, Gatorade and Pringles in hand.

'I'm not following you. This is a small airport.'

His nose wrinkles and when he responds, his words drip with condescension. 'Kind of seems like everywhere I go, you're there.'

'That's not the case. If I never saw you again, I'd be happy.'

Fletcher frowns, but I don't feel bad about being prickly.

'Hallie.' He says my name like we're friends and he's tired of waiting for me to forgive him. 'I said I was sorry, and I agree I could have handled it better, but are you ready for what's about to happen?'

The way he says it makes my stomach knot. What is about to happen? I'm not sure how all the intellectual property stuff works, but there are people to help with that.

'I've been in touch with Harcourt, Dad's lawyer, and his agent. I don't need your input.' I take out my wallet and hand some notes to the cashier. 'Also, what you seem to forget is that I'm an avid fantasy reader. You think I don't have anyone in mind to write it?'

I don't, but I enjoy his eyes widening a fraction of an inch. 'Who?'

'Someone who didn't lure me to a restaurant under false pretences then insinuate that I'm incapable of doing what's best for my father's book series.'

I turn and stalk back to the gate. Fletcher doesn't follow.

Wes is on the phone when I take a seat beside him. He must feel the irritation radiating off me because he hangs up and asks what's going on.

I repeat the interaction, and Wes promises to step in if Fletcher comes near me again.

Wes doesn't have to follow through on his promise because when Fletcher returns to the gate prior to boarding, he sits a few chairs down in the row opposite. He doesn't look poised to say anything, but I'm on guard.

'Hey.' Wes taps me on the shoulder, and I slip off my headphones. 'Where's that power brick thing? My phone's almost dead.'

'In my carry on.' I point to the bag under the seat.

Wes stands up, placing the bag on the seat so he can rifle through it. Out comes my jacket, toiletries bag, and scarf. Fletcher looks up, and it's at that moment Wes pulls out the little pouch containing the charging cables, hauling Fletcher's book along with it. I watch as it tumbles from the bag and hits the floor with a thump.

My eyes snap up to Fletcher, who is sporting a wide grin.

I snatch the book from the floor and stuff it back into the bag as they announce boarding for our flight. It takes forever, but as soon as they call our boarding group I hurry toward the gate. It's the only time I've ever rushed to get on a plane.

Fletcher doesn't miss me though and as we board, he's right behind me. It's a whisper, but when I step into the cabin, I hear him say. 'Want me to sign it for you?'

CHAPTER ELEVEN

Day one in Seattle, I wake to the sounds of a housekeeper banging around in the hall and a pool of dribble sticking my face to the pillow. Thanks to a delay in Anchorage, we got in late and the hotel didn't have any rooms left with two beds. As a result, I was kicked in the shins all night because Wes lacks spatial awareness.

'You're pretty as a picture.' Wes grins as he looks at me from the occasional chair in the corner. 'I got you a coffee.'

'Thank you.' I rub my eyes and pick up the takeaway coffee cup on the bedside table.

'What's on the docket for today?' Wes asks.

'I'm meeting with Harcourt.' I scratch some dried spit off my chin. 'Will you be okay by yourself? I'll be as quick as I can.'

'Yeah, I'll be fine. There's a pop culture museum around here somewhere.'

I crawl out of the bed and reach over to muss up Wes's hair. 'You're the best. You know that.'

'I do.' He gives me a wink as he sips his coffee.

An hour later, I arrive at Harcourt to find Fletcher leaning on the front desk. Has he come to crash my meeting with Jordan now, too? It's unbelievable to me that someone could be this obnoxious. If he wanted a shot in hell at this book, he would leave me alone. Or is my blatant hostility not clear?

Fletcher has swapped the Alaska gear for a wool coat, and it's clearly impressed the receptionist. She keeps laughing and touching his arm, so it takes a second for her attention to shift to me. When it does, she looks inconvenienced.

'Halliday Townsend,' I say. 'I'm here to see Jordan Fisher.'

Her kohl-lined eyes flick down to her desk. 'He's on a call, but you're welcome to wait over there.'

I sit in the chair she gestured to while Fletcher ends their conversation and takes a seat next to me.

'You're definitely following me.' I sigh.

'Hallie,' he says as he adjusts in the narrow, leather chair. 'How are you?'

'Fine.' I pull my phone from my pocket. Wes has texted three times. First to say he's finding somewhere to eat, second to tell me he's lost, and third to say he's worked out where he is and not to worry.

'Before you step into this meeting, I have to say something.' Fletcher interrupts my response to Wes.

I lift my eyes from my phone. 'Really? You don't feel you've said enough? Would you like a larger shovel to dig your grave more efficiently?'

He ignores my quip. 'Jordan wants a decision soon. I already know everything about your dad's work and Harcourt published my book. I have experience with them and Jordan.'

Here we go again. I turn my attention back to my phone and finish my text to Wes before answering.

'Why are you here, Fletcher? How did you know what time I'd be here?' I shake my head. 'No, it doesn't matter. I don't care. Just leave me alone.'

My palms are sweating, so I tuck them into my coat.

'I'm trying to help you.'

I don't appreciate his clipped tone. He doesn't get to be snippy with me.

Fletcher drags his hand through his hair. 'This book is a marathon and you need someone who knows what they're doing. Your dad and I were close, and I have more insight into his sixth book than any other author.'

I study his features, searching for any truth to what he's said. Judging by the complete lack of an outline amongst Dad's things in Alaska, I'm thinking Fletcher has little to no information about book six.

I straighten my back, wishing that the receptionist would call him back over. From the wistful look in her eyes, she wants to keep talking to him.

'You don't know anything about book six.' I narrow my eyes as I call his bluff. 'No one does.'

He doesn't get the chance to respond before I hear my name called.

'Halliday.'

I look up to see a man who must be Jordan Fisher walking toward me with his hand outstretched. He's younger than I thought but exudes the confidence you'd expect from someone who's been in this game for decades. He's handsome. Brown skin, megawatt smile, and onyx eyes that shine under the LED lights. The photo on his Twitter account doesn't compare to the real thing. If Violet were here, she'd be elbowing me in the ribs and making her eyebrows dance.

'Great to meet you.' I stand up and shake his hand. He flashes me another smile before leaning around to speak to Fletcher.

'I'll be with you soon, Fletch.' He smiles. 'Thanks for coming in. I know you're busy.'

Fletcher smirks. Basking in the glory that my assumption of him following me here has been shot down.

I pretend not to notice or care as I follow Jordan into the hallway.

The Harcourt offices are modern and minimalist. Blown-up prints of Dad's book covers line the walls with a prominent space waiting for the sixth.

'After you.' Jordan ushers me inside the door at the end of the hall, and it's obvious he scored the office with the best view. As I sit down, I glimpse the ocean between the buildings. The sky is grey as a thick mist crawls in. Typical Seattle.

Jordan undoes the button on his navy suit as he sits down, and it feels like I'm seconds away from a bank loan rejection.

'How are you doing?' He makes direct eye contact and his dark brows draw together. 'I can't imagine what you're going through right now.'

I wonder if he's trying to gauge my fragility. If he's

invested in Fletcher writing the book, like Anthony said, then I don't want to appear confused or incompetent.

It takes a bit of work, but I steel myself.

'I'm coping, given the situation.'

Yuck. I sound like a recorded message on an answering machine. The alternative is crying, but I'm not keen on embarrassing myself this early in our working relationship.

He leans back in his chair, still surveying me as he taps his chin with his index finger. I'm not sure if I like him or not yet. I'm also not sure if I've made the best first impression.

'We planned on releasing Ellery's sixth book this year, and his tragic passing has us all at a loose end. I, for one, am a huge fan of his and working with him on books four and five was a dream come true. His work going unfinished is something I can't fathom.' He looks away for a second, takes a breath, and clears his throat.

It's this brief display of emotion that softens my resolve. I do like him.

'Sorry.' He clears his throat again and returns his attention to me. 'With the licensing agreements we had in place, certain decisions fall to you. As his beneficiary, Ellery's intellectual property and any notes and outlines for future projects are yours.'

The atmosphere in the office has changed. There's a tingle in my nose, and I wipe my eye with the sleeve of my coat. There are no notes or outlines. And there won't be any future projects from Dad.

'I'm a bit overwhelmed,' I mutter. 'Sorry.'

Jordan nods. 'I understand. We're all rattled at the moment.'

He slides open his desk drawer and produces a small box of tissues. The gesture does nothing for my composure, but I keep the breakdown at bay.

'Do I decide who writes the book?'

'Yes,' Jordan says. 'It's a big decision, so I'll work with you to ensure we appoint the right person. We already have several authors interested in the project.'

'How many authors?'

'Four, as of an hour ago.'

Curiosity burns bright in my chest as I look at Jordan. 'That many? Already?'

He smiles. 'Yes, and I think the selection will impress you.'

'Who are they?'

'Brent Gallagher and Scott Cutler confirmed their interest yesterday, and my understanding is that Fletcher Larson has already been in contact with you.'

I press my mouth into a thin line. 'Unfortunately, yes.'

A smirk plays on Jordan's lips. 'Yeah, I heard what happened. He's tenacious.'

'Tenacious?' I scoff. 'That's not the word I'd use.'

'He's talented.'

'I know he is. I'm a huge fan of *Red Reign*, but after meeting him, I can't see us working well together.'

Jordan scratches his temple as he seems to search for a response.

'Who's the fourth author?' I steer the conversation away from Fletcher.

Jordan's phone vibrates on his desk and he looks down to read the message before glancing down the hallway behind me.

'He's here if you'd like to meet him.' Jordan stands and moves the door, stepping back so I can exit in front of him. We pass a few other offices before he pulls to a stop in front of a spotlessly clean glass door. 'In here.'

I don't miss the sly smile on his face as we step into a modest-sized boardroom. A concrete table dominates the long space, and an angled metal light fixture hangs from the roof, casting the room in a harsh white light.

'Thank you for coming in.' Jordan strides to the opposite end of the table. The man seated there stands to shake Jordan's hand.

'You're lucky you caught me. I'm flying back to San Francisco tomorrow.' His eyes crinkle as he unleashes a familiar smile. My heart races.

'Mason Parrish!' I round the table, stepping past Jordan to shake Mason's hand. 'I'm a massive fan of your books.'

I'm holding Mason's hand for way too long and Jordan clears his throat.

'Mason, this is Halliday Townsend. Ellery's daughter.'

Mason smiles and the lines form around his bright blue eyes again. 'Halliday? As in the English novelist Alice Halliday?'

'The very same. Dad was a fan of the classics. He tried to get Tolkien past Mum, but she wasn't having it.'

Mason chuckles and dips his chin. 'I feel Halliday suits you better.'

'I have every one of your Death Knight books. And the Summoner Series, and the Kingdom of Bone Trilogy.'

'And what did you think of them?' Mason chuckles.

'I love them. All of them. Everything you've ever written, in fact. Dad's work aside, I don't think I've found a fantasy novel with a magic system as well-crafted as yours.'

Mason puts his hand on his chest and beams. 'Well, that is quite the compliment.'

I lift my shoulders. 'I'm not the authority on it, but I'm buying what you're selling.'

'So are millions of other people,' Jordan interjects and gestures for me to take a seat. As I do, I glance out the glass door to see Fletcher in reception. He says something to the receptionist who points toward the boardroom. Fletcher follows her finger, and his brow creases when he sees me.

'I'm also a fan of your father's work. We did a few BookCon panels together. He always had such passion for our craft,' Mason says and my chest swells with unwarranted pride. 'It upset me to hear of his passing. Especially so young and at the height of his career.'

Jordan leans forward in his chair to insert himself into our conversation.

'As I explained to you, Mason, Ellery's death has left *Blood of Gold* in stasis. With Hallie's permission, our intention is to move forward with the sixth book and have it penned by a different author. Last time we spoke you expressed some interest.'

Mason nods. 'I'd be very interested.'

My heart speeds up and I know I'm still starstruck. Mason wants to write Dad's book? I'm not sure I'm on the planet anymore. I may have floated away in anti-gravitational elation.

'Mason is experienced, has brand recognition. All things

that will benefit us when it comes to pleasing our readers,' Jordan says.

'I'd be happy to submit some ideas I have if that would help?' Mason offers.

I want to tell him it won't be necessary but stifle the giddiness rushing through me.

'I'd be honoured to hear your ideas.'

Jordan turns his attention to Mason. 'Mase, we've got a few other authors interested, so we'll give Hallie a chance to assess her options.'

While I *should* assess my options, Mason's credentials are hard to ignore. He's seasoned, with twenty-eight bestsellers under his belt. Not to mention that he's one of my all-time favourite authors.

Mason leans forward and rests his elbows on the surface of the table. 'I understand this is a big decision, so take your time.'

It is, but my brain is screaming to sign Mason right now. What if he changes his mind? I don't want to lose this opportunity.

'All we want is the best outcome possible. Ellery deserves a fitting conclusion to his work,' Jordan says. 'Hallie and I have things to discuss, but Mason, thank you for coming in. I'll be in touch soon.'

Mason stands, grinning as he shakes Jordan's hand and then mine.

'It was great to meet you.' I return his smile.

'You too, Halliday, and again I am so sorry for your loss.'

Mason exits the boardroom and Jordan's eyes are on me, his jaw tight and eyebrows raised.

'What are you thinking?'

'Can we sign him now?' I say. 'He's accomplished *and* talented.'

Jordan nods. 'He is, but I'd like you to talk with the other authors. Assess your options.'

I reluctantly agree as we exit the room and stand in the hallway.

'I'll arrange a video call with Gallagher and Cutler and email you the details,' Jordan says. 'I've got a meeting with Fletcher now about his next book, and I'll see where he's at if you'd still like to consider him for *Blood of Gold.*'

Not really, but I have three other options for the project, and one of them is Mason Parrish. I can push Fletcher aside without too much drama.

'Sure. You can talk to him about it.' I shrug.

Jordan's phone rings and he taps the answer button before covering the mouthpiece. 'Can you tell Fletcher I'll be out in a minute?'

I agree and walk toward Fletcher, who springs up from his chair and crosses the lobby's expanse in a few strides.

'Don't go with Mason.' His voice echoes. 'Ellery wouldn't want that.'

I take a deep breath. 'Jordan had to take a call, but he'll be out in a sec.'

'Hallie, don't go with Mason. He doesn't understand Ellery's work. He'll ruin everything.'

His face is flushed, eyes pleading as I walk past him and press the call button for the elevator.

'Bye, Fletcher.'

He's on my heels. 'Hallie, listen to me. This is a terrible idea. Do not let Mason near Elle's work. Do not do it.'

When the elevator arrives, I step inside and turn just in time to see Fletcher's tortured face before the doors close.

CHAPTER TWELVE

W es and I are up with the sun, and after room service eggs on toast, I read more of Dad's journal. I'm in the groove of not reading it chronologically. The entries seem more impactful when I don't know what's coming or how old I'll be in his memories. I've read the one about Justin over and over. I remember that night clear as anything. I got mint choc chip ice cream and swindled Dad into taking me and Justin to the beach the following weekend. He knew me well, but I knew him better. I crack open the journal to a page closer to the front.

Writing these entries is a thrill. I'll let you read them one day. Then you'll have a history of your life through my eyes. I wish I'd started the day you were born, but you never gave me or your mom a second of peace, so I wouldn't have had the time. You're seven at the moment, and you've started reading obsessively. I think my genes have finally kicked in and I've passed on more than my hatred of zucchini. You are welcome. This entry is only a short one because I'm taking you to the park for Wesley's birthday party soon. He seems like a great kid, but I heard your mom and his mom gossiping about how close you are, it's got me worried. Anyway, I have to go because you can't find your sandals with the silver buckles. I didn't know I was supposed to monitor their whereabouts.

I smile and put the journal back in my bag before grabbing my phone to check Facebook. My smile melts when I see my feed dotted with more articles about Dad. Including one paired with a photo of Mason Parrish leaving Harcourt yesterday. It's poor quality, taken on a phone and zoomed in too far.

The article itself is nothing but filler. Some guy across the street recognised Mason and realised he was leaving Harcourt. Now there are four thousand comments on a blurry photo saying Mason is finishing the series. Most of the comments on the article are positive, and this has my heart singing. I search for more articles and since it's the internet there are two sides to the argument. A select group of Dad's fans seems to share Fletcher's opinion on Mason and they aren't holding back.

'What's going on?' Wes asks as he steps out of the bathroom, drying his hair with the impractically small hotel towel.

'Nothing.' I put my phone down. 'Do you want to go on a city tour today? Or check out Pike Place or the aquarium? We haven't done anything fun on this trip.'

'Not true.' He shakes his head. 'Watching you lay an egg every time we board a plane is fun.'

I toss a pillow across the room and it hits his chest with a soft thud. 'Shut up and get dressed. We're going to visit the otters.'

It's early afternoon when we return to the hotel with a plushie dolphin for Archie and several nondescript t-shirts for Wes. We stumbled on an Old Navy and he stocked up. After that we strolled around Pike Place Market, and Wes talked me into eating oysters at a restaurant on the pier.

Never again.

As payback, I made him pose underneath the public market sign and dragged him through the Olympic Sculpture Garden. That's when he started complaining about his aching feet, and we took a cab back to the hotel to drop off our bags before my appointment with Dad's agent.

The literary agency office is much smaller and less grand than the Harcourt office. From the reception area, I can see a rabbit warren of desks separated by short partitions and a few enclosed offices along the back wall. Casually dressed staff members bustle around while a local radio station pumps pop music through inbuilt speakers. The laid-back atmosphere puts me at ease, and I tap my foot on the carpeted floor in time with the music while waiting for Cecelia to appear. I've been told she's on a call, but she doesn't keep me waiting long.

'Halliday.' Cecelia breezes into reception and I recognise the angled structure of her face and ocean blue eyes from the 'about us' section of the agency's website. She's in her early forties, dressed in jeans and a white button-up shirt with her light brown hair twisted into a messy bun.

'It's great to meet you, Cecelia.' I shake her hand and cock my head in Wes's direction. 'This is my friend Wes.'

'Please, call me Cece. It's great to meet you both.'

We follow Cece along the front of the cubicles and into a small, windowless office with an L-shaped timber desk taking up most of the space. The first thing I notice as I sit down is the collector's editions of Dad's books on the wall-mounted shelving above the desk. She has a few other nods to Dad, including a poster from the TV show and a figurine of Princess Halladora wielding a sword, her dark brown hair blown back by an invisible wind.

Cece starts by offering condolences and the cracks in her cheerful facade are clear. They were close, Dad mentioned her a lot as their careers flourished together. He was an unknown, and she was a new agent. She took a chance on him, and her commitment never wavered. Her glassy eyes look away from me for a second and she apologises. It's unnecessary and I tell her that.

For the next half an hour we chat about Dad. Cece talks about visiting him and Marie in Fairbanks and how it was impossible to get any hints out of him on how he'd end the series. She tells me about the first meeting she and Dad had with the studio that wanted to adapt the series for television. Dad was apprehensive because it's not uncommon for TV shows to deviate from the source material. He'd called to tell me about that meeting, and I remember the excitement in his voice when they contracted him as a producer. It meant Dad would keep a lot of the creative control.

Cece smiles to herself as we trade memories, and it fills me with warmth to talk about him like this.

'I've spoken with Jordan Fisher,' Cece explains. 'They've got Mason Parrish interested in the project. He's a big name.'

I nod. 'Tell me about it. It took all my strength not to lock him in on the spot. Though I thought I should talk to you before deciding. Dad would trust your opinion.'

'I understand. Mason has experience, but Jordan said Fletcher Larson was also an option.' She steeples her fingers. 'He's talented. His voice is fresher, and Ellery was a tremendous influence on him.'

I was hoping she wouldn't say that, but even I can see how Dad has influenced Fletcher's writing.

'Are you saying she should go with Fletcher?' Wes cuts in.

Cece leans back in her chair and contemplates the situation for a moment.

'I wouldn't discount him but sit down with each of the prospects. Discuss what they can bring to the project. It's one thing to use someone else's outline and notes, but it's quite another to get their voice right.'

My stomach roils. She doesn't know about Dad's outline.

Wes looks over at me, his mouth turning down at the corners.

'Did Dad send you an outline by chance?' I ask.

She shakes her head. 'No. Only a rough first chapter. Why?'

'We might have a problem.' I look at Wes. 'We turned his place upside down. There's no outline for book six.'

Cece stares down at the looping wood grain pattern on her desk. It takes a moment for her to speak, but she doesn't seem shocked or even that concerned. More pragmatic. Like it's a small hurdle to jump.

'Well, that's even more of a reason to take your time in choosing an author. They'll use the source material available to outline the last book and construct the ending from whatever Ellery has left behind.'

Her approach to this giant stick in the spokes of the book six bike takes me by surprise.

'Is that even possible? Can someone come in and finish it when there's nothing to work from?' Wes asks.

'There's plenty to work from. We've got five books and from what Ellery told me, Hallie knows more about this story than anyone.'

'I do.' I nod as enthusiasm sparks in my chest. 'I'm sure I can work out the ending. I just need the words.'

'Then make sure you choose an author you can work with. Take some time to think about it and don't let anyone steer you into making a call you're not ready to. Being a literary executor is an enormous responsibility and your dad's work is more important than most,' Cece warns.

'What if they refuse to let Hal go with who she wants?' Wes asks. 'Can she take it to another publisher?'

Cece shakes her head. 'Unfortunately, not. Before Elle died, he signed on for a sixth book. He retains the intellectual property of the work, but he's still contractually obligated to publish it with Harcourt.'

That's not the end of the world. I have no problem with Harcourt, neither did Dad, and ultimately, it's still my decision.

For the rest of my time with Cece, we go over my responsibilities with the TV network. Which is little, considering that they have enough source material for multiple seasons, but she lets me know they will be in contact regarding certain creative decisions once filming resumes in a few months. Cece offers to help me navigate all of this, and she has a contact on the show's production crew we can deal with, but when I think of what's on the horizon, the tension causes my shoulders to bunch. She says it's not as daunting as it sounds, and for now all I should do is focus on book six.

'What's goin' on in your head right now?' Wes asks as we wait for a cab outside Cece's office.

'Mostly that I have no idea what I'm doing.'

'You'll be alright. You've got all these people to help you,'

I tuck my hands into my coat pockets. 'It's still scary.'

'You know what's scarier?' He wraps an arm around my shoulders. 'You've got like seventeen hours of flight time to get through tonight.'

'Oh yeah,' I grumble. 'I feel way better now. Thank you.'

CHAPTER THIRTEEN

In the early hours of Monday morning, Queensland time, we touch down in Brisbane and Wes's phone rings straight away. While he talks to Teddy, I steer him off the plane and through the terminal until we get to baggage claim. Mum messaged to say she'll wait for us in the pickup area outside the terminal.

Unlike me, Wes doesn't flinch when we come in contact with the Brisbane heat. He pushes his sunglasses onto his face and drinks in the sun. In comparison, I am almost breathless. It's stifling, and my clothing feels like cling wrap on my sweaty skin.

Mum arrives a few minutes later and launches herself from the car, grabbing both Wes and me round the neck and pulling us to her.

'Thank God you're back in one piece.' She beams and holds us just long enough to earn a loud throat clearing from the traffic marshal.

In a feat of superhuman strength, Wes goes to work, leaving me fighting jet lag on my own. Violet is useful for the first three hours of this, but Archie's baby swimming lesson means I'm on my own for the afternoon.

I spend the next hour pouring over the emails that landed in my inbox while I was over the Pacific. I'm still feeling like a wrung-out sponge, but my adrenaline spikes when I read the email from Cece.

She's been in contact with the showrunner for the TV series and they've invited me to the set when they re-start filming in two months. I've been a fan of the show since the first episode, and I know they involved Dad heavily to ensure the adaptation was right. I wonder if that will still be the case now that Dad's gone? I know a little about publishing but nothing about television. The thought causes a sizeable knot to form in my belly.

'You're snoring.' I feel a gentle squeeze on my arm and spy Wes through my half-closed lid. He looks more rested than he has any right to.

'What time is it?' I garble through the paste that's formed in my mouth.

'Quarter to eight.' Wes checks his watch before sitting a takeaway container of Pad Thai and a fork on the coffee table in front of me.

'How long have you been home?'

'A couple of hours. I was gonna wake you, but that gurgling noise you make when you sleep is so soothing.'

I grab the fork and start shovelling food into my mouth. 'I tried to stay awake.'

'I'm sure you did.' Wes grabs two cans of Coke from the fridge and on his way back to the couch notices Dad's journal sticking out of my bag. 'Have you finished reading it yet?'

'Not yet.' With a nod, I give Wes permission to look at it. He pulls it out and lets it fall open on his palm.

'Read it out?' I ask and his eyes meet mine with apprehension.

'Are you sure? It seems kinda personal.'

'Wes, you've bought me tampons. I think our friendship can handle this.'

He swallows before turning his eyes back to the book and reading Dad's words aloud.

'*How the hell did you make it to eighteen? You don't know this yet, but I've booked a flight and I'll be there to surprise you! I can't wait to see the look on your face. You're going to cry and then you'll be mad that I made you cry. Mum said you have plans with Wes that involve heavy alcohol consumption. I'm not sure how I feel about that, but either way I'll be there to witness the punishment of your first legal hangover. As opposed to the many illegal ones I witnessed thanks to Wes. How is that kid still alive? He's thrill-seeking and accident-prone, so maybe you shouldn't get too attached to him.*'

I laugh at the pinched expression on Wes's face. 'I'm not accident-prone.'

'You are.' I wrinkle my nose. 'But it's too late. I'm attached.'

Wes looks down again, re-reading the entry, and his brow furrows. 'He didn't come and see you when you turned eighteen.'

No, he didn't. I wasn't even aware that he'd intended to. I shift up onto my knees as Wes comes over and sits on the back of the couch. He holds the notebook so we can both read it.

I'm so sorry I couldn't make it for your birthday, Hal. Mom said she didn't mention anything about my trip anyway to save you the disappointment. I can't argue with her on that one. I didn't realize how much work I'd have to do on this draft for book three, and my publisher has scheduled interviews in the lead-up to book two's release. I'm going to call you as soon as you wake up because I have a plan. Maybe you'll consider taking some time off before you start college, I thought you could come over and stay with me for a few months. You can help me draft and spend some time getting to know Marie a little better. I know it's not the best sales pitch, but I would love to spend some time with you.

Wes says nothing. He stares at me, waiting for a breakdown. I'm teetering and the jet lag isn't helping, but I'm tired of crying. Honestly, I'm tired of thinking about Dad, his book, and all the ways we could have tried harder when he was alive. I'm just tired.

CHAPTER FOURTEEN

I t's grey on the Saturday of Wes's birthday and the promise of a cyclonic afternoon storm is thick in the air.

On the flight home, I suggested getting an apartment on the Gold Coast to celebrate Wes entering the last year of his twenties, but he insisted on a small get-together instead. I still want to show my gratitude, so I bought a new washing machine, the shoot-'em-up game for PlayStation he wanted, and I'm going to cater the shit out of this gathering.

The swollen clouds threaten as we head to the supermarket. It's packed, but Wes doesn't complain as we dodge small children and elderly people in the crowded aisles.

'How'd your video chat go with that other author?' Wes asks as he throws a bag of pre-cubed cheese into the trolley.

'It was alright. Brent is a nice guy and talented. I don't think we'd be a good fit though.'

'Why's that?' He frowns.

'To be honest, I felt like I steamrolled the guy. I want someone willing to push back a little. Someone I can have an honest conversation with that adds some insight to the story and makes suggestions. He just sat there nodding like I was employing him to re-tile my bathroom.'

Wes lifts a brow. 'You know how you want the story to end, right? Doesn't he just have to word it for you?'

I shake my head. 'It's more than that. I know one thing about the ending, and there are so many character arcs and plot threads to follow. The author has to know the ins and outs and help me get the book from Dad's first chapter to Halladora being on the throne. Everything in between is a massive web that needs untangling.'

'And that's Mason?'

'Yeah, it is. He's an epic fantasy writer, so it's in his wheel-house. Even though I'm yet to have my meeting with Scott Cutler, I'm not sure his talent for sci-fi can translate over to Dad's medieval-style fantasy.'

We round the corner into the snack aisle and the trolley fills. 'Fletcher's out of the running then?'

While I haven't said that, I implied it in my last email to Jordan. Fletcher is on his book tour at the moment, but Jordan suggested we talk as soon as possible to clear the air and get Fletcher's thoughts on the book. I reluctantly agreed to have a video chat with him when he gets back from the UK leg of his tour.

'Jordan's leaning toward Fletcher, but he'd be happy if I went with Mason. I mean, how could he not be? I think we're lucky that Mason gave us the time of day.'

'Pick him then,' Wes says. 'Your dad liked him, you like him, and from what you were reading online, the rest of the world likes him. Seems like the right choice to me.'

Wes's insight, while simplistic, is a breath of fresh air and I curse my brain's natural ability to overthink things.

'I'm going to go back to the US soon.' I pick at the frayed hem of my denim shorts. 'It could be for a while.'

Wes nods. 'I know. I didn't say I wouldn't miss you.'

I reach over and squeeze his forearm. 'Looks like you'll have to learn how to iron your business shirts.'

'Fuck.' He grunts as he lifts a pack of Coke from the shelf and deposits it in the space I've cleared at the front of the trolley.

After clearing the checkout, Wes and I struggle to the car, overloaded with grocery bags that contain nothing of nutritional value. With the back of Wes's truck stocked, I climb into the passenger's seat and take out my phone to see an email from Jordan in my inbox.

Fletcher is back from the UK, so Jordan has set up a video conference for nine a.m. tomorrow. Which I work out will be two in the morning for me. I shoot back a response to confirm. A similar confirmation email comes through from Fletcher a few moments later, saying that he's looking forward to it.

He's the only one.

I'm sweating and stick my head out the window in search of Wes. I spot him over by the trolley bay, talking to a young girl with shimmery blonde hair. Even from this distance I recognise her as our schoolmate Fiona's younger sister, Jen. She's two years younger than us, but she often tagged along with Fi to the movies and backyard parties when we were in high school.

Wes leans down and whispers something in her ear, which makes her smile. It's way too familiar.

'What was that?' I ask once Wes slides into the driver's seat and starts the engine. The blast of cool air from the vents is a dream as I flap the front of my shirt to unstick it from my skin.

'What was what?'

'Um, how about you getting real close with Fi's sister?'

Wes scoffs. 'We're mates. I invited her to the party tonight.'

'By nuzzling her ear?'

Wes blushes. 'Come off it. She's come to the pub after work a few times. Fi and Chris brought her along.'

Chris, Fi's husband, has joined Wes and Teddy's business, so this story checks out. I open my mouth to gather more information, but Wes shuts it down.

'If you mention it again, I'll make you hose off the patio furniture when we get home.'

I'm not taking that bullet, so I'll just interrogate Fiona.

That's exactly what I do nine hours later when we've both had a glass of wine and Jen is sitting beside Wes on the couch.

'They've been together for months.' Fi picks at the glorious cheeseboard on my kitchen bench. 'I thought you knew.'

I shake my head as I slather a cracker in French onion dip. 'He hasn't said a word to me. I didn't realise you guys all hung out after work either,'

That comes across more childish than I intended.

'Hang out is a stretch. Jen started working for this event company and they do heaps of functions at the Park Hill

Hotel. She ran into Wes, Teddy, and Chris there one afternoon and brought Chris home for me. She and Wes started texting each other, then he asked her out. They've been together ever since.'

My chest feels heavy. Why wouldn't Wes tell me? We share everything, and recently had two fourteen-hour flights where he had multiple opportunities to talk to me about this.

'Don't tell him I told you,' Fi whispers. 'It might have been a secret.'

I look over at Wes. His arm is over the back of the couch, behind Jen's head. When I get his attention, he pulls it back to his side and turns to talk to Chris.

Wes seems to dodge me for most of the night, always leaving a conversation as I enter it. I'm not angry, so I don't understand what the problem is. I'm not going to ambush him about this now, and I have no problem with him and Jen. She's a sweet girl with a great sense of humour. In fact, she's perfect for him. I want to tell him that, but he keeps dodging me.

At one-thirty in the morning, most of the guests have left with only the diehards remaining. Fi, Chris, Teddy, and Jen are lazy drunk and sitting around in the backyard, looking at the stars and talking about investment properties and retirement savings plans. Not topics that should be discussed with that high of a blood alcohol level.

'Hold up, you.' I corner Wes as he comes out of the upstairs bathroom. He flattens himself against the hallway wall and looks down at me. There's no fear in his eyes, more resignation.

'Ah, shit.' He sighs, shoulders slumping.

I open my mouth just as my phone rings.

'Dammit.' I pull my phone from my pocket. Jordan is calling me early.

'You should take that,' Wes says as he slips past me and hurries down the stairs.

I run to my room and close the door as I press the answer button. Jordan's face appears. He looks well rested and his smile is bright. I'm certain he didn't calculate the time difference before arranging the call.

'Hey, Hallie.' He leans forward and, in the background, I can see the view out of his office window. 'I'll patch through Fletcher in a moment, but I wanted to see where you're at now that you've met Brent and Mason.'

I lock the door and settle on my bed, holding the phone at face height and silently thanking God that my makeup held up tonight.

'I'm invested in Mason. He knows what he's doing and as soon as I get back, I'd like to have a meeting with him to brainstorm some ideas.'

Jordan strokes his chin. 'That's fair. You didn't have time to talk with him in the office. We've still got Fletcher and Scott though, so let's speak with them first, then we'll contact Mason and set something up.'

A jolt of electricity hits my blood. I'll be brainstorming Dad's book with Mason Parrish. It's ridiculous. Unfathomable and incredible.

Jordan says he's going to get Fletcher on the call, and I use the momentary distraction to fix my hair. The waves have fallen a bit flat, but it looks alright in the tiny square on the screen.

A few seconds later, Fletcher's face appears beside Jordan's and he looks dishevelled by comparison. He gives me a brief hello before Jordan asks about the tour and I get closer to falling asleep. Fletcher must notice because he turns the conversation back to the book.

'Halliday, I'd love to be the one to finish Ellery's series. I know his work inside and out. He mentored me when writing *Red Reign* and compared to Mason, my voice is more similar to Ellery's.'

He has a point. I loved *Red Reign* because his prose is like Dad's and even though my anger toward him has softened, I still want Mason.

Jordan and I decided that we wouldn't tell the prospective authors about the lack of an outline until we could gauge their commitment to the project. In the meeting with Brent Gallagher, I told him about fifteen minutes in and he clammed up even more. That's not something Mason would do. Jordan even said Mason had sent through some notes without being prompted.

With Fletcher, I want to play the no outline thing differently. I know he knows Dad's books, but does he know Dad? With no hard evidence on what leads up to the ending, it's not about how we think the story would play out, it's how Dad would have had it play out.

'Your voice is like his,' I admit. 'But what about the story? Where do you think it's going?'

Fletcher smiles and his whiskey coloured eyes lock with mine through the tiny lens.

'Halladora's going to sit on the throne.'

That's an easy one and Dad probably told him that, just like he told me. You'll have to do better than that, Fletcher.

'And how's she going to get there? She has no allies, coin, or army. She has Vengul, and that's it.'

'Vengul is all she needs.' He smirks.

Jordan leans back in his chair, removing himself from the conversation.

'Right, so you think Halladora and her guard can take Lorden's keep from the Karrakan King on their own?'

'Have you read book two?' Fletcher leans a little closer to the camera, and the light from the window beside him makes his dark hair shimmer. 'It's alright if you haven't. I can fill you in.'

I narrow my eyes and clench my teeth. I want to slap the grin off his face.

'Because if you had read book two, you'd know that Vengul's grandfather was the commander of the sovereign forces in the West. He can call in that favour anytime he wants.'

Now it's my turn to smile. 'And if you were familiar with book four, you'd know that the sovereign forces were from the kingdom of Biltarnya. A kingdom which dissolved after the Princes' Rebellion and became the Free States of the West.'

My chest swells as I bask in the glory of my victory. Fletcher doesn't let me enjoy it though.

'The Free States still have military strength, and the Northern Provinces support Halladora. If Vengul gains the support of the former sovereign forces and the North back Halladora, they'd have enough military might to storm the keep and kill the Karrakan King.'

I want to put him through his paces but it's clear I have my work cut out for me.

'The North won't come,' I say. 'The Shadow Gate is unstable. They're preparing for the blight.'

He doesn't miss a beat. 'A blight they could fight with the sovereign forces and the Second King's army. Don't tell me you forgot about Winshaw?'

I prickle with irritation. I would never forget about Winshaw. The golden-haired rebel with the rugged good looks of an old Hollywood movie star, the heart of a poet, and the ability to sever a head from a body with unmatched precision.

'You think he'd give up his cause so easily?' I say.

'I never said it would be easy,' Fletcher replies. 'But he does love Halladora.'

He does. More than anything. Before she was captured and taken to the Tower of Blood, Winshaw told her that his love for her was like a river, carving a path through mountains to get to the sea. Nothing would stop him. Nothing would keep him from her.

Jordan clears his throat. 'As much as I enjoy watching you two argue, we need to discuss logistics here.'

Fletcher takes his eyes off me and focuses on Jordan. 'I'm ready to start immediately.'

'Hold up,' I cut in. 'We still have another author to meet with, and I haven't talked in depth with Mason yet.'

'There's no need. I'm happy to take on the project,' Fletcher says, unleashing another broad smile.

'Aren't you tired?' I ask. 'It must be exhausting maintaining this level of self-importance. I'm tired just listening to you.'

'Alright, that's enough.' Jordan sighs. 'Fletch, you know what you're talking about with this series. Let Hallie think it over and I'll call you in a few days.'

Fletcher agrees and offers a smug goodbye before disappearing from the call.

'You've got some thinking to do.' Jordan scratches his temple.

'I really don't,' I say. 'I want Mason.'

CHAPTER FIFTEEN

Two days after the Fletcher meeting, Jordan and I have a video chat with Scott Cutler. He's a nice guy, but I've only read one of his eight novels, so it limits my knowledge of his work. Jordan takes the lead, but about ten minutes into the conversation it's clear that Scott isn't the guy for the project. He kept bringing the conversation back to the TV adaptation, and we all agreed that he should bow out of consideration. After the meeting, Jordan asks if I'm certain Mason is the author to go with and I give him an unequivocal yes.

It's been over twenty-four hours since I told Jordan to pull the trigger and I'm tightly wound over it all.

'Gardens are looking good now.' Wes inspects the hydrangeas as we settle on the back patio of the townhouse. We're expecting Brad and Violet any minute for afternoon drinks, but I can't hold in the words that bubble up in my throat.

'I can't believe you didn't tell me about Jen.'

Wes sighs. 'Here we go.'

'You've never hidden anything from me before. Not girls anyway.'

'It was early days.'

'I asked Teddy, and he said it's been months.'

'For fuck's sake, Teddy.'

'At least he was honest.'

'Since when do you talk to Teddy.'

'Since you stopped talking to me about stuff.'

There's a light knock on the front door, and Wes scrambles to his feet, making a break for it. 'Brad and Vi are here.'

I roll my eyes as he swings the door open with a flourish.

'Friends! Come in.' He ushers them inside and there are drinks in their hands before they can take a breath. Wes even sets Archie up with some ABC Kids on his phone while we gather outside around the low table laden with nibble platters. Brad scoffs down one water cracker before asking me about Dad's sixth book. I tell him I've picked an author, but since nothing's confirmed yet, we can't talk about it. He looks more upset than the time Archie tossed the remote and it hit the TV at the exact right angle to crack the display. He doesn't let up though and tries to trip me up all night. Violet gets in on it at one stage, but I don't break. Wes, on the other hand, almost lets Mason's name slip, but I slap him across the stomach before he gets it out.

Not long after that, Archie gets grizzly, and when he can't be calmed Brad and Vi head off, leaving me and Wes alone to watch the sunset and continue to scrutinise his new landscaping.

After dinner, Wes ducks out to see his parents. He's a

dutiful son, but it's a ploy to get away from the Jen questioning. With Wes gone, I shower and go to bed. I'm aggressively jostling my hair with a towel when my phone vibrates on my bedside table. In my haste to answer, I stub my toe on the bed frame and let out a screech. By the time I recover, the ringing has stopped, but I see Jordan's name beside the missed call notification.

'Shit.' I swipe my finger over the screen and call him back.

'Halliday.' He sounds chipper. 'I hope it's not too late to call.'

'Not at all.' I drop onto the bed, holding my throbbing toe. 'What's going on? Have you heard from Mason?'

'I have.'

'And?'

Jordan's voice is muffled as he covers the mouthpiece and says something to someone else. It takes far too long for him to come back to our conversation.

'Sorry, where was I?' He clears his throat.

'Mason. What's happening with Mason?'

'I spoke to Mason and told him you wanted him for the project. He's going to come up to Seattle for a few days, have a bit of a brainstorming session with you, and then we can sign him on for *Blood of Gold*.'

My hands tremble, but the excitement and the relief I feel makes tears appear out of nowhere.

'How soon can you get back here?' he asks.

'I'll look up flights straight away.' I keep my voice even. 'I've got some things to sort out before I come over, but that won't take long.'

'Great. Let me know when you'll be back, and I'll organise it with Mason.'

As soon as I'm off the phone, I research flights. I don't want to leave Mum in the lurch, so I select a flight just shy of two weeks from now and enter my credit card details. She's already hired two new casual staff for the store, and I can help train them up before I leave. I don't know how long I'll be gone for, but I'll have to butter Mum up with a nice dinner and then break the news over dessert.

I call Mum the next day and we agree on dinner at my place on Friday night. Wes is taking Jen out on a date, which is still a weird concept, so I'll talk things over with Mum alone.

When Friday rolls around, she informs me she's made garlic chicken and will bring it around at seven. Thank God she's supplying the food because whatever atrocity I plate up would only add to the anguish of me leaving. She doesn't need to be picking eggshells out of her food while she cries.

'This is nice,' Mum says as she sits down and runs her hands over the silver tablecloth I bought for the occasion.

'Kmart,' I say as I scoop chicken out of the casserole dish and ferry it to each of our plates. I can't wait till dessert. I have to cut to the chase.

'Mum, I have to tell you something.'

'You're pregnant,' she blurts out and my eyes widen so much I almost snap an optic nerve.

'What? No, I'm not pregnant.'

She looks more disappointed than she should. 'Well you're around that age so I thought there was a chance.'

'That I'd be pregnant?' I cut up my chicken but pause with the cutlery in the air. 'Wait, who did you think the father was?'

'Wes, obviously.'

'Gross, Mum.'

'Hey, you could do worse than Wesley Randall.' She points her fork at me. 'He's a sweet young man, and he's good to you.'

'I know, Mum.'

She's still pointing the fork. 'He's good-looking too. You'd have nice babies.'

While this is true, it has never been, nor will it ever be, on the cards, she knows this.

'No, Mum. What I was going to tell you is that I've picked an author for Dad's book and I'm going to go over to the States for a while to help with it.'

She puts down her cutlery, ensuring it doesn't slip off the plate and smear sauce on my eight-dollar tablecloth.

'How long is a while?' Her voice is a whisper. I kind of wish I was pregnant to soften this blow for her.

'I don't know. Probably a couple of months.'

'Oh, a couple of months. Okay.' She nods. 'When are you leaving?'

'Next weekend. So, I have some time to help you with the new staff.'

She's still for a long time, and I worry she's forgotten how to breathe.

I filled her in on all the details about my various meetings while I was in the US, and she almost choked on her own tongue when I told her how much money Dad left me. She hasn't brought it up since though, because she thinks it's unseemly to talk about it. She did, however, ask questions about what's expected of me now, so an extended stay in Seattle isn't entirely out of the blue.

'I'll keep you in the loop with everything. I don't know how long it will take to get the book done, but I'll come back to visit in a couple of months, regardless.'

She's still nodding, but I'm not sure she's taking it in.

'If you could check in on Wes while I'm gone, I'd appreciate it. Take him for walks even.'

Mum doesn't smile at my joke and I reach over the table and take her hand.

'It's going to be okay. I'll be back before you know it.'

She's quiet for almost the entirety of dinner. Only piping up now and then when a thought pops into her head. She's in panic planning mode so most of her comments are things like 'make sure you sign up for paperless billing for all your utilities' and 'can Wes be trusted to water the pot plants, or should she come over and do that?' I tell her that Wes has kept himself alive for twenty-nine years, so I think he can handle some watering.

It's a hollow assurance because, even though Wes is alright with the yard maintenance, my succulents are not long for this world.

'When are you off then?' Wes asks as he leans on the doorframe with his arms folded over his chest. He arrived home not long after Mum left and has been downstairs polishing off the last of the garlic chicken.

'Next Sunday.' I gather the clean clothes I've folded and

put them in the walk-in wardrobe. Wes steps into the room and collapses on my bed, arms by his sides, staring up at the ceiling fan. I lay down next to him and angle my neck, so my head rests against his. He leans into me and lets out a sigh. 'I'll be lonely without you.'

'Really?' I exhale. 'You've been avoiding me since your birthday.'

'I know and I'm sorry. I know you're mad about Jen.'

I pull my head back and look at the side of his face. 'I'm not mad about Jen. I'm confused why you didn't tell me about Jen.'

'Well, now I know that, I wish I had told you. Especially now you're going and who knows when you'll be back. I've wasted the last week dodging you.'

'I'll message and call you all the time, and you have Jen to look out for you.'

'Yeah, she's pretty cool, I guess.' He grips my hand and holds it to his side. 'I'm proud of you for doing this.'

'I'm not sure how much help I'll be. I didn't inherit Dad's writing skill.'

'You're looking out for him. That's all that matters.'

I squeeze Wes's fingers and roll onto my side, so I'm cuddled into him. It reminds me of when we were kids and I would jump on my bike and ride the three streets over to Wes's house. Every night he'd pop the fly screen out and leave his bedroom window open a crack so I could climb in. We'd lay on his bed for hours and ponder the complexities of our small universe.

'I told Mum about going to Seattle today.'

'Mmm, what'd she say?' Wes's voice is low and sleepy.

'She was okay with it. Shocked, but she can't say no.' I look up at him, his eyes are closed, and his chest rises and falls slowly.

'I'll keep an eye on her for you,' he mutters.

'She's going to bring you so much food.'

'I know and I love it.'

I exhale. 'Please tell me why you've been so weird about Jen. I hate that you felt the need to dodge me for a week.'

He opens his eyes and rolls his head to the side to look at me.

'At first there was nothing to tell, we were just hanging out after work. Then we started seeing each other away from Chris and Fi. I took her out to dinner a couple of times, and it went from there.'

'I cannot picture you on a date.' I laugh. 'Wait, is that why you got your haircut and started buying those tins of hair wax?'

'Maybe.' His mouth twists up into a slight smirk.

'You could have told me.'

He lifts his shoulders. 'Didn't feel right. I was all excited for what was goin' on with Jen and you were coming home after all those shitty dates and then your dad died. It didn't feel right to be so happy when you're not.'

I feel a lump rise in my throat. He should never have felt that way, not for a second.

I sit up, leaning over him so he can see my face.

'Wesley.' I narrow my eyes. 'Your happiness isn't contingent on mine.'

He rises to rest on his elbows. 'I just thought it'd upset you.'

'Seeing you happy never upsets me, you idiot.' I push him back down. 'I love you.'

'I love you too,' he says forcefully as I lay back down and rest my head on his shoulder.

'And thank you,' I mumble.

'For what?'

'For being my best friend.'

'Teddy is my best friend.' His words are garbled as he yawns. 'We're roommates at best.'

CHAPTER SIXTEEN

The late February chill of Seattle is more than welcome when I step off the plane. I'm still shaking even though it's my seventh flight of the year and I Google flight anxiety hypnosis while waiting for Jordan to pick me up outside SeaTac.

He was kind enough to help me sublet a small apartment close to the Harcourt office on a month-to-month basis, and from the pictures it's a little hipster dream. I'm looking forward to collapsing on the bed and sleeping until I don't know what day it is.

'I'll drop you off at the apartment to get settled, then we've got an author event tonight in Fremont,' Jordan explains as we enter Downtown.

'What author event?'

'It's a get-together the company puts on twice a year for our authors. There's only one speech and an open bar.'

He sways me with the words 'open bar'.

'Sure. I'd be happy to tag along.'

'Mason is going to be there. He flew up from San Francisco early.'

On Friday, Jordan called to say Mason had agreed to a one-on-one brainstorming session with me before discussing contracts. I know he's capable. I've been sold on him from the start, but I've had no contact with him, and I haven't seen this elusive notebook full of ideas that Jordan's mentioned on multiple occasions.

We pull up outside a three-story, red-brick building in Belltown. The concrete sidewalk is dotted with small trees and I look up to admire the arched black windows that symmetrically decorate the building's exterior. I'm guessing it used to be a warehouse.

Jordan takes me into the building and up to my apartment on the second floor. The lock is a little tricky, so he shows me how to tackle that before dropping the key in my palm and promising to be back at six-thirty. He mentioned in the car he was on his way to see Fletcher and was not looking forward to breaking the news that I've chosen Mason. It could make for some tense cocktail conversation if they're both at the event tonight.

I drag my suitcase into the bedroom section of the studio. Overall it's cosy, with a frameless bed pushed up against one of the arch windows and a spindly metal side table. An over-stuffed emerald couch dominates the rest of the apartment, facing a flatscreen TV that's been mounted to the exposed brick wall. Along the far wall is a small kitchen with a double burner stove and a decent size fridge. Whoever decorated the place forwent a dining table and instead filled the remaining space with a dark timber desk and narrow bookcase.

The place is perfect, and I shoot Jordan a message to thank him for organising it all.

By six o'clock, I've napped, showered, and spent far too long choosing something to wear. Jordan said business casual, but that makes little sense to me, so I wear the only fancy item of clothing I brought with me. It's a tight, black dress that hugs my thighs and ends at my knees. The top is a thick panel of black lace that cuts across my collar bones, and since it's February, I throw on my cream wool coat. And to think I almost talked myself out of bringing my sensible black, patent leather heels. I don't think my grey sneakers would have paired as well with the outfit.

'Wow, you look great,' Jordan comments as he hurries around the side of his Audi to open the door for me.

'Is it a bit much?' I hold open the coat to show him the dress. 'I don't know what business casual is.'

'The dress is perfect,' he assures me as he climbs into the driver's seat and starts the engine.

We scarcely make it out of the street before I ask about his chat with Fletcher.

'He's disappointed,' Jordan says. 'He's not a fan of Mason.'

'Yeah, because he lost the gig to Mason. That's all it would be about.'

Jordan doesn't look convinced, and I'm worried there is more to this than either he or Fletcher is letting on.

'I'd steer clear of Fletcher tonight, just to be safe.'

I'm able to put the Fletcher drama out of my head by the time we reach the venue. It's an industrial building in Fremont that's now a multipurpose event space. Thick, steel girders run across the ceiling and around the top of the two-story concrete walls. It's already a hive of activity when Jordan walks me in. Smartly dressed people are clustered around tall tables holding champagne flutes in one hand and undersized canapés in the other.

Jordan takes my coat and guides me over to a table where I'm introduced to Ruth Portsmith, an elderly romance author who seems genuinely delighted to meet me. I've read none of her books, but Mum has a couple on her shelf. The covers feature stock images of twenty-something girls either on a beach or in an open field. I bumble my way through some light conversation with Ruth before we're joined by Whitney Farris, a young adult fantasy author whose work I am familiar with.

'Jordan is excellent,' Whitney tells me as she takes a sip of champagne. 'He was the editor for my third book, and his dedication was inspiring.'

'He's been really helpful so far. Considering how far out of my depth I am.'

I explained my situation in the first three minutes of our conversation. Largely because I felt the need to justify my being here.

When Whitney heads off in search of canapés and Ruth

needs to use the bathroom, I scan the space for Jordan. I want to latch myself onto him because networking is not my strongest attribute. I went to a trade fair once with Mum and somehow got talked into stocking a line of lobster-shaped oven mitts because I got flustered and perpetuated the conversation past its natural endpoint.

'Halliday.'

I turn at the sound of my name and see Mason moving through the crowd toward me. My smile is almost manic as he grips my bare shoulders firmly.

'It's wonderful to see you again, my dear. I'm very much looking forward to our meeting on Tuesday.'

'Me too,' I say as I take the glass of wine he offers before steering me out of the walkway and toward a table in the far corner. It's quieter and the candle on the table lights up his flushed, ageing face, exposing his look of wide-eyed excitement. This isn't his first glass of wine this evening.

'I can't stop thinking about this book, Halliday. I've hardly slept. Every time I try, I get another idea. And another, and another. It's taking over my life.'

I chuckle as he stares down at the flickering candle, seemingly consumed by more thoughts.

'We could stretch it out to at least three books.'

For the next fifteen minutes he throws questions at me. I hardly have time to articulate an answer before he moves on to the next. It's a whirlwind that solidifies my decision to have him write the book. He's so passionate, and a real departure from what I imagined him to be like based on a first meeting.

I asked Dad on countless occasions what Mason Parrish

was like, but he never gave me an answer. They spoke on panels together and Dad said he was nice and professional. Though there was a rather heated argument between them about villain redemption arcs on last year's BookCon panel. It has two hundred thousand views on YouTube and doesn't paint either of them in a good light but it's not the first time I've seen authors of that calibre disagree on something like that.

I'm onto my second glass of wine, and deep in a thorough analysis of the political structure in Dad's fantasy world, when the repeated ting of a knife against glass echoes through the venue and the room falls silent.

Mason stills beside me as a middle-aged man in a crisp grey suit garners everyone's attention from the centre of the room. He has a glass in his hand and his eyes look a little glazed over.

'How many old fashions have you had tonight, Greg?' someone shouts and the man in the grey suit points to the source of the comment, a grin splitting his face.

'Watch it, Stu. I haven't signed off on your memoir yet.'

The guy in grey must be Greg Strickland, the owner of Harcourt, and it's time for that one speech Jordan warned me about.

Greg opens with a joke about the art department that I don't understand, but it tickles the crowd. He then thanks everyone for coming and raises his glass. I follow along with the rest of the room, pretending I belong.

That's when I see him.

Fletcher is standing at a table on the other side of the room, dressed in an exquisitely cut charcoal suit and a black button-up shirt with no tie. The swept back style of his hair reminds me of the author photo on his book jacket.

I keep my face expressionless while his irritated gaze shifts from me to Mason, who is laughing at whatever nonsensical anecdote Greg has just come out with.

When the speech is over, Jordan makes his way over to Fletcher. They talk for a few moments and Fletcher's focus moves back to me several times. His lips press together and even from this distance I can see his jaw clench.

'Mason, would you excuse me for a sec?' I don't wait for an answer before I shuffle off through the crowd to a service entrance that leads to the parking lot. It's positively freezing outside, but at least I can dodge Fletcher's silent hostility until Jordan takes me back to the apartment.

I lean on the concrete wall and clench my teeth to stop them from chattering. It's futile, and a second later the door swings open and Fletcher steps out into the parking lot, spotting me immediately.

'Did you choose him out of spite? Is that what's happening here? Are you that petty?'

'Petty?' My eyes go wide. 'I chose him because he's more experienced, and I don't have to justify my decision to you.'

I push off the wall and turn to walk inside, but Fletcher lowers his voice. I hardly hear it over the squeak of the ancient hinges.

'He would hate what you've done.'

My blood heats, anger rippling through my stomach and up into my chest.

'You have no right to say that. No-one knows what he would want because he wasn't supposed to die at forty-eight.

This whole thing, this book, it was his job to finish it and now it's on my shoulders. I'm doing the best I can.'

I bare my teeth to fight the tears, and I can't be sure if I'm shaking from rage or the zero-degree weather.

'He hated Mason. Right from the second he met him.'

'That's bullshit. He bought every one of his books.'

Fletcher stares at me. 'For you. Not for himself.'

I shake off the comment.

'I'm not arguing with you about this,' I say. 'I know you wanted this job, but you weren't a good fit. That's life. Get over it.'

'Mason Parrish is going to destroy everything your dad built. He has his own agenda, he always has, and if you think he's going to let you have a say in anything, you're delusional.'

I wrap my arms around myself as the wind picks up and bites my exposed skin. 'I still have creative control. He can't do whatever he wants with the story. That's up to me.'

Fletcher forces a laugh. 'Mason will get around that. He'll butter up Jordan and convince you you're in control the entire time. Then you'll have another Death Knight book with the names changed.'

'Do you not see how inappropriate you're being? You're not a part of this. You aren't the literary executor. I am, and I've made my decision, so the sooner you make peace with it the better because right now you're embarrassing yourself.'

There's fire in his eyes and the muscle in his cheek twitches as he looks down at my shivering arms.

'Oh, for fuck's sake.' He whips off his coat and throws it around my shoulders. 'You're going to freeze to death before we finish this conversation.'

I want to rip the jacket off and throw it on the ground, but it's already warming me up.

'I haven't made a mistake. I chose the person with the most experience. Mason's already come up with stacks of ideas for book six.' I pull the jacket closer and get a whiff of the sea-salty smell that lingers on the lapel.

'And you think I don't have ideas as well? You never gave me a chance. You were never going to.'

'Not based on the impression you made when we first met.'

He drags his hand through his hair. 'Tell me you wouldn't have done the same thing? If there was something you wanted more than anything, tell me you wouldn't push for it. Tell me you wouldn't take that shot.'

'I would take the shot,' I bark. 'But I wouldn't take it a week after your dad died and then expect you to be okay with it. I don't know you, Fletcher, and you don't know me. So we don't owe each other anything, and if you think arguing with me outside a party is going to make me change my mind then you're more out of touch than I realised.'

His arms drop to his sides and I stand there watching disappointment consume him.

'You don't know what you're doing Halliday. You barely know Mason and if you did, trust me, you wouldn't be signing your dad's work over to him.'

Fletcher looks into my eyes and we're both motionless for far too long. If there's honesty in his words, I have no way of knowing. He wants something from me and that makes him harder to read.

'I'm sorry, but I'm choosing Mason. I chose Mason. Accept it.'

I slide his jacket off my shoulders and hand it back to him. He looks down at the pavement and his voice is nothing but a whisper.

'You didn't know your dad either. At least you haven't for a while.'

I turn back to face Fletcher; I can feel the blood climbing into my cheeks.

'Excuse me?'

'If you did, you would know he'd want anyone but Mason. You aren't doing what's best for Elle or the book and I can't tell you how devastating that is to witness. Especially when what's at stake isn't yours to mess with.'

That's a direct hit to my solar plexus. The pain ripples through my body and the frozen night air is heavy in my lungs. It takes a second to find my voice again.

'I knew him better than anyone and you can't stand there and tell me I don't have Dad's best interests at heart. What happens to his work is my number one priority.'

'I'm not saying that you don't care about Elle. I'm saying that you're so blinded by your adoration of Mason Parrish that you're willing to ignore the fact that your father hated him. There is no way on earth Elle would want that man anywhere near his work. You'd know that if you'd seen him in the last six years.'

I am blinded by the rage I feel for the man in front of me. I hate his face. I hate his voice, and I hate the guilt that slices through me at his words.

'Fuck you,' I hiss, stepping back toward the building.

'Hallie, wait.' Fletcher steps around in front of me, his hands up defensively.

'No. I will not stand here and listen to you criticise my relationship with my father. I'm also done having you beg me to choose you to write this book.'

'I'm not begging you to choose me.' His shoulders fall and he takes a deep breath. 'But I am begging you not to choose him.'

CHAPTER SEVENTEEN

Halliday,

I can't believe book five is out in the world. I still have to pinch myself to make sure it's not my vivid imagination. That's actually becoming something of a habit for these book releases.

I had a signing in Fairbanks tonight, and I met this young author named Fletcher. We talked for a while and long story short: I have the manuscript for his debut novel. It's brilliant, Hal, right up your alley. I considered asking him if you could read it, but he seemed nervous to have anyone take a look. I'll send you the first finished copy I can get my hands on though.

Love Dad

On Tuesday morning, Mason enters the Harcourt meeting room with a coffee in one hand and a tattered notebook in the other. Every cell in my body wants to know what he's written in that notebook. He said he'd been brainstorming since we approached him about the project, and I can only imagine the ideas in there.

'Halliday, great to see you again, my dear.' He flashes a smile as he sets his notebook and coffee cup on the table. 'Are we ready to get started?'

For our meeting today, Jordan has allocated us a small room in the far corner of the office. It has a wide window that looks out over the city below and chairs purchased for the aesthetic over comfort. There's a circular table in the centre and, at Mason's request, Jordan sourced us a whiteboard on wheels. It takes up most of the back wall and restricts the swivelling capability of my chair.

'Let's get cracking,' I say as I open my bag and pull out Dad's books. They're a little worse for wear and littered with colourful tabs.

'You've been busy.' Mason laughs.

'I've marked all the major plot points, impactful character moments, certain intricacies of the world-building that we'll need to remember to ensure continuity. Those yellow tabs are threads that I'm sure Dad intended on following up in the last book,' I explain.

Mason pulls book four toward him and idly flicks the tabs. 'And he left nothing for book six? No notes or even a brief outline?'

I shake my head. 'All I have is a rough draft of chapter one.'

Mason scratches his greying beard and stares at the blank whiteboard for a few moments. He says nothing, but I'm startled when he leaps up and uncaps a marker in one fluid movement.

'How about this,' he taps his chin, 'we'll map out where each character was left in book five and plot their arc to the end.'

I extract my tattered notebook from my bag and flick to the section where I've already completed this task. 'Like this?'

Mason takes the notes and his eyes narrow as he skims them. 'This is good.'

I feel a swell of pride in my chest. 'There are still so many moving parts to each character's story, but I think we should start with Halladora and work back from there. She's out of the tower now and is travelling to Lorden's Keep with Vengul. The final siege should take place there, but if Halladora is to be crowned at the end, she'll need to gain support from the lords of the other provinces.' I take a breath and let my brain catch up. 'She's been gone for over a year and thought to be dead, so I think she should send word to the lords, have her meet them individually. Show that she can take control of the situation and that she has a plan to gather forces and stop the blight.'

Mason is still reading over my notes and shakes his head when he looks up at me.

'Halladora is flighty and inexperienced. She'll never be the queen.'

'She is the queen, though. Rightfully. By blood.'

Mason purses his lips. 'She's been through a lot but having her survive the inevitable siege on Lorden's Keep is unrealistic. She can't fight and has no military experience. At this point, all she has is plot armour.'

'Plot armour?' I stammer.

'Halladora should be killed before they reach the Keep,' he

says. 'Vengul and Winshaw have a more compelling arc. I mean, the disgraced guard trying to protect his queen, and the rebel, questioning the merit of his cause over a woman, only to have her die. It writes itself.'

'Wait…wait.' I hold my hands up. 'We can't kill the main character now. She's alive because she's smart. She let herself be captured because being held in the tower meant she was safe. She's a bargaining chip and knows she has leverage. That's not plot armour.'

Mason's attention is back on my notes and he taps his chin, not having listened to a word I've said.

'Yes, we'll kill off Halladora. Think of the emotional impact it would have on Vengul. After all his efforts, his queen dies, anyway. Winshaw wouldn't be aware of it until he meets with her company. She's always been his enemy, but when they became lovers, it resulted in a crisis of conscience for him. He chose to help her. That point is moot now. He doesn't have to hold up his end of the bargain because she's dead. Does he honour the promise he made or return to the rebels and take the now empty throne for his King?'

Mason jots notes on the whiteboard and my mouth goes dry when he puts a big, wonky circle around *Death of Halladora*.

'I get what you're saying, and the impact it would have on Vengul and Winshaw would be an interesting aspect to explore, but think of everything Halladora went through in the first five books. She's a fighter, and she's already shown so much growth. Don't cut her off at the knees when she's so close to the end.'

Mason continues writing notes relating to the demise of our heroine. He also writes something about Winshaw poisoning himself to be with Halladora, and I make a mental note to shut that down later.

'Can I have a look at the notes you've written?' I ask and Mason turns around to face me. He thinks for a second, probably wondering which other beloved character he could kill prematurely.

'Of course.' He hands his notebook over and I open it to the first page. His handwriting is abhorrent, and I wonder if he trained as a doctor before this. I make out a few musings, namely relating to Halladora's demise. I only make it to the second page before I interrupt his brainstorming again.

'You want the blight to happen?' My eyes go wide. 'You want the Shadowspawn to open the Gate completely? They'll destroy the entire kingdom.'

Mason caps his marker and sits down at the table. 'Yes, and I'm insistent on it.'

I shake my head and stumble over my words. 'No, no… that can't happen. It makes the battle for the throne redundant because there'll be no land to rule over.'

'Exactly. The rebels are fighting for nothing. They were too busy with their border skirmishes to see the real threat. Shadowspawn have been trickling in, gaining strength before they blow the Shadow Gate open and become a plague on all those who were too blind to see them.' He folds his arms across his chest, rumpling his powder blue polo shirt.

What the fuck? That was never Dad's vision for the story. What Mason is suggesting will destroy everything Dad built. Burning it to the ground with everyone inside.

'I know it's a bold choice, but no one will see it coming,' Mason says. 'And if we're being honest with ourselves, Ellery wrote himself into a corner when he killed the Red Knight in book five. The Shadow Gate can't be closed without his blood.'

'I'm certain Dad had a plan for how to stop the blight. We just have to find it.'

Easier said than done. I've read these books time and time again, and I still don't know how to get around that hurdle without breaking a lot of the strict rules Dad created for his flawless magic system.

'Let's just start with killing Halladora off and go from there.' Mason is back at the whiteboard again. 'She's on her way to the Keep so we'll have some bandits ambush the convoy and slit her throat. Vengul can mourn for the rest of the journey, holding her shrouded body or something. Maybe shed a few tears before burning her remains and sending them down the Utheran River.'

I'm breathless. My head is spinning and I can feel sweat beading on my forehead. What's happening?

There's a knock at the door and Jordan's face appears. 'How's it going in here?'

Jordan doesn't register the silent distress that cripples me.

'Things are going great. We've made real headway,' Mason responds.

'Great to hear.' Jordan smiles and glances at the whiteboard. 'Oh, wow, death of Halladora. That sounds intriguing.'

'That's not happening.' I find my voice, but it's weak.

'Come on, Hallie.' Mason sighs. 'Don't be difficult.'

'I'm not trying to be difficult,' I scramble. 'She's the main character. You can't kill her off. There are plenty of other ways to raise the stakes in this story and create emotional impact for the characters. Halladora is supposed to sit on the throne at the end.'

Jordan steps into the room and takes a seat in Mason's vacant chair. 'I have a meeting in ten minutes, but this debate is fascinating.'

'I don't think there is anything to debate,' I say.

Mason looks irritated and turns to Jordan. 'The debate is in its infancy. I'll get it over the line.'

Irritation flares hot in my blood when Mason winks at Jordan. It's like I'm not even in the room.

Jordan finally picks up on the panic in my eyes. 'How about you pitch me both sides of the argument?'

Mason starts and his argument is more of a dramatic reading than anything else. He talks about tugging on heart-strings, rebels questioning their cause, and a deeper under-standing of what makes a villain tick. It almost swayed *me* for a moment, and Jordan is lapping it up. When Mason finishes, both men turn to me, and my rushed argument loses steam on its way from my brain to my mouth. Dad always said Halladora would wear the crown, but I don't know how she gets there, and I can't articulate it in a way that sounds as interesting as Mason's vision. Nevertheless, I clear my throat.

'It's her story. She faces so much adversity but confronts her fears and uses her brain to overcome it. She's an active protagonist with flaws and realistic emotions who fights for her people and isn't afraid to do what she has to in order to protect them. But you want to cheapen that complexity and use her death to force the personal growth of others. There's enough tension and turmoil in the world to affect them without using the most important character as cannon fodder to spur the male characters into action.'

'Halladora is too chaotic and emotional. Why would anyone want her to rule when they could have the rebel king on the throne? A man who has experience and ambition.' Mason speaks directly to Jordan.

'You don't understand her.' I bring their attention back to me.

'Of course I do.'

I shake my head. 'No, you don't. If you did, you would see that the things you don't like about her are what make her interesting. She's pure chaos. It's beautiful.'

Mason's posture stiffens. He shifts his weight from one foot to the other while Jordan rocks forward in his chair and drums his fingers on the table.

'I'm with Hallie.' Jordan stands and opens the door. 'Long live the Queen.'

The victory that momentarily lit Mason's features disappears immediately.

CHAPTER EIGHTEEN

Protecting Halladora from Mason was the least of my problems in the brainstorming session. I ended up stopping several assassinations, a plague, three dragons entering the story out of nowhere and the entire magic system being flipped on its head thanks to some McGuffin amulet that sends Winshaw back to the Borderlands.

When it's over, my brain feels like it's been toasted in a panini press.

'I take it the session didn't go as well as you'd hoped,' Jordan says as he presses the down button on the elevator.

'To be honest I'm just really confused by his methods.' I sigh. 'Tell me they won't all be like that?'

'For your sake, I hope not, but to be honest, Mason has a lot of sway around here and he knows it. He earned that respect though.'

The elevator dings and we step out into the basement parking lot. Jordan invited me to dinner to give him a rundown of the day and now I'm wondering if I'm capable of rehashing it.

'I love his work. He's one of my favourite authors, but he doesn't seem to understand that this book is the finale. Everything has been building to this, Dad laid the foundation, we can't and shouldn't change that.'

Jordan nods as he unlocks the car and we both slide in. 'Let me play devil's advocate for a second. Mason has his own process and we've dropped him into someone else's. It's a big change and it might take some time for you two to find your groove.'

He's right. Mason and I have just started navigating these waters, and it's going to take time. The grace period is short, though, and soon I'll need to sign on the dotted line. I hope we find that elusive groove before then.

After dinner, we return to the apartment and start tearing through my notes for book six. I'm on the right track, Jordan confirms it, but says we should consider some of Mason's ideas. I want to be flexible so I agree to work them in where I can.

'I still don't know how we're going to get around this Red Knight problem.' Jordan loosens his tie and undoes the top button on his dress shirt.

'I don't know either.' I put my head in my hands. 'Dad screwed us over with that.'

Jordan scoots forward on the couch and grabs his phone off the coffee table. A smile plays on his lips as he opens his email. 'Do you want to see what Fletcher came up with?'

My eyes widen. 'What do you mean?'

'Fletcher sent me some ideas before I told him you'd

chosen Mason. They don't solve your Red Knight problem, but I've got to admit, some of them are good.'

He holds out the phone and I snatch it, skimming the email as fast as my brain can take it in.

'Oh my god, of course! We can use the Council of Magi to help with the blight.'

Jordan grins. 'You'll have to rebuild the council using Halladora's influence in the East but think of how powerful that last battle will be. The mages storming the fields around the Gate while Vengul leads the Free State army and Winshaw brings the rebel forces.'

I'm giddy with excitement as I continue reading Fletcher's email. He wants to dig deeper into the rebellion and flesh out their cause. But it's his final plot point, at the end of the email, that makes my heart skip a beat.

'Winshaw is the rebel king?' I whisper. 'He's been the king all along?'

'I thought you'd like that one.' Jordan takes his phone and slips it back into his pocket. 'It's a hell of a twist.'

I slump back into the couch cushions. 'He was the king all along. That's why he never meets with the king and refuses to disclose the king's whereabouts to Halladora. She even points out how loyal the rebel forces are to Winshaw. They all know who he is but keep it a secret.' My synapses are firing all at once. 'But what's he gonna do when the Karrakin King falls? Will he take the throne or give it to Halladora like he promised?'

I grab my notebook off the coffee table and start scribbling. 'What if he doesn't? He loves her deeply, so what if he goes with her to the Gate? He fights beside her and dies for her.'

Jordan holds his hands up. 'Take a breath.'

'No!' I scramble to my feet again and begin pacing. 'We have to dig way deeper into all this.'

He stands too and collects his coat from the end of the bed. 'On that note, I have to get home. But run some of this by Mason tomorrow. See how he feels about it before we sign that contract.'

I nod furiously as I cross the room and open the door for him. 'I need to write all this down.'

'And maybe get some sleep?' Jordan encourages.

'Yeah, that too.'

I do not sleep a wink, but I fill the rest of my notebook with the seed that Fletcher, of all people, planted in my head.

It takes a freezing shower and two coffees to get me to Harcourt. Mason is already in the meeting room when I arrive, and he looks irritated that I've kept him waiting.

'I'm so sorry, my cab got stuck in some traffic.' I drop my bag on the table and start rifling through it. 'Anyway, I was up all night brainstorming and I've got some great stuff to go over today.'

Mason uncaps the whiteboard marker and draws another circle around the Death of Halladora. 'We're going with this. It's the most interesting idea we have.'

'It's not, trust me.' I skim the pages of my notebook to find what I'm looking for. I feel a little bad not crediting Fletcher for the Winshaw discovery, but it needs to be in the book.

'Winshaw is the rebel king,' I announce. 'If you look at all of his chapters in previous books, the clues are there. They're subtle—thanks, Dad—but they are there.'

Mason scratches his beard and his eyes have lost the wild spark they had the other night at the party. I wait with bated breath as he considers what I've said.

'No, Halladora will die. The blight will happen, the amulet will close the Gate, and they will elect Vengul to rule after his victory in battle.'

'This amulet doesn't exist anywhere in the other books. You can't invent some magical object to get us out of a bind. It's lazy, and if Dad hinted at Winshaw being the king then there must be a clue to the Gate.'

This argument carries on for so long my coffee wears off and I lose volume control.

'Why do you want Vengul to sit on the throne so much? He doesn't want to rule and it's not in his character to pursue it,' I snap.

Mason leans over the desk, head in his hands as he grinds his teeth.

'Halladora has no experience, there's no way she'd survive that battle.'

'She would. She has allies and a small council to guide her. I'm not saying she'll accomplish all this on her own.'

I haven't even gotten to Winshaw dying, but I already know there's going to be pushback on it. 'If anything, Vengul should die.'

Mason slaps his hand on the desk. 'Absolutely not. He is a commander and a leader. Halladora is a naïve woman and I'm not pandering to some feminist agenda where an unskilled and outmatched woman becomes the most powerful being in the universe by default, while the men around her train tirelessly and fight hard, only to be slaughtered for shock value.'

My mouth is agape and over Mason's shoulder I see a few people peering over their partitions at us. Whatever composure he had yesterday is gone, but I need to push back. Dad's work depends on it.

'Halladora is smart. That's her weapon, so let's work out how to use it.'

Mason's jaw tightens, causing the veins in his neck to stretch in the most unflattering way.

'You're impossible.' He rises to his feet and stares down at me. 'And ignorant, just like your father.'

I stand up from my chair to meet his eyes, but I'm still a head shorter than him. 'Ignorant?'

'Yes, ignorant, spoiled, and misguided. You know nothing about cohesive storytelling, and I don't have time to explain it to you.'

My mouth hangs open as the image I had of the great Mason Parrish dissolves before my eyes.

'Are you serious?' I splutter. 'This is supposed to be a team effort. We're meant to trust each other. You haven't listened to a word I've said.'

Mason's face pinches and his eyes narrow and I take a step back. He sucks in a deep breath, stepping forward to crowd my space.

'I don't need to listen to you and if you want this book written, I suggest you sit down, shut up, and let someone who knows what they are doing take over.' He lowers his voice. 'There is a big difference between reading a fantasy book and writing one, and the sooner you get that through your thick head the better off we'll be.'

He uncaps his pen and circles Halladora's death one more time for good measure. 'I'm feeling generous, so you can decide if her throat gets cut or if she gets kicked in the head by a horse.'

I think of Dad and the way his face lit up when we bounced ideas around for this story. He loved these characters, and while we both understood that some would be sacrificed, their deaths have to mean something. Because their lives meant something.

'She isn't dying.' My voice shakes but I hold my ground.

The marker squeaks as he scribbles on the board. 'Slit throat it is.'

'No. That's not how the story will go.' I swallow the lump in my throat. 'I'll die on this hill, Mason. Just watch.'

He forces a laugh. 'I'll be honest, a small part of me admires your tenacity but you're bordering on petulant. So why not save yourself further embarrassment and walk away? It's clear you're incapable of having a mature conversation.'

An angry pounding starts behind my temples and my vision blurs at the edges. I've made a huge mistake.

'We're done. Just get out.' I exhale.

Mason turns and snatches his notebook off the desk, flushing red as he reefs open the door. 'Fine. This overblown, uninspired drivel your father produced isn't worth my time anyway.'

He storms off down the hallway and as soon as he's out of sight I collapse into a chair and suck in as much air as my lungs can handle.

CHAPTER NINETEEN

Jordan drags his hand down his face as he paces his office.

'I know this isn't ideal, but it's lucky we haven't signed the contract,' I ramble. 'That would make it way more complicated.'

Twenty-five minutes ago, Mason stormed out of Harcourt, calling me 'the architect of modern fantasy's demise'. It's not the worst thing someone has called me, but when it comes from my favourite author after an almighty fall from grace, it stings.

I've been sitting in Jordan's office for eighteen minutes and talking for sixteen of those minutes. Jordan is yet to have any kind of outward reaction, and I don't know him well enough to predict what's going on in his head. Maybe he'll see this as a good thing. We dodged a bullet and now we can move on and find another author. Maybe he'll be thankful that I pushed for the brainstorming session before signing Mason. Maybe I'm better at this than I thought.

'Fuck.' Jordan drops into his chair with a thud.

Scratch that. I am not good at this.

'I couldn't let him kill Halladora, and he dismissed Winshaw being the rebel king. Then he called me ignorant, like my dad. I am not leaving Dad's book in his hands. I'm sorry, I won't do it.'

That little pluck of courage dies because this is putting Jordan through the wringer. He's been great through all of this, and I'm becoming reliant on his friendship. I genuinely hate disappointing him.

'I know, I know.' He leans forward and puts his elbows on the desk. 'I understand where you're coming from, and you're right about the contract.'

'Can you put some feelers out, see if we can get another author who might be interested?'

Jordan nods. 'Or we could go with Fletcher. He's finishing up the US leg of his tour in a couple of weeks. You could have a brainstorming session with him.'

I haven't told Jordan about the altercation Fletcher and I had at the Fremont party, even though I had to text Jordan and ask him to bring my coat outside while I waited for a cab. The excuse was 'the flight took it out of me' and he seemed to buy it.

I spent my entire first night in Seattle stewing over what Fletcher had said. I'm still furious about it now. He had no right to pass judgment on me not seeing Dad for six years because he has no idea what it was like being on opposite sides of the world.

'I don't want Fletcher.' I dig my nails into my knees. 'Every interaction I've had with him has upset me and if we don't get along, then the project will suffer.'

Jordan leans back in his chair and sucks in an exaggerated breath. 'Alright. I'll see what I can do. Give me a few days and I'll round up some more authors for you.'

'Thank you.' I reach across the desk and place my hand on his. 'I'm not trying to be a dick here. I just want to get it right.'

He puts his other hand on top of mine and squeezes. 'I know. But my God girl, you're testing me.'

His dark eyes crinkle as he lets out a laugh.

'Now get out so I can work.'

A day later, Jordan calls to let me know he's working on finding another author. With writing, touring, and publicity schedules, he's struggling to lock someone down. When he asks for a week to arrange something, I agree and book a flight to Fairbanks.

Since arriving back in the US, I've had one brief phone call with Marie. I told her I'd get back to Alaska as soon as I could to help with the rest of the cabin cleanout but couldn't give her a firm date. To my surprise, she seemed excited when I said I was flying up and staying the week. She told me where to wait outside the terminal for easy pick-up and even asked me to send through the flight number.

Marie always came across as a woman who doesn't long for the company of others. It explains why she and Dad maintained separate houses. But I suppose I can understand why, given the circumstances, she would want some company. After everything that happened with Mason, I need time to decompress. Alaska is perfect for that, and when I see Marie's smiling face through the car window outside the airport terminal, I know this is where I'm supposed to be right now.

'I can't get rid of his clothes yet,' Marie says as she pulls up in front of Dad's house. 'It's too soon.'

'That's okay. We don't have to get rid of anything if you don't want to.' I reach over and squeeze her arm. 'The house isn't going anywhere.'

She nods and stares up at the house for a while before ushering me inside for food and to see the new pet bed she sewed for Clover.

It only takes two days for us to move the boxes up into the loft and return the main living area to a functional space. Not that there's anyone here to use it.

'What are you going to do with the house?' Marie says as she closes Dad's closet door.

It's the first time she has alluded to what Dad left me, but there's no bitterness in her tone. There should be, and the fact she isn't bothered perplexes me.

'Why didn't he leave you anything in his will?' I ask. 'You were in a relationship for over a decade, but it all went to me.'

She lifts her shoulders lazily. 'I didn't ask for anything.'

'It's not about asking. It's about him wanting you to be taken care of if something happened.'

'I don't think he expected to die at forty-eight.' Her voice has a sharp edge to it. 'It wasn't really a concern.'

Colour springs to her cheeks and she folds her arms across her chest.

'Are you angry with me, at least? I haven't seen him in years then I swoop in, take his money and his book series.' Tears prick my eyes as I take in her blank expression. I want her to be mad at me because, aside from Fletcher, no-one else is. I wasn't that good of a daughter, so I don't deserve all this.

'It's his money. If he wanted you to have it, then that's his choice.' Her eyes meet mine. 'And I honestly don't care that much about the book. It seems selfish, but if he can't finish it then why does it have to be finished at all?'

Her mouth presses into a line but it slackens as she seems to realise how angry she looks.

'Now that's enough talk on the subject.'

I reluctantly agree as my phone dings with a message.

JORDAN

> We have a problem. Mason's gone rogue.

At the bottom of the message is the link to a podcast. I click on it and read the description. It's a fantasy novel podcast and I've listened to it before when Dad was a guest. The guest of this episode is Mason Parrish, and my stomach sinks like a stone.

I apologise to Marie and hurry to my bedroom, fishing my headphones from my bag before crawling onto the bed and pressing play.

After the tinny theme music and the introduction by the two hosts, Mason's voice is crisp and clear in my ears. They chat for a few minutes about his last book, his writing process, and what's next on the horizon. That last question opens a floodgate.

'Well, as you know, Steven, it was rumoured that I was to pen the final book in the *Blood of Gold* series,' Mason says. 'Those rumours were true, however after several meetings with Ellery's daughter, I walked away from the project.'

Okay, that's kind of true.

Steven, one of the hosts, makes a scandalised 'oooh' noise into the microphone before Drew, his co-host says, 'Sounds like there's more to this than you're letting on. *Blood of Gold* is one hell of an opportunity, and not something any author would walk away from easily. Would you care to delve a little deeper into your decision to leave the project? Was the enormity of the world Yates built a factor?'

There is a beat of silence that lasts long enough for my heart to climb into my throat. Please don't delve deeper. Let sleeping dogs lie, Mason.

'The problem was not the sheer magnitude of the project. I have no qualms penning a two hundred-thousand-word novel. The problem is that Halliday, Ellery's daughter, has such a stranglehold on this book, she refuses to listen to the opinions of others.'

This time Drew makes the 'oooh' noise and Steven steps in. 'I didn't know he had a daughter. I'm sure few people did. Can you explain her involvement?'

Mason clears his throat. 'You see, Ellery appointed her as his literary executor, and rather than leaving the project in the capable hands of Harcourt Press, this young woman, with no experience or qualification, has exercised her right to creative control over the project. We had two meetings to discuss the direction of the story, and throughout both she was difficult, ignorant, and offered nothing of value. I pity whoever takes on the project because they'll be dealing with a spoiled brat who doesn't care about the art of a fantasy novel. She's only looking to drain more money out of her deceased father's estate.'

I stop breathing and my body caves in on itself.

'Wow.' Drew laughs nervously. 'That's quite an accusation, Mason.'

'It's not an accusation, it's the truth, and this is why literary executorship should be put in the hands of professionals. Not a young girl with no knowledge of the craft who, if we're honest with ourselves, is only part of this because she wants to visit the TV set and rub shoulders with celebrities.'

I rip the earbuds from my ears and throw the phone across the bed. How could he say those things? How could he comfortably lie like that? My whole body trembles as I pick the phone back up to call Jordan. He answers after the first ring.

'Are you alright?'

I shake my head and throw it back, hoping gravity will stop the tears. 'Why would he say any of that? It's not true.'

'You're a thorn in his side and now he's lashing out,' Jordan says. 'I wish he'd kept the truth about Ellery not having an outline to himself, though.'

'What?'

'It's going to complicate finding another author. Not to mention the fan backlash now they know whoever writes it isn't working from Ellery's plan.'

I drag my hand through my hair. 'I didn't listen to the

whole podcast. I shut it off after he said all I wanted was Dad's money.'

'That's for the best,' he says. 'I've got another call coming in, but I'll be in contact in a few days when I have some author options for you.'

I thank Jordan for his efforts before hanging up the call.

If only I could successfully convince myself that no one cares about that podcast and that Mason will be seen for the sexist, egotistical, and petty man that he is. Unfortunately, any defence I offer would have zero merit. I'm not an author, publisher, or editor. I'm just Ellery's daughter, and thanks to Mason, I'm now on the world's radar.

<h1 style="text-align:center">CHAPTER TWENTY</h1>

Four days later, I'm on my way back to Seattle and doing my best to stop my heart from skipping every time my phone rings. Thanks to the release of my uncommon name, it didn't take long for private messages and comments to flood my social media accounts. It's an even split between Dad's fans telling me to remove myself from the project and Mason's fans calling me an idiot for not listening to him. It takes all my strength not to respond with exactly what happened in those meetings. I even drafted a message saying that Mason wanted to kill off Halladora, who is the most popular character in the series. There would be riots in the streets if she died.

Instead, I say nothing and delete all of my accounts. I don't want to make life more difficult for Jordan and Harcourt by blasting keyboard warriors and having my childish behaviour retweeted over and over.

Everyone at home has gotten wind of the apparent 'online

beef' I have with Mason as well. It doesn't matter that it's one sided. Wes called me straight away and let me cry for a solid fifteen minutes before I managed coherent conversation. He said not to worry and to stay off the internet. I do that for about an hour before I'm back on news websites and fantasy forums.

When I arrive back at the Seattle apartment, Jordan is waiting for me. He offers a hug and a sympathetic smile as I invite him inside.

'It's easier said than done, but you have to ignore all the bullshit you see online. Mason doesn't deserve the time of day he's being given to criticise you.'

I drop onto one end of the couch and Jordan takes the other. Mason is lashing out because I bruised his ego, but so far no one has come to my defence publicly, and the longer it goes on the more truthful his words appear. I'm not in the public eye, I don't have a massive platform to defend myself. I'm a twenty-eight-year-old assistant store manager from Brisbane whose Dad died.

'When do we meet with other authors?' I ask as I stare at the Aztec pattern on the woven rug beneath my feet. Jordan doesn't respond and when I look up, he's tugging on his earlobe.

'We don't have any other authors.'

'As in, they can't make it into the office for a meeting? We can video chat or I can go to them.'

My stomach is already in knots at the thought of flying again, but I push through.

Jordan shakes his head. 'I've called everyone I know, even authors who aren't with Harcourt. I don't know whether

Mason got to them directly or if they heard the podcast, either way they're reluctant to work with you.'

I close my eyes and take two deep breaths.

'This is so unfair. I've done nothing wrong.'

'I know that, and the company knows that.'

'So, what do we do?'

Jordan leans forward, resting his forearms on his thighs and linking his fingers together. 'We've only got one option.'

It's Fletcher. He knows it and I know it.

'I can't call him,' I whisper. 'I just can't.'

'You have to if we want this book published.'

Not publishing the book at all seems preferable to crawling back to Fletcher with my tail between my legs.

'He's in Chicago for the next two days wrapping up his book tour. It would be better if you asked in person rather than have me call him. It'll also give you a chance to explain what happened with Mason.'

Jordan's right, but that doesn't make it an easier pill to swallow.

'I'll book a flight,' I concede.

The flight to Chicago is exhausting, but I pass the time reading the remaining entries in Dad's journal. While my heart is heavy, my connection to him feels stronger than ever. Unfortunately, on my walk to Fletcher's signing in River North, I realise those entries are the last words of Dad's I will ever read and I wish I'd rationed them.

I try to push that thought out of my head as I step into the bookstore. It's larger than I expected. The main floor has rows upon rows of shelves, all constructed from polished mahogany, and according to the colourful map on the wall beside the counter, there's an upper level and a lower level that are as expansive as this one.

I work my way forward through the growing crowd until I'm on the outskirts of a large open space with rows of chairs and a low stage with one white-clothed table on it. Every seat is occupied, so I slink around the side and position myself next to a large poster with Fletcher's author photo printed on it.

We aren't waiting long before the crowd erupts, and I see Fletcher making his way from the other side of the room to the table in front. I admit to myself that he looks good in his dark suit and white shirt with his hair pushed back neatly. He waves to the crowd and shakes hands with the host who I recognise as Xavier Kirkman, a YouTube personality who amassed thousands of subscribers by reviewing popular books. He's a fan of Dad's and a huge number of his videos are about *Blood of Gold*.

It takes a beat for the crowd to settle and when they do, Xavier introduces Fletcher and thanks everyone for coming. My focus stays on Fletcher, and I try not to smile at the witty responses he has for the questions he's asked.

'This is easy.' Xavier grins as he looks at the notes in his hand. 'Biggest influence?'

Fletcher smiles. 'That *is* easy. Ellery Yates.'

Xavier asks a few more questions about Dad, but Fletcher doesn't talk too much about him and pulls the discussion back to *Red Reign*.

'When can we expect a sequel?' Xavier asks, and the

crowd ripples with excitement. Fletcher says it's in the works, prompting loud chatter to break out across the room.

Xavier swiftly brings this back to Dad and kicks off the line of questioning I've been dreading.

'Fletcher, what are your thoughts on Mason Parrish and the freefall that the final *Blood of Gold* book is now in?'

Fletcher pauses for a second before lifting the microphone to his mouth. It takes all my strength not to leave the store. I don't need to hear this.

'Yates is prolific, so they would be big shoes to fill. Maybe Mason wasn't up to the task?'

The crowd rumbles and Xavier's dark eyebrows creep toward his hairline.

'That's an interesting take. Mason's been outspoken about the way Harcourt is handling the series' conclusion. He's slammed Ellery's daughter and her involvement in the project. What are your thoughts on that?'

Fletcher doesn't sit on this question. 'I don't envy Halliday. She's in a difficult position, and like myself and many others, she wants what's best for the series. If Mason Parrish isn't it, then we can't blame her for that.'

That's not what he said at the Fremont party, and if the crowd knew, would they be so starry-eyed?

When the question-and-answer portion of the night is over, the store employees stack copies of Fletcher's book on the table and I watch from the side as the people form a queue to have their books signed. It takes him a while to get through everyone, but I wait until he gets up from the table and moves to the side of the room. Xavier is already bending his ear, and as I get the courage to walk over, something tears through my peripheral vision.

A small boy weaves his way through the chairs, colliding with Fletcher's legs. He's being tailed by a beautiful woman with thick, dark hair cropped to her shoulders. She smiles as she watches Fletcher pick up the child, who promptly collapses against Fletcher's chest.

'It's past bedtime, buddy,' Fletcher says and as he looks up at the woman, he sees me hovering across a row of chairs.

He seems surprised and I don't know what to do. I stay rooted to the spot, clutching my copy of his book in my hand. Considering the hostility of our last encounter, I expect he's going to make this one as miserable as possible.

'Hallie?' His forehead wrinkles. 'What are you doing here?'

The dark-haired woman takes the kid from Fletcher, depositing him on her hip and reaching for Fletcher's arm. I don't remember anything on his website bio or social media that suggests he has a wife and kid. He doesn't wear a wedding ring.

'Fletch, I've got to get Luca home.' The woman glances at me. 'Our ride is outside.'

He nods, pats her arm, and kisses the young boy on the head. 'I'll call you later.'

She dips her chin and secures her handbag on her shoulder before leaving the store. Fletcher is already on his way over to me.

'I came to get my book signed.' I hold the book out and he looks at me for a long moment before taking it.

'Halliday, is it?' he jokes as he uncaps a pen, leans on a

chair, and scribbles his signature on the page bearing the dedication to my dad.

Fletcher hands the book back and I stash it in my handbag.

'I know you didn't come all the way to Chicago for that.'

'Can we talk?' I ask and he gives a resigned nod.

※

It's almost ten on a Friday, and the bar in my hotel is evidently not the hottest spot in town. It's an opulent space with panelled walls and dark upholstered furniture. The soft lighting from the intricate gold wall sconces makes it more romantic than I'd like.

I order a white wine and Fletcher asks for a bourbon as we settle into a pair of high-backed velvet chairs in the corner of the room. I'm feeling underdressed in my black jeans and plum coloured jacket. Fletcher looks right at home.

He flashes a grin as he unbuttons his suit jacket. 'I hope my signing wasn't a disappointment.'

'It wasn't, which is surprising,' I say. 'Considering every other interaction I've had with you.'

He raises an eyebrow. 'I know what you're here for, so maybe you shouldn't lead with an insult.'

I take a deep breath and wipe my sweaty palms on my jeans. I didn't realise how much I'm still seething about what he said in Fremont until I saw him again.

'Maybe if you were less insufferable, I might be less inclined to insult you.'

I'm not proud of the hostility, but it's my MO now, so I have no choice but to steer into it.

'See you're doing it again.' He leans forward. 'You want something from me, but you're doing your best to piss me off. That makes me think you want me to say no then you can go back to Jordan and tell him you tried to sign me on for book six, but I was the one that refused.'

Dammit. He's onto me.

'Astute, aren't you.' I take a sip of my wine. 'I'll be honest. I don't want you to write this book because I'm looking for an author I respect. Which was you, right up until you opened your mouth.'

'You should have listened when I opened my mouth. I told you Mason was a mistake and now look where you are. Begging me to reconsider because your reputation is blown to hell, and no author wants to put themselves through working with you.'

I grit my teeth. 'Mason is full of shit and I am not begging you to do anything.'

'You don't have to. Of course I'm going to write the book, because Ellery's legacy is more important than whatever is going on between me and you.'

'There's nothing going on between me and you.' I straighten my back. 'I think you're a dick but a talented author, and as much as I hate to admit it, I need a talented author right now.'

Fletcher pinches his bottom lip as he leans back in his chair. 'You're not good at this.'

'My interpersonal skills aren't a priority. You want to write the book, then congratulations, I choose you. As soon as you're back in Seattle, I'll get Jordan to set up a meeting, and we can go through what we have so far and push on from there.'

My hands tremble as I take another sip of wine. He notices and it brings a smile to his face.

'Jordan showed you my ideas, didn't he?'

'I skimmed the email.'

'And...'

'They're fine.'

'Come on.' He pins me with a stare. A warm, glittering bronze look that causes something to spark in my chest. 'What did you think of the Winshaw thing?'

I am stubborn, but not to a fault. Still, I manage to hold on to my excitement.

'It's interesting. We'll talk more about it next week.' I down the rest of my wine and stand up. 'I'll see you in Seattle.'

'You will.' He nods but stays seated as I leave the bar.

I make it to the lobby elevator before my curiosity becomes too much. I swallow my pride, walk back into the bar, and find him fixing up the bill I walked out on.

'What about the Shadow Gate?' I say as he turns to look at me. 'How do they close it?'

He searches my face for a second and with the most sincere expression I've ever seen, he says, 'I don't know. That secret died with him.'

CHAPTER TWENTY-ONE

Jordan wastes no time getting the ball rolling. I touch down in Seattle on Saturday afternoon and he immediately invites me to dinner to go over the press release and contract, and talk about the publicity relating to my less than stellar reputation. Fletcher took the red-eye back to Seattle and has already confirmed he'll be joining us.

Here I thought that getting the book written was going to be my biggest issue. Now people are contacting me, trying to get interviews and statements about the trashing that Mason has given me in the media. I've ignored all of them and called Cece, Dad's agent, to see if she'd be interested in helping with everything that's about to happen. Even though I'm not an author, she agreed to represent my interests with the Harcourt contract and the TV adaptation. It takes some pressure off, that's for sure.

Fletcher and Jordan are seated when I arrive at the steakhouse a few blocks back from the waterfront. It's a long, rectangular space lined with bottle green, button-tufted booths and floral-patterned carpet. While the decor is dated, it's well presented, and it doesn't smell like old cigars, which is the vibe it gives off.

'Hallie.' Jordan slides sideways so I can get in next to him. 'I hope you don't mind, I ordered you a drink.'

He pushes the tumbler of amber liquid toward me.

'Thank you.' I take a sip and enjoy the smooth burn of what has to be the best scotch I've ever tasted. Turns out, if you spend over fifteen dollars on a bottle, it's not that bad.

We hold off on discussing the book until meals are ordered, which means Jordan is working overtime to avoid dead air between me and Fletcher. He's magnificent at it, but as soon as the server walks away, the stalling is over.

'They're going to announce it on Tuesday after we sign the contract. I'll email you the press release to look over, but I think you'll both be happy with it.'

'Sounds great.' Fletcher rubs his hands together. 'When do I start?'

'When do *we* start?' I correct him and he gives me the side-eye.

'You know what I mean.' He fires back.

Jordan rolls up the sleeves of his dress shirt. 'Is this how it's going to be? Really?'

Fletcher and I look at each other before turning back to Jordan and answering in unison. 'Yes.'

'Fine. But you two are on your own. I want to see an outline as soon as possible, then frequent chapters. Greg is already breathing down my neck about this book.'

'We'll get it done,' Fletcher says, exuding confidence from every inch of his body.

I agree with a firm nod.

'Good. Now the next matter is the press. Hallie is going to hate this, but the PR department has booked you both on a morning show next week to talk about the book and what it's like working together.' Jordan looks pointedly at me. 'Which is an absolute dream, in case either of you are wondering.'

'Does this mean I finally get to tell the world how much of an arsehole Mason is?'

Jordan puts his head in his hands. 'Hell no. Fletcher's experienced with this, just let him take the lead and say nothing that's going to come across as bitter about the Mason thing. It's a clean slate now. Fletcher is the man for the job, and you support each other creatively.'

'Don't worry, Jordan. I can make her look good.' Fletcher winks and I fight the urge to toss my drink in his perfectly proportioned face.

'The other matter is the set visit. Filming resumes in Ireland in five weeks and two Harcourt staffers are going to fly out there with you to develop some content for our social accounts. We want to build some positive buzz and show the two of you working together.'

'That's fine,' I say. 'We can handle that.'

Fletcher smirks like he doesn't think I'm capable, but I want this book to be a success more than anything. It also wouldn't hurt to rehab my image considering it's still taking a beating.

How is that even something I have to worry about now?

This whole thing is getting out of control, and I'm glad Dad kept me out of all this for as long as he could.

After dinner, Jordan has to rush off because his fiancée, Lara, is upset that he cancelled seeing a wedding venue tonight in favour of sorting out my mess. I know little about Lara, but I get the sense that this isn't the first time Jordan has ditched her for work.

'Get her flowers on the way home,' I call out as he hurries from the restaurant.

I turn back to face Fletcher, who is refilling his water glass. 'We should go over this interview then,' he says. 'To make sure you don't sink my career in a ten-minute television appearance.'

'I think, if provoked, you'd do that yourself.'

'And what gives you that impression?'

'Come on,' I scoff. 'I saw you at the signing. All diplomatic when asked about me and Mason. That's not what you're really like.'

'You don't know what I'm really like.'

'I know enough.'

He folds his arms. 'You know nothing about me because you don't want to know. I made a questionable first impression and you refuse to look past it. How immature does that make you?'

I look him in the eye. 'Let me remind you, it wasn't just the first impression. How about the Fremont party where you said I don't know what my own father would want and that I don't care about him because I didn't see him for six years. That fucking stung.'

Fletcher swallows and his expression softens. 'I'm sorry

about that. It was out of line. It frustrated me that you didn't seem to care that he hated Mason and you chose him because you liked him.'

I roll my empty glass between my fingers and stare down at the table. 'I didn't know Dad hated him, but now I see why he would have.'

Fletcher says nothing and we sit in heavy silence until the waiter returns, clears our plates, and asks if we'd like to see a dessert menu. I decline and turn my attention back to Fletcher.

'Was that your wife and son at the signing?'

He nods. 'Luca is my son and Mia's my ex-wife.'

'Does she live in Chicago?'

'No, but her family does. She was out there visiting.'

That oppressive silence takes us over again, so I revert back to a dynamic we both seem much more comfortable with. 'I can't believe someone would marry you. Or did you trick her into it, and then she realised how much of a pain you are?'

His mouth cracks into a wide grin. 'I've gotta say I'm warming to all these insults you throw at me. Maybe we will work well together.'

'Maybe,' I concede. 'I would like to know you better before we're locked in a boardroom for the next few months.'

'Alright, what do you want to know?' Fletcher relaxes back into the padded booth and the poor lighting turns his eyes a richer brown.

'When was the last time you spoke to my dad?'

He swallows but still focuses on me. 'An hour before he died.'

I move my attention to the glass in my hands as tears prick

my eyes. I don't want to cry in the middle of a restaurant when the people around me are trying to enjoy their fifty-dollar steak.

'You were the last one to speak to him then?'

Fletcher nods slowly. 'Marie was with him, but yes, I was one of the last people to speak to him.'

'Did he sound happy?'

'Yeah. I called to tell him they'd added Dallas to my tour and that Chicago, New York, and Boston had all sold out.' He smiles. 'He said he was proud.'

We both fall silent as we remember what it was like to hear Dad say those words. It didn't matter how small the achievement was because there was something in the way he said it. His voice lifted, and he made you feel like you'd hung the stars.

'You were close then, by the sounds of it.'

I don't understand the pang of jealousy that hits when I vocalise that fact. Dad didn't know he was going to die, but my chest constricts because I wasn't the one he spoke to an hour before it happened. It's a moment that Fletcher gets to keep forever, and I don't.

Fletcher clears his throat. 'I went up to Alaska a few times this past year. Spent time with him working on edits for *Red Reign*. He helped me through a lot of shit.'

'What kind of shit?' I ask as a waitress walks by with a tray of drinks for the table behind us. When she's out of earshot, he turns his attention back to me and answers my question.

'My divorce. It was being finalised around the time I met Elle.'

He says it with ease but seems to notice that I've shifted in my seat. I can't work out why but talking about his wife makes me uncomfortable. Probably because in my experience marriage doesn't work, and if you don't talk about it, then no one has to relive any heartbreak.

'We were separated for two years before we bothered with the paperwork, and we're on good terms,' he assures me. 'We wanted it to be amicable because we have Luca to think about.'

I arch a brow. 'How old are you?'

'Thirty-two.'

'And how old is your son?'

'Five.'

He was younger than me when he became a father, and I can't fathom that level of responsibility. I'm anxious when Violet leaves the room and I have to monitor Archie for a few minutes. I don't even have to feed him. I just have to make sure he doesn't stick a fork in an electrical outlet.

'Why don't you tell me something about you?' He folds his arms on the table and the way he smiles with eager curiosity somehow makes me feel like I'm the only person in the room. Though, nothing about me seems interesting enough because he already knows who my dad is.

'Not much to tell. I studied Business and English at university, bought a house when I was twenty-three, and I run a homewares store with my mum.'

'Any marriages?'

I shake my head. 'Not that I know of.'

'Serious relationships?'

'Nope, and I'm fine with that.'

The waitress appears at our table, asking if we'd like another round of drinks, and Fletcher seems annoyed by the interruption. I ask for the check and when she scurries off, I turn back to see he's looking at me. When he isn't being condescending or rude, he kind of looks like a Disney prince.

'Why do you want to write Dad's book?'

'We don't have to talk about the book.' He leans in, closer to my side of the booth. 'We can just talk about Elliot as a person.'

'But his books are all anyone wants to talk to me about.'

His expression softens, and it's definitely pity. 'Why would you say that?'

'Because it's true. Whenever anyone finds out who my dad is, they ask me questions about his books and how it's going to end, and they dump all these insane theories on me and study my reaction to see if they can pick up on a clue. It's tiring.'

The waitress returns with the check and I go sifting through my bag for my card. Fletcher beats me to it, slapping his credit card in the billfold and signing the receipt.

'You didn't have to do that,' I protest.

He shrugs his broad shoulders. 'I'll get Jordan to reimburse me later.'

CHAPTER TWENTY-TWO

On Monday morning, I arrive at the Harcourt office before Fletcher. Jordan's day is an absolute disaster, but he sets me up in the meeting room and wishes me luck.

While I wait, I pull out my phone and see a handful of messages from Wes. He wants an opinion on some bathroom tiles for the house he's working on, wondering how to turn on the vacuum cleaner and asking if we can keep a cat that's scaled the fence in our backyard. He's supplied a photo of the cat, which looks well-groomed and is definitely the property of someone in the neighbourhood. I press the little camera icon to start a video chat, and it rings for far too long.

'Hey,' Wes answers, holding the phone well below his chin so I can see straight up his nose.

'How's it going?' I lean back in my chair and cross my legs. Wes looks up and says something to someone I can't see before the camera flips, and I catch a glimpse of the house he's at today.

'You're not keeping that cat,' I say as the camera shakes and pans the floor before he works out how to turn it back to his face.

'But the cat likes me.' He looks off in a different direction and gives someone an instruction. 'What's new with you?'

His attention is dragged away again before I can answer. I feel like I'm imposing, but one of his messages said to call when I had a chance.

'I'm being interviewed on some morning show on Friday,' I say to Wes's cheek as his heavy footfalls crackle through the speaker.

'You what?'

'Yeah, I'm terrified. Fletcher is signing on to write the book after the Mason mess, and we need to make it look like it isn't all a giant clusterfuck.'

Wes brings his attention back to me and laughs. 'This is gonna be mint. I can't wait to watch.'

My forehead wrinkles. 'Thank you for your support.'

'You're welcome.' He scratches his brand-new beard, and I can see that he's now sitting on the steps outside. 'I gotta get back to work, but I'll give the cat a cuddle for you.'

'No. You're not keeping the cat!' I call out, but he hangs up the phone.

I'm firing off a cat-related text to Wes when Fletcher steps into the room, laptop under one arm and a well-worn messenger bag over the opposite shoulder.

'Morning.' He yawns as he drops into a chair and looks up at the whiteboard. Mason's scribblings are still there, including the death of Halladora note. Fletcher's brow furrows as he turns back to me.

'He wanted to kill off Halladora?'

I nod. 'It was one of our more significant creative differences.'

'I'm glad you stood your ground. We're getting Hal to the other side of this. She'll get her crown.'

'Not without closing the Gate,' I point out. 'We still have no idea how that's going to work.'

He picks up the bag and pulls out five tattered and heavily annotated paperbacks. They're Dad's but I can scarcely make out the name on the severely cracked spines.

'There will be a clue in here somewhere. We just have to find it.'

Wild enthusiasm sparks in his eyes as he picks up the first book and thumbs through the pages.

We're at it for four hours before Jordan sticks his head in to drop off the sushi he got us for lunch. Neither Fletcher nor I am interested in slowing down, so Jordan leaves the plastic containers on the desk and wishes us luck for the afternoon ahead.

By the time the sun dips, we've been through book one in its entirety and are yet to find any clues for the glaring problem Dad laid out.

'Did he even know what he was going to do about the Gate?' I huff. 'When I read his initial chapters for book five, he said it would work out, but now I'm wondering if he'd even thought that far ahead.'

'He had.' Fletcher scratches his temple. 'Trust me, he thought of everything. He has notes about this somewhere in that house. I'd put money on it.'

I don't know if it's the tone of his voice or the comment,

but it rubs me the wrong way. I'm tired of him insinuating that he knew Dad better than I did.

'Why do you do that?' I sigh.

'Do what?'

'Try to drive home this idea that you were closer to him than me?'

His eyes narrow. 'I don't do that.'

'What do you call it then?' I close my notebook. 'Because you behave like it's a competition. You get a thrill out of knowing something I don't.'

Fletcher leans back in his chair, and I expect the customary smug grin in response. It doesn't happen though. Instead, he looks me in the eye and lets out a slow, near painful breath.

'Are you going to spend this entire project picking fights with me?'

Now the smug grin arrives.

'It wasn't my intention but picking fights with you is gratifying. Especially when I know I'll win.' I force a menacing smile in return.

'Trust me when I say you aren't winning.' He leans closer. 'Because as you can see, I'm unaffected. You, on the other hand, that's a different story. Your neck flushes when you're irritated, and it's quite fun to see how red I can make the tops of your ears.'

He's so close that I can smell his sea-salt cologne and see the caramel strands in his dark hair as the last of the daylight streams into the cramped room.

I clear my throat. 'How about you get back to doing what you're being hired to do. Unless the Winshaw revelation was lightning in a bottle and you've realised you're incapable of coming up with another good idea.'

He barks a laugh. 'King Winshaw is better than anything you've come up with.'

'The clues were in the book. Stumbling upon something that was there for you to find isn't the same as creating it.'

'You didn't find it.' His knee bumps mine under the table and I feel the flush crawl up my neck. His eyes drop to my collarbone and he smiles.

'I may not have found that, but there is a lot of me sprinkled throughout that text.'

He raises a brow. 'Like what?'

'Dad didn't come up with the trade war that sparked the Princes' Rebellion and caused the provinces to secede from one another. That was all my idea.'

I thoroughly enjoy the look of admiration he's trying to hide.

'Then where are all these other ideas? Because from what I can tell,' he points at the whiteboard. 'All that up there, is Mason.'

I drum my fingers on my notebook before flipping it open and pushing it toward him. His knee is still touching mine as I watch his eyes scan the thought-dump I had after I read his email. It sparked something and I couldn't stop. I scribbled every tiny spark on that page.

Fletcher shifts in his chair and our contact dissolves. He's still studying the pages, brow furrowing and mouth pulling tight. If this is judgement, then I prefer the smirk.

'Thoughts?' I prompt, folding my arms across my chest and bracing for a Mason-esque reaction.

He closes the book, taps it against his chin, and stares at the whiteboard. Anticipation builds in my body and I realise that I want him to like it. I've become attached to Winshaw dying to complete his arc, and I'm not sure what I'll do if Fletcher doesn't see how fitting that ending would be.

He stands up, collects a marker from the table, and uncaps it. I hold my breath as he takes a step toward the board and uses the side of his hand to erase Mason's words. He jots something down and fixes the wonky circle before capping the pen and stepping back to admire his handy work. The board now reads *Death of Winshaw*.

It's well after ten p.m. when we leave the Harcourt office with a rough outline in hand and a much higher tolerance for each other. There were some clipped tones, heated debates, and minor sulking on my part when Fletcher refused to include a sex scene between Halladora's lady-in-waiting and Vengul. He said he'd be no good at writing it, but *Red Reign* had some steamier moments, so I know that's not true.

'I think we can expand on this idea that Zios wants to join the acolytes.' Fletcher struggles to contain the volume of his voice as we exit the building and meet the frigid Seattle air.

'He needs a morally grey trajectory, otherwise what's the point of having his POV at all? It'll also give us some insight in the Karrakan King and what his plan is when the siege kicks off.' I tuck my hands into my pockets for fear of frostbite.

'Exactly.' Fletcher runs his hand through his hair. He's so amped up his teeth aren't even chattering in the cold. Where was this guy when we first met? This is what I imagined the author of one of my favourite books would be like. He's all passion and fire.

'I won't be able to sleep tonight.' He exhales. 'I have to keep working on this outline.'

We come to a stop on the corner of the block, and I hesitate to pull out my phone and order an Uber.

'I don't have anywhere to be.' I shrug. 'We can keep working on it.'

He tucks his hands in his pockets. 'Wait, you're saying you want to spend more time with me?'

'Don't get cocky. This outline needs polishing and we're already on the back foot with the Mason debacle.'

'Where are we going then?' He moves, so he's standing in front of me. 'My place is fifteen minutes that way.'

He points north, and even though my apartment is five minutes the other way, I nod. I want to see where he lives.

On the walk we talk almost exclusively about fantasy novels. He's interested to know what Brent Gallagher is like and is underwhelmed with my assessment. I don't have any other gossip to provide, so conversation turns to my moniker and I take my Tolkien joke out for another spin. He laughs harder than Mason did.

'But are you seriously telling me you haven't read Lord of the Rings?' he scoffs. 'I thought you were a fantasy fan.'

'I'm sorry. I tried, but I couldn't get through it,' I explain as I narrowly avoid stepping off the edge of the pavement. I was too focused on Fletcher and not what's in front of me.

He shakes his head. 'I'm so disappointed. You need to rectify this immediately.'

'Sorry to burst your bubble, but I won't. I tried and have accepted my failure.'

'I take it you wouldn't be impressed by my collector's edition of The Fellowship of the Ring then.'

I shrug. 'Not as much as you'd be hoping for.'

He shakes his head and comes to a stop outside a quaint little bar with a sign on the front that reads Whiskey Double. It fills the lower level of a free-standing brick building and has a handful of occupied tables on the sidewalk.

'You live in a bar? Is this to really emphasise that tortured artist vibe?'

'I'm not tortured, and no, my brother owns the bar. I live in the apartment above it.'

He guides me around the side of the building to a paint-chipped door with an intimidating deadlock.

'I've only written one bestseller. I'll get a bigger place when the sequel hits number one on the Times' list.' He pushes the door open with his shoulder and as we walk up the narrow staircase, I'm reminded of all the questions I have about *Blue Horizon* but decide to shelve the subject for later.

'This is it,' he announces as he steps to the side and ushers me into his apartment. It's about half the size of the ground level of my townhouse, but the layout is similar. The kitchen is along the left wall with a fridge at the end and enough bench space to make a sandwich. In the centre is a small, round table and beyond that, a compact living area with a two-seater couch and a unit that doesn't look structurally sound enough to hold the widescreen TV sitting on top of it. Through an alcove a few steps from the back of the couch, I can see the end of a small bed behind a dinosaur patterned room divider.

The true treasure of the place is the custom-built bookshelves that span almost an entire wall. They're built around two doorframes, and I'd hazard a guess there's at least a thousand books tightly packed into the shelves.

'Holy shit,' I breathe as I take a few steps forward and study the spines. He's got everything. Epic fantasy, thrillers, graphic novels, and a much smaller section dedicated to contemporary romance. I've discovered the inspiration for *Red Reign's* romantic subplot.

'Not much of a reader then,' I joke as he steps up behind me and helps slide my coat off. He folds it over the back of the dining chair before ushering me to sit, and I pull out my notebook while he sets down a glass of water and some questionable crackers he found in an overhead cabinet. I thank him for the spread but return to the task at hand.

By two-thirty in the morning we've been through the outline multiple times, fleshed out the major plot points, and transferred it from my notebook to Fletcher's laptop.

'I'm gonna call a cab.' I stand up and put on my coat, giving the bookcases another look.

'You have all the leather-bound editions.' I point at the shelf and his eyes follow my gaze. Above the door to his bedroom are five shiny black spines with gold lettering. I have a matching set and know they're worth an absolute mint because Dad signed every one of the limited run produced.

'Yeah, Elle sent them to me to celebrate *Red Reign* getting published.'

His focus moves to my eyes and for the briefest moment, down to my mouth.

I take a step back because I don't like the funny feeling

that's rising in my chest. It doesn't stop it from spreading through me like a poison, though.

He senses the atmospheric shift and appears to relax. It's been at least five hours since we last dropped a snide comment toward one another, and I hadn't even noticed. Maybe this is the groove. We're in it.

'How's calling that cab going?' He raises an eyebrow because I'm staring at the table.

'Superb. They'll be here any second.'

'You haven't even gotten your phone out.'

'Don't need to.' I shrug. 'I'm telepathic.'

'That's a neat trick. You'll have to show me how it works.'

'One day,' I say. 'I'm going to get out of your hair now, but thanks for a good first day.'

'You're welcome.' He chuckles as he holds out his phone. 'Add your number.'

I do as instructed because having his number will be handy throughout this project. Especially when I can't sleep because ideas are bouncing around my head and I need someone to suffer along with me.

He dials my number so I have his before stuffing the phone into his pocket. 'Make sure you telepathically let me know that you got back to your apartment safely.'

'I'll think about it.' I take a few steps toward the door as he shakes his head.

'That's a bad joke.'

'It's a great joke.'

'Is this what working with you is going to be like?'

'Yes.' I give him a wave as I open the door.

'Looking forward to it then,' he calls out after me.

CHAPTER TWENTY-THREE

The days leading up to the morning show interview are wall-to-wall meetings. It's only been two months since I lost Dad and already so much has changed. I show up at a Seattle office building every day. I have a favourite Seattle coffee shop. The Amazon Spheres are just another building on my walk to Harcourt, and the Thai restaurant across the street knows my order.

It's all so far removed from my old reality, it causes knots to form in my stomach.

This is especially true when the Harcourt publicity team preps Fletcher and me for the interview. They've already submitted off-limit topics to the producer at Channel 17's morning program and they remind me that I'm not to say anything negative about Mason. It's not good for my image, and since Mason is still a high-profile Harcourt author, it reflects poorly on everyone. I assure them I won't blow up live on air, but even the intern doesn't seem convinced.

Somewhere between the progress meetings with Jordan, interview prep, and social media strategy meetings, Cece and Anthony stop by to oversee the signing of the contract that officially puts Dad's work in Fletcher's hands.

It doesn't take long to go over, but I read the pertinent information. Having Cece there makes me far more comfortable, and when she reads over it, she's happy with the terms. I continue to read while Anthony, Fletcher, and Jordan talk about deadlines and press releases.

'Sign here when you're ready.' Cece lowers her voice and points at the dotted line on the last page. If she notices my hand is shaking, she doesn't say anything. Once I put pen to paper, it's done. I'm giving Dad to Fletcher. I take a second to let it sink in.

'Do you have questions about the contract?' Jordan says, noticing my hesitation.

'It's all good.' I scribble my signature on the line and slide it across the desk.

On the morning of the interview I'm pacing the apartment, trying to keep my breakfast down. Fletcher and I did some final prep on the phone last night and I talked a big game. I told him several times I don't need him to answer questions for me, but now I'm worried that, in front of the cameras, I'll be catatonic and make a dick of myself.

'Stop picking at your eyebrows,' Fletcher scolds as he drives us to the studio at the crack of dawn. 'They look fine.'

'I think I over-plucked them last night. Now they look like little caterpillars.'

'You're going to go straight into hair and make-up. They'll make you look perfect. Not that you don't now, but...you know what I mean,' he grumbles.

I slap the sun visor closed and claw at my thighs. I spent most of yesterday trying to decide on what to wear. I watched some clips from the show, and they seem to always seat their guests on uncomfortable-looking stools, so a short dress was out of the question. I opted for navy skinny pants and a loose white sweater. It's more suburban mum than my usual getup, but it covers my cleavage and the little stomach rolls I get when I sit down.

As Fletcher predicted, when we arrive at the studio we're taken to hair and makeup. I stare at myself in an oversized mirror while a young guy with a comforting smile curls my hair into waves that fall to my shoulder blades. When he's done, an older woman appears and paints my face in silence, using an array of products from her intimidating tool belt. At the end I'm pleased to see I still look like myself, albeit with much thicker lashes and smoother skin.

Before our segment is due to start, Fletcher and I reconvene in the hallway outside the dressing rooms.

'Is it always so hot in here?' I say to the production assistant that fits me with a lapel mic and earpiece. 'My hands are so sweaty I can't hold my phone.'

The assistant takes my phone and reaches over to snatch Fletcher's. 'I'll return them after.'

We don't get the chance to object because the assistant scurries off down the hall.

'Harcourt has released the statement.' Fletcher exhales. 'It's out there now.'

He looks down as he taps his shoe on the bundle of thick cords that run along the side of the walkway.

'You're not having second thoughts, are you? Because it's too late now. We've signed and we are three seconds from talking about it on national television.'

Those brown eyes flick up to me, and he sighs. 'No. I'm not having second thoughts. Why are you so dramatic all the time?'

'I'm not dramatic.' I cover the mic on my chest and whisper, 'This process hasn't exactly been smooth sailing, so I'm a little on edge.'

Fletcher covers his mic too. 'It's fine. *I'm* fine. Can we just focus on not embarrassing ourselves out there.'

'I won't embarrass myself. Are you sure you're fine, though? Your hand is shaking.'

He stuffs his hand in his pocket. 'I've done this before, so let me take the lead and we'll get through this.'

I exhale. 'If you insist, but I can speak for myself.'

'Yes. Speaking is something you can do.' He steps out of the way of a passing crew member. 'The problem is you don't know when to *stop* speaking.'

'God, you're rude,' I hiss.

'And you're entitled.'

'And you're condescending. Which is not as endearing as you think it is.'

He folds his arms across his chest and leans back against the wall. 'I'm not trying to be endearing, and to be honest, I don't care if you think I'm rude or condescending. I'm here to write a book, not stroke your ego.'

My mouth falls open. 'Stroke *my* ego?'

'That's what I said.' He steps toward me. 'I know as much about this series as you do and I can write. You need me, not the other way around.'

I hold his stare, but I know he's right. I do need him and I need to stop letting my first impression of him dictate my behaviour.

'What are we doing?' I whisper.

Fletcher takes a deep breath and stares at the floor. 'I don't know.'

I don't have time to respond before a portly producer ushers us down the hall towards the stage.

'Halliday, Fletcher.' A well-groomed Asian-American woman crosses the room and shakes both our hands. 'My name's Hope. I'll be interviewing you today.'

I'm already paling under the invasive lights, so Fletcher takes the lead on pleasantries before the producer sits us down and double checks our mics.

My hands are shaking as Hope stares down the barrel of a large camera and introduces the segment. In my head it's a garble of nonsensical words, and I feel disconnected from everything that's happening around me.

'Early this year, the world was rocked by the sudden passing of beloved fantasy author, Ellery Yates. His series, *Blood of Gold*, has taken the world by storm, with interest in the books at its peak since the TV adaptation hit screens early last year. However, his tragic death has raised questions about the end of the series. I'm joined here today by bestselling author of *Red Reign*, Fletcher Larson, and Ellery Yates' daughter, Halliday Townsend.'

The corners of my mouth stretch as I mimic the smile Fletcher is firing at the camera that's trained on us.

'Thank you so much for joining us today,' Hope says.

My brain has disengaged from my mouth and in that beat, Fletcher steps in. 'It's great to be here.'

I nod in agreement, and Hope takes over.

'Now Fletcher, this morning Harcourt Press announced that you will be penning the last book in the *Blood of Gold* series. How daunting of a task is that? Do you have any reservations about the project?'

Fletcher's voice is smooth and relaxed as he answers the question. He hits all the beats we went over in the prep meeting. Things like 'Ellery has big shoes to fill' and that with my help we can 'have the best outcome possible'. Hope doesn't dig much deeper before turning to me.

'Halliday, my understanding is that you've had no involvement with your father's work until now. What's it like being thrust into this world?'

No involvement? It sounds like Mason's viral rants are the source of her information. My focus shifts from the blinding studio lights overhead to Hope and her forced smile.

'That's not strictly true.' My throat is bone dry and my face is burning. 'While I haven't had involvement in the publishing side of Dad's career, he always involved me in the creative side. I read all of his drafts and offered feedback before he would submit them to his editor. We often discussed the direction the story would take and how each of the characters were going to develop.'

Hope nods and smiles, but her eyes are widening like I'm taking up too much time. When I stop speaking, she turns her attention back to Fletcher and asks more inane questions about how he's going to tackle the project.

The interview seems to go in circles with the same questions being asked ten different ways. Hope doesn't dig deeper, but it's clear she's building up to the line of questioning she doesn't have permission to ask.

'Halliday, let me come back to you for a second.' Her forehead wrinkles. 'Finding someone to write this book fell to you and you chose Mason Parrish, but then backflipped and went with Fletcher. Mason has been outspoken about what it was like to work with you and, if we're honest, has painted you in a rather negative light. What are your thoughts on this?'

Fletcher looks over at me; under all these lights his eyes are a comforting golden brown. He gives me a nod of encouragement.

'It was always going to be difficult to find someone to write this book. The publisher gave me options, and I met with each author to discuss how everything was going to unfold. From there I spoke with Dad's editor and agent, and, being a big fan of Mason's work, I thought he would be a good fit. We had two brainstorming sessions, but he wanted to take the book one way and I wanted to take it another. I have a lot of respect for Mason as an author, and our creative differences over this project haven't affected that at all. But, ultimately, Fletcher is a better fit. He was friends with my dad, and I know Dad would trust him with the conclusion of the series.'

My voice cracks at the end because I know there's truth in it. Fletcher reaches over and takes my hand, squeezing it as the camera focus moves back to Hope.

She wraps up the interview and a moment later we're having our mics removed and our belongings returned.

CHAPTER TWENTY-FOUR

In the days following the interview, Fletcher and I lock ourselves in the Harcourt office during business hours and Fletcher's apartment outside of that. We go over our outline several times and Fletcher edits Dad's first chapter. It's all a welcome distraction from the fallout following the morning show interview and Harcourt announcement. Jordan assured me I handled the Mason question well, but it didn't stop the disgruntled author from doubling down on his scathing attacks. Fletcher's been drawn into it and, thanks to a screenshot of him squeezing my hand on the show, the rumour is I scrapped Mason because I'm sleeping with Fletcher. It didn't take long for my reputation to spiral from there. Before I was inexperienced and money hungry. Now I'm a whore too. At least that's what a stack of comments on the Harcourt press release say.

It forced me into an uncomfortable Skype call with my

mother. Specific questions were asked, and it will be at least six months before I can make eye contact with her again.

I've tried to ignore it all, but even without social media, the toxic nature of the internet keeps finding its way in. Even Violet called to ask if the Fletcher rumours were true. I assured her that, until a week ago, I didn't want to be in the same room as him and our working relationship is still in its infancy.

I'm not sure if she believed me. I'm not sure if Wes believed me either.

It's late when Fletcher and I take a well-earned break. He leaves me alone in his apartment while he goes to get some baked potato soup from the supermarket down the road. I contemplate calling Wes or Mum to get some things off my chest, but after reading another scathing article about Fletcher and my inadequacies I'm too close to tears. I feel like a punching bag and now, after every hit, the bruises are taking longer and longer to heal. I want to focus on the book, but the pull to get back online is too strong. What if someone has something nice to say and I'm missing it?

It's a lazy justification, but it doesn't stop me from opening up the podcasting app on my phone and seeing that Mason is the returning guest on Steven and Drew's fantasy chat show.

I get less than three minutes in before I turn it off. I don't know why some sliver of my being thought Mason might have something nice to say. Instead, he went in on Fletcher and criticised everything about *Red Reign*. It makes my blood boil and I turn it off when he talks about Fletcher and my perceived relationship. I can't decide what pisses me off more, that he's shitting on one of my favourite books or that he's touting with absolute certainty that Fletcher slept with me to get the job, and that I'm an idiot for falling for the gross manipulation of it all.

I put my head in my hands and the storm that rages inside me is released in a flood of tears to the point that I can't catch my breath.

'Hey, hey.' Fletcher puts the containers of soup on the table and drops to his knees in front of me. 'What happened?'

I drag my hands down my face and heave, but it still feels like no oxygen is getting in.

'Were you online again? I told you not to believe anything you see on there.'

I splutter out the details of the podcast before Fletcher stands up and pulls me into him. His jacket is cold from the night outside and I take a deep inhale of his sea salt smell.

'I haven't done anything, so why does he keep attacking me?'

'Because he's a worthless piece of shit who thinks everyone on the planet cares what he has to say.'

'It seems like they do.'

Fletcher leans back, puts his soup-warmed hands on my cheeks and looks me in the eye. 'Who gives a fuck? We only have to get this right for one person, and you know that.'

Tears are still spilling down my cheeks as I nod in agreement. 'I wish I could ask Dad what he thinks of this. What he thinks of me.'

Fletcher moves his hands down to grip my shoulders and I miss the warmth of his hands on my face.

'He'd be so proud. You know he would. The things Mason

is saying are classic Mason. Your dad knows that, and there is no way I could write this book without you.'

My heart beats differently at seeing the honesty in Fletcher's eyes. Since the morning show, our working relationship has improved, but I need to stop letting Mason get to me. Every ounce of my focus needs to be on the book, and consoling me whenever Mason opens his mouth isn't something Fletcher should be worried about.

I take his wrists and lower his arms to his sides. His gaze is fixed on my face, honey-gold and a little dejected.

'I should go home.' I turn to the table and close the lid on the laptop I bought a few days ago when I got tired of my every thought being in a notebook. 'Thanks for being so good about this.'

My cheeks flush with embarrassment at how unprofessional it was to let him see me fall apart over a podcast. He reads the expression and makes me swear I'm okay before he bids me goodnight.

I continue to cry the entire cab ride back to my apartment.

Over the next week, Fletcher and I get into a productive groove. We don't talk about any of the shit that keeps cropping up online and with our noses to the grindstone, turn four superb chapters into Jordan.

I'm riding high on the success of the late nights Fletcher and I spend in his apartment. While he's writing, I work on the in-depth outlines for future chapters and make sure we don't run into continuity issues with the other five books. It's all a rip-roaring success until Mia has to go to Nashville for work and Fletcher's five-year-old son invades our expertly curated workspace.

At first, we work around it. Staying at the office until Fletcher picks him up from school, then I come around after dinner to get cracking on the book. The routine works but five days into Mia's ten-day trip, Luca pushes the boundaries on everything from bedtime to the acceptable use of Fletcher's computer. It was impressive to watch Fletcher keep his cool when Luca deleted three paragraphs of chapter five because he wanted to watch toy reviews on YouTube.

To his credit, Fletcher does his best to keep Luca entertained, but there's only so much time he can spend doing jigsaw puzzles and watching cartoons. Every time Luca yanks on Fletcher's sleeve, stress levels rise, and the circles under Fletcher's eyes have their own postcode now. I try my best to take some pressure off, but I don't know how to manage a five-year-old, and he isn't that interested in hanging out with me, anyway.

When we reach the last day of full-time Luca, we've accomplished little on the book. Though, I did construct an enviable fort out of bedsheets, and it's enough to keep Luca distracted while Fletcher and I complete the detailed outline for the beginning of act two.

'We've got a problem.' I lean over the back of the couch. 'It was late Spring when Halladora escaped the tower and now we have Winshaw meeting her at the Crossroads a week later.'

Fletcher looks up. 'Dammit, he's down in the Borderlands. It would take him over a month to get to the Crossroads.'

'He needs to stay down there to convince the Warden of the Borderlands to side with him.'

Luca screams some kind of battle cry from the bedroom.

Fletcher looks at me and wrinkles his nose. I've come to learn this is his thinking face, and even though he's looking at me, he's miles away. I still watch him though, like maybe if I look deep enough into those eyes, I'll see a whole fantastical universe in there.

'We need to add a turning point in Farron's storyline that involves Halladora and the Shadowspawn. Something they can't ignore that kicks off the need to close the Gate before the blight hits. It can prompt the northern provinces to support Halladora in her quest to meet with the Karrakan King and secure his forces to fight the Shadowspawn. And it would buy some time so Winshaw can arrive with the rebel and Border-lands armies.'

'I love it.' I smile.

Luca runs out into the living room, still chanting his battle cry as he collapses on the floor. Fletcher looks at his son.

'Hey buddy, can we play quietly please?'

Luca pokes his tongue out as he upends a small plastic case of Lego and spreads them across the rug. He then picks up several plastic bricks and hurls them at the window, sending them pinging off the glass in all directions.

'Luca, that's enough.' Fletcher looks defeated as he watches his son pick up another fistful of blocks. Luca grins but doesn't toss them again.

Fletcher turns his attention back to me for a second. 'We still need to work out how to close the Shadow Gate.'

'I'm re-reading book three at the moment, but so far I

can't find a way of closing it without the Red Knight. His sacrifice is part of the ritual.'

Fletcher drags his hand down his face. 'We'll have to keep looking.'

Luca throws another handful of blocks and laughs maniacally. Fletcher stares him down and I try not to get involved, even though I want to tell Luca to shut up so I can think.

'How about for now we work on Winshaw's demise and then figure out the Red Knight issue.' I settle back on the couch and pick up my laptop.

Fletcher's brow wrinkles again as he looks at his own computer. 'I think Halladora should lose her arm too.'

I scramble to stop my laptop from slipping off my legs. 'What? No, she's keeping her arms. Why would you do that to her?'

'She's part of the battle and has no skill with a sword. Actions and consequences,' he explains. 'It's just from the elbow down.'

'No.'

'Wrist?'

'No.'

'What about a couple of fingers?'

I rub my eyes. 'Just leave her arms alone.'

'Hal, there is no way she's getting out of it unscathed.'

I know that, but he doesn't have to be so cavalier about it.

I lean over and look him dead in the eye. 'One non-fatal wound to the abdomen that looks bad, but she recovers in a timely fashion and is left with a scar. That's my last offer.'

Fletcher considers this for a moment before he shakes my outstretched hand. 'Deal.'

On my periphery I catch a sudden movement followed by a giggle that can only mean something terrible is happening.

'Luca, no.' I turn to see him filling my already brimming coffee cup with Lego. He startles and knocks the coffee over, sending dark brown liquid splashing across the table and seeping into the handwritten notes for book six.

'Shit,' I hiss as I scoop up the cup. The damage is done, and Fletcher is wide eyed and flushed with embarrassment.

'Dammit.' He grabs a towel from the bathroom and tries to mop up the mess. 'Luca, apologise right now.'

Luca looks down at his toes. 'Sorry, Hallie.'

I take a deep breath and count to three because I want so desperately to vocalise how irritating he's being.

'It's okay,' I manage. 'Accidents happen.'

Luca runs back to the bedroom to hide in his fort while I put the empty mug in the sink.

'Mia is picking him up in two hours, then we'll spend the rest of the night trying to work out how to close the Gate,' Fletcher says.

If only it was that easy. We've been dealing with this Gate problem from the start and I doubt we'll crack it tonight over coffee-soaked notes. I think what I need is some space from Seattle and the insanity of the last month. A place to take a deep breath, get into Dad's head, and let the forever firing circuits of my brain make the right connection. I need the snow. I need the lights.

I need Alaska.

'How about we take a break?' I suggest. 'I'll head north for a bit and figure out the Red Knight problem.'

'Let me come with you,' Fletcher blurts out. 'I'll talk to Mia about it when she gets here.'

I gather my laptop and my handbag. 'You can come if you want to.'

He grins and it's refreshing to no longer find it smug.

'Great. I'll call you later to make a plan.'

I agree and slip out through the door just as Luca yells his battle cry again.

CHAPTER TWENTY-FIVE

Fletcher and I talked on the phone at length about the details of the trip. I asked about Mia, and he said she's supportive of his decision to go to Alaska. I assumed we'd only be going for a week, but Fletcher and Mia arranged for him to come back to Seattle every other weekend to see Luca for the foreseeable future. As sad as it sounds, I keep waiting for her to be nasty or difficult, but it doesn't happen. I think she might be a genuinely nice person who cares about her ex-husband's career. It's bizarre, but so is thinking of Fletcher as someone's husband.

I'm not complaining about the plan because I'd rather be working in Alaska than Seattle. It's secluded, and Fletcher and I will get the peace we need to work on the book or tear each other apart. It's anyone's guess at this point.

I called Marie to let her know what's happening, and she was almost too excited to hear that Fletcher was joining me.

She offered to collect us from the airport and said she would go over to Dad's house and get it ready for our stay.

On the morning of our departure, I ring the bell beside Fletcher's paint-chipped door. It doesn't take long for heavy footsteps on wooden stairs to sound behind it. Fletcher appears, impractically small suitcase in hand and a smile on his face.

'Cab's waiting.' I throw a glance over my shoulder at the irritated man behind the wheel of a Toyota. I think he's mad because I spent the ride here fitfully moving around in the back seat, dragging my nails across my thighs and trying to breathe. He thinks I'm on something, even though I assured him it's flight anxiety. I explained the affliction to Fletcher when we arranged the flight in case it's a bad one and I have to curl up in the footwell for take-off and landing.

My anxiety grows on our ride to the airport, and Fletcher writes notes about Shadowspawn while I lament the rifting of Pangea. I hate flying so much, and I decide once I'm in Alaska, I'm staying there. People can visit me if they want, and if I have to leave, I'm doing it by boat. I don't care that Fair-banks is in the Alaskan interior, I'll drive to the coast.

Once we've boarded the plane, I close my eyes and listen to the chatter and shuffling of passengers getting to their seats. Fletcher shifts beside me, leaning over and then back as he pulls something from his pocket. I open my right eye and peer at him.

'Here.' He holds out some folded paper. 'This might help.'

I take the paper and unfold it while he watches me.

'I did some reading and sometimes understanding what's

happening can lessen flight anxiety. I printed out the fact sheet and it has some breathing techniques on the back.'

He directs my attention to the second page that features cartoon images attempting to illustrate relaxed breathing. My heart swells at this act of kindness and I watch as he retrieves his phone from the seat pocket, tapping on the screen to bring it to life.

'The website suggested a breathing exercise app too. I installed it on my phone so you can try it.' He taps on a little blue icon.

My heart is in my throat. No one takes my fear seriously. I get told to calm down and that it's fine, or have statistics fired at me.

When his eyes glance up, my heart squeezes, and I know I'm in trouble.

'Thank you,' I whisper.

'You're welcome.' He hands me his phone, swiping through the exercises he thinks might help.

I use the app during take-off, and even though I have reservations, it seems to help. To be fair, this is by far the most turbulent flight I've ever been on. They stop the drink service because it's unsafe, and the seatbelt sign is on permanently. It's hard to focus on the info sheet about turbulence or the app, or breathing in general, let alone deep breathing. Fletcher does his best to distract me by talking through some more ideas for the book.

'I think Winshaw will go out with a spear through the chest.'

'God, really? A spear?'

I let my head fall back as the turbulence picks up again.

'He dies alone on the battlefield with Halladora's ring clutched in his hand.'

'No, that's too sad. Can she hold him as he dies?'

'It's unlikely they'll even see each other during the battle. She can hope that he'll survive, but when it's all over, Vengul can bring Winshaw's helmet to her or something.'

My chest is heavy as I play the scene over in my head. It's gut-wrenchingly perfect.

When we touch down in Fairbanks, I fight the urge to fling myself onto the tarmac and kiss the frozen earth. My muscles are aching from being tensed for three hours, and we still have the drive to Dad's place. Thankfully, Marie is already waiting to pick us up.

'How was the flight?' She beams as she pulls Fletcher down for a hug.

'It was fine,' he says and I scowl at the unadulterated lie that has spilled from his gorgeous mouth.

Marie moves over to me and squeezes my upper arm. 'It's good to have you back.'

Our drive north passes quickly, and I listen to Fletcher and Marie's conversation. She's thrilled that Fletcher is writing the book and reaches over, pats his arm, and says, 'You're the only one he would trust it to.'

The realisation that I'm the outsider is heavy when Marie asks about Mia's job—she's the collections manager at an art gallery—and whether Luca liked the train set she got him for Christmas. Fletcher tells her all about his book tour and how much he wishes he could tell Dad about it, and how excited his parents are for their stay at the lodge, post renovation. A wave of jealousy hits as their dynamic becomes clear. They're a makeshift family, and I am suddenly homesick.

When we arrive at the house, Marie invites us over for dinner, but I'm struggling to hold in a yawn. Fletcher declines on my behalf and promises we'll be over for breakfast if she'll have us. Marie agrees and hands me the key to Dad's house.

'Sleep well.' She gives Fletcher another hug, and I hear her say, 'It's so good to have you back.'

Light snow dusts the path leading up to the house, and it makes dragging suitcases that much harder. Fletcher is behind me, struggling with his own belongings, and we're both out of breath when he joins me on the porch. The pink flush in his cheeks is sort of cute.

I open the door and we trudge into the blackness, suitcases leaving trails of snow on the timber floorboards. It takes a moment of sliding my hand over the wall until I find the light switch. When I do, it floods the lounge with tungsten light. Nothing has changed since Marie and I tidied the place, but the air is stale and it's painfully still.

'It's weird being here without him,' Fletcher mumbles as he looks across the living room. 'It doesn't feel right.'

'Yeah.' My voice is thick. 'I keep expecting to hear Cat Stevens and tapping on a keyboard.'

'The First Cut is the Deepest?'

I nod. 'On repeat.'

'Yep.' He takes a deep breath.

We stand side by side in silence for a long time before Fletcher's hand brushes against mine. It's feather light, his knuckles grazing the back of my hand before I turn my palm out and he links our fingers together.

It's a comforting gesture and I return the gentle squeeze he gives my hand.

The silence stretches on, but when he lets go, I offer him my room for the duration of our stay while I take the loft upstairs. He declines at first, but I insist and eventually he gives in.

After we bid each other good night, I wait at the bottom of the stairs until he's in my room with the door closed.

The space upstairs is cluttered. Marie and I didn't make it this far on my last visit so the floor is strewn with stacks of books at varying heights, like a cityscape of tiny, colourful skyscrapers. The long mahogany bookcases that stretch the length of the left wall are empty, and a layer of fine dust has settled on each of the shelves.

An hour later, I lay on the fold-out couch and stare at the piles of books illuminated by the weak moonlight. I need to sort them out, they're already gathering dust.

Ignoring the exhaustion, I crawl off the bed and gather up as many hardcovers as I can. I place them at the end of the sofa bed and grab a t-shirt from my suitcase to wipe the covers before lining the books up on the bookcase. I collect another stack, Mason Parrish's complete works, and throw them into an empty box. Kindling for the fire pit up at the lodge.

I keep dusting and stacking until the shelves are full and all that's left on the floor is one last cardboard box. It contains a stack of papers and I lift out the first sheet to see it's a copy of my birth certificate. One of the official reprints that has to be applied for through Births, Deaths, and Marriages. I put it to the side and pick up the next document. A copy of Mum and Dad's divorce paperwork and something about the division of assets. I skim over it and see that he gave her everything. Not that he had much to offer at that time. I keep shuffling; there are a few other documents relating to Dad's contracts with Harcourt, his ownership of the house, and some old birthday cards. Toward the bottom there are copies of all the forms relating to my dual citizenship. I continue looking through the paperwork, wondering where to store all of it when a small envelope falls from between some pages. It's sealed and addressed to me.

My heart thunders in my chest, but I tear it open.

Halliday,

I hope you're well. I know you're busy and it's harder and harder to get hold of you these days, so I thought I'd write you a letter. I might not be fifty yet, but your dad is still old school. I want to apologize in advance for my lack of contact in the coming months, I need to get stuck into this final book. I've been putting it off, thinking about how much of a master-piece it has to be. To be honest, the pressure is getting to me. I thought I knew the ending; I've sprinkled clues through all five of the books, but now I'm concerned that it won't be enough. What if it's unsatisfying? What if I can't give these characters the ending they deserve?

I'm drowning in the expectations I read online. Sometimes I worry that these fan theories might be better than anything I could write. I'm sure you could come up with the perfect ending for all this. For now, though, I'll take it a day at a time and remind myself that I can't please everyone, and I shouldn't try. You're the only person I want to make proud. It's all for you. When this book is done, I can breathe again, and we will finally have our time together. I miss you, and I'll see you soon,

Dad

Everything hits me at once, and it feels like my body is collapsing in on itself. I'm shaking. Tears stream down my face and I can't hold them in long enough to take a breath. Why didn't he send this? Why hadn't I just called him back when I missed his calls? Why was I so selfish, thinking whatever I was doing was more important than taking the time to visit my dad? Why did he have to fucking die at forty-eight years of age?

'Hallie?' Fletcher's voice is rough and groggy as he lowers to the floor beside me. He rubs my back, worry lines appearing on his forehead. 'What happened?'

'I want those six years back.' I continue to sob. 'He was forty-eight, Fletch. That is so unfair.'

'I know.' He pulls me to him, and I look up to see tears in his eyes. 'It's not fair.'

I don't know what this feeling is. The emptiness in my chest is so much worse than before. All the happy memories are more painful than the sad ones. I'm broken, and the pieces left behind are microscopic. I've never dealt with loss like this and until now I've been holding back. Cracking, but not breaking apart. The break is here and the pressure that's been building will soon be free.

Fletcher's body tenses, and I hear him try to catch his breath as he listens to me cry. The one thing we can agree on is that Dad deserved a better ending.

CHAPTER TWENTY-SIX

The next morning, I wake to find Fletcher sitting in the bay window with a stack of books beside him. He's engrossed in what I recognise as Dad's first book and tracked down some sticky notes and a blank legal pad to assist with his frantic note-taking. He must be exhausted because we sat on the floor for hours last night. There was little talking, but he held my hand while I cried, and I'm embarrassed to face him after such a display.

'I didn't know you wore glasses,' I say as I descend the stairs.

He pushes a pair of black-framed glasses up the bridge of his nose, looking very Clark Kent.

'I left my contact solution at home.' He closes Dad's book and clears a space for me to sit beside him. 'How are you feeling?'

'Better,' I answer flatly and change the subject. 'But I think we should get some groceries after breakfast. Marie can't feed us the entire time we're here.'

With our bellies full of pancakes, Marie directs us to a supermarket in Fairbanks and thankfully Fletcher offers to drive. I can't drive on the wrong side of the road while sitting on the wrong side of the car *and* dealing with snow. Even with Fletcher driving I'm nervous, but it might have something to do with Dad's car being a forest green Range Rover that's as old as me. It's no wonder he had so much money, he never spent it on anything.

It takes a while for us to get supplies because Fletcher keeps hijacking the trolley and taking off in search of snacks. I gather up some meat, vegetables, and pasta and throw it in the trolley when he's on his way from the chip aisle to ice cream. I only know four recipes, so he's about to become acquainted with spaghetti bolognese, chicken parmigiana, mushroom risotto, and beef casserole. He says he's excited to try some Australian cuisine, and I laugh at the idea that we even have a discernible cuisine. Either way, he's about to be disappointed.

When we're back at the house with groceries away, we dive back into the book. With no solution to the Gate on the horizon, we press on with chapters six and seven, one of which includes an emotional scene between Vengul and Halladora. We've mapped out how the scene will unfold, and I can leave Fletcher alone while he drafts it. I decide to check in with Marie and see how renovations are going up at the lodge.

There's less snowfall than last time I was here, but the little we had last night is more than welcome. Despite the cold, I enjoy the crunch of fresh snow under my boots. It breaks the silence of the cloudless day.

The lodge is a quintessential Alaskan log cabin, only on steroids. It has a wrap-around porch with thick log railings, and a third of the facade is enormous windows. I can see the cathedral ceiling through them and the antler chandelier that's more cobwebs than antler at this point. Stairs lead up to the carved front door and I turn to glimpse the view as we climb them. The incline of the property has us looking over the houses down the front. Beyond that there's nothing but an expanse of snow-dusted trees and small hills.

'We've made a little progress.' Marie unlocks the door and ushers me into the building.

The main part of the lodge is one enormous room with those tall windows mirrored on the other side. The fireplace on the far wall has had some stone chipped away to prepare for its upgrade, and there are benches set up with various power tools and equipment strewn around them. Like Marie's place, the kitchen sits on the right, and a set of stairs in the entryway leads up to the second level.

'At the moment, I rent out the lodge as a whole.' Marie walks halfway up the stairs before turning back to face me. 'But I'll add a bathroom at this end and two bedrooms at the other end so it can accommodate two groups instead of one.'

'What about this space?' I ask as I gesture toward the central area.

'I'll set it up with couches to create a few sitting areas and a dining area. That way, it could cater to tour groups who want to relax in the lodge while they wait for the Northern Lights. The kitchen needs gutting, and Elle wanted to extend the deck on the front, so it's more useful in the summer.'

The stairs creak as Marie descends them and comes to

stand beside me at the front window. She twists her mulberry coloured beanie between her fingers as she looks down at her house.

'I enjoy having you here,' she whispers. 'And Fletcher, too.'

We stare out over the landscape, and it's easy to imagine Marie and Dad working up here together. He mentioned it in some of his later journal entries. Marie taught him how to lay the tiles in the laundry room, but he sucked at it and she had to take over.

'Can you tell me a story about him?'

Marie nods. 'I'd love to.'

We sit down on the dusty floorboards and lean against the cold windowpane. She tells me about how, even on deadline, Dad would take her to the city every Friday night for a restaurant dinner. He said it was important they make time for each other because he had a tendency to get wrapped up in his work and forget about the real world. He always took her to Seattle for meetings with Harcourt and on book tours. They would stay in nice hotels and explore the city and find somewhere to buy a coffee mug with the city's name on it for me.

'Yeah, I have a box of unused coffee mugs in my garage thanks to that habit,' I joke.

'I suggested fridge magnets, but when he found that seagull mug in San Diego there was no changing his mind.'

'Oh, that poor seagull mug. Wes accidentally broke the beak off it when he dropped it on the bench.'

'Don't tell Elle, he'll be devastated.' She smiles to herself.

'I won't. I promise.'

We lose track of time, and she opens up enough to tell me about the day he died. He was on her couch, watching the weather report when he slipped into unconsciousness. She thought he was asleep, but when she tried to wake him, he didn't stir, so she called an ambulance and sat with him while waiting for them to arrive. I hold her hand tight as she tells me how useless she felt when it all happened.

'I love talking about him,' she whispers as she squeezes my fingers. 'And I still feel him everywhere.' She looks at me, eyes brimming with tears but a smile on her face.

'Marie, I want you to use Dad's money to finish the lodge.'

She pulls her hand away like she's been scalded. 'Absolutely not.'

'He was going to spend money on it, anyway. It's written in his journal.'

'I don't want to talk about this Halliday. It makes me uncomfortable.' She stands and straightens her jacket.

I pull myself up off the floor, wiping the dust off my jeans. 'Please let me help you.'

She makes a choking noise, and I look up to see her fanning her face. It does nothing to stop the emotion that's welling up. A tear rolls down her cheek, and she doesn't wipe it away. It falls from her face and lands on her linen shirt, darkening the fabric.

'How long were you together?' I'm not sure the words come out as gently as I intended.

She's hesitant to answer and doesn't look at me when she does. 'Six years before he left, then we started things up again when he moved back.'

'Six years and he pissed off to Australia, got a girl pregnant, and then didn't come back for fourteen years?'

'It was a little more complicated than that,' she argues. 'I was the one who told him to go. Neither of us knew what we wanted, so he left to work that out.'

She rubs her eyes and looks away from me again.

'That didn't go as planned,' I point out.

'I didn't think it would take him fourteen years, that's for sure.'

I'm wracked with guilt that he put his life on hold for me.

'If he didn't love Mum, he shouldn't have married her.'

'He loved her. No one can say he didn't, and marrying her made it easier to stay in the country. He wouldn't leave you.'

He wanted to though, I knew that. He was homesick, missing his family and his life back here. He never settled in Brisbane, and it must have been confronting when he admitted that to himself, and Mum.

Marie exhales. 'He wanted you to move over here, but you couldn't leave the country without your mom's permission. By the time you were eighteen, you had your own life. It was hard for him to accept that staying in Australia was the best thing for you. He missed you so much though, and I know he had regrets about not being able to see you more.'

'I should have made more of an effort too,' I admit.

I look over at Marie and try to picture them together, standing in this spot and talking about the future that would never come to fruition.

'You were together for so long, but you still lived in separate houses?'

Her shoulders lift in a casual shrug. 'After his mom died, he talked about selling it but took no steps to make it happen. He lived with me but liked his own space over there for writing. It was his family home for so many years, he couldn't part with it.'

As she talks more about their years together, I feel even more guilty about the sixty million dollars in my bank account and know she is probably scraping together savings to pay for the work on the lodge. I'll find a way to help even though she's fighting me on it.

'I'm glad he was happy,' I say finally. 'I'm glad you made him happy.'

She wipes her eyes as she looks up at me.

'No, please don't cry,' I hold up my hands, 'it makes me uncomfortable.'

She laughs before pulling me in for a hug. It's comforting and genuine, nothing like the hug from weeks ago when she picked me up at the Regent Inn.

CHAPTER TWENTY-SEVEN

wo weeks and thirteen chapters into the Alaskan writer's retreat, Fletcher makes plans to go back to Seattle for a few days. He misses Luca and his mum's cooking. I try not to take offence at the confession and bring the focus back to the scene we're revising. It's a pivotal love scene from chapter fourteen where Halladora and Winshaw are finally reunited. I'm of the belief they should make the most of their night at the inn, but Fletcher isn't sure he's up to the task.

'He's going to die,' I point out. 'The least you can do is give them a night of passion before he cops a spear in the ribs.'

Fletcher chews at the inside of his cheek. 'I can't do it.'

'Um, yes you can. I still have dreams about that scene in *Red Reign*. The one with Elaro at the lake.' I press my hand to my heart. 'So hot.'

He rolls his eyes. 'Don't remind me of that scene. I'm still embarrassed that my mom read it.'

'What's hot?' Marie steps out of Dad's kitchen with a

baking dish of lasagne in her hands. She offered to cook us dinner, and we would not look a gift horse in the mouth on that.

'That scene from *Red*.' I wiggle my eyebrows as I hang over the back of the couch.

Marie places the dish on the table and slaps her oven mitts together. 'Oh, the one in the lake.'

'Yep.' I grin and Marie stares off across the room, her mouth slightly open.

'That scene,' she breathes. 'The water running off their bodies. His hands in her hair as they slide under the surface. It was a sexual awakening for me.'

Fletcher almost spits his beer across the living room. 'Marie!'

'What?' She looks confused. 'You wrote it, not me.'

She saunters back to the kitchen and I enjoy the blush that colours Fletcher's cheeks.

'See. I told you it was a magnificent scene. Was "writhing" the word you used? I also remember tensing, sliding, biting, and my personal favourite...thrusting.'

Fletcher grabs a cushion and tosses it at me. I cackle as I slap it away.

'No more talk about thrusting,' he says through gritted teeth. 'Especially not in front of Marie.'

As if summoned, Marie returns. 'I liked the thrusting. That and Elaro's sculpted body and the way his—'

'Nope. I'm out.' Fletcher stands up and disappears down the hallway.

'You need to own it!' I call out behind him.

'No, I don't!' he shouts back before my bedroom door closes.

Marie and I are still laughing when my phone rattles across the coffee table. It's a Fairbanks number, and curiosity spikes.

'Hey, this is Hallie.'

'Fuck, it's cold up here,' the familiar voice on the end of the line grumbles.

'Wes!' I screech. 'Are you in Fairbanks?'

'That's what the pilot said when we landed.'

'What are you doing here? Are you at the airport? Or a hotel? I'll meet you,' I babble. 'Send me an address. I'm about to have dinner, but I'll head straight over after that.'

Even though I'm rattling with excitement, knowing that Wes is here sets me at ease.

'Yeah, alright. Settle down.'

'No!' I shout. 'Send me the address now.'

After the call, I receive a message with Wes's hotel details. He's staying in the same hotel we did last time, so I have a rough idea where I'm headed.

I put away my serving of lasagne in record time.

'Careful, you don't choke,' Fletcher chides as he lifts his fork to his lips.

When I'm finished, I throw on my coat and grab the keys to Dad's car.

'Do you want me to drive you?' Fletcher offers but Marie gets up from the table.

'I'll drive her,' she says.

'No, it's fine. Fletcher, keep going on the book. Marie, dinner was amazing. Can you wrap some up for lunch tomorrow?'

I don't hear their responses before I'm running down to the garage.

My knuckles are whiter than ever when I pull into the parking lot of the hotel. There wasn't much traffic, but the entire drive I had to concentrate so hard on doing the exact opposite of everything that comes naturally to me when driving. I take a couple of minutes to compose myself in the car before I go inside.

'You made it.' Wes flings open the door and I am on him like a shot. Crawling up him and wrapping my arms around him so tightly he makes a pained grunting noise. 'Settle down.'

'I'm so glad you're here,' I mumble into his shoulder before sliding back down to the floor. 'But why are you here?'

His hair is a floppy mess and his beard has filled in. His eyes are heavy and ringed purple. I know that feeling all too well.

'Missed you and I thought I'd come over for a visit. I'm here for a bit, then I'm meeting Jen in Los Angeles for a few days before we check out San Francisco and Vegas.'

'You should have said something. You could have stayed at Dad's place with me.'

'And miss all this.' He gestures at my face. 'Look at you. All in shock with a face like a slapped arse.'

I close my mouth to look less like said 'slapped arse.'

'Well, I'm glad you're here.'

I take a few steps into the room so Wes can close the door. The layout is the same as the room we stayed in last time, complete with two queen beds and those awful floral bedspreads. I lay back on the nearest bed and Wes follows.

'God, that flight takes it out of ya.' He stretches his long limbs and closes his eyes.

'I'm surprised you made it here all by yourself.' I poke him in the ribs.

'Ha-ha. I'm a lot more capable than you think…' He trails off before blurting out, 'And I have to tell you something important. Something that didn't feel right to tell you over the phone.'

I pull myself up to sit and search his exhausted face for clues. He looks content as he drags himself off the bed and over to his suitcase.

'I'm scared now.' I crane my neck up to see what he's doing, but his body is blocking the view.

He rummages around for a few seconds before turning to face me with a small red box between his calloused fingers. My breath catches as he flicks it open to reveal a sparkling diamond ring.

'Wes, I don't know what to say.' I grin. 'I had no idea you felt this way.'

He plonks down beside me on the bed and bumps my shoulder.

'Don't be a dick. Do you think Jen will like it?'

I take the box and inspect the ring. He did good. Really, really good.

'She's going to love it,' I confirm. 'But isn't it a little too soon? It's only been like, six months?'

He lifts his shoulders. 'When you know, you know.'

I hand back the ring. 'That's such a Wes thing to say. What's the plan for the proposal?'

'A Californian beach at sunset.'

My heart flutters at the excitement in his voice. 'Perfect.'

'Yeah, hopefully she says yes.'

'She will. Of course she will.'

A girl would be mad to say no to this man and that ring.

He tucks the ring back into his suitcase, then lays down on the opposite bed. I ask him for more details on his proposal plan, but he admits they're loose. He nods off a few times while waiting for the wings and burgers to be delivered from the sports bar downstairs.

Aside from the change of scenery, it feels normal to be hanging out with Wes, watching an overacted action movie while licking buffalo sauce from between our fingers. It's a welcome reprieve from all things *Blood of Gold* and the vitriol I'm still getting online.

'Has Mum been checking up on you?' I ask as Wes comes out of the bathroom, now dressed in track pants and an old band t-shirt.

'Yeah, like four times a week. I've got no room left in the freezer with all the food she's been bringing over.'

I laugh at the thought of Wes trying to politely decline a frozen lasagne. 'I'll get her to dial it back.'

'No, just buy a bigger freezer,' he says. 'I don't know where she finds the time to mother me so much. With the store and Eric, she's got a lot going on.'

I sit up and tuck my legs under myself. 'Eric? That guy she went on one date with?'

'One date? They've been together for ages now. I think he's

talking about moving in. He's always there when I go and see her on Tuesdays and Thursdays.' Wes pulls back the covers on the other bed and climbs in. His jaw almost unhinges with a deep yawn.

'What?' I blink. 'Why didn't she tell me about it? Also, why are you going over there so much?'

'I pick her up for our Italian cooking class on Tuesday, and Thursdays is Pilates at that studio near her house.'

'Wesley?'

'Halliday?'

'You're taking a cooking class and doing Pilates with my mum?'

He nods. 'Yeah, and I'm really good at making bolognese now.'

'Why are you doing these things?' I laugh and he shrugs.

'She misses you, so I hang out with her. I think it makes her happy.'

I move to the other bed and curl up behind him. As adorable as this is, I feel left out and hurt that Mum didn't tell me any of this. We message each other every few days and there's been no mention of her and Eric becoming a real thing.

It's all a bit much to get my head around. Mum has a boyfriend. My mum. A woman who rearranges the linen cupboard for fun and has far too many opinions on Master-Chef contestant backstories. Opinions she's very vocal about. Not to mention that Wes has replaced me as her child.

'You're a better daughter to her than I am.'

He pulls himself up to lean against the headboard and tucks me into the nook under his arm. 'I've sneakily been replacing the photos of you in her house with pictures of me.'

I wrinkle my nose. 'You what?'

'Kidding.' He chuckles. 'But she has our prom photo framed in the living room. I look incredible in that photo and one of your eyes is closed, so read into that what you will.'

It's dark when I get back, and I've broken a stack of road rules because my head is a fuzzy mess. Wes has reminded me of home, and Dad's house feels foreign again.

With the car safely in the garage, I sit for a few minutes to make sense of the longing building in my chest. I miss Mum and Violet, and hearing about her and Wes taking classes together has filled me with irrational jealousy. I'm an exhausted ball of confusion and emotion, and this slow, poisonous homesickness taints everything around me.

I close my eyes and take a deep breath as I pull out my phone to call Mum. Talking to her will make me feel better, but as soon as I swipe the glass, I see a news alert for Dad's book. I shouldn't have signed up for the alerts, but since I deleted all my social accounts, I wanted a way to stay in the loop.

The alert directs me to several new articles. There are a few more that mention me, but most of them are going in on Fletcher. They hate him as the author of Dad's book, and now it's drawn negative attention to *Red Reign*.

I feel sick to the pit of my stomach.

A second later, my phone buzzes in my hand and I see a message from Violet with a photo attached.

VIOLET

Surprise! Wes swore he wouldn't tell,
so hopefully he kept his promise.
We're due in October.

I open the photo of Archie, looking bereft after being forced into a t-shirt that says *World's Best Big Brother*. I stare at it for a while before forcing my fingers to type a reply.

HALLIE

CONGRATULATIONS!! That is the best
news!!! And Wes managed to keep
your secret. Archie doesn't look super
pleased in that pic.

VIOLET

Brad was holding a biscuit just out of
frame because Archie's a bit of a diva.
We've got everyone over for a
celebratory brunch otherwise I would
have called to tell you. Aunty June
can't keep her mouth shut and will
send out a broadcast text any minute.

HALLIE

Dammit, June. I have her number too,
so she would have spoiled it for sure.
Congratulations and we'll talk soon.

That overwhelming homesickness claws its way up my throat, coupled with the anger from the news articles and the email that came in afterward with a social media plan to stop people from hating me.

I smack the steering wheel with my palm between guttural sobs.

Amidst my anguish there's a knock on the car window, and I clutch my chest to make sure my heart stays in there. Fletcher's forehead creases, and he waves at me as I reach over and push the door open.

'Cool, so driving yourself went well then?' he says as he slides into the passenger's seat.

I wipe the tears off my cheeks and sniffle. 'Really well.'

'What happened?'

I close my eyes and take a breath. 'Wes is proposing to his girlfriend, my friend, Violet, is having another baby, and my mum is getting serious with a guy she's seeing.'

Fletcher looks confused. 'These all sound like good things.'

'They are, and I know it's selfish, but I'm not a part of it.' I wipe my cheek. 'I'm missing out on so much good stuff at home while I'm here being hauled across the coals, thanks to Mason's wounded pride.'

'That's not selfish. It's normal to miss home.'

'I like being here though,' I say. 'I feel close to Dad and I'm getting to know Marie. There's just a lot going on and I'm overwhelmed, so I wanted to have a cry for a bit.'

'We can do that.' He opens his arms as wide as the confines of the car allows. The gesture doesn't feel intimate, more friendly, and after the few months I've had I do want to be held.

I slide over onto his lap and he wraps his arms around me as I rest against his chest, my legs still dangling over the console, feet resting on the driver's seat.

'Can I cry too?' he asks.

I look up at him. 'Oh, no. You've been online too, haven't you?'

'Yeah. Today I watched a forty-five-minute video that broke down every chapter of *Red Reign* and explained in excruciating detail what was wrong with it.' He swallows hard. 'The worst part is, I think they're right.'

'They're fucking idiots.' I lean back into him and notice that he's only wearing a t-shirt, and his skin is cool.

'Are you cold?' I say. 'We can go inside.'

'In a minute.' He presses his mouth into a line. 'Marie is taking me to the airport soon and Mia called to tell me Luca has a cold and hasn't been sleeping.'

I raise a brow. 'You want to spend this time in silence, don't you?'

'Absolutely I do.'

He tightens his arms around me, and suddenly, home doesn't feel that far away.

CHAPTER TWENTY-EIGHT

Fletcher is in Seattle for four days, and my mind is still racing with thoughts about the book. I bounce some ideas off a confused Wes while he helps Marie tile the bathroom up at the lodge. He doesn't know what I'm talking about but, in his typically supportive fashion, says I'm knocking it out of the park.

With Fletcher gone, it doesn't feel that way at all, but I promised myself I would not call him. He needs time with his family.

'It is a dreamland,' Wes says as he stares out Dad's living room window at the gentle shimmer of light in the sky. 'I see why you like it here.'

It's late April, so the Northern Lights displays are petering out each night. I'm still glad Wes got to see it, though.

'Would you care to relocate? I think we could make a go of it here. Bring Jen if you want to.'

'Hell no, it's too cold.' He grunts as he drops onto the

couch with a beer in his hand. 'You're not thinking of moving here, are you?'

I lift my shoulders and take a sip of my drink. With the book still unfinished, everything is up in the air. I like it in Alaska, but once the book is done, I figured I'd be going home.

'I feel close to Dad here, but I miss home too.'

Wes leans forward and sets his beer on the coffee table.

'If you move here, you'll be all alone having to deal with minus fifty winters and not being able to leave this house half the time,' he says. 'And Hal, your dad isn't here anymore. Don't change your entire life because you feel guilty for not visiting him.'

Wes's bout of wisdom causes my stomach to knot. How can he breeze in and be right about everything? It's infuriating.

'It's not only being here that I like. I like being in Seattle and working with Jordan and Fletcher on the book. I've never had this kind of purpose before.'

I stretch my legs out and tuck my toes under Wes's thigh to warm them.

He sighs. 'How serious is it?'

'What?'

'I talked to your mum and Vi and we think there's something you're not telling us. Something about Fletcher.'

I shake my head and wrap my arms around myself. 'There's nothing going on. We're just working together. That's it.'

Wes raises a blonde brow. 'I don't believe that for a second.'

'You can believe whatever you want. Our focus is the book, and nothing is going to get in the way of it.'

It sounds forced even to my ears.

'Okay. I trust you.' He pats my legs. 'All I'm saying is, if you like *Seattle* that much, then maybe home isn't where you're meant to be.'

He casually lifts his beer to his lips like he hasn't given me something to stew over obsessively.

Wes's visit passes too quickly and before long he's hugging me goodbye at the airport. I wish him luck for his proposal, and he promises to message me as soon as he does it. I can tell from his excitement that he might drop to one knee the second he sees Jen. Either way it will be perfect, and she's the luckiest woman on earth to have him.

Later that night, Fletcher texts to tell me he's boarding and that he's almost finished another chapter. He wants to go over it with me as soon as he gets back to the house.

Eagerness pools in my belly when Marie goes to pick him up, and the moment he crosses the threshold, I'm asking to see the chapter.

'I love it,' I say as I hand back his laptop. 'But I wish you'd included the scene with Farron and Vengul. Her wanting him to leave Halladora and escape to the Free States is an important part of his arc.'

Fletcher shakes his head as he stifles a yawn. 'They don't know each other well enough for Farron to be asking that of him. I think we should scrap that subplot altogether.'

'But Vengul has to have something else going on outside of Halladora. In book three, when the prince was assassinated on his watch, that was a turning point for Vengul, and this can be another. It makes him more than a guard or a soldier and having someone love him, despite what he's done, adds depth.' I attempt to plump up my argument, 'I'm sure you can find a way to at least push the two of them in that direction. You're a skilled writer.'

The side of his mouth turns up in a coy smile. 'I bet you say that to all the authors.'

'I don't,' I scoff but consider this for a few seconds. 'However, if given the chance, I would say it to Dietrich Kennedy.'

He raises an eyebrow. 'The guy that wrote *Raven Winter*?'

I nod. 'I love that book. His writing is so poetic, and he seems so down to earth.'

'I've met him. He's a dick,' Fletcher says. 'His name isn't even Dietrich. It's Dennis.'

I stretch my leg across the couch and pinch the sleeve of his hoodie with my toe. 'Oop, someone's jealous.'

'I'm not jealous. I don't care if you like his work, but know that he's not a nice guy. He's pretentious and thinks he reinvented the fantasy genre.'

'Well, I dodged a bullet then.' I smirk. 'To think I could have given Dad's book to him and then he'd be sitting on this couch debating Vengul's love life.'

'As if he'd work with you. You're difficult, remember.' Fletcher grabs my foot and drags me closer, bending my legs over his stomach and pinning me there.

'And I'm ignorant like my father.' I don't break out of Fletcher's hold. 'You called me entitled, too.'

'You are.' He pinches my calf.

'And you're still rude and condescending.'

'Get used to it,' he says. 'I'm too old to change.'

I tap my chin. 'You are old, aren't you? I forget because you act like a child most of the time.'

'There's a difference between acting like a child and having a sense of childlike wonder. I wouldn't expect you to understand because your default setting is either domineering or self-destructive. Do you have any redeeming qualities?'

'That depends? Do you?'

He laughs. 'Ouch. Way to clap back.'

I dig my heel into his side, and he laughs harder.

'And now you're reverting to violence. Unsuccessfully, I might add.'

I wriggle, but he's still holding my leg. 'Do you have Dennis's number by chance? There something I'd like to ask. Mainly how he conveys so much emotional depth in his scenes. It's honestly, poetry.'

'Hey, that's not fair.' His brow furrows. 'You know I'm sensitive about my ability to write emotional depth.'

'Tables have turned now, haven't they?' I poke him in the cheek.

Fletcher frowns as his eyes meet mine. 'You think his writing is poetic?'

'Yours is poetic, too.' I assure him. 'Half the time Dietrich —Dennis—gets bogged down in metaphors, and everything is a damn allegory.'

Fletcher nods in agreement.

'Your work is elegant, not over the top, and your exposition runs rings around his.'

He considers this for a moment, and I smile at the little wrinkles that appear on his forehead.

'But you love his book?'

'Not as much as yours.' I notice that his thumb is gliding over the back of my knee as he enters a state of quiet contemplation.

I'm accustomed to these detached moments he has. It's Fletcher chasing a good idea.

'Hey.' I reach over and yank on the drawstring of his hood. 'Can you tune back in for a sec?'

He looks at me and I adjust my position, leaving my legs over his lap but sitting up so our faces are closer.

'I'm glad things went south with Mason. Swallowing my pride and coming back to you was about as pleasant as walking across carpet covered in Lego, but I'm glad I did it. Everything that we've accomplished in the last few weeks is better than anything I would have gotten out of Mason.'

His eyes fall to where his hand rests on my shin.

'So, you forgive me for what happened when we first met?'

'Oh, no. I still think you're an arsehole.' I smile. 'But a talented one.'

I expect him to poke me in the ribs or tickle my foot. Since that night in the car, we're more comfortable with each other. More physical, with his hand on my back when he leans over to see what I'm burning on the stove. When we look over notes on the couch, he sits close enough that our legs press together.

He doesn't move his hand from my shin, but instead squeezes it as if to get my attention.

'I like how protective you are of Elle.' He lowers his voice. 'When I met you, I thought it was my responsibility to make sure nothing bad happened to his book, and it took a while for me to see you were doing the same thing. I wrongfully assumed I could do it better.'

I finally pull my leg back and curl it under my body, so I sit taller. 'We can take care of Dad together. No one will ever know how good this book would be if he was here. But at least we're doing everything we can to create something worthy of him.'

'Yes, we are.' He takes off his glasses and rubs his eyes before his attention shifts to the window. 'The lights are out.'

I squint into the blackness to see a faint shimmer and move closer to inspect it. 'I think you're right.'

'Hang on.' Fletcher gets up and flicks off the main light switch, plunging us into darkness. The Aurora is more vibrant now, and I push open the doors that lead out onto the rear deck.

'Dreamland,' Fletcher says as he joins me outside. We're woefully underdressed, but I barely notice the cold with that emerald green light dancing across the sky.

I've seen it many times before, but this display is different. More magical, like the heavens have opened. It's likely the last good show of the season.

'How does the world not stop when this is happening?' I whisper, eyes fixed on the shimmering rivers of light. The sky is so electric it takes my breath away.

'It feels like the world *has* stopped to me.'

Fletcher moves closer and even with all this beauty right above our heads, he isn't looking up. He's looking at me.

I shouldn't like it as much as I do, but something about holding his focus squeezes my heart. I could face him, a slight turn of my head, and we'd be kissing. Does a kiss matter that much?

I close my eyes for a second and suck icy air into my lungs.

Every time I read something defamatory about us, I'm absolved by the fact that we haven't crossed that line. Rumours are just that: rumours. To cross it now would partially validate what Mason said, and I don't want him to be right about anything.

Fletcher leans down and presses his forehead to my temple. The chill of the night and the sweet smell of him has my chest constricting, like a thick band is wrapped around my body.

I lean into him.

I don't want to feel anything, but with this slight touch, I feel everything. A warmth spreading through my limbs. A tingle on my cheek as he breathes.

'Fletch, we can't.' My words hit the air in a thin cloud, and I look down to see our fingers laced together. I can't let go, so I squeeze a few times and he matches the pattern like it's our language.

'I know,' he says. 'I just wonder how often I cross your mind.'

I squeeze his hand again, but he releases me and steps away. A new wave of cold hits my body.

'It doesn't matter,' he says. 'I still feel stupid admitting that you're on my mind, all the time.'

CHAPTER TWENTY-NINE

'Whatever you two are doing up there, it's working,' Jordan's animated voice comes down the phone. 'I was up till three in the morning reading. I can't get enough of Vengul and Halladora's banter.'

I look over at Fletcher. He's sitting at Dad's desk, glasses on, and typing away on his laptop. Chapter sixteen is close to being done, but we had some major creative differences on the last scene.

Since the almost-kiss three days ago, we've been tiptoeing around each other. Keeping conversation about the book only and sitting at opposite sides of the room while we work. I brushed off what happened, but I'm worried I've handled it wrong. Fletcher doesn't seem embarrassed about it, more irritated, and I don't know how to fix it.

'We should have chapter sixteen to you in the next day or so,' I assure Jordan.

'Great. I need more.'

There's a pause and Jordan says something away from the phone before coming back to our conversation.

'I just got confirmation from Patrick Coleman, the showrunner. They're filming some scenes outside Dublin next week and would like you and Fletcher to be on set. I've got the team arranging your flights and I'll send you through the details as soon as I have them.'

My pulse quickens and the adrenaline spike brings a wide smile to my face.

'Is it the scene where the farmers come across the first Shadowspawn?'

'Yes, and they're filming it on location in this valley,' Jordan explains. 'The marketing team has asked that you increase the amount of content on Fletcher's social. He got a good response when he posted that photo of himself in the window. Maybe some more content like that would be great. Some photos or stories of you on his account would garner interest, too.'

I took the photo of Fletcher in the bay window. Mostly because he was looking incredibly handsome. He caught me doing it, so I made up a flimsy excuse about creating social content. He's nowhere near as skilled as Violet when it comes to detecting my lies.

My eyes lift to the desk again and Fletcher has stopped writing. He's off in Dad's world, and I wonder if his imagination sometimes feels like a curse.

'It doesn't have to be invasive. Just show that you're working well together,' Jordan adds. 'I'll have another social media plan drawn up that will cover the trip to Ireland and the set visit. We can capitalise on all that and generate some interest from fans of the show who haven't read the books.'

'Sounds great.' I feign enthusiasm, knowing that Fletcher won't be keen on pasting my face all over his accounts. It will certainly stir up more Mason-related drama.

After the call, I ask Fletcher if I can look at the chapter. He says no, he wants to finish it first, and it opens up an old can of worms relating to the final scene.

'Having Zios leave The Keep doesn't make sense.' Fletcher drags his hands down his face as we square off across the living room. 'He's the eyes into the King's movements. If he leaves, we don't know what's going on in there.'

'The King's Guard are about to discover Zios, so if you want to keep him alive, he has to go,' I fire back.

'Then we don't let them discover him.'

'That makes the guards seem inept.'

'So?'

'The Karrakans are conquerors. They're smart. Not to mention that the king is paranoid about a spy in his ranks, and Zios ain't discrete by any means.'

Fletcher lets out a laboured breath. 'No. I'm writing it my way. We're keeping Zios at the king's side, at least until Halladora's army arrives.'

A flush crawls up my neck and I wonder if he's being difficult for the sake of it.

'Have I done something to piss you off?' I put my hands on my hips, pressing my fingers into the bone. 'Because if this is about the other night…'

'God, it's not about the other night. You can be wrong about this book sometimes. I've read the series as many times as you and I've made a career out of this. How about you back off and let me do my job without inserting yourself into everything?'

I reel back at the fire that rages in his eyes.

'This book is my responsibility, and I will not back away from it.'

'You're supposed to trust me. You signed a contract to that effect.'

I take a step closer to him. 'I still have creative control.'

'Well, maybe you shouldn't.' He pulls himself up to his full height. 'You're not an author. You don't understand every facet of this process.'

'And that's why you're here to help. We don't have an outline from Dad, so I'm doing my best to push the story in the direction he would want it to go. Now it feels like you're fighting me on it because of whatever that was the other night.'

He clenches his fists at his sides and groans in frustration. 'This has nothing to do with the other night. Yes, I wanted to kiss you, but that moment has passed so forget it and focus on this book.'

That shouldn't hurt me as much as it does.

'My focus *is* on the book, that's why I don't want to take it further with you. Having you act out because I rejected you is counterproductive to what we're trying to achieve.'

His eyes widen. 'Rejected me?'

'How else would you describe it?'

'I put myself out there and you said no. I'm thirty-two, not some teenager who's going to skip school for a month until this all blows over. You turned me down and it won't affect our work. I started having feelings for you in Seattle and it hasn't been an issue so far.'

My mouth goes dry as he looks at me. The cloudless day outside pushes beams of sunlight through the window and it lights up his eyes in a way I've never seen before.

'You've liked me since Seattle?' I whisper. 'Why?'

'What do you mean, why?'

'Why do you like me?'

'I don't know.' He sighs. 'I mean, you are kind of infuriating.'

'That's our dynamic.'

'Yeah, it is, and I don't know when it changed.'

I take another step toward him. 'Why didn't you tell me back in Seattle? Especially if it could affect us working together.'

'It won't affect us working together.'

'It will. It already is.'

Fletcher shakes his head. 'It won't and it's not, because it's obviously one sided.'

Panic needles my veins because that's not true. I have to hold firm, though. 'So, we agree to forget all of this? Go back to the way things were before?'

'You mean you insulting me at every opportunity? Yes.' He grunts.

We're in each other's faces and tension wracks my muscles. I give in to the urge to deflect the intensity of this situation.

'Apparently that's a massive turn-on for you. Now I'm worried that if I hang shit on you all the time, it will make you want me more.'

He rolls his eyes. 'I wouldn't worry about it. More often than not, you drive me crazy.'

'Is that right?' I prod. 'What about me drives you crazy?'

He sucks in a breath, like he's winding up. 'For starters, I hate the way you chew on pen lids. It's disgusting. You don't know when to shut up, even when I agree with you. You seem to be incapable of moving laundry from the washer to the dryer. When it makes that beep noise, it's done. Move it from one appliance to the other. It's not that hard.'

We're even closer now, chest to chest as he stares down at me.

'It's infuriating that you make me smile all the time. You're smart and funny, and do you know how frustrating it is to think about you constantly? I have to shut off an entire section of my brain just so I can sleep at night.'

The butterflies inside me are nervous, fluttering around on the brink of terror. But amidst that sensation, there is a warmth in my soul. It soothes my nerves, placates the worry, and breathing becomes easier. I don't understand this feeling. It's a sensation I've never felt before.

'Fletch, you can't say that shit to me. Not when we're about to spend several long-haul flights together.'

'I know. I'm sorry.' He exhales. 'I'll stop.'

I press my teeth into my bottom lip. A confession crawls up my throat, burning like acid, and I can't stop myself from releasing it.

'It's not one sided.' I step away from him. 'But that changes nothing. At least not while we're working together.'

He nods, and I don't miss the half smile that tugs at his mouth as he turns away.

CHAPTER THIRTY

Getting me from Fairbanks to Dublin is an exercise in patience from Fletcher and a real testament to the durability of an aeroplane armrest. We have three flights in total. One from Fairbanks to Seattle, where we stay for two days so Fletcher can see Luca and I can collect some stuff from my sublet to take on the trip.

From there we fly to Boston with two members of the Harcourt publicity team. One is Andrea, a friendly woman around my age who laughs too hard at Fletcher's bad jokes, and is responsible for getting us from point A to point B without a media crisis. Thanks to Fletcher and my public interest, it's important that we present a united front. Especially since Mason did an interview on commercial radio where he insinuated that the project is tanking and the public should not be misled by staged photos of me and Fletcher working at Dad's place in Alaska.

The fourth member of our party is an intern named

Henry. He's here to assist Andrea and snap photos of everything we're doing for Fletcher to post on Instagram. Henry also likes to keep me up to date on what the internet is trashing me for at the present moment, and after three updates Fletcher asks him to stop.

The flight from Boston to Dublin is fine, but due to cloud cover we have to circle over Dublin airport for forty-five minutes while Fletcher holds my hand. By the time we land, get through customs, and make it to the hotel in the centre of Dublin, my legs ache and my stomach is rumbling. Andrea confirms our early wake up to get to the set in the morning, and straight after dinner the four of us retire to our separate rooms.

It isn't long before a gentle knock sounds at my door and I open it to see Fletcher, eyes hanging out of his head, and his open laptop in his hand.

'I'm stuck.' He sighs. 'We need to sort out this Shadow Gate issue before I can move on.'

I knew this was coming, and even though we spent most of the transatlantic flight discussing it, we didn't get any closer to solving our blight problem.

'Come in.' I usher Fletcher inside and he takes a seat on the king-sized bed. He's in a grey Seattle Mariners t-shirt and black track pants but didn't think the twenty-metre walk from his room to mine warranted shoes. Thankfully I was testing out the fluffy robe supplied by the hotel before he arrived and it's covering my less than presentable singlet and pyjama shorts.

'Is there a chance we can get around the issue by not

closing the Gate?' He scratches his temple. 'Maybe the blight could happen, and they fight it.'

'I don't think we have the page count for that. Dad built it up as this massive threat throughout the series and unless they had the Karrakan King on board to fight alongside them, they'd have no chance. He already knows about the plans to depose him and that Gate gets weaker every day.'

Fletcher puts the laptop down and scoots up so he's leaning against the headboard. I perch myself on the end of the bed and scroll through the notes he has opened on the screen.

'There has to be a clue somewhere. Dad's magic system has strict rules, so my guess is that the Red Knight isn't the only one able to close the Gate.'

'Elle doesn't have that many notes on the Red Knight. We know little about his history because he's supposed to be an enigma.'

'He was.' I exhale as I close the lid of the laptop.

'Until Winshaw slashed his throat.'

I fall back on the bed. 'Fucking hell, Winshaw. You gorgeous idiot.'

Fletcher pulls himself up off the bed and starts pacing the room, scratching the dark stubble that covers his jaw. 'Why did he kill him, though? Aside from the Knight kidnapping his love interest.'

I frown. 'Umm, Halladora isn't his love interest. She's his soulmate. His beginning, middle, and end. The only woman who has ever held his heart. She is his universe.'

'Yeah, besides that?' Fletcher says. 'The Red Knight was working for the Karrakan King, but he was a mercenary, and after Zios discovered that the king didn't have enough gold to fund the takeover of the Southern Isles, why would the Red Knight serve him knowing he could get paid handsomely somewhere else?'

'There's something else keeping him there.' I stand up to face Fletcher. 'Something personal?'

'Exactly, but it's not Halladora. He wouldn't have kidnapped her and taken her to the Tower of Blood on the king's orders if she was important to him.'

Our conversation goes back and forth for almost an hour before we both fall asleep under the soft glow of Fletcher's laptop, surrounded by Dad's books.

It isn't a peaceful sleep because my brain isn't close to switching off, though. My subconscious is replaying Halladora's story on a loop. I can see the Red Knight's death and every moment in the Tower of Blood. Every single moment. From Halladora's capture to the moment she escapes. I can see the guards dressed in their ornate silver armour. I can see the other prisoners. The old woman sentenced to death for stealing a horse and the boy with cuts on his feet. I picture his innocent face. Locked away without committing a crime. Why was he even there?

Around three in the morning, my eyes flutter open. Every conversation Fletcher and I have had dissecting this issue is in the forefront of my mind. It's an odd sensation. Like fog is rolling back and I can see a perfectly clear image underneath. It's a realisation so big it sends wild pulses through my entire body. I've solved the Gate problem.

'Fletcher!' I shout and he scrambles off the bed in a panic, throwing on the lamp to meet my wide-eyed stare.

'I've figured it out.'

'The Gate?' He rubs his eyes.

I stand up on the bed, leaning down to grip his shoulders. My blood hammers in my veins and I take a moment to arrange the idea in my head.

'What if the Knight's bloodline didn't end with him? What if he had a son?'

I dive for book four and start flicking through pages.

'There's nothing about him having a kid. All we know about him is that he grew up in Andosia and fought in the Prince's Rebellion before he became a mercenary.'

I find the passage I'm looking for and flick my eyes to Fletcher. He fights another yawn.

'The Red Knight never took his helmet off, but what was the one feature Dad always pointed out about him. He mentioned it so many times.'

Fletcher thinks for a moment, and his nose wrinkles as he tosses out the answer. 'Golden eyes?'

'Exactly.' I hand the book over, my finger pressed against the paragraph halfway down the page. Fletcher scans it and reads the passage aloud.

'Halladora dragged her nails over the stone. Ragged, chipped, and bleeding. The young man cowered, pressing himself into the piss-soaked corner of the cell they shared. As the moon passed over, released from the whisper of clouds in the night sky, a light cast over the boy's face. He was feeble, bucktoothed, and freckled. The cuts on his skin were deep and his golden eyes disappeared behind heavy lids.'

Fletcher looks up at me. 'No.'

I nod firmly. 'Yep.'

'No.'

'Yes. The Red Knight doesn't care about Halladora. He put her in there knowing the kid would be safe with her.'

'The kid says he's from Andosia, he tells her that when they first speak.'

I squeeze Fletcher's arms, holding tight to keep my balance on the edge of the mattress. 'That huge chunk of book two about the Andosian genocide and the Red Knight being the only survivor isn't true. He's not the last King of Andosia. His son is.'

His eyes light up and he drags his hands down his face. 'Fuck.'

'I know.' My shoulders drop. 'We're going to have to sacrifice that kid. If we can find him first.'

'He fled to the coast when Halladora broke out of the tower.'

We stare at each other for a moment, silent ideas bouncing between us as our heart rates quicken. It has lifted a metric tonne of weight off our collective shoulders and I see it in Fletcher's eyes. This cloud that's been hanging over us since we started the outline has lifted.

'Halladora should send scouts to the coast after she figures out how he's the Red Knight's son.'

Fletcher's breathing is ragged, and his eyes are alight. 'I can't wait to write it. We need to brainstorm now.'

I nod, but my focus is on the rise and fall of his chest. My own pulse is racing as I reach out and lay my hand on his heart. It's a rhythmic drum beat under my palm. All the excitement of the last few minutes manifesting, turning the air electric and rendering us both silent.

In a matter of seconds, his mouth is on mine as he hooks his hands behind my thighs, dropping me to the bed, and sliding over me. His lips are soft, but it's frenzied. He wants to be gentle, but if this is as far as it goes, we can't waste a second of it.

His hand moves down to the front of my robe and yanks on the sash around my middle. I force my fingers into his hair, tugging gently as his mouth moves across my jaw and down my neck.

'This is still a bad idea,' I mumble as my hands slide under his shirt.

'Do you want to stop?'

'No, but we should.'

He leans back to look at me. 'Why?'

I take a breath, my lips still tingling. 'Because I don't want this to be about us. It just adds fuel to the fire Mason started.'

Fletcher's hand comes up, holding the side of my neck, and his thumb skims my jaw.

'We both know all that stuff he said was bullshit. What does it matter?'

'It matters to me. I don't want people to think I chose you because I wanted to sleep with you.'

'Do you want to sleep with me?' He raises one brow.

'That's not the point.'

His mouth comes back down, kissing the hollow of my throat, and I close my eyes, knowing I'll see stars.

I relish the feeling for a second before pushing against his chest.

Fletcher lifts his weight off me. 'Halliday?'

'We can't do this right now.' I pull my robe closed and move away. 'I'm sorry.'

He shifts into a sitting position and reaches for my hand, lacing his fingers through mine.

'Don't apologise. I understand,' he says. 'I think tonight got away from us.'

I nod. 'It's not that I don't want this. I do, but our circumstances haven't changed.'

'I know.' He leans down and kisses my temple, and as I curl into him it takes every fibre in my body not to ask him to stay.

In the end, I say nothing as he collects his laptop and leaves my hotel room.

CHAPTER THIRTY-ONE

'What's going on?' Andrea looks from me to Fletcher as we wait in the hotel's lobby. 'Something's off.'

Her icy grey eyes narrow, and even though she's at least a head shorter than me, I feel intimidated.

'Nothing is going on,' Fletcher deadpans. 'We were up late thanks to a breakthrough with the book.'

Andrea doesn't believe it, but her phone rings and she turns her pinched, accusatory face away from me.

She's replaced by Henry, who snaps pictures of us waiting for our transport to the set and asks Fletcher to add them to his Instagram story. To which an exhausted Fletcher hands over his phone and tells the young intern to do it himself.

He uploads three unflattering photos of Fletcher and me looking like shit as we climb into the van the production company sent to collect us.

The set is an hour and half outside Dublin in a glacial valley. Fletcher has been there before, years ago, and assured me it's even more spectacular in person than it is on the show. It's the perfect place to stand in as Dad's evergreen Northern Province.

Henry takes photos the whole way and uploads a handful to Fletcher's accounts. He's gained forty new followers before we reach outer Dublin, and it appears to be going to Fletcher's head.

'They're only following you to see me,' I chide, poking him in the ribs.

'Please, I looked at your accounts before you shut them down. I'd describe your online presence as bland at best. Nobody cares that you're at a bar and your beer glass is covered in condensation. It's not deep or moving.'

'It's like that is it?' I mock. 'Well, mate, you aren't exactly engaging on social media either. The view from your apartment window isn't as captivating as you think.'

I poke him again, but he snatches my hand and links our fingers, keeping it out of view of Andrea and Henry in the seat in front of us.

I squeeze three times and he squeezes back. It soon becomes a game. The sequence growing more complicated until Fletcher can't keep up.

'I win,' I whisper.

'Don't worry.' He kisses the shell of my ear. 'I'll get you back.'

Every nerve in my body ripples and for a second it feels like my blood is running backward. Trying not to like him is more challenging than I thought. The less I want to like him, the more irresistible he becomes. I'm not sure how long I can hold out.

We spend the rest of the drive listening to Andrea return phone calls. Henry snaps a few more photos, but they don't make the cut. I ignore what's going on in the van and devote my attention to the endless rolling hills of County Wicklow. Now and then Fletcher chimes in with a fun fact or just to point out something beautiful in the Irish countryside.

When we arrive on set, we're met by a production assistant who ushers us over to a large tent set up in the valley. There's an army of crew members rushing around, dragging equipment from one spot to another, and a holding area with a group of extras in costume.

Inside the tent we're introduced to Patrick, the showrunner, and the director, an older woman with dark hair that's silvering at the temples. Her name is Elizabeth, and she gives us a quick rundown of the scene they're about to shoot. It's the one where a farmer discovers the Gate that allows terrifying monsters made of shadow to pass from the death plane to that of the living. It was cool to hear about when Dad came up with it, but now Elizabeth's vision for the scene is blowing my mind.

In reality, a lot of the action is CGI, so there are a million takes of the farmer falling into the grass in shock while someone holds a stick with a green ball on the end above his head.

It is underwhelming, to say the least.

When those scenes wrap, they move on to a scene that takes place a little further up the valley that acts as the village where Halladora has been hiding out. This scene is infinitely more interesting because Halladora and Winshaw are in it, and I'm about to fangirl like never before.

Patrick walks us through what's happening. The scene takes place at the edge of the lake, and it's about three minutes long with a few lines of dialogue. Winshaw and Halladora meet, only she doesn't know he's working with the rebels. He's trying to confirm if she's the missing heir to the throne and their terse conversation leaves him reeling. She's sharp-tongued and beautiful. Winshaw is not prepared.

Neither am I when I see Oliver Montgomery, the actor cast as Winshaw. They've lightened his hair to a golden shade that shines on this unusually sunny Irish day. He's in full costume, holding a takeaway coffee cup in one hand while a crew member fixes the fall of his hair. It looks perfect from where I'm standing.

'Put your tongue back in your head please.' Fletcher stands behind me and nudges my arm. 'He's just an actor.'

As soon as the words come out of his mouth, we both spot Rebecca Reid, the actress playing Halladora. Now Fletcher is fighting the urge to stare.

Rebecca is a carbon copy of Halladora from the books, tall and svelte with bright green eyes. Though her natural blonde hair is hidden under a long chestnut wig.

The scene is brief, but it still takes over an hour to shoot. With every 'cut' and 'reset' a flurry of activity descends on the lake. They primp the actors, and the cameras, lighting, and sound equipment are reconfigured before they start the whole thing over again. It looks tedious, but between takes Rebecca and Oliver chat animatedly to each other while scrolling on their phones and taking photos.

This triggers Henry to get back to work, and soon Fletcher and I are posing for photos as well. Henry takes a few candid shots of us watching the scene being filmed, along with some posed pictures while we play around with weapons and shields. The content gains Fletcher heaps of new followers but also a swag of hateful comments. I can't stop my back teeth from grinding as I read some of them over his shoulder while we wait for Patrick to join us. There aren't many about me, they're mostly dragging Fletcher for everything from his writing to his hairstyle.

Patrick wants to talk about the series end, and because it's such a closely guarded secret, we're taken back to the van to talk about it. After ten minutes of waiting, we're told Patrick has been called back to the set and will be with us as soon as possible. He can take his time because I'm enjoying being alone with Fletcher.

'Have you told anyone about how it's going to end?' I ask as he tucks his phone back into the pocket of his jeans.

'No. Have you?'

I shake my head more vigorously than necessary. Aside from him and Jordan, I haven't been exposed to anyone else. Violet has asked for spoilers a few times but seems to have got the hint I'm not spilling.

'Have you been tempted?'

He looks at his hands. 'Yeah. My sister is a big fan and threatened to break into my apartment and steal the manuscript if I don't give up the goods soon.'

'You have a sister?' I shift in the van seat, unsure why this fun fact surprises me.

'Leah. I also have an older brother, Nolan, and two younger brothers, Danny and Miles, who owns the bar.'

'And where do you fit into this plethora of children?'

'Second oldest.'

'But not the wisest?'

Fletcher rolls his eyes as he grabs my arm and pulls me closer to his side. The warmth from his body spreads through me and the setting sun that streams in through the windscreen highlights the fine cut of his jaw and the smoky caramel colour of his eyes. The recent shift between us is seismic and I can't explain what's happening inside my body.

When I look at him, really look at him, my heart beats a little funny.

He leans closer and his thumb skims my knuckles. We haven't talked about what happened in my room last night, but our situation hasn't changed. Except that I can't stop thinking about his lips, body, and eyes, and how I want all three on me immediately.

'Did you bring your laptop?' I clear my throat and pull my hand away. 'We can work on chapter seventeen. Jordan is asking for it.'

Fletcher's quiet for a second before he digs a messenger bag out from under the seat and produces the laptop.

With the book as a healthy distraction, we pass the time waiting for Patrick. It isn't that long, but we still knock out two paragraphs before he slides open the door of the van and climbs inside.

He's a tall man, meaning he has to fold himself in half to fit inside, and even then, his thinning black hair is still grazing the roof.

'I am so ready for this,' he says as he rubs his hands together. 'Tell me how it ends.'

Fletcher and I spend the next twenty minutes explaining

the ending we have devised for the book series. Patrick is on board for the most part but suggests a slight deviation from the plan to align with the show. Dad gave the all clear to add a violent battle when the Karrakan King takes Lorden's Keep, which in the books is a stealthy display of conquest using three strategically placed assassins within the castle. An overpriced battle is more cinematic, so Dad agreed to the change back when they were planning season two. The TV show's version of the Karrakan King's rise to power creates some small continuity issues with the narrative of the book, but Patrick assures me we can cross that bridge in four seasons' time.

When the meeting finishes, I thank Patrick for allowing us to visit before he heads back to the set to send Andrea and Henry our way.

'Now four people know how it's going to end,' I point out as Fletcher puts his laptop away.

An uneasy feeling builds in my stomach. Jordan is happy, I'm happy, Fletcher is happy, and so is Patrick, but what if the buck stops there? What if the rest of the world doesn't like it? This realisation is a storm cloud, and it's growing dark.

'No turning back now,' Fletcher says. 'Do you trust me?'

'I do.' I bury my concerns beneath an amiable smile.

His eyes travel down to my mouth and once again we're way closer than we need to be. How that keeps happening, I don't know. At some point we morphed into magnets and seem incapable of being separated.

'Fletch.' My eyes dart to the window but I can't see Andrea and Henry, only a few crew members milling around.

'Yeah?' He raises a brow as I place my hand on his leg and press my nails in.

'About what happened last night—'

He cuts me off. 'It's fine, you don't have to explain. We should keep this professional, and I don't want to make you uncomfortable. You know how I feel about you and you're under no obligation to share your feelings.'

I lift my hand to his face, tilting his chin up, and press my lips to his. If I'm honest, it's an excessively enthusiastic kiss.

He reciprocates, and my heart is on the verge of cracking one or two of my ribs. He brushes his hand over my cheek until it's buried in my hair and he's holding me to him. It's all consuming like it was last night, and if we were back in the hotel room, there's no way I could stop. I don't want to stop.

But I have to, and with my forehead pressed to his, I lower my voice to a whisper.

'If I could explain what I feel for you, trust me, I would not use words.'

The intensity of the moment is blown to smithereens when I look over to see Henry's wide-eyed expression through the barely tinted window.

CHAPTER THIRTY-TWO

The ride back to Dublin is uncomfortable. Henry told Andrea what he saw and the pair of them weighed the pros and cons of going public with our 'relationship'.

I don't know what relationship she's referring to because we've kissed twice and even though our bodies haven't gotten the message, we both know we should cool it down. I'll work out a way to suppress my irrational desire to jump Fletcher, and we'll leave it at that until the book release and the heat on us has died.

'You're lucky no one else saw you,' Andrea berates us as we wind our way back through County Wicklow. 'Especially with Mason tweeting some snide comment every time you two pop up on Instagram.'

Fletcher looks at Henry who, bless him, seems to have finally grown a backbone.

'Fletcher's fans love them together. Every photo of them gets more engagement than anything Fletcher puts up.'

'Hey,' Fletcher huffs and I stifle a laugh.

'Sorry, but you're not that interesting.' Henry presses his mouth into a line. 'It's Halliday that makes you interesting.'

I grin and Fletcher pinches my thigh.

'Henry, the answer is no, we're not going public,' Andrea cuts in. 'It's all about the book. Mason is stoking the fire with this vendetta he has against Hallie, and it's generating a lot of interest in the project. Sales on the first five books are up, so let's get book six written and then we can talk about tours and publicity.'

When we arrive back at the hotel, Andrea watches us enter our separate rooms from the far end of the hall. I feel like a hormonal teenager at a school camp.

'You know we have to write the book together? We have to work somewhere,' I call out to her.

'Business centre,' she calls back and points toward the elevator.

'Fuck that,' Fletcher mumbles and, in a half-arsed act of defiance, suggests we hit up the quaint little pub beside the hotel.

On the walk over, he grumbles about Andrea. If the confusing feelings and the online comments weren't enough, having an overzealous PR manager hovering around takes it to the next level.

Andrea doesn't crowd us in person though. She sends Henry to do her bidding and he sits across from us at the pub, forcing down Guinness and hissing after every sip.

'Jordan sent his notes on chapter sixteen,' Fletcher tells me as I return from the bar with a beer in each hand.

'Finally. What did he think?'

I watch Fletcher as he skims the document. Jordan knows the whole outline and loved it, he's also happy with the execution. Chapter sixteen is pivotal, and the last scene between Winshaw and the Warden of the Borderlands is something that Fletcher and I came to a number of heated blows over. Fletcher wanted the Warden to agree to Winshaw's terms and back the rebel army. I thought that was too easy and wanted to see Winshaw fight for the Warden's allegiance.

A wide grin splits Fletcher's face, and he slaps his hands together.

I know what that means.

'I'm calling Jordan.' I pull my phone out of my jeans. 'No way are you winning this one.'

He stands up, bringing his laptop with him to read from the screen.

'Fletch, love the last scene. Perfectly executed, completely in line with the Warden's character and the tension is on point. Tell Hal she's lost this round. Can't wait for chapter seventeen. PS Enjoy Dublin.'

'No!' I say. 'Dammit Jordan, you traitor.'

'I told you it was perfect.' Fletcher laughs. 'Now we can get Winshaw up to the Crossroads to meet Halladora.'

I put my phone down in defeat. 'Fine. Take him to the Crossroads, but they're going at it like rabbits at that inn. None of this fade to black shit. I want caressing, biting, and Elaro in the lake levels of thrusting.'

Fletcher drops his head back and chuckles. 'You drive a hard bargain.'

'Nice choice of words.'

'Get your mind out of the gutter.' He hooks his finger into

my belt loop and yanks me forward before we both remember that Henry is sitting across from us.

He's holding Fletcher's phone and my eyes go wide. 'Stop with the photos.'

'I didn't post anything. But there are some I took before while you were working that I think Fletcher should post.'

Henry hands the phone back and when Fletcher sets it next to his laptop, I see a screen full of notifications. They're all web alerts for *Blood of Gold* and *Red Reign*.

'I think you should call it a night,' Fletcher says to the young intern who takes the not even remotely subtle hint and returns to the hotel.

Fletcher and I remain at the pub, keeping our hands to ourselves until last call.

We finish chapter seventeen and I respond to a few messages from Mum and Wes while Fletcher goes through his alerts. I don't miss the downward pull of his shoulders when an article picking apart *Red Reign* appears, followed by a video about all the ways book six will fall apart without Dad.

Seeing the hurt in Fletcher's eyes at these attacks breaks my heart.

'What do you think about Vengul sustaining an injury? I know you want to grow that bond between him and Farron, and she's always been nurturing. At the moment he escapes the bandit attack unscathed, but I could change that,' Fletcher muses on the way back to our hotel rooms.

I adore the wrinkle in his brow as he contemplates the idea.

'Yeah, I think that's great,' I agree as we come to a stop outside the door to his room. He pulls the key card from his pocket and swipes it over the sensor.

I'm not at all ready to leave him. I don't want to lie on cold sheets thinking about him a few doors away. I don't want to brush aside these intense feelings when we don't know for certain what will happen if we explore them. In secret, of course.

My ability to justify this is astounding.

Almost as astounding as the sight of Fletcher's chest straining against his t-shirt when he put his jacket on in the pub. From what I felt last night, I think he's built, and I'll gladly rip off the shirt with my bare hands to confirm it.

The lock releases with a clunk and he nudges the door open with his shoe before looking up and down the hallway.

'Do you want to keep working?'

I shake my head. 'No.'

'Oh. Okay.' He pushes the door open wide and I move past him to enter the room.

It's the same as mine. King-size bed in the middle with the same crisp, white sheets and swirl patterned carpet. I leave him on the threshold and cross the room to close the curtains.

'Are you going to stand in the doorway for the entire night?' I ask. 'Andrea might walk past.'

He closes the door and flips the metal latch over for good measure. He doesn't progress further than that, simply standing by the door, idly turning the key card between his fingers.

'Fletch.' I breathe in. 'Can I ask you something?'

He nods, still rooted to the spot.

'Are you happy?'

His expression softens, like he's relieved that my question isn't as complex as he feared. He doesn't understand how important this is.

'I saw the articles you were reading and all the alerts on your phone.'

'I want to stay updated. That's all.' His brows draw together. 'I'm happy with how it's going, and I'm glad I get to write it with you.'

I take three steps toward him. 'Are you sure? Because I know how much it hurts to read horrible shit about yourself. Especially when it's a complete lie.'

'It does hurt, but I don't know what to do about it.' He sets the key card on the small table by the door. 'Sometimes it feels like knowing what people are saying is better than not knowing. No matter how bad it is.'

I close the distance, standing so close I can feel the heat of his body. 'Do you want to talk about it? Maybe we could find a car, sit in the front seat, and I could hold you while you cry?'

The corner of his mouth lifts. 'I think I'm okay.'

'Are you sure?' I arch a brow. 'Because I'll do it.'

He pinches my chin between his fingers. 'I believe you.'

I roll up onto my toes and bring his mouth down to mine. It's sweet and slow, like we have all the time in the world. I revel in it.

Fletcher pulls back and our eyes meet. I run my hand up his arm and squeeze his bicep before my hands move to his chest, and I can feel his muscles flex beneath my fingertips. He pulls me back in, his lips moving against mine, then along my jaw and to the side of my neck until the neckline of my shirt brings him to a halt.

'Can we get rid of this?' He tugs on the cotton, and I tear it over my head like it's on fire. His shirt joins mine on the floor immediately.

'Are we doing this?' I ask as my fingers continue to trace his muscles. I was right, his body is amazing. Toned and lean with a fine dusting of dark hair across his chest.

'Do you want to?'

I slide my hands up to wrap around his neck, and kiss him in a way that is a lot more suggestive than any of our others. 'Yes, I do.'

'Thank God.'

I squeal when he picks me up and drops me on the bed before climbing on top of me. I close my eyes and let him explore, soaking in the feeling of his hands and mouth on my rapidly heating skin.

Every sexual encounter I've had before seems like a bumbling mess compared to this. Fletcher knows what he's doing, every movement is exact, and I hope he doesn't notice that I'm trembling. I plant a gentle kiss on his cheek, pressing my lips along his jaw until I reach his mouth. He takes control, sliding his hand between our bodies, and his fingers spread across my stomach, tracing a line from hip bone to hip bone before continuing down. I press my head back into the pillow and close my eyes. I can't help it; his precise, slow touch has every one of my nerves curling.

The world is a haze of soft skin and warm kisses. It's almost out of body, like I can see us from above, but I can't pinpoint how I got here. Now I can't imagine not wanting him, and my brain is turning to mush.

I gain enough composure to explore his body with my hands, while pressing kisses to his neck. Our breathing is ragged and when a groan builds in his throat, I don't want to wait anymore.

'Do you have anything?' I ask against his mouth when we pause long enough to take a breath. He nods, and even though it's the answer I wanted, I laugh.

'What's so funny?' He holds himself up so he can look me in the eye.

'I'm surprised you're prepared, considering we kissed for the first time yesterday.'

He's blushing. 'I didn't know this was going to happen.'

I laugh again. 'Seems like maybe you did.'

'Maybe it wasn't for you.' His brows lift. 'Maybe I was hoping for a nice Irish girl who knows when to shut up.'

'Please. That's not your type.'

He rolls onto his back, and the cold air hits my skin. 'What's my type then?'

'Me.' I roll over and press my body into his side. 'In all my stubborn glory.'

He groans. 'Dammit, you're right.'

'But if you're holding out for an Irish girl, then we'll call it a night.'

I'm enamoured with the smile that graces his lips. 'Sounds good to me.'

He moves up the bed to rest his head on a pillow, pretending to sleep. I am living for this game.

'Sure. Whatever you want.' I stand and begin to unbutton my jeans.

He sits up on his elbows and in the dim light I can see the crease in his brow. 'What are you doing?'

'Going to sleep.' I shrug as I remove the rest of my clothing and toss it to the side. 'It's just hot in here now.'

He watches as I slide back into bed and lay on my side, facing away from him. I feign disinterest as Fletcher gets up off the bed and returns a moment later.

He slides in behind me, completely naked too.

'I thought we weren't going to bother,' I joke.

His skin is soft, but the muscles stacked beneath are solid. I press my back against him as he drags his finger down my arm and along the dip of my waist to my hip. 'I want to bother.'

My blood heats when I feel his breath on my neck. Moving onto my back and running my hands over his skin, I explore every inch of him again as his mouth moves against mine. I know we won't come back from this, but I can't stop. He kisses me, and as his body relaxes, I push him back and throw my leg over him. He lets out a groan and I pull myself up, kissing him with intent.

That's when a hint of panic snakes its way around my spine and drags me up like a puppet. I look down at him, dark hair sticking out every which way, and his eyes are so filled with warmth as they gaze at me. He lifts his hand, curling a loose tendril of my hair around his finger before lowering his hands back down. I'm not sure anyone has looked at me like this before, and I can't place its intention. It's desire, but something else mixed in. I want to ask, but choose to appreciate the moment, staring down at my fingers splayed across his chest.

His fingers press into my thighs, and I feel him against me.

'Are you alright?' he asks as he lifts his hand to my cheek.

I turn my head, pressing a kiss to the palm of his hand. 'I've never been better.'

With a sharp intake of breath, I sink onto him. He groans and grips my hips harder as I move. His head is back, eyes closed tight, and I'm looking down at my hands on his chest again, nails biting his skin. He pulls himself up and buries his hand in my hair as he drags my mouth to his. It's frenzied, and I roll my hips, whimpering into his mouth as I push him back down. There is something about the control that makes it feel more intense. I love looking at him, seeing his eyes snap shut and then open again as he watches me.

I will not be okay at the end of this, and for a second, I'm angry with him. I'm mad he made me care about him this much. I'm mad at myself for wanting him, when we both know how complicated this could get. Not to mention that he has a son and an ex-wife. Two things that will always be a part of him. Monumental life moments that I'm yet to experience and that he'll never again experience for the first time. I will have to share him forever.

In one fluid movement, he flips me onto my back, eases my thighs apart, and settles between them again. I gasp as he hooks me behind the knee and pushes my leg up, resting my ankle on his shoulder. My eyes open to meet his and I am here completely. Every inch of skin where we connect is alight as I move with him. My back arches, and he drops my leg as his mouth crashes down on mine. It's over for me now, and I will happily die with these stars behind my eyelids.

CHAPTER THIRTY-THREE

'I hate panels.' Fletcher reads Jordan's email off my phone as we taxi to the gate at SeaTac. 'Can't I just write a book and not have to speak publicly about it?'

Somewhere over Wyoming, we were invited to take part in a panel at a book convention in LA. It's in a week's time and the last-minute invite is the direct result of Henry, a one-man social media machine, thoroughly documenting the trip to Ireland.

Henry's content was impressive, especially on the day we visited the film studios north of Dublin where most of the show is shot. Fletcher and I got to spend the day with Oliver and Rebecca, who did their best to pressure us for information on the ending. To our credit, neither of us caved, though Fletcher was close at one point.

'You were great at the signing in Chicago. Well-spoken and engaging. The crowd loved you.'

'Well, I'm glad I came across that way. I was nervous as hell.'

The seatbelt sign dings, and we stay seated as passengers cascade into the aisle.

'Fletch, you're brilliant and people love your work. They want to hear you talk about it.' I lean into his shoulder. 'Plus, you look adorable in your suit with your hair all swooshed back.'

'Why, thank you. I swoosh it myself.' He grins and his eyes sparkle under the overhead cabin lighting. It takes all my strength not to reach over and pinch his cheek.

'How did you get to be so cute?'

'I don't know.' He shrugs and kisses the tip of my nose. 'You can ask my parents when I take you to meet them.'

My stomach flutters. 'What?'

He slides out into the aisle and collects my bag from the overhead bin. 'Let's go. We're holding people up.'

'How did I get talked into this?' I grumble as we pull up outside a two-story mid-century home on a narrow street dotted with craftsman bungalows. I now have a moderate knowledge of North American residential architecture and need to lay off the HGTV for a bit.

'I've told them all about you,' Fletcher says as he opens my door and helps me out.

'Oh, no. I really am in over my head then.' I tuck my hands into the sleeves of my cardigan as he pulls me to his side.

'It's too late to back out.' He smiles. 'Also, all my siblings and their kids are here too.'

My backbone stiffens as ice forms in my stomach. 'What?'

'Come on.' Fletcher takes my hand. 'They're waiting.'

We climb the concrete steps toward the bright red front door. A warm glow emanates from the front windows, and Fletcher has to knock twice so they can hear us over the raucous laughter coming from inside. A few moments later, the door swings open, and I'm face to face with a tall, dark-haired man who looks a few years older than Fletcher.

'Mom, they're here!' The man calls out as he reaches for Fletcher and drags him across the threshold into a hug.

'Nolan. This is Hallie.' Fletcher turns back to me. 'Hal, this is my older brother.'

'Nice to meet you.' I shake Nolan's hand and step into the house. The entryway opens into a large living room with a stone fireplace on the far wall and a modular couch in front of it. Every available surface in the room is laden with framed photographs, handmade pottery, and flower arrangements in twisted vases. Fletcher said his mother is an artist, so I'm assuming the many abstract paintings that cover the walls are hers.

Nolan wipes his hands on the tea towel over his shoulder. 'Perfect timing. We're about to eat.'

'Are you sure this is okay?' I take a step toward Fletcher as Nolan skirts around us to get back to the festivities.

'Yeah, it's fine. Mom's excited to meet you.'

Nerves twist in my stomach as I follow him through to the dining room. Upon entry, the chatter dips and there are too many sets of eyes looking up at me. This is worse than the TV interview and possibly the panel tomorrow.

'Everyone, listen up.' Fletcher claps his hands once, and the attention shifts to him. 'This is Hallie.'

They say hi to me in unison, like they've been practicing for this performance. Fletcher puts his arm around my shoulders and starts at the head of the table for his introductions.

'That's my dad, William. My mom, Judy. Nolan, you met, and that's his wife, Estelle. Then you've got my younger brother Miles, my sister Leah, and her fiancé Ben.'

I give them all a smile before Fletcher directs my attention to the small, circular table at the end. It's been tacked onto the main table and covered with a matching floral tablecloth. It's six inches shorter, and a sandy-haired guy in his mid-twenties looks disappointed to be seated at it.

Fletcher steps over and musses the man's hair. 'At the kid's table we've got my youngest brother, Danny, and Nolan's kids, Nate, Taylor, and Gemma.'

I'm committing the names to memory when Gemma holds out her hand and shakes mine with the confidence of a mid-forties stockbroker.

'It's a pleasure to meet you, Halliday.'

'You too.' I beam, but her eyes narrow.

'I think we'd all like to know what your intentions are with my uncle.'

Fletcher barks a laugh as I look at him for help. Gemma isn't having it though.

'It's not a hard question, Halliday. I want to make sure you're nice to him. He's my favourite uncle.'

'Hey,' Danny grumbles as he leans back in his pink plastic kid's chair. 'I thought I was your favourite.'

Gemma looks at Danny and her mouth presses into a line. 'I say that so you'll eat my carrots.'

The dynamic of this family is adorable, and I grin as Gemma forces Danny from his chair and makes me sit beside her at the kid's table.

'It's nice to meet you all,' I say as I attempt to get comfortable in a seat designed for an arse half the size of mine.

'It's great to meet you,' Judy pipes up from the other end of the table. 'Finally.'

Finally? Why finally?

I consider asking for clarification, but Judy grins so excitedly I feel like I should have prepared a magic trick or something. I'm not that fascinating up close.

'Sorry to barge in. Fletcher didn't tell me you were having a big family get-together.'

'Enough of that.' Judy waves off my apology as she wheels a computer chair over for Fletcher. 'Everyone is welcome.'

Gemma does not allow Fletcher and me to sit together, so I'm sequestered to the kid's table for the entire meal while Fletcher throws me apologetic glances from the place next to his dad.

The seating arrangement doesn't stop Judy from making me the centre of attention, though. I field a barrage of questions about my job, my home, and my family. By the time dessert is served the conversation has turned to the book.

'I'll admit I haven't read the books.' Nolan's wife, Estelle, looks rueful. 'But I love the show.'

'I read the first three but haven't caught up on the rest.' Nolan takes a swig from his beer bottle. 'They're long.'

'It's okay, there won't be a test at the end of dinner or anything,' I joke, but my joviality dies when I see the look on Fletcher's face. That cloud of doubt is heavy tonight thanks to an opinion piece on his work that some thoughtless 'fan' private-messaged to him. It was hard to read and harder to watch Fletcher read it.

I change the subject and get Judy talking about the art in the living room. It's all her work, and she tells me about an exhibit she has at a small gallery in the city. Fletcher's dad beams with pride at his wife's achievements. It's a small reprieve before Dad's book becomes the topic of conversation again.

'What happened with that Mason guy?' Miles asks. 'Why'd he really ditch the project?'

'He didn't listen to any of my ideas.'

'Well, I'm glad Mason's gone.' Leah taps the base of her wine glass with her pink lacquered nail. 'Fletch is a way better writer.'

I shrug. 'He's alright I guess.'

There's a chorus of laughter around the table, but Gemma levels a stare in my direction.

'Can you at least tell us how it's going to end? Fletcher is being a real stick in the mud about it.' Estelle pouts.

Fletcher beams, like he deserves a medal for remaining tight-lipped on the subject.

'We've been sworn to secrecy, I'm afraid.'

'Just tell us if they close The Gate,' Miles pipes up.

I shake my head and throw Fletcher a pleading glance. His

smirk has returned, and if it wasn't so adorable, I'd flick ice cream at him.

Nolan points at me. 'She shook her head. They don't close the gate.'

'No, they do,' I blurt out. 'Shit.'

Nate giggles before shouting, 'Shit.'

Estelle's eyes widen at her four-year-old and the table breaks into another fit of laughter. Nate is living for the attention and shouts 'shit' three more times before I bury my face in my hands.

When the meal is over, I'm ushered to the living room by Fletcher's dad and instructed to relax. I do as I'm told and take great pleasure in looking at all the family photographs that crowd the mantle above the fireplace. There's a selection from various camping trips, weddings, and even a few from Estelle's baby showers. I keep scanning until I stop at a picture of Fletcher in a suit with his arm around Mia. She's dressed in a form-fitting white gown, and her chocolatey waves fall over her shoulders. She's as stunning as the first time I saw her and the heavy weight of jealousy pools in my stomach.

'Come with me.' Fletcher takes my hand and leads me through the kitchen, which is bustling with his siblings attempting to help with the dishes. No one notices as we slip out through a sliding glass door onto the back deck.

It's a clear night, and the suburban neighbourhood is quiet, save for the occasional honk of traffic in the distance. It feels like we're a world away from the city.

'This dinner was supposed to just be me and your parents,' I say as we sit on a timber bench at the opposite end of the deck, far away from the residual kitchen light and prying eyes.

'It's never just my parents. If there's a free meal on offer, my siblings will travel for it.' His smile fades, and his shoulders slump; I can tell he's thinking about that article.

'I had a great time, though. Your family is wonderful.' It's the truth, and I feel robbed that I've never experienced something like this before. 'You're really lucky.'

He nods as he looks down at his feet. 'I know.'

I want to lift this weight from him, but I wouldn't know what to do with it. If the last few months have taught us anything, it's that we have no control over what people say about us. They're almost always wrong, but I understand how much it stings.

'We're almost there, Fletch,' I whisper after a long while. 'Just a little longer and everyone will see how well you've done with this book.'

'Let's hope they like it.' He rests his elbows on his knees and turns his head to look at me. 'God, it makes me sick thinking about it.'

I shuffle over on the seat, loop my arm under his, and cuddle into him. His sea salt smell is sweetened by the vanilla bean ice cream we ate for dessert, and my body warms as he holds me close.

'Thank you for being so good throughout all this. The book and getting used to not having Dad.' I take a breath. 'It's nice to have someone to talk to about him. I mean, Mum tries and Wes has been great, but I'm not sure they understand. I feel so guilty about not seeing Dad more and all my memories of him are from when I was a kid. You and Marie knew him as he was now...being around you makes me feel closer to him. I know that sounds weird.'

'It's not weird at all and if I'm honest, being around you makes it easier for me to come to terms with losing him. My family has always been supportive of my work, but none of them have an interest in writing. When I met your dad, I found someone who understood me. He was someone I could talk to about my book because he got what it was like to have writer's block and manage plot holes and build worlds in your head, then struggle to get it all out on paper.' He turns to face me. 'I just really miss him.'

I reach out and take his hand, linking our fingers together. 'We don't have to do this panel.'

'Do you not want to?'

I lift my shoulders. 'I'm nervous about being on display while people ask questions about Dad, but I want his fans to know how well this is going. If there's a chance we can rebuff Mason's claims without coming across as petty then I want to do it. I'm getting tired of his shit.'

Fletcher squeezes my hand three times and I match the pattern. Our special language brings a smile to my face and a sense of calm washes over me when he kisses my temple and says, 'We'll go to LA and get through it together.'

CHAPTER THIRTY-FOUR

L os Angeles is bright and comfortably cool. I watch the thin palms sway in the breeze as Fletcher drives us from the hotel to the convention centre. The traffic is a nightmare, but Fletcher is unperturbed by the chaos of the freeways. I stay quiet so he can concentrate, but I'm also trying not to throw my guts up. It's like the TV interview all over again but my brain dampened the memory of those nerves when I agreed to do the panel. Jordan forewarned us that Mason will be in attendance, but it's unlikely that we'll run into him because we'll be ducking out as soon as we're done and heading back to Seattle.

Upon arrival at the convention centre, we follow the instructions and check in with one of the event coordinators. From there, we're ushered to a curtained-off holding area behind the stage while they wait for the audience to be seated.

'There are so many people out there.' I peer out through the curtain as my stomach surges up into my throat. A chunk of the audience members are dressed like characters from the books and they're pretty spot on. My concern is that microphones are set up in the aisles for people to ask questions.

'We'll be out of here soon.' Fletcher stands behind me and rubs my shoulders. I can feel the tension in his body.

As we're about to go on, the moderator, a middle-aged man with tight brown curls, steers Fletcher away to discuss some topics we'll be covering in the panel. Fletcher's going on first to discuss *Red Reign* and *Blue Horizon* before I'm introduced.

I can't help but pace the small holding area. Twisting my fingers into the side seam of my navy jumpsuit while listening to Fletcher's muffled voice through the speakers at either end of the stage.

I don't know how he does it. It's like a switch flips when he's in front of an audience, and he's all calm and collected. I wish he'd toss some of that bravado my way, but I don't think it's transferable.

My pacing has escalated when the curtain draws back and Mason steps inside. He pins me with a smug grin.

'Halliday, nice to see you again.'

I'm still as he takes a seat on one of the fold-out chairs and hooks his ankle over his opposite knee, sliding down and getting comfortable.

'What are you doing in here?' I clamp my back teeth down so hard it hurts.

'My panel is on after yours and I was told that the holding area was available to wait in.' He's still smiling. 'How are things going with the book?'

'Don't ask me that,' I spit. 'Not after all the things you said about me.'

He puts his hand to his chest in mock outrage. 'As opposed to the things you said about me privately? You should thank me. Since I started talking about the project, book sales have been up on the first five books and, correct me if I'm wrong, but there's a swarm of people out there clamouring to hear you speak. You don't deserve any of these things I've given to you.'

The moderator's voice echoes through a mic behind the curtain and the crowd cheers.

'I don't want all that.' I grind my teeth again. 'All I wanted was to finish my dad's book series with an author I respected. Give Dad's fans closure and have some for myself too. You've poisoned all of that. Painting this selfish, money-hungry picture of me to the world that I'll never be able to get away from. Few people knew that Dad even had a daughter—he kept it quiet to protect me, and I'm so thankful that he did. But in a matter of months, you've blown up my life because you couldn't handle the fact that your ideas weren't good enough.' I get closer and lower my voice. 'But my stubbornness and inexperience weren't affecting the book enough, so you took it further with these lies. You are a sad little man and I'm so glad you walked away. This book is better for it.'

I don't expect the wide smile that splits his face, or the slight chuckle as he stretches his arms over his head and stands.

'You think the book is better for it?' He shakes his head, still grinning. 'Have you been online today?'

An immediate weight hits my stomach and all the muscles

in my body bunch. Fletcher's muffled voice echoes through the room as Mason turns and pulls back the curtain to leave.

'They may have been lies at the start, Hallie. But you made them all true.'

As soon as he disappears, I pull my phone from my pocket and frantically search Fletcher's name. The first headline turns my insides to stone.

Blood of Gold *chapter leak. What the internet is saying about Fletcher Larson's continuation of the series.*

With shaking fingers, I tap on the article. It's filled with screenshots of text documents, emails between Fletcher and Jordan with outline details, and photos of me with Rebecca and Oliver on set, laughing and messing around between takes.

That isn't the worst of it, though.

At the bottom of the article is a clear shot through the van window of me kissing Fletcher.

My skin crawls, prickling hot as I look at the photo. I feel violated. I want to smash my phone but as I scroll back up, my attention catches on something.

The response was swift, with thousands of fans saving the images that were leaked via Instagram this morning before the anonymous poster removed them. Within minutes, online forums exploded with comments on what appears to be the first four chapters of the sixth book, along with emails discussing potential outcomes for the story. The fan response was less than glowing—many are saying that Larson doesn't have the same technical skill as Yates and there are already signs that the character behaviour is deviating from Yates' original creation. Overall, it's a disap-

pointing look into what we can expect from book six, with some fans already cancelling their pre-orders.

This leak was coupled with images of Larson and Yates' daughter, Halliday, rubbing shoulders with the cast on the set of the TV adaptation in Ireland. Several other leaked images show Larson and Halliday kissing in a car and an intimate moment between the two on O'Connell Bridge in central Dublin.

I scroll back and forth until I find the Dublin photo. Fletcher whispering in my ear, telling me how glad he was that we'd found each other, before we continued our city tour and he started flexing his knowledge of The Battle of Dublin and the Irish Civil War. I took an elective on the subject at university and some of his facts were slightly off, but I didn't correct him. Instead, I pointed out how similar Trinity College is to Dad's description of the fictional Therendall Palace. That sparked an idea about the book, and we had to rush back to the hotel for Fletcher to write it down. It was so us and so perfect. Now that moment is sullied.

I keep scrolling further down until I come to another screenshot of an email and scan the paragraph underneath.

To make matters worse for the author's embattled daughter, an email also leaked where she blasts Mason Parrish's behaviour, calling the respected best-selling author delusional, misogynistic, and an insult to the genre. And those are the kinder words she offered.

• • •

Fuck.

That email is the most hateful, expletive-filled rant that has ever come from my mouth. I sent it to Jordan after Mason slammed me in another podcast, only to double down on the slander in a radio interview the following day. I was already on the edge and that shoved me right off it.

'Halliday, you're up.' A young girl with a headset cocks her chin toward the stage, and I stuff my phone back into my pocket. My legs are jelly, barely able to carry the rest of me to the stage, and when the chatter of the crowd hits my ears, it feels like an unpractised orchestra is playing in my head.

Fletcher smiles wide as he pulls out my chair and pushes it in when I sit. I reach out and grip his hand under the table, squeezing three times, which he reciprocates as he watches the crowd. There's no way he's seen any of it, and I wish we could have a moment alone to talk before this crowd hurls the new information at him.

The moderator introduces me, and I force a smile before he launches into his first question about the book. I stare at my hands and pick at my nails as Fletcher tells everyone how well the project is going and that he's proud of the chapters we've turned over to Harcourt.

These superficial questions continue until the moderator changes course.

'And how are you both feeling in the wake of this chapter leak? Ellery's fans had some rather strong opinions about those first four chapters. Would you care to comment on it?'

Fletcher's cheeks pale, and he looks over at me, his brow wrinkled because he doesn't understand the question or the severity of what the moderator is referring to.

He mouths, 'Chapter leak?'

Based on every PR-related exercise I've ever seen portrayed on film, I know that we shouldn't talk about any of this until we hear from Jordan. While the photos are impossible to deny, we might be able to salvage the chapter leak, so I steel my spine and lean into the microphone.

'We won't be answering questions about the alleged chapter leak on today's panel.'

The moderator seems temporarily confused, but he recovers. Unlike Fletcher.

We bumble our way through the rest of the panel, with me fielding most of the questions. I pivot the discussion onto Dad, his writing process, and what it was like growing up with him. I don't shy away from the subject of him leaving Australia and the challenges we faced in the years after he left. I tell them how proud I am for everything he accomplished and that I miss him every day.

The question-and-answer portion is endless, and it takes all my strength not to toss the mic when the leak keeps coming up and people ask invasive questions about mine and Fletcher's relationship. To his credit, Fletcher shuts those down because it's clear how uncomfortable I am.

'Fuck,' he later groans as he reads the article on his phone. 'Where did they get it from?'

I shake my head. 'I have no idea. Is there a chance someone hacked our emails?'

We've been sitting in the car outside the hotel for half an hour, waiting for Jordan to call us back. He got wind of the leak and has been working with Andrea to do some damage control. From all reports we did the right thing by refusing to address it, but we still have to get back to Seattle to come up with a plan.

Fletcher's mouth presses into a line, and he pulls his phone even closer to his face.

'Are you reading the email I sent about Mason?'

He looks up at me and nods. 'Shit, Hal.'

'I know. I know.' I press my fingers into my eye sockets. 'I was angry.'

'Angry? You said he's so conceited he probably jacks off to his own audiobooks and with an ego that big he has to be compensating for something.'

'Look, I'm not proud of the dick-related content. Again, I was angry.'

'He won't let this go.' Fletcher groans again as he drops his phone into the cup holder and starts the car.

I book first-class seats on the next flight from LAX to SeaTac, so we have some privacy on the plane to talk about it. Fletcher is a mess when we drop off the hire car and hurry to the first-class lounge. He keeps reading the articles and every time I see the photo of us in the van, my stomach rolls. Abhorrent invasion of privacy aside, all I have done is confirm the rumours Mason has been spreading. Now everything that comes out of his mouth seems even more reliable in the eyes of the public.

A few people have jumped to our defence saying they liked the chapters and that early drafts shouldn't be taken as gospel. Which is what I tell Fletcher while squeezing his hand during take-off. He's devastated by the hundreds of hurtful messages he's received and all the petitions that have sprung up to remove him from the project.

'We'll go back to Alaska,' I say as he rests his head on my shoulder when we reach cruising altitude. 'Jordan can help sort all this out and we'll head north and keep doing what we're doing.'

Fletcher draws in a shaky breath but doesn't consult his phone for the rest of the flight.

CHAPTER THIRTY-FIVE

Harcourt stays quiet about the leak for a week, and it's unbearable. Jordan says they're looking for the source before saying anything publicly, but since only the three of us had access to the chapters, I don't understand how it got out. Fletcher and I busy ourselves with the rest of the book, but even as we move into the third act, the comments on the first four chapters weigh on him.

To make matters worse, Mason is up to his old tricks again. Since the leak appears to confirm everything he said about us, I'm once again taking heat online, and Jordan said Harcourt is getting calls and emails daily to have Mason put back on the project. It makes my blood boil, so I book the next flight to Fairbanks. Fletcher promises to join me after he spends some time with Luca.

We talk every day and night over the next two weeks to keep the project going. I can see that he's struggling and promise that when he gets to Fairbanks, we'll get this done, and we can address every concern being raised online about the work in the edits. We're so close to the end of the first draft that if we bog ourselves down with going back and rehashing the first part of the book, we'll never get it finished.

I spend the night before Fletcher arrives sitting on the couch staring at the fire. It took me a while to get it going because I wasn't paying attention during the orientation Fletcher ran me through last time. He was in charge of the fireplace, so it didn't feel necessary to learn. For the last two hours, my attention has been shifting between the flames and my phone. I shouldn't go online, it will only make me feel like shit, but there's merit to what Fletcher said, it might feel better knowing what's being said than not.

After my second cup of tea and hundredth lap of the lounge, I plonk down behind Dad's desk. The phone still taunts me as I give everything a quick tidy. Post-its stacked, notebooks closed, and pens in the empty mug with *WRITE ON* printed on the side. I'm dusting the back of Dad's computer monitor when my phone rings, and it just about separates me from my skin.

'Hey,' I answer after the first ring, and it's more of a startled yell than a greeting.

'Everything alright?' Fletcher says.

'Yeah, I'm fine. Just doing some tidying around the place.'

'It's one in the morning there.'

'Is it?' I lean back in Dad's chair. 'Why are you calling me so late then?'

'I was working on the draft and time got away from me,' he says through a yawn. 'I wanted to hear your voice before I fell asleep, though.'

'This voice? The voice you once called shrill?'

'I would never call you shrill.'

I pull my legs to my chest. 'You did. You told Jordan I was shrill. I heard you say it on my way back to the table at the steakhouse.'

'In my defence, I didn't think you'd hear me.'

I laugh. 'It's a weak defence, so you still have to make it up to me when you finally get back here.'

'You miss me then?'

I tilt my head back and let out a sigh. 'Yes, I miss you.'

'I know. I wanted to hear you say it.'

'Will you always be this obnoxious?'

'Yes.' He lowers his voice and goosebumps prickle my skin again. 'Goodnight, Halliday.'

There's a heavy beat of silence and I don't want him to hang up. An ache builds in my chest at his absence, and suddenly the conversation feels unfinished.

'Wait,' I blurt out with nothing to follow it up.

'Yeah?' he says.

My body relaxes at the sound of his voice and a serious confession rests on the tip of my tongue. It's threatening, but he's so far away I can't bear to let it out. I'm not even sure when I started feeling the need to say anything more than goodnight. It might have been when his mother told me about the short stories he writes for his nieces and nephew. She was so proud and all I could think was, what am I supposed to do with that information? It made me want to have his babies.

I'm skipping too many steps, so I keep this madness to myself.

'I can't wait for you to get up here.' I close my eyes.

'One more sleep,' he replies. 'Goodnight.'

'Night.'

I hang up the phone before downing the rest of my whiskey and staring out the oversized window at the blackness beyond. At least Fletcher didn't sound as stressed as he has the last few days. Maybe we'll both get some sleep for a change.

I wake up on the couch with Netflix on that judgemental 'Are you still watching?' screen. To stop myself from reading hurtful comments, I binge-watched teen dramas for far too long.

'Rough night?' Marie says as she steps into the house and gives me a once-over.

'Just a late one, that's all.' I amble into the kitchen with her on my heels. She says something about the floorboards up at the lodge, but her talking spurs the ache behind my temples.

'What's happening with you?' she asks. 'What's all this?'

She waves her hand at me, and I frown. I know I'm not looking my best.

'Nothing is happening.' I press the button on the coffee machine and pull out two mugs.

With coffee in hand, we step back into the living room and take a seat amongst the pillows and blanket I used as bedding last night, both looking out at the blinding blue day.

When I turn back to Marie, she's sipping her coffee and eyeing me like she has a conversation in mind but wants me to initiate it. It's disconcerting.

'You've looked online, haven't you?'

Marie lowers her mug. 'Maybe.'

'I told you not to,' I groan. 'And the day I got here, you promised you wouldn't.'

'I know, and I held out for as long as I could, but then Suzanne from my painting class sent me the link to an article…'

I suck in a deep breath. 'Look, it's not ideal.'

'Ideal?' Marie splutters. 'That email is horrendous.'

'Yes, it is, and like I told Fletcher, I was angry.'

'So many penis references, Halliday.'

'Because Mason is a dick. There's another one for you.' Marie stifles a laugh and I rub my eyes. 'Why is this so hard?'

'That's enough, Hal.'

'Wasn't a pun. I'm genuinely asking,' I grumble. 'I'm trying not to get bogged down in this mess because Fletch and I need to focus on getting the draft finished.'

No matter how many times I say that, it doesn't get easier. Seeing my private moments splashed over the internet and constantly being dragged for things I haven't even done is grating me to the bone.

'Poor Fletcher,' Marie says. 'It will be good to have him back here. Ellery always said Alaska was an escape from the rest of the world. It eased the sting of criticism.'

I raise a brow. 'He never cared what people thought of his work.'

'Of course he did. He had more down days than I can count.'

I turn to look at his empty desk and my mind conjures him into existence. His laugh and his wide smile. It wasn't painted on. At least I never thought it was. That pane of glass between me and Dad has thickened, and once again I'm out of the loop.

'I had no idea.'

Marie places her mug on the coffee table before she moves over to sit beside me.

'He was good at hiding it.' She takes my free hand. 'Don't let it worry you. He pushed through it and he knew that not everyone would be a fan of his work. It doesn't make it hurt less, but it's something that has to be dealt with. He kept moving forward, and that's what you and Fletcher have to do.'

I look down at my hand in hers. 'I'm trying.'

'I know you are, and your dad knows that too.'

Tears prick my eyes. 'I'm worried about Fletcher. The chapter leak has been hard on him.'

Marie's lips press into a line. 'Yes, that is unfortunate, and it's going to shake his confidence. You just have to hold his hand and make sure he knows you're on his team.'

'I'll always be on his team.' I don't hold back. 'I love him.'

A slight smile plays on my stepmother's lips, and her eyes are alight with unnecessary victory.

'I knew it,' she whispers.

'You knew what?'

'I knew you'd fall in love with him.'

My confession is an exposed nerve.

'No, you didn't. No one did. We didn't like each other.'

She grins. 'He liked you.'

'No, he didn't.'

'He's always liked you.'

'He never met me.'

Marie collects her coffee off the low table and sips it casually. 'He overheard a handful of phone calls between you and your dad, and Elle showed him pictures of you all the time. Honestly, it was embarrassing to witness. I half expected Elle to engineer some plot to put you both in the same room so you'd get together.'

I cringe at the thought of my dad trying to set me up with Fletcher. Marie finds all this incredibly amusing.

'My first meeting with Fletcher was a disaster.'

'Yeah, he fucked that up.' Marie shakes her head and I'm taken aback by her language. 'I knew he'd salvage the situation, though.'

'He barely salvaged it. If Mason wasn't such a phenomenal piece of shit, Fletcher wouldn't have gotten the chance.'

Marie winks. 'Aren't you glad he got the chance, though?'

'Alright, that's enough of that.' I wrinkle my nose. 'Let's change the subject.'

I shift on the couch, resting my arm along the backrest.

'Have you talked to him about what happens after the book?'

'That's the same subject, Marie.'

'It is not.'

I press my teeth into my bottom lip. 'Has Fletcher said something to you? About what he wants to happen.'

'Not directly, but with you he's taking things seriously. As far as I know, he hasn't been involved with anyone since his divorce.'

That thought hadn't crossed my mind. Nor would I have wanted to ask if it did. I've had a tough time dealing with him being married to Mia, let alone anyone that may have come after her.

'How often do you speak to him?' I raise a brow.

She lifts her shoulders in a lazy shrug. 'Couple of times a week at least. Though that has dropped a little since he started things up with you.'

'I'll talk to him about it once this chapter leak stuff settles down. We're both under enough pressure so I won't add to it.'

I'm so distracted with all this falling in love business, I hadn't stopped to think about what a relationship with Fletcher would look like in the long term. Our brief trip to Ireland granted me another ninety-days in the US, but pointless trips out of the country every three months isn't sustainable. If I sort out residency and move to Seattle, what would I even do there? I'd spend most of my days sitting around and watching my friends and family carry on living their lives at home.

'Before you decide, make your peace with everything that comes with Fletcher.' Marie's expression softens. 'Luca is part of the deal and that's quite a commitment.'

I let out a long breath, feeling a weight lift. Of course, she's been through all this with Dad and me, and Luca *is* a thought I've pushed from my mind whenever it creeps in.

'I can't say anything about that to Fletcher. It's his son. I just have to keep any concerns like that to myself.'

Marie looks me in the eye, nodding. 'You can say something. It's no small thing, committing to someone who has a child, and bringing you into Luca's life in that capacity isn't something Fletcher should take lightly either.'

It doesn't feel right to think of Luca as an inconvenience. An obstacle that adds another level of complexity to a blossoming relationship.

'What was it like for you when Dad moved back here?' I ask, and Marie's focus shifts to the embers in the fireplace.

'It was hard. He thought he made a mistake leaving Brisbane.'

'Do you think he did?'

The muscles in her jaw tighten. 'No, and I know that's a selfish answer. I wanted him back here, I always did, and even though it meant leaving you, I didn't care. I wanted things to be about me for a change.'

My head swims as I take in her words. They're so un-Marie-like.

Her forehead wrinkles. 'I'm sorry. I wanted to be honest.'

'Don't be sorry. I appreciate it. In fact, I'd like it if you were more honest.'

She tugs at the cropped ends of her auburn hair.

'He came back a few times over the years. The first time was the hardest. He sat me down on the steps of his parent's house. God, it must have been ten below and I was in a sweater and jeans. He gave me his jacket and when he looked at me, there was such sadness in his eyes. I didn't know what on earth could make this man so sad because he was back home now, and we could talk about our future. My only plan was to take over the lodge, and I'd enrolled in business management classes at night school. I was excited to tell him about it. He smiled and listened while I spoke, but he wasn't focused, not on me anyway. That's when he told me he'd met someone, a young girl from Brisbane. I asked if he loved her and he said not yet. I asked if he was going to love her and he said hopefully one day because she was pregnant with his baby.'

A lump forms in my throat as Marie tears up. 'What did you say to him?'

'I told him I never wanted to see him again. I was young and dramatic back then, you see. But I didn't have the right to be so mad at him; I broke up with him before he left, so he was free to do what he wanted, and your mother being pregnant forced his hand. He never regretted it though, not for one second.'

'And you forgave him when he came back?'

She nods and looks down at her hands. 'Not at first. He came back when my parents died and the day before he was due to fly out to Australia, we talked about everything. I told him how much it hurt that he'd been so irresponsible and that it kept him there for so many years. That was when he told me he wasn't doing great. He wanted to come home.'

I remember that. It was post divorce and he and Mum were barely speaking.

'It wouldn't have been easy having me here the few times I visited.'

She drags the back of her hand across her nose. 'It was difficult. A reminder of something I never had with him. He had a whole life without me, and I was coming in at the end with nothing new to offer.'

I take a deep breath, aware of the parallel.

'You were happy with him though?'

'The happiest I've ever been. Even if I did only get fourteen years.'

Marie takes a large gulp of her coffee and wipes a fictitious gathering of fluff off her jeans.

'With all that said, is a move to Seattle an option for you?'

I drag my teeth over my bottom lip again, pressing harder. 'Is it too soon to be thinking about that? Think of the pressure it would put on both of us to make it work. Fletcher has a life there and all I would have is him.'

'I guess you need to decide if it's worth the risk.' She nods. 'You could always find something to occupy your time. You do own part of a publishing company there.'

'By default, and I don't know enough about working in publishing.'

She sips her coffee again, wrapping her hands around the mug and swirling the liquid inside it as she swallows. 'Wouldn't hurt to learn, if it's something you're interested in. You've got the money.'

I let out a sound that borders on cackling. 'Are you saying I should spend Dad's money on buying Harcourt?'

'Yeah, as an investment.'

'An investment?'

She smiles. 'It isn't as ridiculous as you're making it seem. You could be a silent owner while you learn the ropes.'

'Marie, you're joking, right? What do I know about running a publishing company?'

'You'd have people to run it for you.'

My fingers tingle, and I realise I've been pressing them into the side of the hot mug. Marie nods with encouragement at the ludicrous idea. That's what it is, ludicrous. Bat shit insane and borderline impossible. What's more insane is that I'm wondering how I could make it less impossible.

'Can I even buy a company if I don't live in the country?'

Marie waves off the question. 'Let Dana Robinson worry about that stuff.'

We sit in silence for a few moments and she knows I'm considering it.

I slink back down into the pillow as her phone chimes with an incoming message.

'Bob the builder is up at the lodge, so I have to go.'

I smile and nod. 'I spoke to him yesterday. Apparently he doesn't like it when we call him Bob the builder.'

'Yes, so we won't say it to his face.' She collects her mug and rinses it in the sink before coming to a stop at the front door.

'Hallie?' she says, eyes narrowing and her hand hovering above the door handle. 'Make sure you talk to Fletcher as soon as he's back. I won't tolerate you hurting that boy.'

She breezes out of the house in a flash of green nylon, leaving the thinly veiled threat in her wake.

CHAPTER THIRTY-SIX

I t's late afternoon when I make the bold decision to pick Fletcher up from the airport by myself. Marie is waiting on Bob to come back with decking boards, but she insists I take her car because, and I quote, Dad's car is a death trap that a roadside ditch is too good for.

The drive is less stressful now that I'm a little practiced. I also changed the voice on the GPS to the Australian lady which, while soothing, only amps up my homesickness.

'Where's Marie?' Fletcher raises his eyebrow and inspects the back seats of the Chevy as he opens the passenger door.

'At home.' I lean over and kiss him. 'But I made it here in one piece.'

My hands grip the steering wheel and I'm still shaking.

'You want me to take over?' he asks.

I sag back into the seat. 'God, yes. I thought you'd never ask.'

We jump out and swap sides. My heart rate returns to

normal the second my butt hits the passenger's seat. Fletcher, by comparison, looks as wound up as I do when I'm boarding a flight.

'Is everything alright?' I reach over the console to take his hand. He squeezes my fingers briefly before returning to the wheel.

'Fine.' His voice is even but a muscle twitches in his cheek. I pull my hand back and rest it in my lap. I had planned on spending the drive back broaching the subject of what's happening with us, but clearly something else is going on.

'Did something happen in Seattle?'

He shakes his head. 'No. I'm fine.'

I don't press the issue and as a result the thirty-minute drive to the house is silent, save for the folksy music that hums through the car speakers.

'I need a shower,' Fletcher announces as he drops his bag on the bed in my room. The house feels complete now he's back, but he's hardly said a word and I'm worried he's been checking news alerts all day.

'I invited Marie over for dinner.' I slip my cardigan off and hang it in the wardrobe. 'But if you're tired, we can do it tomorrow night.'

'Dinner sounds good.' He kisses me on the forehead before stripping off his shirt and heading to the bathroom.

I pull out my phone and scroll through my contacts until I find Marie.

'Don't worry, Hal, I'm already roasting a chicken to bring over,' she says upon answering.

'Well, first off, that's insulting. I was going to make a risotto.' I frown. 'And second, I think something is wrong with Fletch.'

I make my way to the kitchen and begin sifting through the pantry for risotto ingredients. We have no rice.

'Are you trying to get out of talking to him about staying in Seattle?'

'No, I'm not, but has he said anything to you? Anything that might be bothering him?'

She clears her throat. 'No, but I'll talk to him after dinner.'

'Thanks, Marie.' I pull open the vegetable drawer in the fridge and notice the mushrooms have turned. 'Also, can you bring the chicken with you?'

She's still laughing when the call disconnects.

With dinner sorted, I head down the hall toward the bathroom. The door is ajar, and I step into a wall of steam that bisects the small room.

'Marie's bringing a roast chicken,' I call out over the thunderous sound of water hitting ceramic tile.

'Great,' he calls back as I take a few steps forward, sucking in more humid air. He's turned away and I see soapy water sliding down his back and over his butt. It's not enough to distract me from the issue at hand, though.

I swing open the glass shower door and it startles him.

He wipes his eyes and stares at me. 'What are you doing?'

'You've barely said two words to me since you landed. Is everything okay with Luca?'

'Luca's fine. I'm fine.' His voice shakes. 'Can you let me shower?'

'Have you been reading articles again? We'll polish everything when we edit.'

He drops his head back and grits his teeth. 'I don't want to talk about the book.'

My gut seizes with worry, but I doubt he's going to budge. Especially when he's all naked and vulnerable and we haven't seen each other in ages.

'Alright, no book talk.'

I step closer, causing spray from the shower to cover my face and neck. He leans down and pecks me on the nose.

'I missed you.'

I smile. 'I missed you too.'

'Get in here.' He cups his hand, filling it with hot water and threatening to splash me with it.

'Don't you dare.'

'Then get in.' The smile lines return to the corners of his eyes. Whatever we're about to do is a temporary distraction from the serious conversation we need to have.

I pull my shirt over my head and toss it to the floor before the rest of my clothes join it. Fletcher pulls me close and kisses me, steam rising as I'm caged between his body and the cool tiled wall. All the frustrating shit that keeps disrupting my life dulls when we're together and I'm thankful for it. I'm still furious the photos of us leaked, but not because I regret what we've started, it's because it took away something sweet and pure that was ours. Splashing it on blogs and news feeds only cheapens it. Turns it into salacious gossip when it isn't. It's very real, and that is clearer than ever.

I pull back to look him in the eye. Water trickles down the side of his face and across his stubbled jaw. I reach up and put my hand on his cheek. 'I'm so glad I found you.'

He places his hands on either side of my neck, thumbs pressing down as he kisses me. It's intense, but nurturing, and I revel in it.

He moves, letting his forehead rest on mine as his fingers brush my cheek.

'We'll be together at the end of this,' he whispers. 'Please tell me we'll be together at the end of this.'

My answer is a decisive kiss.

'All I'm saying is that you should be careful when you do that, Hal. The way you had your leg up was dangerous…the tiles in that shower can be slippery. Especially with soap on them.' Marie raises an eyebrow at me. 'Also, the door has a lock, so it wouldn't hurt to use it.'

'Well, I didn't say come in, did I?' I scoff.

Marie steeples her fingers and the six-foot-two bundle of nerves beside me looks like he wants the earth to swallow him whole.

'It sounded like that's what you said.'

'Trust me, that's not what I was saying.'

'Hal.' Fletcher drags his hands down his face. 'Can we forget this happened? Please?'

He's reliving the moment when Marie's startled face came into view amidst our guttural moaning twenty minutes ago.

Fletcher dropped me like a hot potato and faced the wall as Marie backed out, saying she'd wait at the table. I've seen the funny side, but Fletcher hasn't come around yet. I'm not sure he will.

'It would have been more embarrassing if one of you slipped and hurt yourself. Imagine the EMTs bursting in and seeing what I saw.' Marie tries to contain a laugh.

I fail to hold in a chuckle of my own, but I am saved from Fletcher's irritated glare when Jordan's name flashes across my phone screen.

'Sorry. I should get this.' I tap the green button and lean back in my chair. 'Hey, Jordan.'

'Hallie, fuck, I'm so sorry.' His voice is low and muffled, like he's in a confined space.

'What are you sorry for?' I scratch my temple and Fletcher looks over at me, brows drawing together.

'Haven't you heard? Have you spoken to Cece?'

'No. I missed a call a while ago, but I haven't called her back. What's going on?'

Jordan sucks in a laboured breath and my heart races, my nerves raw.

'I'm not supposed to speak with you. Please call Cece right now.'

He hangs up the phone, and I immediately call Dad's agent.

I stumble over my words when she answers. 'Cece, what's happening? Jordan told me to call you.'

'Hallie. I'm so sorry.' She sounds as strung out as Jordan. 'I tried to call as soon as I heard.'

'Heard what? What is happening?'

She hesitates before taking a deep breath. 'Harcourt is suing you.'

A sudden coldness spreads from the centre of my body to my limbs.

'They're doing what?'

'They're suing you for executorship of Ellery's literary estate. Citing that you're not competent enough to act in your dad's best interests.'

I dig the heel of my hand into my eye. 'They can't do that.'

'They can, and I'm so sorry.'

Fletcher takes the phone from me.

'Cece?'

I can't hear what she's saying but Fletcher closes his eyes and drops his head back. How much worse could this possibly get? Every step forward results in ten steps back.

I stand up, ignoring a confused Marie as I hurry to the bedroom.

Fletcher says something into the phone before chasing after me.

'Halliday.' My name leaves his mouth in a morose whisper and he places my phone on the bedside table before sitting beside me. Silent tears are already rolling down my cheeks.

'I was on a date,' I whisper. 'Can you believe that? I was looking across at this perfectly preened idiot and ignoring Marie's calls. Dad was dead, and she was trying to let me know. I ignored it and instead heard about Dad on a news bulletin.'

Fletcher reaches over and takes my hand.

'I just wanted to get this right for him. I hadn't seen him in so long, and I loved him so much. With him gone, all I can do is make sure I get this right, but someone is always trying to drag me down. If it's not Mason, it's Dad's fans, and now it's Harcourt.'

I want to cry harder than ever before. I want to let everything that has built inside me over the last five months out before having to face this spiteful new turn of events.

Fletcher clears his throat. 'Cece said that after the leak Harcourt's worried about their image and what their association with you is doing to it.'

'For fuck's sake.' I stand and start pacing the room, my devastation warping into anger. 'When will this end? No matter what I do, it's wrong. Even when I don't say or do anything, I still get blasted over it. I know these books and I know my dad. I made a mistake with Mason, but I'm proud of what we've done, and Dad would be too.'

Fletcher stands up, grips my shoulders, and runs his hands down my arms. 'I know, I know. I'm proud of what we did too, but if they take it away then you'll lose everything. There might be something we can do to stop that.'

'What are you saying?' I narrow my eyes.

'I'm saying that if I step aside and you work with Mason, then at least you're still involved. It might not be the exact vision we had for it, but you'd still have a hand in it.'

I step away from him. 'We're not doing that, Fletch. We'll work out some other way.'

Fletcher pinches the bridge of his nose. 'I understand that you want to fight but people hated my work and Harcourt has deep pockets.'

'So do I,' I counter, not knowing the lengths I might need to go to.

✳

I lay in bed, alone for some time. Eventually the sound of the TV fades away, replaced with hushed voices. Marie says something I can't make out, and Fletcher's muffled reply sounds panicked.

I'm thankful for the well-oiled door hinges as I take a step into the hallway. I peek around the corner to see Marie with her back to me and Fletcher sitting on the adjacent couch. His hair is a mess, like he's been pulling at it.

'Tell her, Fletch. She'll find out soon, anyway.' Marie sighs.

'I can't.' His voice is pinched, and he runs his hand through his hair again. 'She'll never forgive me.'

'Maybe not, but if this is what you want, then she should hear it from you.'

I wrinkle my nose and lean closer, hoping I've misheard whatever is being said and the 'she' they're referring to isn't me.

'Jordan said I'm letting the backlash from the chapters get to me, but it's more than that. I wanted this so bad, but what if I'm the wrong choice?'

He stares at Marie and she reaches over and pats his knee. Fletcher releases a frustrated breath and drags his hands down his face.

'You're not the wrong choice.' I say and they both turn to face me as I step out of the hallway. I notice the dark circles under Fletcher's eyes.

'I'm going to go.' Marie sets her mug down and weaves around me as Fletcher and I continue to stare at each other. She bids us goodbye and hurries out the door.

'What's going on?' I ask and Fletcher hangs his head.

'I called Jordan,' he whispers. 'And told him I'm leaving the project.'

My heart thunders against my ribs but I take a deep breath as I sit on the end of the coffee table and face him.

'Why would you do that?'

He hesitates, head still bowed. He can't look at me.

'I'm sorry.' He exhales. 'I don't want you to fight them on it. You could lose everything. Mason might be a piece of work, but he's a skilled writer, and if they want him and it means you keep control then that's what we have to do.'

I attempt another deep breath but my lungs feel like slabs of concrete. He's taken this decision away from me. He's abandoned me. Left me to suffer with Mason.

'It's *not* what we have to do, and now you've made this massive decision when I told you a few hours ago that it wasn't what I wanted.'

His eyes finally come up to mine and they're filled with shame and disappointment.

'It's what I want…all of this is too fucking hard. Every day a new petition launches online to take me off the project. One of them has over half a million signatures. How am I supposed to process that? No matter what I produce, people will hate it because Ellery didn't write it.'

There are tears in his eyes as he slumps forward, elbows on his knees and head in his hands. I slide forward, gauging his response, and when I'm close enough, he leans into me, his head against my chest.

Tears sting my own eyes as I run my hand through his hair.

It takes a moment to find my voice, not because I don't know what to say, it's that I don't know how to say it.

'Fletcher, I don't care what other people want. *Blood of Gold* is mine. He wrote it for me.'

I pull his head back gently so I can look into his dark eyes.

'When I was a kid, Dad told me this story to get me to sleep. It was about a queen who wanted to keep her throne when no-one believed she was strong enough or clever enough to rule. He added magic and dragons and a stoic knight for the queen to fall in love with. He called it Dreamland, and every night the next instalment started with the phrase, "In the land of shimmering jewels where snow meets sky."'

Fletcher's expression softens.

'When I read his work, I hear his voice; like he's reading it to me the way he used to tell me those stories. I loved *Red Reign* because it felt like he was reading it to me. Your style and your voice reminds me so much of him.' I take a deep breath and run my hand over his cheek. 'I made a huge mistake getting Mason involved because I was thrust into all this and I didn't know what it entailed. I saw someone I respected and thought his success and talent were all I needed to get this book out there. I was wrong, and even though we didn't get off to the best start, it was always you, and I think Dad, from wherever he is, had a hand in that.'

Fletcher looks at me and I hate how powerless I feel. No matter what I say, I can't take away his self-doubt; for every kind word from me there are a thousand spiteful ones from people who should be scrambling to buy the book he wrote.

'We'll go back to Seattle.' I stand and pull him up into my arms. 'I need to talk to Jordan.'

CHAPTER THIRTY-SEVEN

Dana drums her nails on the surface of her desk as she reads over the letter that arrived at Dad's house this morning.

'In short, yes, they are seeking to remove you as executor of Elliot's literary estate. They won't be able to make any decisions about what happens with any of his assets, it simply revokes the creative control you have over his last book.'

I rub the back of my neck and groan. Jordan hasn't answered any of my or Fletcher's calls, and panic has set in.

'What are the chances they'll win?'

Dana's mouth presses into a line as she drops the letter on the desk. 'They aren't seeking royalties from the sales or asking for the advance that was paid before Elliot died. All they want is the book, so they may have a good shot considering you're inexperienced and it doesn't look like it's going well. Removing you is the easiest way to reinstate Mason and make the boatload of money they're hoping for.'

Fletcher leans forward in the seat beside me. 'What if I step away and we let Mason write the book? Can we convince them to drop it?'

'That's up to them,' Dana says. 'It would spare you a lengthy legal battle that may result in a loss and delay the book further. They might argue that Hallie is responsible for a delay in publication and enforce the deadlines in Elliot's contract. Then you'd be responsible for lost revenue.'

I slide down in the chair. 'Fucking hell. What about my stake in Harcourt? Can I do something with that?'

'Elliot wasn't on the board or a majority shareholder. He chose a silent partnership that expressly states that his only involvement is financial. They're offering to buy out your stake as part of this, so you'll be removed completely.' She sighs. 'I'm sorry, Halliday. I wish I had better news for you. I have some old colleagues in Seattle that I could refer you to?'

I nod and take the letter she hands back. 'That would be great. Thanks, Dana.'

On the ride to the airport, I try calling Jordan again. He doesn't answer.

He doesn't answer when I call him from Fletcher's apartment either, and every hollow ring is like a needle in my spine.

That night, I'm lying in bed beside Fletcher when a quiet knock sounds on the door. Fletcher sleeps like the dead, so I slap his shoulder to wake him up.

'Someone's at the door.'

He rubs his eyes and gathers some track pants from the floor, pulling them on as he disappears into the kitchen.

The voices are muffled, but I can tell it's Jordan. I spring out of bed, throw on some clothes myself, and hurry out of the bedroom.

'Hallie.' Jordan sighs as he pulls me into a tight hug. 'I'm so sorry I haven't been answering your calls. I've been told not to talk to you.'

I pull out a chair from around the table and usher Jordan into it. 'It's fine, just tell me what's happening.'

Jordan sucks in a breath. 'It turns out Henry was the one that leaked the chapters and photos. He screen-shotted it all off Fletcher's phone, including the emails we sent back and forth, workshopping the outline. His intention was to leak the chapters as a teaser to generate some interest. I still don't know who leaked the email you sent to me saying those things about Mason, but anyone in the building could have stolen it off the server and put it online.'

I look over at Fletcher, who is pinching the bridge of his nose.

'Mason's been getting some criticism, thanks to what you said about your meetings in the email, and he's acting out in the worst possible way. He doesn't want to write the book. He just doesn't want you to be a part of it. Greg Strickland, the publisher, is in Mason's back pocket because his books bring in a fortune for Harcourt, and since they haven't had a successful release since Fletcher's book, they need the revenue.'

Fletcher stands up and starts pacing his shoebox apartment. 'Fuck. This is all my fucking fault. I shouldn't have given that kid my phone.'

'Fletch, it's not your fault. I shouldn't have antagonised Mason at the convention or said those things about him in that email.' I reach out and grip his wrist, pulling him to a stop. 'We'll work this out. I'll talk to Greg and get all this sorted.'

Jordan looks dubious and sweat beads on his brow. 'I have to go, and you can't call me anymore. Just come to the office and ask to see Greg. They'll want to avoid a lengthy legal battle and they can't lose Mason, but whatever you do, make sure there is something in it for them. As it stands, I'm certain that Mason is fronting the money to buy out your share, anyway.'

Fletcher's hand clamps down on my shoulder as I take in the genuine fear in Jordan's eyes. He's taken a risk telling me any of this, and there's no way I'll let him be punished for it.

Jordan leaves soon after, and Fletcher and I sit opposite each other at the kitchen table for what feels like hours.

'Even if you spend all this money fighting them, you'll still have to publish the book through Harcourt,' Fletcher says. 'And we've already seen how unimpressed Elle's fans are with my work, so if you keep control, I think you should look into another author.'

'I'm not doing that,' I say. 'It just needs editing and Jordan can handle it. He did it for Dad's other books and he'll do it for this one.'

Fletcher leans back in his chair and drags his nails down his thighs. While I've been grappling with the lawsuit, Fletcher's stuck on the feedback from the chapter leak. I don't blame him because the shitshow from those four chapters is still raging online.

'Can I show you something?'

Fletcher looks up, dark eyes curious as he nods. I cross to the lounge where my suitcase lies open. I intended on showing this to Mason when we first started working together, but since that fell apart, I kept it to myself. I don't want to keep it to myself anymore.

I take out the thick stack of paper. It's crumpled but the spiral bindings hold it together.

'What's this?' Fletcher asks as I hand it over.

'This is the draft for Dad's first book. Read it and tell me with a straight face that it isn't a steaming pile of garbage.'

He takes the manuscript and scans it. His forehead wrinkles as he reaches the end of the first page and moves on to the next. He keeps going until he finishes the first chapter.

'It's terrible.' He exhales. 'Like worse than mine.'

'Exactly, and he submitted that to publishers.'

'And it worked?'

'Fuck no. He got enough rejection letters to wallpaper our house. But the point is he didn't stop trying to make it into something great.'

I crouch down, resting my hands on Fletcher's thigh and looking into his eyes.

'All I want in the world is to write this thing myself, but I can't. You don't understand how lucky you are to have the talent that you do.'

His expression softens.

'You and Dad build entire worlds from nothing. You make people fall in love with fictional characters they'll follow to whatever end. It's incredible. It will always be incredible.'

Fletcher sits the manuscript on the table and stares at it like it might scurry away if left alone too long.

'I have something else to show you.' I reach for my handbag on the table and pull out a folded piece of paper. It's been in my bag since I found it with those documents at Dad's house.

'It's the letter Dad wrote me. The one I found upstairs that night in the house.'

He unfolds it, eyes moving across the words I couldn't read a second time.

Halliday,

I hope you're well. I know you're busy and it's harder and harder to get hold of you these days, so I thought I'd write you a letter. I might not be fifty yet, but your dad is still old school. I want to apologize in advance for my lack of contact in the coming months, I need to get stuck into this final book. I've been putting it off, thinking about how much of a masterpiece it has to be. To be honest, the pressure is getting to me. I thought I knew the ending; I've sprinkled clues through all five of the books, but now I'm concerned that it won't be enough. What if it's unsatisfying? What if I can't give these characters the ending they deserve?

I'm drowning in the expectations I read online. Sometimes I worry that these fan theories might be better than anything I could write. I'm sure you could come up with the perfect ending for all this. For now, though, I'll take it a day at a time and remind myself that I can't please everyone, and I shouldn't try. You're the only person I want to make proud. It's all for you. When this book is done, I can breathe again, and we will finally have our time together. I miss you, and I'll see you soon,

Dad

I tug on Fletcher's hand and pull him up from the chair. He

wraps his arms around me, and I unravel. After a long moment, I lean my head back to look at him again.

'Everything you're feeling, he felt it too.'

Fletcher drags his hand across his eyes as he reads the letter a second time over my shoulder.

'Please tell me you'll do this for him,' I say. 'I'll sort out everything else. I just need you to finish this.'

CHAPTER THIRTY-EIGHT

I do what Jordan suggested and arrive at Harcourt the following morning asking to speak to Greg. The receptionist is new, scattered, and doesn't look entirely sure who Greg is. Thankfully, Jordan appears right on time and ushers me to the boardroom.

'I've got a plan,' I say as I take a seat.

Jordan holds his hand up. 'Don't tell me. I'll have to sit in on the meeting and I don't want Greg to know we've been in contact.'

He leaves the boardroom and I'm left to my own devices for at least forty-five minutes. I turn the plan over in my head several times, practicing what I'm going to say and how I'm going to say it. I didn't tell Fletcher what I'm about to do and snuck out while he was taking Luca to school. By now, he's probably worked out where I've gone and is on his way here.

'Halliday.' Greg Strickland enters the room. He's in yet

another crisp grey suit and he's flanked by Jordan and a portly woman I don't recognise.

I stand and hold my hand out. He shakes it before undoing the button on his jacket and moving to the other side of the table. I catch Jordan's eye, but he gives nothing away.

Greg gestures at the woman next to him. 'This is Colleen McFarlane, she's from our contracts department.'

While I've never met Colleen, I remember seeing her name on the contract I signed when I authorised the use of Dad's intellectual property.

'Nice to meet you, Colleen,' I manage while trying to keep my hands from shaking under the table. Greg once again takes control of the conversation.

'I understand you've been notified of our intention to remove your executorship. It's nothing personal, Halliday, but with the way you've handled all this and your vendetta against Mason Parrish, we have no choice but to step in and protect our assets.'

I look back at Jordan, his eyes are soft and he gives me an encouraging smile. I have to remain calm.

'I understand, and my intention was never to cause problems with Mason. I thought he was the right fit for the project, but we didn't work well together.'

There are barbs in my throat as I force down the hate that threatens to spill from my mouth. It's infuriating that Harcourt and I have to pander to that prick.

'That much is clear.' Greg chuckles. 'But as you know, Mason is our most high-profile author, and he has three projects we're in the process of acquiring. His dealings with you have put a strain on our relationship with Mason and therefore cutting ties with you is in Harcourt's best interest.'

It's insulting, but Mason's vindictiveness isn't a surprise. It's sad that a man I had so much respect for is going to such lengths to bring me down. I'm not an author and I'm perfectly happy working on the book with Fletcher then stepping away from Harcourt when it's done. If I had my way, I'd take the book to a different publisher. Hell, I could even start my own publishing house.

'I'm sorry that he's put you in this position,' I say. 'It's a shame that a man of his talent has an ego so fragile that he can't handle even the slightest bit of criticism. What's more disappointing is that you, Greg, a man with decades of experience as a publisher and a businessman, are allowing yourself to be pushed around by someone like Mason. He might have three projects in the works, but do you know the quality of that work? Because I'll tell you, when I spent two days working with him on *Blood of Gold*, his ideas were palatable at best. He's a has-been, and you should focus your resources on fresher voices. Have you even been looking to see what's out there?'

Greg shifts in his chair. 'With all due respect Halliday, that's easier said than done.'

'It's not, but I'm sure you'll continue to use that as an excuse while you publish another three Death Knight books that, at this point, are the literary version of a police procedural on network television.' I link my fingers on the table. 'You can do so much better than Mason.'

Colleen pushes her glasses up the bridge of her nose as she clears her throat. 'That's not why we're here. Harcourt is offering a sizeable sum for your father's holdings in the company. We're prepared to take you to court to overturn your executorship, and considering the negative media attention you've brought to the project, you could be liable for damages.'

My stomach seizes even though I was expecting this. I don't want to use Dad's money and fight only to lose, but I want them to believe I will.

It took all night staring at Fletcher's ceiling for me to come up with my course of action, and after a phone call with Cece outside Fletcher's apartment this morning, I know this is the best way forward.

I want Dad's book to be in capable hands, even if those hands aren't mine.

'If you refuse to stand up to Mason, then I have an alternative.'

Greg raises a brow. 'Let's hear it then.'

'I'll step away from the project.' The words sting coming out. 'If Mason is going to behave this way, then I won't waste more of my time trying to change him. I'll step down so you can keep working with Mason on his projects.'

Jordan drags his hand down his face and lets out a sigh. Greg's attention is fixed on me, so he doesn't notice.

'Why do I feel there are some conditions to this arrangement? Conditions I won't like.'

'I have two conditions. One is that Fletcher finishes the book. He's almost there, and he knows the full outline and how it ends.'

Greg looks at Jordan and Colleen before giving a stiff nod.

'What's the second?' Colleen leans forward as she asks.

'The second is that you drop the lawsuit and I'll willingly sign over my literary executorship to someone else. They'll have control over the project and work with Fletcher to get it finished.'

'And who will you be signing it over to?' Greg's mouth pulls into a line.

'Jordan.' I take a deep breath. 'Not Harcourt Press. Jordan Fisher, personally.'

'Hallie,' Jordan cuts in, almost jumping out of his seat, 'you can't give it all up like that.'

Greg flashes him a look of irritation. 'Of course she can. We'll drop the suit and then we'll need proof that you've handed it over to Jordan.'

I nod. 'I'll also need it in writing that Jordan will have creative control and publication of the final manuscript is subject to his approval.'

'Now it's more complicated than that. We're a team here and this book is important, so I'm afraid there are some other factors to consider.'

'No, there aren't. I want Jordan to handle all of it and not at the expense of his job at Harcourt. I don't want him coerced into doing something he disagrees with because it serves your agenda.'

Greg scoffs. 'What you're asking for is limiting to us. I'm afraid you might have to sweeten the deal.'

A smile curves my lips. I knew this was coming and I only have one card left to play.

'I'll sell you back Dad's stake in Harcourt for half its value.'

Colleen opens her mouth, but Greg cuts her off. 'Done. We'll get it drawn up as soon as possible.'

He stands up, shakes my hand, and he and Colleen leave me and Jordan at the table.

My throat is tight and I tear up as I look over at Jordan.

'Why did you do that? You could have fought them on it.' he says.

'I'm tired, Jordan.' I let out a shaky breath. 'I'm so tired of trying to do what's best for this book and being cut off at the knees at every turn. Spending Dad's money on a court battle will not make Mason less of an arsehole, and it won't make Greg give a shit about anything other than money. I did the best I could with what they've dealt me and if it means that you and Fletcher get to take care of this book then so be it.' I stand up and walk around the table before Jordan pulls me into a hug.

'You've been so great through all of this and I trust you to do what's right for my dad,' I mumble into his shoulder.

He pulls back to look at me, and I see the conviction in his eyes. 'I won't let you down.'

CHAPTER THIRTY-NINE

'You're sure about this?' Jordan pulls the pen away and looks down at the contract on the table. It's early evening so Whiskey Double hasn't sprung to life yet and I know I'm going to need a drink after this.

Three days ago, I received two documents, one signing over my executorship to Jordan and another outlining the revised terms of my deal with Harcourt. As promised, Greg came through with my conditions and the contract includes an agreement with Jordan, as executor, that Fletcher will author the final book. I covered my bases with the TV show, ensuring that I maintain a consultancy position. It's more complex than I imagined so I had it looked over by Cece, Dana, Marie, and Mum. Even Wes had a look, but he admitted he didn't understand any of it, and he frequently puts together tenders for large-scale building projects.

'I'm sure.' I take the pen from Jordan's hand and scribble my signature on all the required pages of both documents. I don't regret this decision, but the finality of it makes my chest heavy. I'm giving away the last piece of my dad and the emptiness that follows is not something I prepared for.

Jordan puts his arm around my shoulders and pulls me into his side. 'I've got this.'

I know he does, that's why I chose him. Over the last six months, Jordan has been something stable to hold on to while the ground shifts beneath my feet. He listens to me, speaks to me not as the inexperienced daughter of a former colleague but as someone of value. As a friend, a genuine friend.

'Take care of Fletcher for me, too.' I nudge Jordan in the ribs. 'He's still struggling with the backlash and we've only got three chapters to go. He needs to focus on what's ahead.'

Jordan nods. 'I'll take care of it all.'

I look over the booth to Fletcher, who's talking to his brother at the bar. The shifts in his mood are becoming more and more unpredictable. One moment we're finishing a chapter and his eyes are alight with uncontrollable excitement, and the next he's tagged in another think piece about how impossible it is to finish another author's book and I have to pick him up off the floor. He said he knew what he was in for, but it doesn't take the bite out of it.

'What are you going to do?' Jordan takes a sip of his beer. 'Since you and Fletcher are together now.'

I shake my head at the cheesy grin on his face. 'You knew it was going to happen didn't you?'

'Yes. The second I met you, I knew it was going to happen. Even when Fletch told me about his disastrous first meeting with you, I knew it was going to happen.'

I huff. 'And you still let me go with Mason?'

'Now him being such a pain in the ass, I did not see coming,' Jordan admits. 'He's always been easy to deal with. You brought out the asshole in him.'

I tap my chin. 'Like a superpower.'

'Yeah but one with no practical use.'

I shrug. 'Better than nothing.'

We both watch as Fletcher comes over and slides into the booth beside me. I lean into his body and he kisses my temple.

'Did you sort out the contracts?' he asks. I give a silent nod and Fletcher taps the neck of his beer bottle against Jordan's. 'Guess it's up to us now.'

'Guess so.' Jordan grins. 'How do you feel about Mason Parrish coming on to consult?'

I lean away from Fletcher and narrow my eyes at Jordan.

'That's not even a little bit funny.'

It takes three solid weeks for Fletcher to finish the first draft of the manuscript. While I no longer have creative control, there's nothing in the contract that prohibits me from being involved in the writing process. I am, however, prohibited from speaking publicly about the book or anything relating to Harcourt's involvement. This is more challenging than I thought when Harcourt announces that I've stepped aside and that the book is being handled internally. I'm not upset with their statement. It was fine. I wasn't presented negatively, and it reads as though I willingly stepped aside. Which I technically did.

I am upset that I'm now being painted as the reason for

the book's premature failure. Countless news articles, podcasts, and YouTube videos have identified me as the roadblock that's stopping the series from having a satisfying conclusion. It grates on me like nothing else.

In the announcement's wake, I go back to Fairbanks and spend some time with Marie. It's been six months since Dad passed away and we celebrate his life sitting side by side, drinking wine and looking up at the line of trees where his ashes are scattered.

The lodge is finished now, and Marie already has guests booked well into early winter. I don't like the thought of her being alone up here, but she says she'll never leave Dad. That brings more than one tear to my eye.

Upon returning from Alaska, I'm three weeks out from exhausting my allowed time in the US. It's a tough decision, but Fletcher and I talk about what's going to happen from here. He wants me to pop up to Vancouver so I can come back and have another ninety-days without a visa since I entered on my Australian passport and haven't gotten a US one. As much as I don't want to leave him, I still miss home and it's time to go back.

It takes some convincing, but he agrees, even though it's laden with a thousand invitations to move to Seattle.

'Can I drive you to the airport at least?' Fletcher asks as I haul my suitcase over to his front door.

'Don't you have to get Luca from school? I don't mind taking a cab.'

He runs his hand into my hair and pulls me forward for a kiss.

'We'll pick him up on the way.'

For most of the car ride, Luca's distracted by a book series about a forgetful elephant. According to Mia, he's slightly obsessed.

'He won't go to sleep unless we read at least two of those books.' Fletcher rolls his eyes, and I glance at the dark-haired boy, who's invested in Eddie the elephant's trip to the supermarket.

'You mean they aren't as intellectually stimulating for you, an adult man, as they are for a five-year-old child?' I feign shock.

'Not even close,' Fletcher says. 'Eddie's always getting himself into avoidable situations and blaming his problems on those around him.'

'You've put some thought into this.'

'They're poorly structured stories, too. No discernible plot, no character development, or defined arc.'

I laugh. 'Sounds like Dad's first draft.'

'Ouch. That's brutal.'

'Don't act like it isn't true.'

When Luca's attention strays from the book, I take the opportunity to talk to him. We discuss a boy in his kinder-garten class that eats crayons, and he tells me how cool it is that he gets to live in two houses. He doesn't like tomatoes, which I agree with, but he says he loves cauliflower, which I do not agree with. He shows me his book and tells me about the two new ones his mum bought him yesterday from the book-store near their house.

'My dad writes books,' he announces. 'They don't have pictures.'

'But all the best ones do.' I hand Eddie the elephant back

to Luca, and he holds it against his chest with his chubby little fingers, like he'll protect it for as long as he lives.

When we arrive outside SeaTac, Fletcher climbs out of the car to collect my bag. I unbuckle my seatbelt and turn to face Luca, whose beautiful brown eyes dart from the building to my face and back.

'My dad says you don't like airplanes.'

My nerves are already frayed. 'No, I don't like them at all.'

'Are you scared?'

'Yes.'

'But you're flying in the clouds.' He swoops his hand through the air like it's a plane.

'I know, that's what's scary about it.'

He considers my response and looks at his dad, who's waiting on the curb. I'm about to say goodbye when he leans as far forward as his car seat straps allow and fishes something out of the seat pocket. He holds his hand out, showing me a small elastic bracelet threaded with blue and yellow beads.

'What's this?' I ask as I take it.

'My friend Abigail gave it to me when I was scared to go to school. She said when you hold it, you feel better. I like school, so I don't need it now. It will help you on the plane, so you don't feel scared.'

'Thank you.' I slide the bracelet onto my wrist but see that Luca's attention has returned to his book. 'I'll see you next time.'

'Bye.' He waves without looking up.

I step out of the car as the beautiful July breeze sweeps across the front of the terminal.

'Can you let me know when you've landed?' Fletcher pulls

me into a hug, and I wrap my arms around his waist. We don't have long because the parking marshal is hovering nearby with the intention of ruining our moment.

'I will, and I want you to promise you'll talk to me if you're feeling overwhelmed,' I whisper against his chest and listen to the laughter that rattles his ribs. 'And stay off the fucking internet.'

'I'll do my best.' He kisses the top of my head.

We hold each other for a second longer before we're told to move the car. Fletcher glances in through the car window to confirm that Luca is engrossed in Eddie the elephant's misadventures before he pulls me to him and kisses me like these few seconds are all we have left.

'I love you,' I say when I'm able to take a breath. 'You know that, don't you?'

'Yeah, I know.' He chuckles. 'I love you too.'

CHAPTER FORTY

Once again, I'm wrecked when I arrive back in Brisbane. Wes kindly collects me from the airport but has to race back out because he and Jen are going to look at a wedding venue. They've set the date, it's eight weeks from now and they're both surprisingly good at organising the whole thing. Jen says it won't be a huge affair, but Wes's mum has other ideas. Wes asks me to be his best man while we're stopped at a set of lights, between mouthfuls of bacon and egg McMuffin. I thought I was his *roommate at best* but he says I'd be better than Teddy at making sure everything goes smoothly. It's not true, and Wes can't make it sound convincing, though he follows it up by saying it was always going to be me.

I get a little downtime at home before Violet is luring me over with ice cream. She wants the rundown on everything that's happened, so I give it to her, sparing no detail.

It's a bit of a rollercoaster, and she gets emotional about the beaded bracelet that's still on my wrist. There might be some merit to what Luca said: it made my flight a little easier, even though I cried on and off after parting ways with Fletcher.

'When are you moving there?' she asks.

'I'm not sure. We agreed the book is taking priority. Once that's done, we'll circle back to the Seattle thing.'

'You've changed. You're more sensible than I remember.' She frowns and checks the little video baby monitor to make sure Archie is still asleep. 'If you aren't immediately going to Seattle and you aren't helping with the book, what are you going to do with yourself?'

'Well, I've been thinking about that.' I sit forward on the couch and grip my knees, ready to pitch my idea. Violet mimics my pose. 'I'm going back to uni.'

Her shoulders slump. 'What?'

'I'm going back to uni,' I repeat and her mouth pulls into a frown.

'Are you yanking my chain cause if you are, I don't get it?'

'I'm going to study editing and publishing. It's two years, full time and online. I'll have to sit two exams in person though.'

'That sounds…fun.' She speaks slowly, unconvinced that this is something we should crack open a bottle of Dom for.

'What's your problem? You look like I've slapped Archie.' I lean back on the couch while she contemplates her response.

'I just thought you'd do something more exciting. Not upskilling to get a job.'

'See, that's where it gets exciting. I sold my stake in Harcourt, which removes any conflict of interest.'

Violet tilts her head to the side. 'Conflict of interest?'

'Yeah. To start my own publishing house.'

She hesitates and a crease forms between her brows. 'I don't know what to say.'

'I know more about the inner workings now and coupling my business degree with an editing course gives me the confidence to make a go of it.'

She nods and taps her chin in contemplation. 'Where are you setting this up?'

'Seattle,' I confirm. 'I want to poach Jordan as soon as he's done with Dad's book. If he's willing.'

The next day, after the jet lag has eased, I'm standing outside Mum's house. She isn't home from work yet, so I settle on the step, soaking up the sunshine and reading through my text conversations with Fletcher. It's mostly me scolding him for texting when he should be writing, but to his credit most of our conversations are book related. He's heading up to Alaska with Luca and his parents to celebrate finishing the manuscript. It's with Jordan at the moment who is constructively tearing it apart with all the love and attention we need from him.

I'm firing off a text to Jordan for a sneaky update when Mum pulls into the driveway and sees me taking up space on her front step.

She slams the car door and rushes over to give me an overdue hug. 'God, I've missed you.'

She holds me for so long and it reminds me of when I was

a kid. It's warm, honest, and what I've been needing. Seattle feels far away, both geographically and in my head.

'Come inside.' She pulls away and rummages through her bag for her keys.

Aside from a few minor decorative changes the house is the same. I follow her through to the kitchen where she makes me a coffee and stares at me for so long it's unnerving.

'You okay?' I ask as I blow the steam off my drink.

She smiles and looks away for a second like she's embarrassed. 'I've been seeing someone.'

'Yeah, Eric,' I say. 'Wes told me it's getting serious. Which I'm pissed I didn't hear about from you.'

Her neck flushes. 'I'm sorry about that. You've had a lot on your plate, so I didn't want to bother you. Anyway, I'm not talking about Eric. I meant I've been seeing someone else. A counsellor.'

'What?'

'Her name's Margaret and I see her once a week for an hour.' Mum says this with such pride it forces a grin out of me.

'What brought this on?'

'It was Wesley, actually. I've been missing you a lot and since we found out about Elle, I've been at a bit of a loose end. Not sure how to handle it all, you know? You got to go over there and be in his world, and I felt a bit left behind.'

Mum goes quiet and looks at the tiles, dragging the toe of her shoe along the grout.

'Mum, I wanted you to come. Right from the start. You could have stayed in Alaska with me. Spent some time with Marie and come to terms with all this.'

She presses her teeth into her bottom lip, leaving a red indent.

'I want to support you and speaking with Margaret has really helped me work out my own feelings about your dad. I wish I'd started seeing her years ago.'

She shifts her weight from one foot to the other and back again, and in this state of vulnerability, I've never been prouder of her.

'Mum, that is fantastic.' I reach for her, and she envelopes me in her arms.

'I loved him so much.' She sniffles. 'And I miss him every day.'

'Me too, and I know this might not make any sense, but being in that house in Alaska made me feel so close to him.' I wipe away my own tears. 'And I love Marie. She's a wonderful person who loved him too. It would be great if you'd get to know her.'

Mum nods, her cheeks wet as she runs her hands down my arms. 'I would like to.'

My response is interrupted by the sound of a key in the front door. An unfamiliar male voice calls out, followed by a familiar one. Mum wipes her cheek and takes a deep breath as the two men enter the room.

'Oh hey, what are you doing here?' Wes asks with a look of surprise as he pulls my mum into a side hug.

'Um, visiting my mother,' I answer. 'What are you doing here?'

'It's stir-fry night and Eric needed help to bring his fish tank over.'

A bespectacled man, around my height with reddish-brown hair, holds out his hand. 'I'm Eric. Nice to meet you, Hallie.'

I shake his hand. 'You too.'

'Hal, can you help carry some stuff? There's a bag of rocks and the filter that needs to come in from the car.'

Wes directs us all out to his truck and loads up my outstretched arms with various fish paraphernalia while he and Eric take opposite ends of the large tank and manoeuvre it out of the tray.

'So, Eric's moving in then?' I say to Mum as soon as he's out of earshot.

Mum smiles, her cheeks going pink as she watches Eric. He groans loudly as he and Wes come to a stop in the middle of the yard and adjust their grip on the cloudy glass box.

'We've been talking about it for a little while and it makes sense at our age.'

'Mum, you're forty-six.'

'And I live alone in a four-bedroom house. He lives alone in a five-bedroom house that's over an hour away with traffic.' She bristles. 'It just makes sense, okay Halliday. I don't want to be alone for the rest of my life and I appreciate Wesley spending time with me, but he has Jen and I don't want to be a charity case.'

'Eric moved in a while ago, didn't he?' I raise a brow.

'Yeah, it's been a month.' She looks down. 'I didn't want to tell you over the phone.'

I put the bags of rocks back in the tray and pull Mum in for a hug.

'I'm glad you're happy and I'm looking forward to getting to know Eric.'

'Me too.' Mum smiles at her new roommate but it turns to a wince when he bumps the corner of the tank on the door frame.

'I'll fix that.' Wes calls out as they clear the doorway and disappear into the house.

'Mum, you hate fish,' I say. 'You said their bulgy eyes make you uncomfortable.'

'They do, but Eric loves them.'

'You're going to put them in the garage, aren't you?'

'Yes.' She picks up one of the rock bags and crosses the yard to inspect the damage on the front door.

CHAPTER FORTY-ONE

The lead up to Wes's wedding passes in the blink of an eye and spending time with my friends has taken some sting out of not seeing Fletcher. Even though the heat died down from the leaked chapters and Fletcher is active on social media again, trying to put the mess behind him, I still worry. But he was growing tired of me asking if he was okay all the time, so now Jordan is acting as an informant. According to my reliable source, they're onto the second edit and Fletcher is positive about all the feedback. Jordan has been drip-feeding me little snippets of the revisions and they're nothing short of perfect.

Dad would be proud. I know that much.

I signed up for my course as soon as I could and in between study and helping Mum at the shop, I've been sorting all the ins and outs of starting a business in the US. Something that is much easier since Dad insisted on dual citizenship. Way to go, Dad.

I'm yet to pitch my bold idea to either Fletcher or Jordan, but from what I've been told, Greg Strickland is hesitant to sign off on the sequel to *Red Reign* and I figure it's out of lingering spite. *Blue Horizon* might be my first acquisition.

I've also attended two counselling sessions with Mum and it's been comforting to discover that Mum and I often felt the same way about Dad, but neither of us knew how to communicate it. From time to time, over the past fourteen years, we were on the same page. She didn't want to lose him and was worried I'd want to go too. I'd enjoyed my trips to Alaska as a teenager and Mum and I had our fair share of fights in those years, so I understand her worry. At any time, I could have been on a plane and deemed legally competent to decide not to come back.

All the sharing of feelings with Mum has lifted a weight off me and it's been a genuine joy getting to know Eric. He's a furniture designer with three adult children and he's unbeatable at Scrabble. Competition-level unbeatable. Every Friday night the Scrabble board comes out and they coax me into playing. After getting my arse handed to me six weeks in a row, I've taken a backseat to the action and instead watch reality dating shows in my old bedroom.

Mum and Eric are polite, so they refuse to tell me I'm a burden for spending most nights at their place. It's clear I've been lonely since Wes moved out. He and Jen bought a house that's miles from mine and got the keys three weeks ago. I wanted to make a fuss about the distance, especially in traffic, but we're about to be a lot further apart so for now the thirty-five-minute drive is a godsend.

'I can't find my tie!' Teddy calls down the hall as I button up my 'best man' tuxedo dress.

'It's in here,' I call back. 'Is Wes ready yet?'

Wes comes barrelling in, beer in hand and a grin on his face. 'I'm waiting on you.'

'I'm ready.' I gesture at my dress. 'We're waiting on Teddy.'

Teddy wanders in, black hair swooped back, and scoops the tie off my bed. Wes snatches it, swigging his beer and laughing as Teddy lunges for it. When Wes goes for another sip and narrowly avoids sloshing beer on his shirt, I've had enough.

'Stop!' I scold. 'My only job today is to get you to the venue on time, not covered in beer, and I will not fail at it.'

The fun stops the second Violet enters the room, eight months pregnant and irritable after having squeezed her swelling feet into heels. She is not to be trifled with.

'Hurry up. Brad's been sitting in the car for ages,' Vi snaps.

'We're ready,' I assure her as we all file out of the house and join Brad in the car.

Wes and Jen decided on a small wedding at the golf club close to her parents' house, and when we arrive, we're greeted by Fiona, who takes us through to a small courtyard decorated with rows of white chairs and white rose bouquets. We have one last run-through, and we aren't waiting long before guests arrive.

Wes looks as calm as ever when we're ushered up to the front to wait for Jen.

It's hot under the Queensland sun, but the ceremony is short. Jen looks stunning in her fitted lace gown, and Wes's vows are trademark Wes: blunt and hilarious. I even manage not to drop the rings, which I stressed about through most of the proceedings. Before I know it, we're filing back down the aisle toward the waiting photographer as Teddy compliments me on a job well done.

The rest of the afternoon is spent taking photos before we return to the giant marquee beside the main clubhouse. I sip champagne and listen to the speeches before switching to vodka and making a speech of my own. Between the interview and the LA panel, I'm not that nervous to speak in front of Wes and Jen's families.

When we reach the dancing portion of the evening, I step outside the marquee into the fresh night air. I wish I'd brought a glass of bubbly with me and contemplate going to get one before I spot Violet hobbling across the grass.

'Are you okay?' I call out.

'Yeah, just had to change my shoes,' she replies, but I know she already changed into pastel ballet flats after the ceremony.

I open my mouth to question it but notice a person next to her, and as they get closer to the light spilling from the marquee, I recognise the dark suit, broad shoulders, and pushed-back hair.

I choke on the breath I was trying to take in.

'Fletcher.' I break into a dangerous run across the grass, my ankles at high risk of serious injury in these shoes. When I'm close enough, I see the wicked smile on his face.

'What are you doing here?' I wrap my arms around him. 'You said you couldn't make it.'

He holds my face in his hands, studying me before he leans down to kiss me. It's tender, sweet, and long overdue.

'You're welcome!' Violet calls out as she trudges up beside us.

'Violet, this is Fletcher.' I grin.

'Yeah, I know. We talked all the way back from the airport.' She presses the button on her keys to lock the car and high-fives Fletcher before returning to the reception.

'God, I've missed you.' He holds me so tight I forget to breathe.

'How long are you here for?' I ask as I pull back.

'A week.' He runs his fingers through my hair. 'Sorry, it's not long, but Mia has to work, so I have to take Luca.'

'A week is great, better than great. How's the book? Where are you at with it?'

Fletcher pinches my chin between his fingers and kisses me again. 'Of course you want to know about the book.'

The joke's on him. I already know where it's at because I've been messaging Jordan for most of the day.

'Let me rephrase. How are you going?' I wrap my arms around his midsection, and he rests his chin on my head.

'I'm great and so is the book,' he says. 'I've missed you though. Especially with the edits. I need your input.'

'I thought you'd never ask.'

'There is something I want to show you.' He untangles himself from me long enough to pull out his phone. The light from the screen illuminates his face and I can't resist reaching out to brush my thumb over his cheek. I've missed the feel of him and that sea-salty cologne smell that makes my heart beat faster.

'What's this?' I raise an eyebrow as he hands me the phone.

'The dedication.'

I look down at a photo of a crisp white page. Tears build as I read it.

For our Halliday
You were right, Elle. She is magic.

Fletcher's dedication has me sobbing in a miserable heap outside Wes's wedding for a good half an hour. By the time Fletcher makes it into the marquee, I'm puffy eyed and worried that if I let go of him, I'll float off the planet. I still can't believe he's here and I take him around, introducing him to everyone I can find.

Mum is smitten with Fletcher to the point where Eric gets bored and heads off to the bar. I follow and return to the table to make sure Mum isn't asking for Fletcher's blood type or something.

'People aren't into original art anymore.' She shakes her head. 'They all want mass-produced posters at a cheap price.'

'It's a shame,' Fletcher agrees, and around all these Australians, his accent stands out. Mum has clearly turned what was some introductory small talk into something about the store, and Fletcher, the sweetest man alive, is engaging out of politeness.

Wes's mum is as taken with Fletcher as mine and soon the pair of them have him cornered by the buffet asking questions about Rocky Mountain rail packages in Canada. I don't know how they got onto that topic, but I save him from it.

'Mind if I steal you for a moment?' I grip Fletcher by the elbow and pull him away.

'Sure.' Mum smiles and gives me an embarrassingly obvious wink of approval.

I usher Fletcher away toward the dance floor only to be intercepted by Brad who is absolutely beside himself.

'Man, I am a huge fan.' He shakes Fletcher's hand. 'I'd love to pick your brain about *Red Reign* if you've got a sec.'

'Yeah, he's got time.' Wes appears at Fletcher's side and claps him on the shoulder. 'Nice to officially meet you, mate.'

'You too.' Fletcher takes the beer Wes holds out. 'Congratulations.'

'Thanks.' Wes grins. 'Now you can chat with Brad here for a bit while I steal my best man for a dance.'

Wes hooks his arm around my waist and Fletcher's hand slips from mine. I watch him and Brad sit at a table as Wes pulls me onto the timber panelled dance floor in the centre of the marquee. Father and Son by Cat Stevens is playing as Wes and I move around in a slow, uncoordinated circle.

'What's the plan here Hal?' he says.

'You've worked it out already.'

'Of course I have. Ages ago.'

'I know.' I lay my head on his shoulder. 'Mum will think it's too fast, but it feels right even if Fletch and I don't know exactly where it's going yet.'

Wes rests his cheek against the crown of my head and takes a deep breath. I memorise everything. The slight crackle of the speakers, the smell of his fancy wedding cologne and how it feels to hold each other. Because deep in my belly I feel us breaking apart. I can't put into words how much I'll miss him, but after all these years our paths have deviated. We're looking at vastly different horizons now.

'Maybe we're not meant to know where we're going,' he says. 'We'll just be pleasantly surprised when we get there.'

'When did you get so wise?'

He chuckles. 'Halliday, my wisdom is like a firework. It's bright, fleeting, and sets off all the dogs in the neighbourhood.'

'What?' I wrinkle my nose.

'I don't know.'

'Your analogies need work.'

'They do.' Wes pulls me close as the song fades out. 'You better come back and visit all the time, because I just got married and I'm not fit to be anyone's husband without guidance.'

'I'm not fit to be anyone's husband either. What makes you think I have any advice to give?' I laugh into his shoulder. 'Mind you, I am glad I can clock out. It's been a gruelling twenty-three years trying to keep you alive.'

There's a tap on Wes's shoulder, and we part to see Fletcher standing there. He's sporting a hopeful smile, and I'm curious to know how he escaped Brad.

'Take good care of my roommate please.' Wes pats him on the back before hurrying to his wife and pulling her into a sweeping kiss that causes people to clink their glasses and cheer.

'Finally, I get to have a moment with you.' Fletcher places his hands on my waist, stroking my ribs with his thumbs as we move from side to side.

'Everyone's heard a lot about you. They're keen to meet this famous author I've been gushing about all year.'

'I hope I'm not a disappointment.'

I wrap my arms around his neck and pull his face close to mine. 'You could never be.'

Fletcher moves me around the dance floor and I'm still a little detached from reality. My eyes keep catching on all the people in this room that make me want to stay. Leaving won't be easy, but Fletcher is the real thing and I want to be with him for as long as I can.

'So, you're flying out next Saturday?' I look up at him and he nods. 'Reckon I could get a seat on the flight?'

The most beautiful smile graces his lips. 'You're taking me up on my offer then?'

'I have conditions.'

'You always have conditions.'

I ignore the jibe. 'We're getting a bigger place and a new mattress. Your bed sucks.'

He pulls me against him and kisses me so passionately I hope Mum isn't watching.

'I'm keeping my TV though.' He's still grinning.

'Deal.' I cup his cheek with my palm. 'You knew I was coming back, didn't you?'

He shrugs. 'Violet and I spoke about it in the car. Everyone knew you were waiting till after the wedding.'

I look over his shoulder and see Violet elbowing Mum in the ribs and pointing in my direction. Fletcher brings my attention back to him when he presses a kiss to my neck, just below my ear.

'I want you to come back with me more than anything, but I have to make sure it's what you want.'

There is no hesitation in my response. 'You know, I always

thought the right person was going to be someone to complete me, but after everything that's happened this year, I realised I'm already whole. What I need is someone who challenges me.' I pull back and look into his eyes. 'You challenge me. You change the way I think and how I interpret things. You give me what I need. An equal, a partner. Someone who lets me be me but pushes me to be the best version of myself. So, to answer your question, this is what I want. You're exactly what I want.'

I feel lighter, having poured my heart out on this rented parquetry dance floor. His hand comes to my cheek, and he presses his lips to mine.

'Pushing you to do anything is harder than you can ever imagine. Do you know how stubborn you are?'

'I've been told.'

'It might be my favourite thing about you though,' he whispers. 'And that's how I know I'm in love with you. Fighting about character arcs with you makes me happy. Even when you have no idea what you're talking about.'

'I always know what I'm talking about.'

'No, you don't and that's okay.' He laughs as he holds me closer.

We continue to dance until the slow song morphs into a dance track. That's when Fletcher leans down and whispers in my ear.

'Do you mind if we leave? I've been on a plane since yesterday and there are a few things I want to do before we go to sleep tonight.'

'Say no more.' I wiggle my eyebrows. 'I just have to give Wes and Jen their wedding present.'

'Where is it?' Fletcher looks around. 'In the car?'
I shake my head. 'No, it wouldn't fit in the car.'
'What is it?'
'I paid out the mortgage on the house he and Jen bought.'
Fletcher's eyes widen. 'Shit.'
'Yeah.' I nod. 'Want me to put your name on the card?'

CHAPTER FORTY-TWO

1 YEAR LATER

Fletcher has been holding my hand since we boarded in Seattle. I've been on so many flights in the last two years, I had to develop a method of coping. It consists of breathing exercises, noise-cancelling headphones, and a strong belief that one day teleportation will exist. Also, hand holding. Lots of Fletcher hand holding.

As we descend into Los Angeles, it isn't the flying that has my stomach in knots.

'I love you,' Fletcher whispers.

'I love you too,' I reply. 'Are you okay?'

'Better than you.' He smirks.

It's been a week since the *Blood of Gold* release and most of the reviews have been positive. Naturally, there's been a handful that have ripped it to shreds but we're trying to avoid them. Which is a lot easier in the comfort of our apartment with our phones in a separate room. There's no avoiding it now, though. In a matter of hours, we'll be facing a room of Dad's fans and their loaded questions.

'We've done this before.' Fletcher squeezes my hand three times. 'We can do it again.'

I wish I could believe that, but neither of us know what this year's panel will be like.

I don't say much on the drive to the convention centre, nor when we're waiting in the holding area. There are other authors, YouTube personalities, and influencers milling around, a few of whom approach Fletcher for photos. I remain seated in the corner, wishing that Jordan hadn't gone to the effort of convincing Harcourt to let me participate in this. My involvement feels unnecessary and, honestly, a little embarrassing. The issues with Mason were well publicised and Fletcher still takes occasional heat over the leaked chapters. None of this has been smooth sailing, but we're expected to act as though it was effortless.

'Ms Townsend and Mr Larson.' The event assistant covers the mouthpiece of her headset as she addresses us. 'We're ready for you.'

I slip my hand into Fletchers and we both take a deep breath before following the assistant out of the holding area. It's a different set up to last year: our holding area isn't a curtain directly behind the stage, it's a small function room just down the hall from where our panel will be held. Jordan said there was an influx of ticket sales after they announced our appearance, so the organizers assigned us a larger room. I've been trying not to think about it too much. The crowd we faced last year was more than enough for my comfort level.

'It's going to be okay.' Fletcher squeezes my hand three

times and I squeeze back as we approach a door. A flimsy paper sign with *Blood of Gold* scrawled on it is stuck to the polished wood.

'Liar,' I whisper.

'I'm not lying. I've already checked online for any scandals. There's nothing out there to derail us this time.'

I look down at our clasped hands. 'Hold on for as long as we can, please?'

He nods as the assistant swings open the door and we're hit by a wall of sound.

I knew the room was bigger, but I'm not prepared for the number of people they've crammed in. Every seat is filled and the available standing room at the back is a sea of people, craning to see the stage.

'Holy fuck,' I exhale as we're guided up onto the stage.

We have the same panel moderator as last year and Fletcher and I briefly let go of each other so we can shake hands and settle into our seats. As soon as we do, I grip Fletcher's hand under the table.

It takes a while for the buzz to die down and when it does the moderator launches into his questions about the content of book six. They're easy questions and nothing that Fletcher hasn't answered in the countless television, podcast, and magazine interviews he's done over the past few months. It's all gearing up to the book tour that kicks off in two weeks. A book tour I won't be part of.

The panel goes on and I'm basically decoration. No questions are directed at me and I don't mind at all. I'm busy thinking about how unfair it is that Dad isn't here and wondering what he'd think of what Fletcher and I have done.

The fans in the room seem happy, but like I told Fletcher, it isn't all about them.

'Alright. We'll start the audience Q&A over here.' The moderator pulls me from my thoughts as he calls on a tall man wearing an interpretation of the Karrakan King's ceremonial battle armour. I hope the King is drinking plenty of water because it's warm out and from where I'm sitting that looks like a real metal breastplate. The man clears his throat and when he leans forward, his deep voice is accompanied by a twinge of microphone feedback.

'What was the hardest part to write?'

Fletcher frowns for a second, as though his response warrants contemplation. It's another easy question and I'm thankful it's the opening one.

'I'd say the second battle scene. Or the scene where Halladora loses her leg. It felt like the right outcome but getting it down on paper was challenging.'

It was more than challenging for me. We agreed no arms, hands, or fingers, so he got me on a technicality. He spared her the non-fatal abdomen wound though, so I'm thankful for that.

The questions roll on and thankfully no one brings up the email and chapter leak debacle, but no one really brings up Dad either. Almost like he isn't a part of this. It grates on me and when I twist Fletcher's hand to get a glimpse of his watch, I'm happy to see there's only five minutes left before we have to make way for a dystopian YA panel.

'My question is for Halliday.'

My attention snaps to the young girl standing behind the microphone. She can't be more than sixteen with tight curls that tumble over her narrow shoulders, her left hand tugging at the hem of her Scholastic Book Fair t-shirt.

'I'm sorry about your dad,' her small voice shakes as it echoes through the room. 'My question isn't about the book. I just wanted to ask what he was like. As a person and as a dad, I mean.'

My mouth goes dry and my throat tightens. The room's attention is on me, but I'm staring at the girl. She tugs harder on her shirt, blinking rapidly.

'No one really asks me that.' I lean into the microphone. 'Thank you.'

She smiles, exhaling in relief as I let go of Fletcher's hand and sit up straight. A sea of expectant faces look up at me and I know they're waiting for me to say he was kind, generous, and funny. All the adjectives used to describe famous people who have died. That's only the surface though, there's more to the picture. Things that have never been publicised. He made mistakes and was selfish at times. He gave all of himself to his work, often at the expense of spending time with me. I lost count of the times dinner went cold while we waited for him to come out of his office. Or the times he rescheduled flights and Skype calls because he had a deadline. There were a lot of things he missed out on, and I'm now realising that they've eclipsed the fond memories of my childhood for years. Like letting me win while playing Nintendo, building Lego houses, and getting ice cream after school. Reading fantasy books together and picking them apart over waffles on a Sunday morning. Him telling me stories every night before bed and trying so hard to be happy with the course his life had taken even when it wasn't true. For loving me and always trying to make me happy even when I made it impossible.

I clear my throat and look out at the crowd. His life, and mine by extension, have been in service of these books. Of this story. This thrilling, magical, and sometimes heartbreaking story. I believe that it was worth it. But I'm not sure the people that love his story so intensely need to know Elliot Townsend. We already gave them Ellery Yates, so maybe Elliot is just for me, Fletcher, Mum, and Marie.

'He was kind, generous, and funny,' I say. 'He was a wonderful cook, a terrible dancer, and a pretty good writer.'

A chuckle rolls through the crowd and the girl who asked the question gives me a nod and a tight smile.

'I think we have time for one more question.' The moderator checks his watch as the next person steps up to the microphone. My hand is back in Fletcher's and I glance at his profile while we wait for a middle-aged woman dressed as Halladora to ask her question.

'Now that *Blood of Gold* is over, what's next for you both?'

Fletcher looks over at me, our secrets firmly locked behind his lips.

Secrets like the fact that I've registered Dreamland Press in Washington State, signed a commercial lease on an office in downtown Seattle, and Jordan will soon be leaving Harcourt to join me. As of yesterday, my publishing company's first acquisition is *Blue Horizon*, and Fletcher is already halfway through the first draft.

'We have plans,' I say. 'Big plans.'

After the panel, we take the next flight to Fairbanks. We're planning a week off the grid at Dad's place before Fletcher goes back to Seattle to prepare for his book tour.

'A month is a long time to be without me,' Fletcher says as he turns the key in Dad's front door. 'Are you sure you can manage?'

'I'm looking forward to some peace and quiet to be honest.'

He wraps his arm around my neck and pulls me in to kiss my temple. 'I'll miss you too.'

Dad's place hasn't changed since the last time we were here, with the exception of some new throw pillows on the couch. On the car ride from the airport, Marie told us she'd been over to freshen the place up. She even stocked the fridge with prepared meals and said all we need to do is follow the instructions on the attached Post-its.

'You ready to do this?' Fletcher takes my hand as we wander over to the bookshelf beside Dad's desk. We stand in silence for a few moments before I get the copy of book six from my bag and hand it to him.

'Care to do the honours?'

Fletcher takes a deep breath and runs his fingers over the cover where it says his name and Dad's. My arms wrap around his waist as he reaches up and puts his book on the shelf next to book five.

'You did it, Fletch.'

'I wrote the words, but the story, that's all yours.'

He turns around to face me and I roll onto my toes to kiss him. 'Team effort.'

He smiles, taking my hand before we walk out onto the

small deck at the back of the house. The Northern Lights are faint as we stare out over the back of the property to Dad's final resting place.

'Do you want to tell him, or should I?' Fletcher says.

'I think technically you were supposed to ask him first. But you stuffed that up.'

'Please, you seduced me. I was powerless.'

'I have no idea how to seduce you. My plan was just to stand close to you until you gave in and married me.'

Fletcher moves to stand behind me, wrapping his arms around my waist and pulling me against his chest. 'Well, either way, it worked.'

I look up to the tree line. 'Are you gonna ask him or what?'

I feel the chuckle rumble through Fletcher's chest.

'Elle, I'm sorry I didn't ask first,' he says into the blackness. 'But somehow your daughter convinced me I need her. I know, I don't get it either. She's damn near impossible to live with. Leaving shoes everywhere and always thinking she's right.'

I elbow him in the ribs.

'Excuse me,' Fletcher grunts. 'I'm talking to your dad, can you give me a second?'

I take a deep breath and stare up at the sky for a moment before bringing my focus back down to the hill and the trees that stand tall atop it.

'You're taking too long.' I grin into the crisp night and Fletcher kisses the top of my head.

'As I was saying.' He turns his attention back to the darkness. 'I'd love your thoughts on the book if you get a chance.'

I bark out a laugh. 'Can you hurry up and ask? It's cold.'

'Alright, alright.' Fletcher links his fingers through mine, squeezing my hand three times before rubbing his thumb over the solitaire on my left hand.

'Elliot, if you're okay with it, I'd love to take Halliday off your hands.'

I look up at the night sky and even though the question is met with silence, I swear the lights overhead shimmer a little brighter.

ACKNOWLEDGMENTS

I have to start with a massive thank you to my dear friend Marnie. You're a saint for helping me through this entire process. Your feedback shaped this story, and I appreciate that every time I sent you a chapter you'd ask if I wanted you to be honest. I'm so glad you were because this book and myself as a writer are better for it. Also, I'm sorry for recommending books that make you cry… I'm also sorry for writing a book that made you cry.

Thank you to all my Brisbane and Townsville friends who have supported this process. It's been a long one, and I can't thank you enough for all your kind words.

A massive thank you to my mum and dad, not only for my existence but for your enthusiasm, encouragement and paying for Writers and Artists camp in grade 6. It means so much to share my work with you, and I'm so grateful for always having you in my corner. I can only hope that I make you proud, because I am proud to be your daughter.

To Straun, my best friend of twenty years and one of the few people to read the early draft of this book. Hats off to you for reading a 93,000 word women's fiction novel in a few days, not to mention the insightful feedback you provided. You're an absolute legend, and I can't thank you enough for your friendship over the years. You are the Wes to my Halliday, and I love you.

To the person for whom the book is dedicated, my sister Nicole. You've always been there for me, even when I was stealing your clothes, accidentally breaking your arm when we played hockey and telling on you to Mum and Dad. Thank you for all the lengthy phone calls we had bouncing around ideas for this story. You were a tremendous help from start to finish and you've always been my number one cheerleader. The world does not deserve a treasure like you and to have you as a sister is a lottery win the likes of which I'll never see again. This book is for you. Every word, every sentence, every page. It's all yours because I couldn't have done it without you.

And finally, a sincere thank you to my husband, Callan. For someone who has no interest in books, you sure listen to me talk about them a lot. In our almost two decades together, you have never let me down. You make me smile every single day and not a moment goes by when I'm not thankful to have you by my side (except when you leave your shoes at the end of the bed for me to trip over… just pick them up, it's not that hard). You are the love of my life, my soulmate, my other half and all that mushy romantic stuff. Thank you for allowing me to pursue my passion and holding my hand through every-thing. I love you forever and always.

ABOUT THE AUTHOR

Lauren Jones grew up in North Queensland and now lives in Brisbane with her graphic designer husband and two mini dachshunds. She started writing stories as a kid and thought time-travelling high fantasy was an easy place to start, she was wrong. Since then, Lauren has worked on her craft, gravitating toward contemporary fiction. She can be found in her little library, rearranging her books or having an afternoon nap.

To stay up to date on new releases you can follow Lauren on Instagram **@laurenjoneswrites** or sign up to her newsletter at www.laurenjoneswrites.com.au.

www.ingramcontent.com/pod-product-compliance
Lightning Source LLC
Chambersburg PA
CBHW030230120726
47903CB00005B/1431